Codex

Codex

Lev Grossman

W F HOWES LTD

This large print edition published in 2006 by
W F Howes Ltd
Unit 4, Rearsby Business Park, Gaddesby Lane,
Rearsby, Leicester LE7 4YH

1 3 5 7 9 10 8 6 4 2

First published in the United Kingdom in 2005
by Arrow Books

1·644948·21

A CIP catalogue record for this book is available
from the British Library

ISBN 1 84632 387 8

Typeset by Palimpsest Book Production Limited,
Polmont, Stirlingshire
Printed and bound in Great Britain
by Antony Rowe Ltd, Chippenham, Wilts.

For Judith Grossman

Such sorowe this lady to her tok
That trewly I, that made this book,
Had such pittee and such rowthe
To rede hir sorwe that, by my trowthe,
I ferde the worse al the morwe
Aftir to thenken on hir sorwe.

—*Geoffrey Chaucer,*
THE BOOK OF THE DUCHESS

CHAPTER 1

Edward Wozny stood squinting at the sun as crowds of people excused themselves past him in both directions. It was hot and bright. He was wearing a very expensive gray handmade suit, and he had to check what seemed like dozens of inside and outside pockets of various sizes and shapes before he found the scrap of paper he was looking for.

He turned it over. It was roughly triangular, with one clean right angle and one ragged edge, the corner of a piece of copier paper rescued from the recycling bin at his office. On one side was a fragment of a xeroxed memo beginning '. . . insofar as all holders of any equity funds . . .' On the other side was a name and an address written in blue ballpoint pen. He folded it neatly in half and put it back in the tiny inside pocket-within-a-pocket where he found it.

Edward checked his watch and set off up Madison Avenue, stepping over a NO STANDING sign that had been wrenched out of the concrete and lay across the sidewalk. In front of the corner bodega a man was spraying down trays of cabbage and lettuce and

Swiss chard with a hose, filling the air with a ripe, wet, vegetable smell. A branching delta of glittering rivulets ran down toward the gutter. He stepped fastidiously between them and turned the corner onto Eighty-fourth Street.

He felt good – or at least, he was doing his best to feel good. Edward was on vacation, his first time off since he'd started work four years ago, and he'd forgotten what it was like. He was free to go wherever he wanted, whenever he wanted, and could do whatever he wanted when he got there. He thought he would enjoy it, but he felt unsettled, disoriented. He didn't know what to do with himself, with this blank, unscripted, in-between time. Yesterday he'd been a hard-charging, highly paid investment banker in New York, and two weeks from now he'd be a hard-charging, highly paid investment banker in London. For now he was just Edward Wozny, and he wasn't totally sure who that was. Working was all he did, and it was all he could remember doing. What did people do when they weren't working? Play? What were the rules? What did you get if you won?

He sighed and squared his shoulders. It was a quiet block, lined on both sides with expensive limestone townhouses. One of the facades was completely overgrown with a single fantastic vine as thick as a tree and twisted like a rope. A crew of overalled workmen was wrestling a white upright piano down a flight of steps into a basement apartment.

Watching them struggle with it, Edward almost

stumbled over a woman who was crouched down on the pavement.

'You know, if you're going to use that word with me,' she said crisply, 'you'd better be sure you mean it.'

The woman was squatting down on her haunches, her dress stretched taut between her thighs, one hand on the pavement for balance like a sprinter ready to burst out of the starting blocks. Her face was hidden from him by the wide brim of a cream sun hat. A few yards behind her stood a white-haired man with a narrow face like a knife – her husband? her father? – waiting next to a cart piled with trunks and suitcases. His hands were clasped lightly behind his back.

'Don't be such a child,' he replied.

'Oh, I'm a child now? Is that what I am?' she asked excitedly. Her accent was somewhere between English and Scottish.

'Yes, that's exactly what you are.'

The woman looked up at Edward. She was older than he was, maybe thirty-five or forty, with pale skin and dark wavy hair – beautiful in a way that was long out of fashion, like a girl in a silent movie. He could see the pale tops of her breasts in their lacy white cups. Edward hated this kind of public display – it was like rounding a corner and stumbling directly into somebody's bedroom – and he tried to slide past her, but she made eye contact before he could make his escape.

'And what about you? Are you just going to

stand there looking down my dress, or are you going to help me look for my earring?'

He stopped. For a critical moment a simple, diplomatic response eluded him. Almost anything would have sufficed – a graceful demurral, a half-decent witticism, a lofty silence – but he blanked.

'Sure,' he muttered. Slowly, awkwardly, he crouched down next to her. The woman picked up the exchange with her companion – her husband, Edward decided – as if nothing had interrupted them.

'Well, I'd rather be a child,' she said, 'than an old man with a red face!'

Edward frowned, studying the glittering cement sidewalk and pretending to have suddenly gone profoundly deaf. He had somewhere to be and his own business to mind.

But he couldn't help noticing that the couple was impeccably dressed. He had a professional knack for estimating incomes, and he smelled money here. The man wore a perfectly tailored light flannel summer suit, the woman a fitted cream sundress that matched her hat. He was thin and a little ravaged-looking, with a thick shock of white hair; his complexion actually was a little florid, as if he'd just gotten back from a spell in the tropics. The luggage piled up on the cart was extravagant, made of deep green leather with a rough, pebbly texture, and it included pieces of every imaginable shape and size, from tiny cubical vanity cases to giant steamer trunks studded with gleaming metal

4

clasps to a circular hatbox the size of a bass drum. It was old-fashioned, either vintage or a meticulous re-creation thereof – it had the glamorous air of an early twentieth-century transatlantic ocean liner, the kind featured in old news-reels being christened with bottles of champagne amid silent storms of confetti.

A sedan with tinted windows idled by the curb. On each piece of luggage was a label with a single word, in small or large letters: WEYMARSHE.

Edward decided to break his silence.

'So what did it look like?' he asked. 'The earring, I mean?'

The woman looked at him as if a passing shih tzu had suddenly spoken.

'Silver. The backing must have fallen off.' She paused, then added unhelpfully: 'It's a Yardsdale.'

The older man got tired of waiting and knelt down too, pausing first to tug up the legs of his trousers with the air of somebody being dragged into something that was infinitely beneath his dignity. Soon they were joined by the driver, a sallow man with a weak chin – a virtual straight line from his lower lip to his collar – who looked cautiously under the limousine. The doorman finished loading the luggage into the trunk. Edward sensed that they shared the older man's dislike of the woman in the sun hat. They were allied against her.

Something crunched under Edward's right heel. He drew back his foot to reveal the crushed remains of the earring. Judging from its surviving twin it must have been shaped like a delicate silver hourglass, but now it was a scrap of mashed tinsel indistinguishable from a gum wrapper.

Serves her right for dragging him into this, he thought. He stood up.

'Sorry,' he said, without making any special effort to sound apologetic. 'I didn't see it.'

Edward held out his hand. The woman stood up too, her face flushed from squatting for so long. He expected an explosion, but instead she looked like she'd just gotten exactly what she wanted for Christmas. She flashed him a heartbreaking smile and plucked the earring delightedly from his hand. As she did so he noticed something he'd missed before: a drop of blood, swollen and fully formed, dangling tremulously from her delicate earlobe. Another spot of blood was visible on the shoulder of her dress right below it.

'Look, Peter! He utterly demolished it!' She turned gaily to her husband, who was brushing invisible dirt from his sleeves. 'Well, you could at least try to feign some interest.'

He peered at the contents of her palm.

'Yes, very nice.'

Just like that, they were back to keeping up appearances. The woman rolled her eyes at Edward conspiratorially, then turned to the car. The weak-chinned driver opened one of the doors, and she climbed into the back seat.

'Well, thank you very much, anyway,' she called back to Edward from the bowels of the sedan.

The driver shot Edward a warning glance, as if to

say, *that's it, that's all you get,* and the limousine peeled away from the curb with a short, sharp screech. Were they somebody famous? Should he have recognized them? A little triangle of the woman's cream dress was trapped in the door when it closed, and it luffed frantically in the wind. Edward pointed and started to yell something after them, then stopped. What was the point? As the car turned the corner onto Park Avenue, still accelerating, Edward watched it go with a sense of mild relief. But he felt a trace of belated disappointment, too – the way Alice might have felt if she had decided, sensibly and prudently but boringly, not to follow the White Rabbit down the rabbit hole.

He shook his head and refocused on the matter at hand. Edward was officially on vacation, two weeks off free and clear before he took over his new job in the London office, but he had agreed to look in on a client before he left. They were a married couple, colossally wealthy, and he'd had a small part in making them fractionally wealthier, a rather artful deal he'd orchestrated involving silver futures, a chain of thoroughbred horse farms, and a huge and hugely undervalued aviation insurance company. Setting it up had involved weeks of mind-crushingly dull research, but when he'd put all the elements in motion it had worked perfectly, like musical chairs in reverse: When the music stopped everyone else was left sitting down in an uncomfortable position, and he was the one left standing up, free to walk away with an appallingly large heap of money. He'd never even met the clients, hadn't known they knew who he was, but he supposed they'd gotten his name from his boss – probably they'd asked after that promising young lad who'd earned them all that cash, and that was why they'd requested him today. He'd been instructed to keep them happy at all costs. At the time he'd made a fuss about it – what was the point of starting up a new client relationship just when he was about to leave? – but now he was embarrassed to realize that he was almost looking forward to it.

The building the well-dressed couple was leaving turned out to be his destination: an ugly old brown brick high-rise left over from the nineteenth century. The windows were small and crowded close together except for the very top three stories, where they were twice or three times as tall as on the other floors. A cheap-looking, billiard-green awning extended out over the sidewalk with a much-trodden red carpet underneath it.

The doorman stepped forward.

'I can help you please?' he said. He was short and broad, with a thick mustache. His thick accent might have been Turkish.

'Laura Crowlyk. Twenty-third floor.'

'If you are insisting.' His bad English seemed to be a private joke that gave him a certain amount of satisfaction. 'Nem pliz?'

'Edward Wozny.'

The doorman stepped into a tiny alcove to the right of the doorway. It had a little wooden stool in it and an antiquated-looking intercom, all black knobs and Scotch tape and old yellowed slips of paper. He pressed a button and leaned down to speak into a grille. Edward couldn't hear the answer, but the man nodded and motioned him inside.

'I cannot stop you!'

The lobby was unexpectedly dark after the brightness of the day outside. He had a fleeting impression of dark wood and cigar smoke, shabby red oriental rugs and mirrored squares on the walls that were imperfectly fitted together. It was a once-grand building gone to seed. The instant he pressed the elevator button a bell rang and the doors shuddered open. It was a minute or two before he reached the twenty-third floor. Edward took the time to straighten his tie and shoot his cuffs.

When the doors opened again he found himself in a bright anteroom, as sunny and airy and open as the lobby had been dark and shabby, with white walls and a hard, polished wood floor. Opposite him his reflection appeared in a full-length mirror with a heavy gilt frame, its face misted over with age. He checked his appearance. Edward was tall and skinny, young-looking for his age – twenty-five – with sharp, pale features. His hair was short and very black, and his eyebrows ran in two thin, high curves that gave him a slightly startled expression at all times. He practiced his banker's face: pleasant, well-meaning, attentive, with a touch of sympathy – not too much – and a shadow of gravity.

A battered old umbrella stand stood in one

corner, upholstered in some exotic-looking reptile skin. He imagined the beast that had donated its hide, shot long ago in some obscure tropical colony by a cartoon safari hunter with a pith hat and a blunderbuss. A pair of French doors opened onto the apartment proper. Edward let himself into a spacious sitting room. A sturdy young black woman in an apron was fussing with some knick-knacks on an end table. She turned around, startled.

'Hi,' Edward said.

'You here to see Laura?' she said, already backing away. Edward nodded.

She hurried away. Edward took up a position on the edge of an enormous and complicated oriental rug. Sunlight streamed in through a pair of impressively tall windows. The room's opulence was pleasantly at odds with the building's gritty exterior; it was like stumbling onto a secret pasha's hideaway. The ceiling was high and white, and there were some side tables standing against the walls, set with vases full of elaborate arrangements of dried flowers. In a small but expensive-looking painting, a pointillist person sculled.

'Is that Edward?'

It was a woman's voice, a low alto with a light English accent. He turned around. Laura Crowlyk was small and fortyish, with a long and elegant face, bright eyes, and slightly unruly brown hair tied back in a bunch.

'Hello,' she said. 'You're the money person, aren't you?'

'I'm the money person.'

She squeezed his hand perfunctorily and let it drop.

'Eddie? Ed?'

'Edward is fine.'

'Follow me, please.'

The corridor down which she led him was dimly lit, and in a couple of places Edward noticed large dusty outlines where it looked like pictures had hung and been recently removed. Laura Crowlyk was almost a foot shorter than he was, and her light Empire-waist dress billowed out behind her as she walked.

A door on their right was ajar, and she led him through it into a sparsely furnished study. It was dominated by a cavernous fireplace guarded by two large red leather wingback chairs arranged at cozy angles to one another.

'Please sit,' she said. 'Would you like some tea? Water? A glass of wine?'

Edward shook his head. He never ate or drank in front of clients if he could help it.

They sat down. The fireplace was swept meticulously clean, although past fires had left behind a blackened patch on the stone. A bundle of dusty birch sticks stood on the hearth in a wrought-iron cradle, still covered in plastic wrap.

When she was settled in opposite him, Laura Crowlyk spoke.

'I suppose Dan told you something about what you'll be doing for us?'

'Actually, he was a little mysterious about it,' Edward said. 'I hope it's nothing too shocking.' His little joke.

'Not unless you're very easily shocked. You'll be available for the next two weeks, more or less?'

'More or less. I hope he told you, I'm moving to London on the twenty-third. I still have some arrangements to make.'

'Of course. Congratulations on your appointment, by the way. I understand it's considered quite prestigious.' She left open the question of whether or not she herself considered it prestigious. 'How long have you been with Esslin & Hart?'

'Four years.' Edward sat forward in his armchair. Time to dispense with the job-interview chat. 'Why don't you tell me how I can help you.'

'In a moment,' said Laura, unreadably. 'You're originally from—?'

Edward sighed.

'Well, I grew up in Bangor. Maine, that is. I know there's one in England, too.'

'Yes, I think I would have detected a Welsh accent. Your parents?'

'My father passed away recently. I haven't seen my mother in years.'

'Oh.' At least she seemed slightly abashed at that. 'And you took your undergraduate degree at Yale. In English?'

'That's right.'

'How unusual. Did you have a particular area of specialty?'

'Well, the twentieth century, broadly speaking. The modern novel. Henry James. Some poetry, too, I guess. It's been a while.'

Being interrogated as to one's qualifications was an occupational hazard when dealing with the very rich, but he hadn't expected this particular line of questioning. His English degree was one of those shameful secrets he avoided mentioning, roughly on a par with having gone to a public high school and having once tried Ecstasy.

'And now you're in private banking.'

'That's right.'

'Right. Right.' She drew the word out in her upper-class English accent, nodding her long, shapely head.

'Well,' she said, relenting, 'let me tell you a little bit about what we have in store for you. Upstairs in this apartment there is a library. It was brought over here by my employers, the Wents, about sixty years ago for safekeeping, shortly before the Second World War. There was a great deal of hysteria, you understand, everyone thought England would be overrun by the Huns at any moment. I don't remember it, of course – I'm not *that* old – but at the time there was some wild talk of selling up and moving the entire family across to America. Thankfully that plan never came to fruition. But the library came over, and somehow it never went back. It had been in the Went family for quite a long time, since the sixteenth century at least. Not unusual in the grand old families, but they were

13

terribly proud of it. Excuse me, it's rather stuffy in here – would you mind opening that window for me, please?'

Edward stood and went over to the window. It was an old wooden window frame, and he expected it to stick, but when he opened the latch it floated up almost by itself, lifted by hidden counterweights. A breeze moved through the room, and the sound of honking horns drifted up from the intersection below.

'The books were brought over in crates,' she went on. 'Probably would have been safer back in England, all things considered, but never mind that. Once they arrived here this apartment was procured – purchased from a professional baseball player, I believe – and the library was sent here. But then the war ended, and what with one thing and another the crates were never unpacked, or even opened, as far as I know. They've been upstairs ever since.

'Anyhow, that's how things stand. It's scandalous, really, but I think the Wents just lost interest in them. For a long time no one even remembered they were here, and then one day a family accountant was trying to balance the books and thought to wonder why we were paying such absurd taxes on this apartment – remind me to ask you about that later – and sure enough, somebody stumbled on the old library again. By now nobody has the slightest idea what's up there, just that it's very, very old and someone needs to take care of it.'

She paused. He waited for her to go on, but she just watched him patiently.

'And the books are . . . very valuable?' he prompted.

'Valuable? Oh, I wouldn't have the first idea. Not my field, as they say.'

'So you wish to have the value of the real estate they occupy assessed.'

'Not really, no. By the way, did you do any medieval work in college?'

'No, I didn't, but—'

There was a limit to how much storytelling Edward allowed his clients as a matter of professional principle, and Laura Crowlyk was now over her quota.

'Ms Crowlyk, I hope you won't take this the wrong way, but why am I here? If you've come across some historical documents that need evaluating, the firm can certainly put you in touch with a specialist who handles that kind of thing. But I don't really—'

'Oh, no, there's no need for anything like that!' She seemed to find the suggestion slightly hilarious. 'I was just getting to that. All we really need is for somebody to get it all unpacked and onto the shelves. Just to break those crates open, for one thing, and start putting it all in some kind of order. Organizing things, getting them cataloged. Sounds hideously boring, I know.'

'Oh, no,' Edward lied. 'Not at all.'

He sighed. Either this woman was slightly insane,

in some megalomaniacal English way, or a serious miscommunication had occurred. Someone somewhere along the line had Fucked Up. He was a senior analyst with Esslin & Hart, and she was apparently looking for some kind of glorified intern to do her housecleaning for her. Either way he, Edward, was going to have to clear things up, rapidly and if possible without provoking an international incident. He had a reasonable idea of the size of the accounts she represented, and offending her was not an option.

'I think there's been a slight misunderstanding,' he purred. 'Do you mind if I make a phone call?'

Edward extracted his cell phone from his jacket pocket and flipped it open. No signal. He looked around.

'Is there a phone here I can use?'

She nodded and stood up, giving him an unexpected flash of freckled cleavage as she leaned forward.

'Follow me.'

He had to take an extra step to catch up with her as she strode out the door. They turned right down the corridor, heading deeper into the apartment. An intricately woven and apparently endless maroon runner followed them underfoot. Edward frowned behind Laura's back as he caught glimpses of more doorways and hallways and rooms. Even he, a frequent visitor to the abodes of the moneyed, was impressed by the apartment's sheer size.

Laura stopped at a doorway. It was half the width

of an ordinary door, with a miniature glass knob –
it looked like the door to a broom closet, or the
entrance to some secret fairy hideaway. She opened
it to reveal a narrow, musty alcove, unlit and paneled
in dark wood. The floor was littered with old paint
chips and hanks of gray dust. It contained a narrow
cast-iron spiral staircase leading up.

He balked.

'I'm sorry,' he said, 'is this the way to your
phone?'

She didn't answer, just started up ahead of him.
It was dark, and the stairs were extremely steep,
and he snagged his foot on the lip of one of them
and had to catch himself on the delicate helical
railing. The metal rang faintly under their footsteps. The staircase wound around in a tight spiral,
and after two revolutions up into the darkness he
couldn't see a thing. When she stopped he nearly
walked into her. Standing behind her, he smelled
the coconut smell of her shampoo and heard the
jingle of keys and the clicking of heavy bolts and
latches.

She braced her thin shoulders and pulled, but
the door resisted, as if somebody were pulling back
from the inside, somebody who adamantly did not
want to be disturbed. She struggled for a few
seconds, then gave up.

'I'm sorry, I can't do it,' she said, panting a little.
'Please open it for me.'

She stepped to one side and flattened herself
against the wall, and they gingerly changed places

on the tiny metal landing. The keys were still in the metal doorknob. He grasped them, wondering whether this was an elaborate prank, gave them a quarter turn and pulled, putting his back into it, then spread his feet wider apart and pulled again. Behind him he heard Laura take a step down to get out of his way. The door was surprisingly thick, like the entrance to an air raid shelter, and there was a cracking, tearing sound as it started to move, like a tree falling, roots snapping deep under the earth, then a sigh of relief as air began to flow through from behind him. The wind crescendoed as it swung open, then died away again as the air pressures equalized.

It was pitch black on the other side. He tapped gingerly at the floor with the toe of his shoe, but he could see nothing. The sound echoed. There were some glimmers of light, high up and indistinct, but that was all.

What the fuck is this? he thought. Laura stepped past him, putting a hand on his elbow in an unexpectedly familiar gesture. He waited for his eyes to adjust to the darkness.

'It'll just be a moment,' she said.

The hollow sound of her footsteps receded in the darkness. The air was refreshingly cool, even cold, fifteen or twenty degrees cooler than it had been downstairs. There was a strong, damp, almost sweet smell; he recognized it from somewhere as the odor of quietly decomposing leather. It felt like he'd wandered into a church. Suddenly he was far away from the sun-baked Manhattan outside. He took a deep breath, his lungs expanding with the chilly air. Edward walked forward a few steps, blindly, toward where he guessed Laura was standing.

'Here it is,' came her voice in the darkness. There was the plastic snap of a switch being turned, but nothing happened.

'Is there anything I can—?'

Edward let his voice trail off. He put out his hand and touched wood, coarse and splintery.

He was suddenly struck by a sense of the size of the room. The far wall was beginning to resolve itself out of the darkness into one enormous window, a hundred feet away and at least two full stories high.

'For Christ's sake,' he said under his breath.

The light that would have been coming through it was almost completely stanched by masses of thick, dark curtains, so that only a ghostly rectangular glow showed through.

Finally the light snapped on. It was a standing lamp with a brown shade, and it gave out a cozy yellow living-room light. The room was indeed huge – it could have doubled as a ballroom. It was much longer than it was wide – it must have run the full depth of the building – and there were cubical wooden crates piled up here and there, mostly at the far end, in head-high stacks of two and three. An aluminum dolly was still parked next to one of them.

She had brought him to the library. Bookshelves ran along one wall, mostly empty. On one of them, at the end of a long, kinky black cord as thick as a garter snake, was the promised telephone, a squat black artifact from the rotary era.

'I thought you would want to see,' she said. 'Before you called.'

He did see. He folded his arms. It had dawned on Edward that this dotty English woman, this rich woman's lackey, actually thought he would go through with it. Even now she was watching him expectantly.

He looked around, composing a speech in his mind to express his righteous indignation. It was a brilliant speech, couched in terms of the most magnificently nuanced diplomacy, but at the same time mined with slights and insults almost too devastatingly subtle to be perceived; she would only realize decades later, as she sat rocking on the porch of the old lackeys' home, how crushingly he had snubbed her. The speech rose up and hung there, poised for delivery, to be accompanied by a slow, steady backing away towards the door, but he hesitated.

'Nothing's been touched,' she said. 'If you can wait another minute I'll bring you up a few more things.'

The speech was ready, but he still didn't deliver it. He hesitated. What was he waiting for? What was the smart play here? He didn't dare offend the Wents, even if it was by proxy. It was already mid-afternoon. He could kill the rest of the day, a couple of hours at most, then call Dan in the morning and have them send over a first-year associate or one of the more vigorous assistants. Dan had gotten him into this, he'd get him out. Wouldn't that be the safest escape route? And for that matter, what else did he have to do today?

Laura stepped past him again, and he turned to watch her as she walked out the door.

When she was gone he kicked one of the wooden crates, and it boomed hollowly in the silence. Dust floated off it and settled to the floor. He tried his cell phone again. No signal – the whole apartment was in the grip of an evil enchantment.

'Fuck it,' he said out loud. He sighed.

Edward felt his irritation seeping away. He walked the length of the room. He could clean up the mess tomorrow. And it was just a bunch of books – didn't he, in his sensitive, idealistic youth, used to read books? The floor was a fine, expensive-looking parquet with long narrow boards. The weak, angled light brought out tiny imperfections in the finish. A solid old wooden table stood along one wall, and he brushed his hand along it. His fingertips came away dusty. The table had one drawer, with one old screwdriver rattling around in it.

It was the weirdest thing, but he actually felt almost glad to be here. There was something about this grand, romantic old room that made him want to stay in it – some invisible body was asserting its gravitational force over him, an undetectable black hole gently drawing him into its orbit. Walking

21

up to the window, he pushed back the curtain a little and looked out. The windows went all the way down to the floor, so he could look straight down at the gray asphalt of Madison Avenue. From this height all the traffic lines and crosswalks looked very neat and precisely drawn. Sunflower-yellow cabs veered and swooped through the intersection, always managing to miss each other at the last possible moment. The building across the street was a hive of activity. He had a perfect god's-eye view: Each window held a desk covered with paper, a blue pulsing computer monitor, generic modern art, dying ficus plants, men and women talking on the phone, earnestly confiding in and consulting with one another, comically unaware of what was happening in the windows all around them. It was a hall of mirrors, the same scene endlessly replicated. That used to be him. He glanced at his watch. It was almost three thirty, the middle of what would have been his work day.

It was the oddest, most uncanny feeling, not working. He never realized how complicated his own life was until he had to get out of it. It had taken Edward six months to plan for the move to London, delegating projects, handing off contacts, transitioning key clients to the stewardship of his colleagues in an endless series of lunches, dinners, meetings, e-mails, conference calls, braindumps, and mind-melds. The sheer number of threads from which he had to delicately disentangle himself one at a time was staggering, and every time he pulled one out he found more threads attached to it.

'Please keep the curtains closed. For the books.' Laura's prim, expressionless voice came from the doorway, where she had silently reappeared like the hoary old housekeeper in a horror movie. He stepped back guiltily. 'We keep the temperature artificially low for the same reason.'

She went over to the table and laid down a black binder and a laptop in a carrying case.

'These should help you with the cataloging. There are some guidelines in this notebook, and you can keep the records on the computer for now. We had Alberto – he takes care of our computers – install a cataloging program that might be of some help to you. If you have any questions, just ask Margot, she'll tell you where to find me. Oh, and keep an eye out for anything by an author named Gervase of Langford. These would be very early books, I'm told, very old. If you see anything by him, do let me know right away.'

'Okay,' he said. 'Gervase of Langford.'

There was a moment of silence.

'I'm sure I'll be seeing you later on,' she said.

'I'm sure you will.'

Now he just wanted her to leave.

'Good to meet you, then.' She obviously had no desire to stay, either.

'Bye.' Edward felt like he should have asked her something else, but nothing came to mind. He listened to the sound of her footsteps as she descended the metal staircase. He was alone.

There was one chair in the room, an antique rolling desk chair standing in the pool of light cast by the one lamp. He brushed it off and sat down; it was hard, but the back flexed very comfortably on an intricate array of springs. Edward rolled himself over to the window and cheated open the crack in the curtains a little wider, then he rolled himself back with a sound like a gutter ball in an empty bowling alley. The three-ring binder on the table was covered in black leather, and inside were twenty or thirty sheets of onionskin paper closely covered with single-spaced typing. They were old, and the hard keystrokes of a manual typewriter had embossed the words into the paper:

> It is my intention that the books in this collection be described according to the Principles of the Science of Bibliography. These Principles are simple and precise, although the variety of the objects with which they are concerned can give rise to scenarios of considerable complexity . . .

Edward rolled his eyes. He already regretted his impulse decision. He seemed to be developing a dangerous habit of helping strange women in distress – first that woman on the sidewalk, now Laura Crowlyk. He flipped through the pages. They were full of diagrams and definitions and descriptions of different kinds of book-bindings, catalogs of various papers and parchments and leathers, examples of assorted handwritings and scripts and typefaces, lists of ornaments, colophons, imperfections, irregularities, printings, editions, watermarks, and so on and so on and so forth.

At the bottom of the last page was a faded blue signature, absurdly elaborate. It was almost illegible, but the author had typed his name below it:

DESMOND WENT

And then a title:

13TH DUKE OF BOWMRY
WEYMARSHE CASTLE

After the final *e* came a long series of flourishes, meaningless loops and curls and rosettes that stretched all the way down to the bottom of the page.

CHAPTER 2

'Bowmry,' he said. His voice sounded very small in the vast, empty room. 'Where the hell is Bowmry?'

Edward set the binder back down on the table and unzipped the laptop case. Of course, that must have been them out on the street, he thought. Mr and Mrs Went – the Duke and Duchess, presumably. He should have known. He supposed they must be on their way back there now, wherever there was. What an odd couple of birds. Prying up the screen with one hand, gently, he felt with the other for the rocker switch on the back. The computer chimed softly in the silence. While it whirred and clicked into life he opened the drawer and took out the screwdriver.

It was a satisfyingly hefty screwdriver, the kind with a fat clear-plastic handle with sparkles floating in it. Edward shrugged out, of his jacket and draped it over the back of the chair, then walked over to the nearest stack of crates. His cell phone rang – it had mysteriously returned to life. It was one of his lesser lieutenants from the office, a first-year analyst. He listened for a minute or two before he interrupted.

'Slow down. Loosen your tie. All right. Are you sitting down? Tie loose?'

He leaned down to examine the crates. They were made of rough white pine boards that still smelled like Christmas trees. The original shipping labels were still attached, addressed to someone named Cruttenden and stamped with heraldic-looking governmental seals from both sides of the Atlantic. A few stray beads of clear yellow sap had oozed out of the wood and hardened into place. A few thousand years and they'd be amber.

'Put the money in French insurance company bonds. Yeah, I know there's a drought in France. No, the insurance companies aren't exposed. French insurance companies don't cover drought. No, they don't. French farmers have their own federal fund. Federal. Entirely separate.'

The first screw resisted as the metal threads bit into the soft wood, but soon it was out, and he set it carefully aside, point up, on the edge of the table. The next one came more quickly, and he went along the top edge of the crate methodically, the cell phone clamped under his ear, until there were ten or twelve freshly liberated screws lined up in a row. Scratchy wisps of dry straw were starting to poke out from under the top, and the edge of a crumpled, yellowed newspaper that had been used as stuffing.

He was annoyed at himself for having kowtowed

to Laura Crowlyk. He took it out on the assistant, whose name was Andre.

'I'm not interested in Farsheed's problems, Andre. Farsheed's problems happen somewhere very far below me. Understand? If Farsheed has problems, don't tell me about them, solve them. Then he won't have any problems, and you won't have any problems either, and neither will I, and the world will be a wonderful place with rainbows and happy flowers and birds singing.'

That seemed like a good note to end on. He hung up the phone and turned it off.

Edward's wrist ached by the time he got the last screw out. He set the screwdriver aside. The top of the crate was hinged, and it squealed as he opened it, then banged down loudly against the side. He peered down into the dimness. Inside were rows of dark packages, firmly nestled in a mixture of straw and newspaper and wrapped in a brown paper. They were all different shapes and sizes. In spite of himself he felt a prickle of excitement in his palms. He felt like a successful smuggler triumphantly unpacking his cargo in the safety of his hideout.

He leaned in and took out one of the parcels at random. It was heavy, about the size and weight of a phone book, and the wrapping paper was folded and sealed with extreme precision, like a box of expensive candy. It was unmarked. He put it down on the table and took out his keys; one of them had a sharp set of teeth, and he used it to part the tape along the seams. Opening packages was something he'd missed doing since he'd acquired his first assistant at work. Densely packed wads of newspaper bulged out as he slit the paper. He uncrumpled one. It turned out to be from a daily paper in London: HISTORIC CHURCH DESTROYED. Inside were two dense, heavy sub-packages stacked on top of each other, each one individually wrapped in thick sea-green paper.

It took him a minute to unwrap the first one – there was still another layer underneath – but when he was done a small, red, leather-bound book lay in front of him in the middle of a huge blossom of wrapping paper.

He picked it up, handling it with involuntary tenderness. The cover was blank, with only a faint thread of gilt tracery around the edges. The word *Travels* was printed on the spine in golden letters. The book gave off a faint breath of dampness in the chilly air.

He laid it flat on the paper and opened it to the title page:

VOLUME II
Of the Author's
WORKS

containing

TRAVELS

INTO SEVERAL
REMOTE NATIONS OF THE WORLD,

by **Lemuel Gulliver,** *first a* **Surgeon,**
and then a **Captain** *of several* **Ships.**

Some of the *s*'s looked like *f*'s; others were printed long and curving, like integral signs. The date underneath was MDCCXXXV – he tried to work it out in his head, then gave up – and the city was Dublin. On the facing page was an engraved portrait of the author. The paper was speckled like an egg, and a faint brown stain had spread like a billowing cumulus cloud over the bottom third of the title page.

Edward set the book aside, keeping it on the wrapping paper so it wouldn't get dusty, and opened the other package. It turned out to be Volume I. He flipped through the pages, idly glancing at occasional passages. He'd been assigned this book once in college but never read it. Hadn't there been a cartoon of it? The two books were in improbably pristine condition, though the pages were brittle and the corners were a little crushed.

Returning to the crate, Edward now saw that the books in the top layer were just the smaller ones, and that there were larger, more substantial volumes farther down. He checked his watch: It was already four-thirty. He should at least make it look like he'd gotten something done before he took off.

He started quickly transferring the rest of the

smaller packages to the table and shucking off the wrapping paper. He uncovered triple-decker novels, chunky dictionaries, vast, sprawling atlases, nineteenth-century textbooks scribbled on by schoolboys who had long since grown up and died, crumbling religious tracts, a miniature set of Shakespeare's tragedies, three inches high and equipped with its own magnifying glass. He arranged them carefully in tall stacks along the back of the work table. Some books were crisp and solid, others fell apart in his hands. One or two of the older ones had foot-long leather thongs and straps dangling from them. He got side-tracked and wasted twenty minutes leafing through an ancient brown leather *Gray's Anatomy*, with many incredibly detailed and occasionally disturbing illustrations of creatively vivisected corpses.

After a while he stopped to take a break. By this time the floor around him was covered with a heaving ocean of wrapping paper. The room was still lit by the warm, brown light of the floor lamp, but the sunlight coming through the heavy curtains was soft and orange.

Edward looked at his watch again. It was almost six – he'd lost track of time. His hands were covered with brown and red dust from the leather covers. He rubbed off as much of it as he could and slipped on his jacket. He'd send Laura Crowlyk the dry-cleaning bill.

On his way out he walked over to the crate again.

A few of the largest, most massive volumes were still left down at the bottom, buried in the straw like dinosaur bones half-submerged in the earth. He bent down to pick one up. It was much heavier than he'd expected, and he had to lean his gut into the edge of the crate and use both hands to get it out. He cleared a space and set it down on the table with a solid *whump*. Fine dust flew out from underneath it. When he got it unwrapped, instead of a book he found a finished wooden case with a simple metal catch on one edge. He undid it, and the case swung open on small, finely made metal hinges.

Inside was a thick black board about one foot wide by two feet long, covered with leather that had turned black with age. Its surface was overgrown with a dark mass of stamps and filigreed metal studs and bosses, and complicated illustrations had been forcibly stamped into the horny leather: abstract ornaments and motifs, panels with human figures standing in different poses. In the center was an oddly proportioned tree, squat and massive, with a spray of tiny branches at the top. Edward felt the ancient surface with his fingertips. There was a deep scar in the leather, and the wood underneath it had splintered and been worn smooth again. Something had struck it very hard, a very long time ago. In places the ornamentation was so thick and dark the pattern was impossible to follow. It looked more like a door than the cover of a book.

It exerted an odd power over him, freezing him to the spot as if it were charged with electricity. He stood there for a minute in the silence, his hands resting on the worked surface, feeling the indentations with his fingertips like a blind man reading Braille. There was no indication of what its contents might be. What could a book like this possibly be about? Tentatively he tried to open it, but it resisted, and when he felt around the edges he discovered a lock that kept it closed, bolted onto the wooden covers. The metal was crudely worked, and time had rusted it into a single solid mass. He wondered how old it was. He tested it gently, but it wouldn't move, and he didn't want to force it.

He blinked. The spell lapsed as suddenly as it had come over him. Why the hell was he still here? He closed the case, snapped off the light and walked to the door. After the cold of the library, the metal railing of the spiral staircase was warm under his hand as he felt his way down the stairs in the darkness. Back out in the hallway, the daylight seemed offensively bright.

But he felt oddly purged by his industrious afternoon. It hadn't been worth doing, but it could have been much worse. It could have blown up in his face. He headed back down the hall in the direction of the stairs. He glanced into the room where he'd talked to Laura Crowlyk, but it was empty now. The window he'd opened before was closed again. The sunlight slanted in at a shallower angle, and with a golden-orange tint. He smelled dinner cooking somewhere. Did Laura Crowlyk actually live here?

The cleaning woman he'd met before was sitting on the edge of a chair in the entrance hall reading *Allure*. She started up guiltily when he appeared and bustled out through another exit. Edward opened the glass doors by the elevator and pressed the button to call it. He straightened his tie in the clouded old mirror.

'Are you going?'

He turned around, smiling. He'd kind of hoped he could slip out without running into Laura Crowlyk.

'Sorry, I couldn't find you. I lost track of time.'

She nodded gravely, looking up at him.

'When will you be coming back?'

Why even bother explaining? Let Dan do the apologizing. It was his fuckup.

'I'm not sure. I'll check my schedule and give you a call in the morning.'

'Fine. Call us tomorrow.' She glanced back behind her at someone in the other room – she might have exchanged a whispered word or two with whoever it was. 'Hold on a moment. I'll get you a key to the apartment.'

She disappeared abruptly and was gone for another minute. The elevator came; Edward watched impatiently as the doors rumbled open and then closed again. He didn't want the key, all he wanted was to get out of there. Laura returned,

34

crossing the enormous oriental carpet toward him, and gave him a dark metal tube key. Well, he'd just have to take it for now.

'It works in the elevator,' she said. 'There's a special keyhole for it. The doorman will let you in the front.'

'Thanks.'

The elevator gave a muffled ping and opened again. Edward stepped inside and put his hand on the rubber-flanged edge to keep it from closing.

'So I'll call you tomorrow,' he said. 'About my schedule.'

Maybe I should make a clean break, he thought. *Call it off. Do it now.* She watched him steadily, as if she could sense his indecision but knew the outcome in advance.

'Tomorrow then.'

The door nudged him impatiently on the shoulder, then closed.

Twenty-five minutes later Edward was back in more familiar territory, sitting in a tattered armchair in his friend Zeph's apartment. His hand held a sweating bottle of McSorley's Ale. The room had a pleasantly musty smell. It was dark, partly because the lights were off, but mostly because the windows were covered with big kindergarten sheets of construction paper in primary colors. The only light came from a computer screen.

Zeph sat next to him playing a computer game. Edward had known him since college, where they'd been assigned to each other as freshman room-mates and, improbably, stayed friends. Zeph was always slightly too cool for the computer geeks he took most of his classes with, and Edward hadn't been quite cool enough for the moneyed, prep-schooled pre-professionals with whom he spent most of his time, and that shared sense of not-quite-fitting-in had become a bond between them in itself. Zeph looked like a child's idea of an ogre: six and a half feet tall, with the massive, gently rounded frame of a naturally large man who never exercised. He had a big potato nose and lumpy amateur white-boy dreadlocks.

'So I went to see the Wents today,' Edward said, breaking a long, comfortable silence.

'The who?' Zeph's double-bass voice sounded like a record played a little too slowly.

'The Wents. Those English clients I told you about. It turns out all they wanted was somebody to organize their library.'

'Their library? What the hell did you tell them?'

'What could I tell them? I'm organizing their library.'

'You are.'

'Well, I made a start on it. It's a pretty big library.'

Deep horizontal wrinkles formed in Zeph's massive brow as he attempted to negotiate some especially tricky maneuver in the game he was playing.

'Edward,' he said gravely, 'you have just received

the most prestigious appointment of your dull but admittedly lucrative career. You're the Golden Child. You're leaving the country in two weeks. Why would you want to spend your last days in the greatest city in the world cleaning some Jeremy Irons character's attic?'

'I don't know.' Edward shook his head. 'It's some kind of screwup. I'm going to call it off tomorrow. I'll call the office and rip somebody's head off. But it's weird, they took me up to this old library, and once I actually saw all these old books lying around in boxes, in this enormous old room – I don't know. I can't explain it.' Edward sipped his beer. It was true, he really couldn't explain it. 'It was just a courtesy visit. You're right, I should be on vacation.'

'Venice is a vacation. This is like work-release.'

'I'll call it off tomorrow. I'm just a little low on sleep. I pulled a couple of all-nighters right before one of those big SEC sessions. Haven't really bounced back yet.' He yawned. 'It was weird – for once it was kind of good to be doing something that didn't involve any thinking. Nobody watching me. They just left me alone up there. They're some kind of aristocrats – he's a duke or a baron or something.' He sat back in his chair and sighed. 'Plus it's good for me to be around English people. I need to learn how to deal with them.'

'What's to learn?' Zeph took a swig from a can of Diet Pepsi. 'Bad teeth, sexy accents.'

Zeph wore sweatpants and a T-shirt with the

words GOGO PARA PRESIDENTE on it. While they talked he fiddled with the game, his huge hands manipulating the wireless keyboard with surprising delicacy. The computer sat on a long table set up on two flimsy IKEA trestles, and the room wasn't much wider than the table. The walls were papered with posters of the Mandelbrot set rendered in psychedelic colors, and fat, split-spined math text-books were piled up in teetering stacks in the corners.

'What is this, anyway?' said Edward, pointing at the screen. He tried not to encourage Zeph's geeky tendencies, but once in a while he pretended to take an interest. 'It looks like a kid's game.'

'Ever have an Atari 2600?'

'I guess. I had an Atari. I don't know what number it was.'

'It was probably a 2600. This is an old Atari 2600 game called *Adventure*. You're the little square here.' Zeph tapped the keys, and a small yellow square on the screen moved in a circle. 'You're on a quest for the Holy Grail. You need to get the key to open the castle. Then you find more keys, with which you open more castles, until you find the Grail. Bring the Grail back to the yellow castle, and you win. On the way, you run into dragons, like the one that's chasing me right now' – a creature that looked like a green duck was bobbing along behind the square – 'who try to eat you. There's also a magnet, and a big purple bridge, and a bat who picks things up and flies away with them – ah, and here's the sword. Good for killing dragons.'

The square picked up the sword, which was really nothing more than a yellow arrow, and waved it through the dragon. The dragon died, accompanied by a mournful downward glissando.

'Key, castle, sword, dragon. The basic building blocks of a tiny, self-contained universe. Very simple. Nothing ambiguous. Every story ends one of two ways: Death, or Victory.'

The square had the Grail now, a pulsing, psyche-delic goblet five times as big as it was. Edward watched languidly as it brought the Grail back to the yellow castle and the screen lit up with a light show and weird, bubbling sound effects.

'So that was Victory?' Edward said.

'How sweet it is. And that was just Level One.'

'How many levels are there?'

'Three. But the truly cool thing is, this is the original Atari code. Somebody actually bothered to write an emulator program that makes my five-thousand-dollar PC think it's a twenty-dollar Atari console from 1982. Then they sucked the code out of an old *Adventure* cartridge, posted it on the Internet, I downloaded it, and Bob's your uncle.'

'Huh,' said Edward, sipping his beer. It was cold and satisfyingly bitter. 'Is that even legal?'

'Kind of a gray area. Want to take it for a spin?'

'Not really.'

Zeph heaved his bulk up out of the desk chair

and sat down again on a broken-down futon Edward recognized from their college days.

'So when you move to the London office, who's going to do your job here?'

'It's an exchange. There's an English guy who comes here from over there. Nicholas something.'

'Nickleby?' Zeph took another swig. 'You know what he is, he's your fetch. It's a Celtic myth: A fetch is a double, a creature that's born at the same moment as you are and looks exactly like you. Woe betide you if you ever meet your fetch.' He snapped his fingers. 'That's it. Game over.'

'Yikes.' Edward stood up. 'I'm going to the bathroom.'

Zeph and Caroline lived in a long, rambling, dusty apartment in the West Village that they'd bought outright with a truckload of stock options from a dotcom Caroline had walked away from at the right time. Virtually every wall was lined with shelves, including the kitchen and the bathroom, and on the shelves were Zeph and Caroline's collection of small plastic toys: Chinese puzzles, LEGOs, action figures, Happy Meal prizes, Rubik's Cubes, spheres, and dodecahedrons. Edward never understood what they saw in them. Zeph said they were good for his spatial visualization skills, though having seen Zeph's senior thesis on low-dimensional topology, Edward thought his spatial visualization skills might already be morbidly overdeveloped.

On his way back Edward was surprised to find a small man standing in the hallway outside Zeph's study. He was studying Zeph's collection absorbedly. Edward had never seen him before.

'Hey,' said Edward.

'Hello,' the man said in a calm, liquid voice. His head was perfectly round, and he had fine, straight dark hair like a child's.

Edward held out his hand.

'I'm Edward.'

The small man put the pink plastic pyramid he was playing with back on the shelf. Edward belatedly withdrew his hand.

'Are you a friend of Zeph's?' he hazarded.

'No.'

The man-child, who really was tiny, barely five feet tall, looked up at him patiently, without blinking.

'So—'

'I used to work with Caroline. As a sysop.'

'Oh, yeah? Like in an office?'

'Exactly.' He beamed, as if he were delighted at Edward's success. 'Exactly. I kept the e-mail server and the local network running. Very interesting.'

'Was it.'

'Yes, it was.' He seemed to have no sense of irony whatsoever. 'Consider the example of packet data. The moment you click SEND on an e-mail, your message splits up into a hundred separate pieces – we call them "packets." It's like mailing a letter by ripping up a sheet of paper and tossing the pieces out the window. They wend their separate ways over the Internet, moving independently, wandering from server to server, but they all arrive at the same destination at the same time, where they spontaneously self-assemble again into a coherent message: your e-mail. Chaos becomes order. What is scattered is made whole.

'You learn a lot about human nature, too. It's amazing what some people will leave on their hard drives, completely unencrypted.'

The man looked up at Edward and quirked an eyebrow at him meaningfully. Edward considered the possibility that he might be hitting on him. He was suddenly gripped with a burning desire to be back in Zeph's study with his beer.

'Excuse me for just a moment,' he said. He sidled carefully past the man, avoiding physical contact as he would with a dog of uncertain provenance, and slipped back into Zeph's study. He closed the door and stood with his back to it.

'You know there's a gnome in your hallway.'

Caroline was there, sitting on Zeph's knee. She was a small woman with a round face surrounded by a corona of curly, honey-brown hair. She had tiny, squinty eyes behind round steel glasses.

'I see you met our friend the Artiste,' she said. Her voice was the opposite of Zeph's: a breathy, baby-doll, Blossom Dearie voice.

'He followed her home one day,' said Zeph. 'Now he shows up and hangs around sometimes. He's pretty harmless.'

Edward looked from one to the other.

'You just let him wander around your house like that?'

'He'll leave eventually,' Caroline explained. 'It freaked me out at first, but after a while I figured out that you don't have to pay any attention to him. He's mildly autistic, something called Asperger Syndrome. He's pretty functional. It doesn't interfere with his intelligence – he's probably smarter than all three of us put together – but it means he has trouble dealing with people. And he gets obsessive about certain things, like computers. Actually, it's good to have him around. He's an unbelievable programmer. He works freelance.'

'Sometimes he slips into machine language while he's talking,' Zeph added. 'Just ones and zeros.' He shuddered, hugging his massive shoulders. 'Creepy.'

'And so he just has the one name?'

Caroline frowned at him. 'Be nice, Edward. The Artiste does the best he can. Zephram, is Edward coming with us tonight?'

'I haven't asked him. Want to come to a party, Edward?'

'I don't know. I'm kind of tired after all that filing.'

Zeph picked up a chunk of volcanic glass that held down a stack of papers and retrieved a small, cream-colored envelope.

'Do you remember a guy in college named Joe Fabrikant?' he asked.

'Fabrikant?' Edward frowned. 'I guess so. Blond. Prep-school type.'

'We're doing some back-end stuff for his intranet.'

43

Caroline shifted herself down onto Zeph's lap. 'Database stuff. He's dreamy.'

'He makes tons of money,' said Zeph. 'The big success story from our class.'

'He's one of these genetically perfect people. He looks like a giant Norse god.'

Zeph passed the envelope to Caroline, who leaned forward and passed it to Edward. Inside was a simple card with an invitation to a party on it.

'I'm sure he has no idea who I am,' said Edward.

'Actually, he asked us to ask you.'

'Really?' That was odd.

Zeph shrugged.

'You came up. I guess he heard about your London gig. Gave him a hard-on. He remembers you from school.'

Caroline hauled over the keyboard and started another game of *Adventure*.

'Come on,' Zeph said. 'There's free booze. You can suck up to influential people. Uninfluential people will suck up to you. You'll love it.'

Edward didn't answer. Zeph was right, and on any other night in the past four years he would have jumped at the invitation. Why not tonight? He thought about all the people who would be there – people he knew or half knew, like Fabrikant, and people he'd never met but whom he nonetheless knew down to the very bottom lines of their xeroxed, stapled, and collated souls.

It was hot, and he took off his jacket and draped it carefully over the arm of his chair. He took another sip from his beer. On the screen, Caroline's yellow square passed the entrance to a corridor that was blocked off by a plain black line.

'Can you go through there?'

'Nope. That's a force field. *Verboten*.'

Caroline was in the courtyard of the black castle, in front of the portcullis. Three duck-dragons, red, yellow, and green, were chasing her around and around in a circle. She teased them, staying just out of their reach, but after a while she miscalculated and got caught in the red dragon's teeth. The square stopped, vibrating in panic for a moment, then there was a swallowing sound and it slid down the dragon's throat into its stomach.

'Hard cheese, old girl,' said Zeph.

They watched the screen in funereal silence. Absurdly, through a glitch in their programming, the other dragons apparently didn't realize the square was dead, and they kept on circling and biting at it in the red dragon's stomach. The black bat entered the screen from the upper left corner. Off in another part of the apartment music was playing; it sounded like 'Smoke Gets in Your Eyes.'

'Damn it,' Zeph said. 'He's into our CD collection.'

'Hang on,' Caroline said. 'Wait a second – this sometimes happens.'

The bat flew diagonally, apparently unimpeded by walls. It made several preliminary passes through the room, cutting through it at an angle, then it changed course deliberately and without slowing

45

down picked up the red dragon and flew away with it. The square came with it, still in the dragon's stomach, and the camera shifted to follow them. The bat flew them willy-nilly through mazes, castles, hallways, secret chambers. It was like being a ghost on a madcap, high-speed haunting spree, a whirlwind tour of the hidden corners of the universe.

Suddenly Edward realized that he was exhausted. Zeph and Caroline, much as he loved them, were geeks, and it was getting to be a little much. Anyway, he should stop by the office and clear up this business about the Wents before his boss left for the night. He looked at his watch.

'I should go,' he said.

'I'll walk you out.' Zeph pushed himself upright, shoving the futon violently back against the wall.

Edward followed him out into the hallway. They walked out into the small, dark living room. The air was heavy with some unfamiliar spice that smelled like Indian food, probably from the restaurant across the street. Caroline's desk was out here, with her books and files scattered around it.

'Wait.' Zeph stopped. 'Hang on a second.'

He ducked back into the hallway and came back with a small square manila envelope, the kind with a red string fastener.

'For you.'

Edward carefully unwound the string. He opened

46

the flap and tipped the contents out into his hand. It was a CD.

'Sorry I don't have a case for it,' Zeph said.

Edward studied its mirrored surface; he caught a glimpse of his face in it, glorified like a medieval saint's, with prismatic highlights. He turned it over. It was completely blank.

'What is it?'

'Something to keep you busy,' said Zeph. 'Burned it m'self.'

'Is it music?'

'It's a game.'

'A computer game?' Edward said, with a sinking feeling. 'You mean like Tetris or something?'

Zeph nodded.

'The Artiste got me hooked on it, actually. It's amazing.'

Edward did his best to look enthused.

'What's it called?'

'Doesn't have a name. Some people call it MOMUS, I don't know why. It's what they call an open source project. Means it's a collaboration between lots of different people over the Internet. Try it, it's a great escape. Really addictive.'

'Great. Thanks a lot.' Edward put the disc back in the envelope, holding it with his thumb and forefinger like a dead insect, and delicately wound up the string again. Oblivious to his dismay, Zeph offered him his hand, a little self-consciously, and Edward shook it.

'Anyway, congratulations. Happy promotion. I'll

call you later about that party. Have some fun for a change.' Zeph shot the bolt. 'It wouldn't be the end of the world.'

Outside in the street it was early evening. Zeph and Caroline's apartment was in the West Village, near Washington Square Park. Edward strolled over to Sixth Avenue and turned right, heading uptown. He felt tired and strangely passive. Was he going to the office? No, he decided, he was not. He was too tired. He'd call in tomorrow morning instead.

The sun was setting, but the afternoon heat showed no sign of subsiding. Edward took a deep breath. The air had a complicated but not un-pleasant smell, a uniquely New York smell com-posed of smoke from the sidewalk gyro vendors, fumes from the subway, steam from a million coffee cups, the delicate evaporations from the glistening surfaces of thousands of fifteen-dollar cosmopoli-tans. A movie crew was setting up on the busy side-walk, running fat black electrical cables in and out of unmarked white trailers, rerouting passersby into the street. Three card tables stood by themselves off to one side loaded down with pasta salad and veggie wraps and cans of diet soda all mummified in plastic wrap. The crew had sprayed sticky white foam like shaving cream all over the pavement to simulate snow for a winter scene. The surrealness of it all in the heat gave Edward a disconnected, dissociated feeling.

He flagged down a taxi at Fourteenth Street. The

driver didn't answer when Edward gave him his destination – his name on the license sounded Chinese – but he seemed to understand. Edward's cell phone rang: Andre again. He let it ring. The cab's black upholstery had been patched so many times it was more duct tape than vinyl, but it was soft and springy, and the seat was tilted sharply backward. He had to fight the urge to close his eyes and take a nap. He watched limply out the window as the hip facades of Chelsea became the shiny metal-and-glass cliffs of midtown, then transmogrified into the soft gray-green of Central Park, with its lumpy landscaped hillocks and its Victorian folly bridges with their intricate, crumbling, urine-soaked brickwork.

Maybe it was the beer he drank at Zeph's, but he really did feel utterly exhausted, body-slammed, wiped out. He'd been working way too hard these past few months – binging on work, wallowing in it, gorging on it, sixty, seventy, eighty hours a week. The more work he did the more there was to do, and he could always find a little more appetite for it, and a little more room in his belly to stuff it down. The only thing that was finite was time, and you could always fix that by sleeping less. Every evening as he set his clock radio he calculated how little he could get by on, like a diver making a dive plan for a dangerous night-time descent: balancing the pressures, estimating his endurance, rationing his precious reserves.

Images from the past six months crowded into

49

his mind, as if the force fields holding them back had suddenly vanished or given way. The permanent twilight of midtown; the not-unattractive face of his assistant, already at her desk when he came in in the morning; the comfy leather chair in his office; the accusing red eye of his voice mail, glaring at him like the malevolent eye of HAL; the firm handshakes with lawyers; his cell phone ringing everywhere – while he was shaving, in a movie, in a stall in the bathroom at La Guardia. Lately the blinking e-mail icon in the upper right-hand corner of his desktop had started appearing in his peripheral vision even when he was away from his desk, causing him to jerk his head up at nothing like an insane person. Three or four times a month he'd pull an all-nighter, doing push-ups on the carpet to stay awake till six, little muscles jumping in his chest from all the caffeine, his jaw clenched like an iron robot's jaw. He would take a car home in the grim quiet of early dawn, feeling like he'd been clubbed in the head. He'd go upstairs and shower, telling himself he felt fine, perfectly fine, good to go, and put on a fresh shirt. Straightening his tie in his kitchen, leaning on his still brand-new stove – he'd never even had the gas turned on – he could see the company car idling by the curb, sending puffs of white exhaust floating up into the early morning air, waiting to take him back to the office for a briefing at seven thirty—

Edward snapped awake as the Chinese driver

pulled up in front of his building. He had to struggle to get his wallet out of the front pocket of his pants. He was so tired he felt like he could fall asleep at any second, right in the middle of the sidewalk. For a minute he stabbed futilely at his front door with the key to his office before he found his building key. He was going to pass out. Finally he was inside, he was climbing the stairs, he was closing the latches behind him in his apartment. He didn't even make it to the bedroom, just lay facedown on the couch.

CHAPTER 3

Growing up in Maine, Edward hadn't especially wanted to be an investment banker, or anything else for that matter. He wasn't one of those children who had his sights set on being something specific: a doctor, or a fireman, or an astronaut with a mission specialty in long-range sensing. When he thought about his childhood, which was rarely, the image that came to mind was of watching snow pile up on a porch railing in the late afternoon, the line of it holding perfectly steady like the line on a graph, then curving up a little where it rose to meet the corner post, and wondering if school would be canceled tomorrow.

His family lived in an old white-painted Victorian house with a thinning patch of lawn out front and a tire swing in back. His parents were ex-hippies, communards who turned out not to have the stomach for life on the farm, and by the time they went straight they found themselves established in the narrow suburban fringe that encircled the old brick city of Bangor and separated it from the cold, piney vastness beyond.

Bangor was a nineteenth-century lumber capital fallen on hard times. It took a lot of snow to cancel school, but fortunately for Edward, Bangor got a lot of snow. If it started before he went to bed – and the later it started, the better his chances were – he would lie awake listening to the snow-muffled silence, and once his parents were asleep he would shine a flashlight out the window, watching each snowflake gleam once as it passed through the beam and then vanished into collective anonymity on the lawn. He would stare feverishly out into the moonless darkness and try to gauge the frequency and quality of the flakes, factoring in temperature and duration, humidity and wind speed, praying inarticulate but fervent prayers to the Superintendent of Schools. Usually he would wake up to the sound of the snowplow scraping orange sparks from the asphalt as it bulled its way down the street, followed a few minutes later by the roar of the sand truck, burying his hopes in a mixture of dirt and road salt.

Growing up in that black-and-white landscape, with snow on the ground from October to May, it made a certain kind of sense that Edward would have a gift for chess.

Once, while his mother was driving them the five hours south to Boston to see relatives, Edward's father gave him an indulgent ten-minute lesson on a miniature magnetic travel chess set, passing it back and forth between the front and back seats. Edward stalemated his father on the first try, beat him on the second, and never lost again. He was seven. For the next five years he spent every weekend – all of Saturday and most of Sunday – at a chess club in Camden, a once grand, now shabby mansion that smelled of peeling wallpaper and old horsehair upholstery. It was populated almost exclusively by annoyingly precocious little boys like Edward and melancholy old men, including two homesick Russian émigrés who would mutter *Bozhe moi!* and *Chyort vozmi!* through their flowing beards as Edward gracefully trapped their knights and forked their rooks.

By the time he was twelve a Bowdoin professor was coaching him every day after school, and he was traveling to Boston and New York and once, thrillingly, to London for chess tournaments. He had a national ranking and a shelf of chess trophies in his bedroom. The very sight of him – already tall, pale as a white bishop, with starch-stiff posture at the board – struck fear into the tiny hearts of his underaged adversaries.

By the time he was thirteen it was all over. Edward's gift evaporated like dew in the harsh dawn of puberty, painlessly and almost overnight, and though afterwards he could clearly remember what it was like to wander through those gleaming mental corridors, the doors to that secret edifice were now firmly closed, the silver key lost, the path overgrown, never to be found again. His ranking plummeted, and his matches became a series of tearful early concessions. He sometimes caught his parents looking at him as if they wondered what had happened to their brilliant changeling of a son.

But despite the tears, and the puzzled looks from his parents, deep down Edward wasn't devastated by the loss of his gift. It left as mysteriously as it had arrived. He missed it, but it had never seemed entirely his in the first place – he'd always felt like its host, a temporary custodian, nothing more. He wasn't bitter. He only wished it well wherever its invisible wings had taken it.

Nevertheless, there were times when he looked back on his years as a wunderkind with nostalgia. In the years that followed he caught himself again and again trying to recapture the feeling of effortless mastery and easy serenity that he'd known on the chessboard, the sense that he was special and meant for better things. He looked for it in his schoolwork, in sports, in sex, in books, and even, much later, in his job at Esslin & Hart.

He never found it.

When Edward woke up he was still lying on the couch. It was dark out. He sat up and slid off his tie, which was creased and wrinkled from having been trapped underneath him.

A weak, pinkish glow from the streetlights outside lit up the two front windows. Edward's apartment was long and narrow, the shape of the skinny Upper East Side apartment building the top floor of which it occupied. It was all one big room, more or less: Up front was the living room, which gradually became the study, which gave way onto a crawlway-thin galley kitchen, and behind it an ill-lit bedroom and a disproportionately sumptuous bathroom. He could have afforded a place twice the size, but he'd never had the time to look for one, and what was the point? He was hardly ever here. The air-conditioning blew out last summer and he hadn't even bothered to get it fixed.

His clock radio spelled out 9:04 in skinny red trapezoids. Edward stood up and went over to his desk in the darkness, undoing his white shirt with one hand. It was too early to go to bed, but he wasn't sure he really wanted to be awake either. Yawning mightily, he picked up his jacket where he'd dropped it on the floor, and he felt the stiff shape of the manila envelope in the inside pocket – Zeph's present. He took it out and looked at it.

Zeph had written on the envelope, in block letters,

FOR EDWARD, WHO HAS PLENTY OF TIME

He slipped the CD out into his hand. It was completely unmarked, and he had to guess which way up it went. As he tilted it in the light, two rainbow spokes chased each other around the center hole.

Edward sighed. He had a colleague named Stewart, a couple of years younger than he was but still a grown man, who kept a GameBoy in his office. He was addicted to it – he played with it constantly, during meetings, on the phone, by the water-cooler, in the back of a limo. It was one of the jokes around the office, Stewart and his purple GameBoy, but Edward just found it embarrassing. He loathed the slack expression on Stewart's face while he played it – the fixed gaze, the loose, parted lips, like a moron trying to solve a calculus problem. If he ever saw that GameBoy come out in front of a client, Edward swore he would throw it out a window.

But he had no choice: He would at least have to take a look at the game. Zeph would ask. Edward walked over to his desk and felt around under it for the power button on his computer. He yawned and stretched while it booted up, then slipped the disc into the CD-ROM drive. A program calling itself 'imthegame.exe' asked permission to install itself. He consented. The program spent a few long minutes unpacking and copying a series of colossal files to his hard drive, setting itself up, looking around, making itself at home. When it was done there was a new shortcut on his desktop. He double-clicked on it.

The screen blacked out abruptly, and the speakers gave a vicious staticky *snap*. The hard drive chooked and whirred to itself like a hen laying an egg. For a minute nothing else happened. Edward looked at the clock again. It was half past nine. He could still change his mind about that party at Joe Fabrikant's office if he really wanted to. His desk lamp made

57

an island of light in the darkened apartment. He leaned his head on his hand.

Then his computer was awake again. Tiny white letters appeared on the screen, against a black background.

ONE PLAYER, OR MANY?

Edward clicked on one. The words disappeared.

CHOOSE ONE:

* MALE
* FEMALE

He blinked. That seemed a little personal. He toyed with the idea of lying, then went ahead and clicked on male.

CHOOSE ONE:

* LAND
* SEA
* RIVER

RIVER.

CHOOSE ONE:

* EASY
* MEDIUM

* HARD
* IMPOSSIBLE

He was on vacation. EASY.

CHOOSE ONE:

* SHORT
* MEDIUM
* LONG

SHORT.

The CD-ROM drive whined and clicked some more, then went silent. The screen went black again for so long that Edward started to wonder if the program had hung. He was about to try aborting it when the hard drive started thrashing again. He hesitated, his hands poised over the keyboard. The screen cleared.

At first Edward thought he was looking at a photograph, frozen and digitized. The scene was strikingly realistic. It was like looking through a window onto another world. The light was green, and there were trees around him, a grove of slender birches and aspens with sunlight falling between them. A light breeze ruffled their tiny leaves. Beyond the delicate scrim of trees was open air and green grass.

Edward moved the mouse experimentally. His point of view swung to one side like a movie camera. He carefully tilted it down and saw a leaf-strewn path. He tilted it back, toward the sky. It was blue, with a single white puff of cloud dissolving in it like a drop of milk in a pool of water.

It occurred to Edward that Zeph had never called him about that party he was going to. Now he couldn't remember what the address was anyway. They were probably there by now, mingling and chatting and half drunk already. He went to the kitchen, poured himself a glass of cold red wine from a half-full, recorked bottle in the fridge, and brought it back to his desk. The cold wine felt good in the heat.

There was something weird about the game. The images moved perfectly smoothly, with no cartoonish jumping or stuttering. The colors were drawn from an intense, hyperreal palette, like a green landscape seconds before a thunderstorm, and the level of detail was impossibly fine. Focusing in on a nearby branch, he saw that one leaf on it had a tiny, irregular half circle nibbled out of one of its edges. It was less like a movie than an old master painting come to life.

Condensation beaded on the surface of his wine glass. He looked at the clock: It was almost ten.

Edward had just about resolved to stay in for the evening when he noticed a square white shape lying on the floor near his couch. It was an envelope. Somebody must have shoved it in under the door by hand, forcefully enough that it slid a few feet into the room. It was a thick, square envelope with his name and street address on the front in calligraphic handwriting. He thought it looked vaguely familiar, and it was: Inside was an invitation to Fabrikant's party.

'Well,' he said aloud. 'God damn.'

How did they even get into the building? He looked at the invitation for another second, then set it aside on the table and turned back to the computer screen.

Trees and branches crackled around him as he pushed his way through them. When he was in the clear he saw that he was on top of a bluff that dropped off steeply down to a wide river far below. The water was the uniform gray of brushed steel and wrinkled with wavelets. The sun hung above it, a bright gold disk in a blue sky across which more white cotton clouds rushed with unnatural speed.

Further off, gentle golf-course-green hills rolled away from the river on both sides, broken in places by patches of dark forest. Downstream a huge stone bridge stretched across the valley. He looked down and caught a glimpse of his own feet: black leather shoes and brown twill pants. Nearby, on the very edge of the cliff, was a solitary, weatherbeaten wooden post with a mailbox nailed to it. Inside the mailbox was a plain white envelope, a pistol, and a silver hourglass, lying on its side. He knew instinctively that they had been left there for him and nobody else.

He started toward them, but something caught his eye from the edge of the screen, and without thinking he turned toward it and stepped off the edge of the cliff.

The screen reeled around him: blue skies, silver river, red cliff walls, blue skies again. He was falling. He'd been so involved with the game that his body started up a panic response: His neck prickled, and his inner ear spun. There was a last flash of bright sun before he hit the water, then the light changed, becoming weak and murky, brown and green and gray. His body settled slowly down toward the river bottom, swaying from side to side like a falling leaf, and came to rest on his back, facing up toward the shining, wobbling surface.

He pressed a few keys. Nothing happened. His point of view was tilted slightly; he could see a bit of the sandy bottom, some slimy green plant life, the shimmery surface above him. A drab fresh-water fish – a trout? – swam by far above him, momentarily eclipsing the watery sun. He realized he was dead.

The apartment was silent. Tentatively, he pressed another key. The screen cleared.

He was back in the forest, back at the beginning again. A gentle breeze was blowing. The sky was blue. He was alive.

CHAPTER 4

The next day Edward woke up late. His head hurt. The last thing he remembered was wandering around the green landscape in the game, through hills and meadows and thickets, playing with the controls, looking for clues. At some point he'd finished the wine and begun pouring himself nips from a bottle of grappa – Zeph and Caroline had brought it back from a conference in Florence last year – on the principle that sticking to liquids based on grapes would minimize his hangover. He was now re-evaluating that principle in light of new evidence.

When did he finally go to bed? God, he was no better than Stewart and his GameBoy. The apartment was stifling. The windows were all closed, and sunlight was pouring in. He could feel the sheen of sweat on his bare back as he swung his legs down. Edward staggered out of bed, threw open all the windows he could find, and staggered back again.

He looked at the clock: It was two in the afternoon. He shook his head. All that stress and lack of sleep must have finally caught up with him. He rested his head in his hands. Today was Friday – he was pretty sure it was, anyway. Usually he would have been at work for six hours already. Standing in the kitchen, he ran himself a tall glass of water and drank it in one long, unbroken series of swallows. A sweet, oversized green apple sat on the counter, and he sliced off a thin segment with a steel carving knife. He ate it off the blade. The crispness of it hurt his teeth.

There was a message on his answering machine. It must have been left last night after he went to bed.

'Edward. Zeph here.' Loud party noise in the background. 'Everybody else here is talking on their cell phones so Caroline and me – Caroline and I – we thought we should call somebody on ours.' Caroline said something in the background. 'I'm not yelling. This is how I talk. Listen, I'm talking in my normal voice.' Zeph was drunk.

'We're all pissed off at you,' he went on. 'Fabrikant's pissed that you're not here, and we're pissed that you're not here, and that's pretty much everybody – well, there's some other people here, they're probably pissed at you too, I can't say for sure. I don't really feel like asking them. We should go now. All this small talk isn't going to make itself. Oh, the Artiste is here, isn't that a scream? I told him about it. I can't believe he came. He's walking around freaking people out. Wow, what a gloriously slutty-looking woman,' Zeph added.

'Look at those heels,' Caroline said in the background. 'Why doesn't she just wear stilts?'

'I'm gonna . . .'

The call cut off there.

Edward walked back through his apartment to the bathroom, where he splashed some cold water on his face. It had been a couple of days since he'd shaved. *You're letting yourself go*, he thought. *You wasted last night, and you've already wasted half of today. Pull yourself together, asshole.* He should call the office and clear up the mess about the Wents' library, he thought, staring at himself in the mirror. No, it was already too late for that today. He should just go over there. By now they'd be waiting for him. He pictured the cool, dark quiet of the Wents' library.

A fresh bloom of sweat was already breaking out on his forehead. He went to the bathroom to take a shower, then he got dressed and threw a notebook and an old sweater into his leather bag. He wasn't going to hang around here all day. At least the Wents had air-conditioning. On his way out he stopped in front of his computer. The monitor screen looked weak and dusty in the direct sunlight. It was still on – the screensaver was obsessively drawing randomly generated fractal mountain ranges over and over and immediately erasing them again. He hadn't even bothered to quit out of the game. He'd left it on all night while he slept.

Edward tapped the space bar and the screen

cleared. He was still alive. Edward frowned. He would have thought some roving space invader or something would have come along and killed him by now. Or maybe it already had – maybe he'd been killed a thousand times since last night and then brought back to life a thousand times. Did it even matter? How would he even know?

Even though it was early afternoon outside, in the game it was seven in the evening according to a tiny digital clock near the bottom of the screen. Through the trees a thin band of glowing, fading sunset stretched halfway around the horizon, red and gold and green. He moved forward to the edge of the cliff. The scattering of sunlight across the roughened river water was rendered in exquisite detail, veins of fire rippling and shivering. For a while he just stood and watched it.

Not everything was the same as it had been the night before. The letter that had been in the mailbox was gone, and so was the pistol. He thought of the lyrics from that Beatles song about leaves whirling inside a letter box. And there actually were leaves on the ground now – the scene had altered subtly, becoming more autumnal. The silver hourglass he'd seen was there, but it lay broken on the ground, the pale sand inside scattered in the grass, which was looking a little patchy and threadbare. Time had passed here. He looked around nervously.

Downstream, the bridge was in ruins. The span had disappeared, and one of the two stone towers that had supported it was completely gone. The other was scarred and blasted. He ran upstream along the top of the cliff to get a better look. He found that he moved swiftly and smoothly in the game, skimming along over the ground in an even, legless glide, faster than he or anybody else could possibly run in real life. It looked like the bridge had aged, eroded, sagged, and finally collapsed under the sheer weight of years. How could so much time have passed? A long, creamy swath of foam swept down-stream from the base of the one surviving tower. As he got closer he could hear the faint rushing sound the turbulence made. Part of a carved stone lion still crouched at the tower's base.

How could the bridge have aged so much in one night? And what was he supposed to do? Fix it? Was that the point of the game? He glided down a steep embankment, then out to the end of the road, as close as he dared to where the ragged edge of the road sagged precipitately downward. The current piled up against the base of the tower like ripples of thick, heavy glass. There was no sound except rushing water, and a looped sample of crickets chirping. A little cartoon sailboat was creeping up the river, looking absurdly peaceful, leaving a white, perfectly V-shaped wake behind it on the dark blue water. From it came the sound of a clear, silvery bell.

He hit Esc to see if the game would let him out, but nothing happened. He tried Ctrl Q, then Alt F4, then Ctrl-Alt-Delete. Nothing, though it did let him save a copy of the game-in-progress.

'Fuck it,' he said out loud.

Maybe killing himself again would help. He walked down to the edge of the road. It was unpaved, a white gravel track with a crest of green grass running along the center. It felt a little weird, deliberately murdering himself, but after a moment's hesitation he backed away to get up some momentum and ran straight over the edge. He didn't tumble this time, just fell – a moment of stillness, floating peacefully in the dusky air, then a plunge down into the dark water.

Instead of sinking he popped back up to the surface. His point of view bobbed up and down, and the current started to take him. He wasn't sinking. He tried to make himself dive down, but he couldn't figure out how. He was as stubbornly buoyant as a cork.

'Die,' he said under his breath. 'Die, you little fucker.'

After a while he got bored of trying to drown himself. It was getting darker. He swam over to the base of the one remaining tower and clambered up onto it. Very far away, almost indistinguishable now from the shoreline, he watched the sailboat recede into the distance. There was writing on the stern, illegible now, though he thought it might have said MOMUS.

A garbage truck was blocking the Wents' narrow street, so the cab let him off around the corner from their apartment. A hard-faced woman was selling tattered back issues of *Penthouse* and *Oui*, sun-faded and water-damaged, spread out on a card table. The heat was brutal – the city was a cement oven. Sunlight flashed painfully off apartment windows and the side mirrors of cars; even the sidewalk was too bright to look at. He walked straight in past the doorman without even looking at him.

The doorman called out after him halfheartedly, 'In you go!'

After the glare outside Edward was practically blind in the gloom of the lobby, and he barked his shin on a coffee table. The air smelled like leather and potpourri. He picked his way through the darkness toward the elevators and fished the tube key Laura had given him out of his pocket. It fit easily into a circular socket next to the button for the seventeenth floor. The doors rumbled shut.

Edward hoped nobody would be home, that he could slip upstairs without having to talk to anybody. His shin ached. An elderly Chasidic man got on at nine, reeking of sweat under his black coat, and got off at ten. As he approached the twenty-third floor Edward had a strange premonition that the doors would open onto nothingness, or a blank wall, or a sheer drop, but when he arrived there was only the mirrored anteroom, exactly as before, with the cleaning woman vigorously vacuuming the oriental rug in the front room.

Laura was nowhere in sight. He walked through the front room and down the elegant, empty white hall with its ghostly missing pictures until he found the closet with the spiral staircase. The sound of the vacuum dwindled behind him. His shoes rang lightly on the metal stairs. This time the door at the top of the stairs opened easily, and he closed it firmly behind him. Walking into the library was like slipping into a movie theater on a summer afternoon – the same dark coolness, the same air of hushed anticipation. He took a deep breath. The air was chilled and musty, but it felt like a damp towel on his aching forehead.

Under the circumstances the prospect of a long afternoon of quiet, industrious, relatively brainless work seemed incredibly pleasant. He walked through the long room to the table, slowly, enjoying the silence and the solitude. Everything was exactly where he'd left it. The large leather volume from the day before was still lying out on the table, dark and sober as a gravestone. He turned on the laptop and strolled over to the open crate while it booted up. The heavy curtains hung open just a sliver, sending a single line of light along the wood floor.

Edward lifted out a short stack of tightly wrapped books from off the top and carried them back to the table. He opened the first one, a small, thin volume bound in gray-green leather with gold trim. *A Sentimental Journey Through France and Italy*, by Laurence Sterne. The leather was so soft and crumbly it left smudges on his fingers. It was a tiny, delicate thing, barely a hundred pages long. He opened it just as far as the frontispiece. It was printed in 1791.

He unwrapped the rest of them, throwing the paper on the floor as he went. *The Complaint; or Night Thoughts, and the Force of Religion*. A Victorian-era account of the excavation of a frozen mammoth, full of gorgeous illustrations and bound together with a contemporary treatise on meteorites. *Le sofa*, a pre-revolutionary French novel with pink paper covers, turned out to be a pornographic account – with strong revolutionary subtext – of the sex lives of the French aristocracy, written from the point of view of a piece of sentient furniture. An unidentifiable bundle of crumbling old papers tied together with a black ribbon: early American religious broadsides. A mottled, cheap-looking edition of Joyce's *Pomes Penyeach*.

Edward opened the binder with the instructions in it and followed them as best he could. He counted the unnumbered extra pages at the front and back of each volume. He measured each book in centimeters. With his fingertips he gauged the sharpness of the corners, and he *tsk*ed over foxing and broken spines. He counted pictures and illustrations and looked up any ornaments in a big book that listed the more popular ones, along with the names and dates of the printers who invented them. He copied out any marks or inscriptions – the endpaper in the Sterne was covered in arithmetic, written in fountain pen ink gone sepia with age. He spent a long time deciphering a signature on

71

Pomes Penyeach. It turned out to have belonged to Anita Loos.

For each book he tapped an entry into the laptop – the cataloging software had a separate field for each piece of information. Nobody came up from the apartment below to bother him. It was cold in the library, but the old sweater he'd brought kept him warm and kept the dust off his clothes. As he worked his headache gradually faded. The traffic on Madison was so far away that it registered as nothing more than oceanic white noise, a seashell roar punctuated by the occasional musical honk.

He went back for another stack of books: a three-volume English legal treatise; a travel guide to Tuscany from the '20s crammed with faded Italian wildflowers that fluttered out from between the pages like moths; a French edition of Turgeniev so decayed that it came apart in his hands; a register of London society from 1863. In a way it was idiotic. He was treating these books like they were holy relics. It wasn't like he would ever actually read them. But there was something magnetic about them, something that compelled respect, even the silly ones, like the Enlightenment treatise about how lightning was caused by bees. They were information, data, but not in the form he was used to dealing with it. They were non-digital, non-electrical chunks of memory, not stamped out of silicon but laboriously crafted out of wood pulp and ink, leather and glue. Somebody had cared enough to write these things; somebody else had cared enough to buy them, possibly even read them, at the very least keep them safe for 150 years, sometimes longer, when they could have vanished at the touch of a spark. That made them worth something, didn't it, just by itself? Though most of them would have bored him rigid the second he cracked them open, which there wasn't much chance of. Maybe that was what he found so appealing: the sight of so many books that he'd never have to read, so much work he'd never have to do. When was the last time he'd actually finished a book? A real, non-detective book?

A moist and pungent smell billowed softly out from each volume as he opened it. The catalog in the computer lengthened, entry by entry, and he lost track of time. Most of the books were from England, but there were a fair number from America and the Continent, and a few from even farther away. Some of the German books were printed in spidery Gothic black letter which took him twice as long to decipher; books in Cyrillic or Arabic he just set aside as lost causes. A printed card slipped out of a book of Bengali poetry. He retrieved it from off the floor: It said 'With the Compliments of the Author,' above a florid, illegible signature.

When the thin thread of light from the window reached the tabletop, he checked his watch and saw that it was almost six. He stood up and stretched, his spine popping deliciously. The long table was two-thirds covered with even, orderly stacks of old books, and the floor was littered with huge rafts of wrapping paper. He felt gloriously virtuous, like a medieval monk who had finished his daily penance and could retire to the abbey for a beer and some artisanal cheese.

There was still that book that Laura mentioned, by somebody from somewhere. He had it written down: Gervase of Langford. Just for extra credit he ran a search of the entries he'd already created, but it wasn't there. He looked over at the dark shapes of all the other crates still waiting to be opened and wondered if he'd even get that far before he went to England.

There were some reference books in the shelves along the wall, and he walked over for a look. They ranged from xeroxed chapbooks to cheap paperbacks to sturdy volumes to massive ten- and twenty-book catalogs, each volume so fat the binding sagged under its own weight. It was highly technical stuff: *Repertorium Bibliographicum*, *Gesamtkatalog der Wiegendrucke, Incunabula in American Libraries, Eighteenth Century Short-Title Catalogue, English Restoration Bookbindings*. Well, he'd never been scared of a little research. He took down a single large, authoritative-looking book entitled *A Catalogue of English Books Before 1501*.

It turned out to be nothing more than a collection of card-catalog cards from different libraries, all pains-takingly photographed in black and white and laid out in alphabetical order, row upon row, page after tissue-thin page, tens of thousands of them. He cleared a space on the table under the lamp and opened it up. It took a minute to find him, but there he was, right in between Gervase of Canterbury (d. 1205) and Gervase of Tilbury (ca. 1160-ca. 1211): Gervase of Langford (ca. 1338-ca. 1374). There were three cards under his name, two of them for different versions of what looked like the same book, *Chronicum Anglicanum* (London, 1363 and 1366). The third was called *Les contes merveilleux* (London, 1359).

Down at the bottom of each of the cards was a string of two- and three-letter abbreviations indicating the libraries that held copies of the books. The key to the abbreviations was in a long appendix at the back; a little flipping back and forth told him that the *Chronicum Anglicanum* was in libraries in New York, Texas, and England. The New York copy was in something called the Chenoweth Rare Book and Manuscript Repository. He wrote down the name, shut down the computer, and picked up his things. Checking around to make sure everything looked ship-shape, he snapped off the desk lamp on his way to the stairs.

Downstairs, the hallway was flooded with an early evening light that turned the stark white walls a soft candy pink. The windows had all been thrown open, and a delicate, cooling breeze moved through the empty rooms. Earlier on he'd wanted to avoid people, but now, after his long afternoon of silent work, he was in a gregarious mood. He almost hoped he'd run into Laura Crowlyk. He wondered again if she lived here, if she ate her meals here and slept here at night. On his way back to the elevator he glanced through a half-open door and discovered a small, cluttered office. The walls, the floor, the tops of cabinets, even the windowsill were stacked high with manila folders, bundles of paper, black three-ring binders, bursting Redwelds tied shut with string, as if some gigantic paper-loving bird were lining its nest. It was odd to see an office with no computer in it.

Edward hesitated a second, then stepped inside. No time like the present. He picked up the phone and called Information for the number of the Chenoweth Rare Book and Manuscript Repository. Would it still be open? The man who picked up transferred him unceremoniously to another department where he was put on hold. While he waited, Edward browsed the papers spread out on the desk: insurance forms, letters, some kind of legal wrangle about contractors buffing the floors. There were flimsy pink carbon copies of invoices for some computer work, made out to an Alberto Hidalgo.

A woman answered.

'Privileges.'

Edward explained that he was looking for Gervase of Langford.

'Book or manuscript?' she asked curtly.

'Book.' What else could it be?

'Are you affiliated with an institution?'

'I'm with the Went Collection,' he improvised.

76

There was a muffled exchange with somebody else in the room, then the woman was back:

'Are you a member of the Went family?' she asked.

'I'm an employee.'

Something in his peripheral vision caught Edward's attention: Laura Crowlyk was standing in the doorway watching him. He did a classic guilty double take. He wrapped things up with the library.

'You'll need to register when you arrive,' the woman warned him, 'so bring photo ID and proof of address.'

'Gotcha.'

They hung up. There was a moment of silence while Laura Crowlyk looked him up and down, taking in his baggy, dirty sweater and his stubbly face. Edward felt he had made a faux pas.

'Finished?' she asked.

'I wanted to call them before they closed for the day. Sorry. I couldn't find you.' He'd used that excuse once already, he realized.

'I haven't been hiding.' Laura stepped into the room and began pointedly clearing off the desk, putting the papers away out of sight. Edward picked up his bag to leave.

'Don't forget to record your expenses at the Chenoweth,' she said. 'They'll charge a fee when you register. It's quite expensive. And bring pencil and paper, if you plan to take notes. You can't take pens into the Reading Room.'

'You've been there?'

'Oh yes, once or twice. But I can't imagine what they have that would interest you.'

'I thought I'd do some research on Gervase of Langford.'

At this she smiled, showing lots of prominent white teeth.

'Ah.'

'Speaking of whom,' he said, 'I haven't found anything upstairs yet.'

'I'm sure he'll turn up.'

'What else can you tell me about him? I'm not sure I really know what I'm looking for.'

She shrugged.

'I think you'll know him when you see him.'

'I hope so.'

He had the distinct feeling that she was waiting for him to go. Therefore, perversely, he tried to keep the conversation going as long as possible.

'You may be underestimating my ignorance.'

'Yes, well I don't know why she didn't ask for somebody more qualified to take care of this,' she said irritably. 'Myself, for example. But that's the Duchess for you all over.'

'The Duchess?'

'Yes, the Duchess.'

She sighed, settling her hair absentmindedly, and bent down to open a desk drawer full of hanging files. Was that the barest trace of whisky on her breath?

'All right. If it's clues you're looking for, look at

this.' She lifted out a typewritten letter and copied out something from it onto a yellow sticky.

'Here's the title – this is the name of the book they're looking for.'

'Uh-huh.' Her handwriting was neat and refined, no doubt the product of some inconceivably exclusive boarding school. It read: *A Viage to the Contree of the Cimmerians.*

He nodded sagely as he scanned it, as if the words meant something to him.

'Do you mind if I ask you why we're looking for it?'

She regarded him with unnervingly pale, slate-colored eyes.

'Because the Duchess asked for it.'

The molten orange sun was almost down over the edge of New Jersey. He was suddenly very conscious that they were alone together in an empty apartment.

'This project is her idea,' she went on, 'in case you hadn't gathered that. You're her idea, too – you Esslin & Hart people. Whatever it is you did with her finances – don't tell me, thanks, not interested – you all seem to have made quite an impression on her, you in particular. I sometimes wonder if we aren't all her idea, in some complicated meta-physical way. Her world seems somehow more substantial than ours.

'As for the book, I suppose it would be valuable, though how valuable is beyond me. Apart from that, I couldn't say why we're looking for it, just that she was extremely insistent that we do so. It is a little unusual. It's not often that I hear from her directly. This is a fairly remote outpost of her empire – the American Embassy, we call it.'

Her irony had a trace of bitterness in it. He wondered if she wasn't a little lonely.

'You do know about the Duchess, don't you?' she went on.

'Well,' said Edward, with calculated vagueness, 'I do and I don't.'

'Well, you'd better learn, if you're going to work for her.' She seemed less severe now, more collegial, now that she was talking about the Wents. 'Blanche and I were at school together. They advanced us both a year ahead of schedule. I sometimes think it was a mistake for her. She was brilliant, certainly, but she had a difficult time. Hers is a very old family – nobody knows them here in America, but in England everybody wanted to get at her. It had an . . . effect on her. Made her very shy and untrustful of some people, and maybe too trustful of others.' She glanced at Edward. 'It's a cliché, but she really has led a very sheltered life.

'As for Peter, I've only met him a few times, at the wedding and then later. They're very reclusive now. They live on an estate in the north of England, and they hardly ever leave it. It's enormous – they bought up the land all around it for miles, though it's mostly fairly wild. Deer park.'

Next thing you know she'd be telling him about the ancient family curse that haunted them to this day whenever the moon was full. Edward stifled a smile. It all sounded so unreal – like the clumsy exposition in a cheap horror movie. Edward remembered a guy he'd known in college who was supposed to be an aristocrat. He was Swedish and very tall, and people said he was a baron. They were in a Chinese history class together, but the baron never said a word the entire semester. He spent all his time in the basement of his dorm playing pinball and pining – Edward supposed – for his faraway fjords.

'So you've met the Duke?' Edward prompted her.

'Of course I've met him,' she said. 'They're both very kind people. Very kind. I understand he isn't well these days – keeps to his bed, mostly. It's hard for Blanche. She's a good deal younger than he is, you know.'

'Oh,' Edward said. 'Is she?'

'Yes, she is.' All at once she closed up again. She whisked away the paper, shut the desk drawer and stood up. 'But don't get any ideas. You'll never even meet her.'

Edward blinked.

'I can assure you,' he said with complete honesty, 'that my brain is completely devoid of any ideas whatsoever.'

'Good.' She continued shuffling her papers. 'Let me be frank. I don't like this city, and I don't like this godforsaken country, and I don't like you. But if you are successful, if you find the Gervase, the

81

Duchess might just see fit to bring me back to England, and there is nothing, nothing in this life, that would make me happier. As far as this enterprise goes, I'll help you however I can. Beyond that I wash my hands of you. Is that understood?'

She looked up at Edward, a little flushed. He meditated any number of brusque, sarcastic responses before he replied.

'Yes,' he said. 'It's understood. Thanks for being frank.'

It was only a few minutes later, when he was on his way down in the elevator, that he realized that at some point in the afternoon he had decided that he and nobody else was going to organize the Wents' library.

CHAPTER 5

On Monday morning at eleven o'clock Edward stepped out of a cab in front of the Chenoweth Rare Book and Manuscript Repository. It was another sunny day, hot and bright, and the street looked like an overexposed photograph. The air was awash with humidity and fumes. A large metal chemical canister belonging to a construction crew stood by itself on the sidewalk, hissing quietly; in places its bright metal surface was covered over with frost. Edward had to resist an overwhelming urge to hug it.

On the outside the Chenoweth Repository was disappointingly plain, a four-story house made of sooty gray stone jammed between two apartment buildings. The first floor was occupied by a clothing boutique called *Zaz!* The door to the library was off to the right, marked by a polished brass plaque; above the plaque, in a glass-and-metal frame, was a card announcing an exhibit entitled 'RARE RENAISSANCE MARGINALIA,' accessible 'BY APPOINTMENT ONLY.'

The front door opened onto a dark, narrow hall. At the end of it a cinnamon-skinned woman stood behind a lighted lectern at the head of a flight of stairs, looking like the maître d' at a restaurant.

'Leave your bag up here, please,' she said, and made him sign a clipboard.

Edward reluctantly parted with his Hermès briefcase, which she added to a disorderly pile of backpacks in the corner behind her. Instead of leading up, the stairs took him down. He realized that the library's exterior was deceptive: Most of it was underground. When he opened the glass door at the bottom of the stairs it was like passing through an airlock into an alien world, one of cold, scrubbed, triple-distilled air, white walls, plate glass, plush carpeting, and elaborately designed indirect lighting. Banks of computer terminals and blond wooden card catalog cabinets were scattered around an enormous open room populated exclusively by old men and young women, filling out forms or purposefully pushing squeaky-wheeled wooden carts this way and that. Traces of sunlight crept into the room, although Edward couldn't quite figure out from where. The temperature was a blessed twenty degrees cooler than it had been out on the street.

A white-haired man barely five feet tall accosted him and ushered him over to the circulation desk, a massive wooden rampart that ran the entire length of one wall, and gave him a pencil and some forms to fill out. A large leather-bound guestbook lay on the desk, held open by a weighted velvet cord, and Edward was instructed to sign it. He obediently wrote out a check to the library for 180 dollars and was handed a receipt. When he was finished the white-haired gnome immediately lost interest in him, and he was left to his own devices.

He strolled over to a computer terminal with an old-fashioned black-and-green monitor. A few xeroxed instructional pamphlets lay scattered around it on the tabletop. He sat down and typed the name 'Gervase,' then hit SEARCH. Nothing. It took him five minutes with the xeroxed pamphlets before he discovered that the medieval holdings were cataloged in a separate database from the rest of the library's collection. When he'd figured out how to access the medieval database, the two other Gervases, Canterbury and Tilbury, turned up right away, but no Langford. He went back to the pamphlets, where he learned that while 80 percent of the Chenoweth's holdings had been transferred to the electronic catalog, the only record of the other 20 percent was in the old paper card catalog.

Edward crossed the room to one of the many wooden cabinets. Its face was studded with hundreds of tiny drawers with hundreds of tiny gleaming brass handles, each one with a neat little hand-lettered paper tag on it. He walked along thirty or forty feet of drawers before he got to the G's, and then the *Ge*'s, where he found – again nothing. Finally he consulted a diminutive blond library page who informed him that he was looking in the books catalog, and that Gervase's works, which were published before the advent of movable type, were written out by hand, and thus were not considered books at all, but manuscripts. Manuscripts were cataloged in a separate system in another part of the room.

It was there that he found the card he was looking for:

Author: *Gervase, of Langford, ca. 1338-ca. 1374*

Title: *Chronicum Anglicanum: (second part)/Gervasius Langfordiensis*

Published: *London, 1366*

Description: *xvi, 363 p.; maps; 34 cm.*

That was all, plus a long call number. With a stunted, eraserless pencil stub he copied the number out on a slip of scrap paper, on the back of which was a fragment of what had once been a research proposal on John Donne and the English Revolution.

But where were the books? Edward could see only two or three scattered bookcases, holding no more than a couple of hundred volumes each at most. He stood there holding the scrap paper, uncertain as to what to do next. He strolled around the room glancing casually at the other patrons, trying to deduce the local protocol on the fly. Nothing obvious presented itself. He peered through various doorways, none of which looked promising. The whole operation was a model of mysterious, gleaming efficiency, like some incomprehensible ultramodern public restroom.

When he passed the front desk for the third time, one of the attendants, a dark-haired, moon-faced young woman caught his eye.

'Is there something I can help you with?' she asked brightly.

'Yes,' he admitted. 'I, ah—'

Flustered, he mutely proffered the slip of paper with the call number on it. The young woman examined it expertly.

'Gotcha,' she said. 'Have a seat. We'll bring it right out to you.'

The girl, who looked like she was barely out of junior high, suggested that he wait in the Reading Room, which sounded like a reasonable enough idea. He watched her disappear through an incongruously heavy metal door back behind the desk.

The lights in the library were slightly dimmed, like a romantic restaurant. Guessing randomly, Edward half opened a door set in a white alcove and interrupted a lively graduate seminar in full swing. He backed away defensively – just looking, thanks – and closed the door. His next try was more promising: a long, roomy chamber set with fifteen or twenty identical wooden tables, regularly spaced. Behind each table was a single severe, wooden-backed chair, and each table had a laptop on it, carefully aligned with the upper right-hand corner. It was silent in the room, and the light was a little brighter, but the air was glacial, even colder than in the lobby. A row of murky oil paintings in elaborate gilt frames hung along the smooth white walls, each accessorized with its own miniature spotlight.

Five or six people sat scattered among the tables. Edward chose an empty one and sat down. He folded his hands in front of him. Ten minutes passed. The silence was broken only by the small, scholarly noises of academics at work: light coughs, the crackle of a turned page, a throat being cleared, a nose being blown. Nobody spoke. He sketched aimlessly with his pencil on the blank sheet of paper he'd brought with him for taking notes. He'd never been able to draw anything, but he did his best with platonic solids: cubes and spheres and cones lit and shadowed from various angles. The windowlessness of the room gave him a sense of being deep underground. In each corner, safely away from the books, a shaft of sunlight made its way down through a skylight from the world above. Edward walked over to one and looked up. It was a square pane of glass, inches thick and recessed a yard deep into the ceiling; beyond it, looking infinitely far away, was a square of burning blue sky.

A hand touched his shoulder. It was the girl from the front desk. She motioned to him to follow her out into the lobby.

'I'm sorry,' she said gravely, when they were outside. 'The materials you requested are unavailable.'

'Unavailable?'

'They're in use by another patron.'

'Another patron. Somebody here?'

'Well, yeah.' She popped her gum. 'You can't take it out of the building.'

'Can I – do you know how long they'll have it for?'

'Nope. Sorry.'

Edward made a face.

'What if I come back in a couple of hours?'

'It's up to you!' she sang.

'Okay. Thanks.'

She practically skipped away. Annoyed, Edward left the Reading Room and climbed the stairs. What were the odds? How many people in the world had even heard of Gervase of Langford? And one of them was here, today, in person, reading exactly the book he needed? When he opened the door the warm, humid air of the outside world embraced him, and he shuddered gratefully and rubbed his freezing hands together. It was like surfacing after a bone-chilling deep-sea dive. The receptionist handed him back his briefcase.

But then the memory of his conversation with Laura came back to him. With it came the memory of the Duchess. He hesitated, standing in the darkened hallway, holding his briefcase flat in his arms like a cafeteria tray. Then he handed it back to the woman and walked back downstairs into the Reading Room.

There was no telling how long he'd have to wait. Desperate to kill time, he unfolded the laptop that was sitting on the table. It opened with an ominous creaking sound, but none of the other readers even glanced up. He turned it on. The dusty liquid crystal display slowly brightened until the desktop appeared. To his surprise he saw, as if it had been put there specifically for him, a shortcut labeled MOMUS.

He looked around again. He had the momentary sensation of being caught up in an international conspiracy – but he remembered Zeph had said the game was popular among the hacker crowd. Maybe somebody from the library's IT staff had stashed a spare copy on one of the library machines for his personal use. And public machines were always littered with software flotsam and jetsam – maybe one of the library's patrons was such a hopeless addict that they'd installed it on a library laptop on the sly. The laptop was old, cheap, and under-powered, and Edward didn't really expect it to be powerful enough to run the game, but he had nothing to lose. Why not? He had a copy of his saved game on a portable keychain hard drive. He plugged it into the laptop, dragged his saved game onto the desktop, and double-clicked on the icon.

Windows full of code formed and vanished on the tiny screen, faster than the sluggish liquid crystal monitor could render them. There was a powerful electric *snap* from the speakers. A cheap plastic pair of headphones lay on the table, and Edward jacked them into the back of the machine.

He looked around guiltily at the other readers, but they didn't seem to have registered what he was doing. Ten seconds went by, then twenty, then almost a minute. It was starting to look like the program had crashed.

But then, slowly, like the footlights coming up on a darkened stage, the familiar scene appeared, this time painted in ghostly gray and white: the same broad sky, the same wide river, the same grass, the same white road, the same ruined bridge. In spite of himself Edward felt reality fade around him. His vision narrowed, dwindling to a single bright rectangle.

From his perch on the base of the shattered bridge tower he looked down at the surface of the river. The water level was lower than he remembered it, and it was milky now, pale with waterborne silt. It ran fast – in places it broke into standing waves and white water. He had the distinct impression that time had somehow slipped or lurched forward again, ten years or a hundred, a thousand, he didn't know. A tree, almost whole and looking freshly torn from its bank, came lumbering along the river, turning and wallowing in the water. Its branches were still covered with wet green leaves that glistened coldly in the dawn light. For the first time since the game started Edward felt like he knew exactly what he was supposed to do. The tree bumped heavily against the base of the bridge, and he leaped nimbly down from his stone perch onto the trunk. It would have been impossible in real life – the trunk would have been too wet and slippery – but in the game it was easy.

The tree was swept on down the river, carrying him with it, the water foaming all around him. He balanced his way up the trunk toward the branches and found a dry perch. The river was wide and fast, and it carried him along at speed. It was daylight now, the cold, clear light of very early morning. The rocks and trees and sandy cliffs on both sides slid effortlessly past him. Digitized birdsong sounded from clumps of reeds by the river's edge at regular intervals.

Minutes passed, ten, maybe fifteen. The banks of the river smoothed out and became less sheer. Soon Edward found himself approaching the outskirts of a city.

He would have expected a fantasy city, a floating castle of spun sugar or a grim Tolkien fortress, but what he got was something considerably less exotic: It was Manhattan. The river he was drifting down was in fact the Hudson. Soon he passed under the George Washington Bridge, and when he reached the Upper West Side he abandoned the tree and swam to the shore. He crossed the West Side Highway. The streets were empty. Scraps of generic litter, lovingly rendered in three dimensions, tumbled along the sidewalks.

His dreamlike gliding run, his seven-league boots, carried him effortlessly south into Midtown. The weather was as clear and sunny as ever, but the city looked gray and dead. He strode through Rockefeller Center – he half expected the marquee at Radio City to say MOMUS, but instead the letters spelled out I HAVE A BAD FEELING ABOUT THIS. The flags around the famous skating rink each bore a single squat tree on a plain dark background. A sense of unease filled him.

He didn't know why, but he found himself heading across town, walking east on Fiftieth Street, instinctively homing in on – what? Moments before he arrived, he realized where he was going. He was heading for the Chenoweth library, the building he was sitting in right now, in real life. There was something at once dangerous and irresistible about closing the logical short circuit. What would he do when he got there? Go inside? Walk downstairs? Would he see himself sitting there, hunched over a laptop?

He turned the final corner. Where the Chenoweth library should have been there were only ruins: collapsed walls, broken glass, brick dust.

Then something strange happened. Thick-leaved, hairy nettles sprouted from the ruins. Time was speeding up. Across the street the clock on a church tower convulsed, its hands a gray blur, then burst into flame with an audible *woof*.

Edward sat back and rubbed his eyes. He looked around the room: The squares of sunlight in the corners had shifted by a foot. What time was it? He'd been losing track of time lately. A few new people had come in, a few others had left, but nobody was paying attention to him. Okay. Everything was under control.

He stretched and looked at his watch. It was after

one: He'd been playing for almost an hour. He'd have to watch that. He was starting to see what people found so addictive about these games. MOMUS had none of the slapdash inefficiency of reality: Every moment was tense with hushed anticipation, foreordained meaning. It was a brighter, higher-grade, more compelling, better-engineered version of reality. He closed the laptop, and it sighed itself to sleep. He walked back out into the lobby. The same young woman who'd helped him before was still at the front desk, but when he caught her gaze she just smiled sorrowfully at him and shook her head.

Edward wasn't used to waiting. If it was an analyst's report or a bond price or an SEC filing he was waiting for, he would have gone ballistic by now. Or he'd have dug in and done the research for himself. He'd already wasted half a day, and he wasn't about to waste the rest of it. He marched back into the Reading Room and stood in the doorway, hands on hips. There were only five men and women there, each hunched over his or her work. One of them must have Gervase.

Two he could rule out right away, a jowly older woman and a crazed-looking young man with wild hair; they were working on loose papers, letters or documents, not books. At another table a tall black man with pure white hair was studying a yellowed pulp magazine through a jeweler's loup. That left only two more: a tall, severe young woman and the old man with the hacking cough.

94

Edward strolled around the edge of the room, pretending to examine the reference books. The shelves were glassed in, and his reflection made him self-conscious. He tried to look casual. The young woman ignored him, leaning over her book like a gambler protecting her hand. He moved on to the old man. He looked up as Edward approached, his moist red lips parted expectantly. At the last moment Edward saw that the book he was reading was in Arabic. No dice. He turned his head and kept walking.

It had to be the young woman. He circled cautiously around the room back to where she was sitting. She was concentrating fiercely, taking notes in a worn spiral notebook that lay open on the table beside her, putting her whole body into it, her long, gawky frame bent almost double over the wooden tabletop. Her chin-length hair was brown and straight, cut off short and square above her pale neck. She wore a green wool cardigan over a plain white T-shirt.

Edward pulled over a chair and sat down opposite her. The book that lay spread open in front of her was very large; the cover alone must have been half an inch thick. The worn, brindled pages were closely covered with fine black script in neat columns. She didn't acknowledge his presence.

'Excuse me—,' he began, in what he hoped was a discreet whisper.

She looked up at him, quickly but not startled. Her face was long and elegant – not pretty exactly, but with brown eyes and a wide, expressive mouth that turned down naturally at the corners like a cat's. Almost as quickly she went back to scribbling on her pad.

'Excuse me—'

With the eraser end of her pencil she tapped a little printed card that was taped flat on the table. It said:

PLEASE NO
TALKING IN THE
READING ROOM

She went back to examining the book.

Edward stood up, got his pencil and paper from where he'd been sitting, and brought them over to her table. He printed carefully on a piece of paper:

IS THAT GERVASE OF LANGFORD?

and passed it across to her.

This time she looked up for a little longer. She hesitated, then nodded reluctantly.

He wrote:

I NEED TO ASK YOU A QUESTION

She sighed deeply and pursed her lips, as if she accepted the fact that being continuously interrupted in her silent labors was her inevitable lot in life, but she wasn't about to act all happy about it. They stood up together and walked to the door. When she stood up he saw that she was quite tall, as tall as he was. The movement in itself was striking, like some large, endangered heron gracefully unfolding itself into flight. He opened the door for her, and she stepped through ahead of him. The jowly old woman was watching him and frowning. He made a face at her.

Edward had wanted to sit down with her at one of the conference tables that were scattered around the lobby, but the young woman just stood by the door, doing the minimum.

'It's a funny thing,' he began, chuckling as if it actually were funny. 'But I came here to look at Gervase of Langford, too.'

He hoped she would throw the ball back, but she just waited for him to continue. He did.

'And I was wondering what time you thought you might be finished with it?'

She was wearing a small silver watch, but she didn't glance at it.

'I'll be working on it for the rest of the day.'

There was something odd about her voice – it was strangely flat and unexpressive. It held out no apology or invitation to negotiate. Edward scratched the back of his head with one hand. He was straying into unfamiliar territory, protocol-wise.

'What if I just took a quick glance at it.'

Her expression didn't change.

'How much time do you need?'

'Fifteen minutes.'

'Will you be transcribing, tracing, or making sketches?'

'No, I don't think so. I just need to – I just have to check a few things.'

She looked at him impassively. Her long nose had an aristocratic ski-jump swoop to it.

'Can you do it right now?'

He nodded.

'All right.' She stepped aside, unbarring the doorway, as if she'd been considering physically challenging him. 'You have fifteen minutes. Come and find me when you're finished.'

As he settled into her chair, he saw that she'd left some of her things where they were, the tools of the trade, scattered on the table in a half circle around the book. There was a red velvet bookweight; a delicate, serious little magnifying glass that looked like demilitarized Russian spy gear; three pencils, number fours, lined up in a row and sharpened to vicious little points. She'd taken her notebook with her, but she'd left her purse behind. It was open, and her Columbia University student ID lay in plain view. Her name, below her thin-lipped, unsmiling picture, was Margaret Napier.

The clock was ticking. Edward looked the volume over with what he hoped was a professional eye. Its sense of ancient, inanimate self-possession disconcerted him. What was he doing here again? It was large and thick, and the mottled pages had an oddly velvety feel unlike ordinary paper. The

98

cover was made of a very pale gray material that he couldn't immediately identify, and it had what looked like a prehistoric metal belt buckle bolted to it. Three delicate pink rosettes were faintly visible drawn along the edges of the gathered pages. The book was so palpably ancient he was afraid it would crumble to dust as he turned to the first page. When he did there was no title page there, just plain text.

He took a few notes. The writing on the pages was dense and black and almost totally illegible. He thought medieval books were supposed to have pictures in them, but there wasn't even anything much in the way of decoration, just a few curlicues here and there between the columns of writing. He spelled out a word or two, enough to see that it was written in Latin. Turning the pages of a book he couldn't read could only keep him amused for so long, but he felt like he should use the full fifteen minutes just to spite Margaret Napier.

But even spite got boring after a while. Edward found her sitting at a circular table in the lobby with an entire drawer from the card catalog in front of her. She had boldly removed the metal rod that ran down the middle and taken out a short stack of catalog cards. She was sorting them into piles on the blond wood in front of her, as if she were involved in an elaborate private card game, and taking the occasional note.

'Who's winning?' he asked jauntily.

'Winning?' Margaret Napier looked up at him uncomprehendingly. Well, she didn't deserve witty conversation anyway.

'Are you really allowed to do that?'

She continued to sort the cards.

'I used to work here,' she said. 'Anyhow, the paper catalog is largely redundant. Most of its contents are duplicated in electronic form.'

'Do you mind if I ask you a few questions?' he said, sitting down across from her. 'I mean, about Gervase of Langford?'

'Why?'

'Well, I'm doing some research, and—'

'Are you a graduate student?'

'I work for a private collection.'

She plucked another manila card out of the drawer and snapped it down onto the table. He forged ahead.

'Recently I've been looking for a particular book by Gervase of Langford. And as part of the search I've been familiarizing myself with the physical characteristics of his work.'

'You're working for a private collection,' she repeated. 'You're interested in acquiring one of his works?'

'Actually, I think we may already have one.'

She looked up from her work. *Touché.* She seemed to register his presence for the first time.

'You're saying that your employers may be in possession of a new example of the work of Gervase of Langford.' She put down her pencil, still skeptical but definitely paying attention now. 'What is it? Another *Chronicum*?'

'No,' said Edward. 'It's a – I think it's some kind of travel book. Something about the land of the Cimmerians, something like that.'

As soon as he said it he knew he'd made a mistake. Her manner frosted over again, visibly, and she went back to shuffling her cards. Edward waited, listening to the sound of her pencil scratching in the quiet of the library, but she said nothing more.

'You know the book I'm talking about?' he prompted.

'The book you're talking about doesn't exist.'

She sounded almost angry about it.

'My employers think it does.'

'Then they're sadly misinformed.'

'Well, they'll be very sorry to hear that.'

'I'm sure they will.'

'But you do know what I'm talking about?' he said doggedly. '*A Voyage to the—?*'

'*A Viage to the Contree of the Cimmerians.*' She spoke the words fluidly and easily, but with a weird sing-song pronunciation. She placed the stresses differently than he would have expected, and she gave 'Cimmerians' a hard *c*, as if it were spelled with a *k*. 'It is a well-known hoax.'

Edward blinked.

'I'm sorry to have to say this,' he said, 'but I don't have the slightest idea what you're talking about.'

'You're not a medievalist, are you?'

She said this without any real scorn. He had the impression that she simply desired a clearer understanding of the situation she was dealing with.

'No,' said Edward. 'I'm not, I'm a—' What was he exactly? 'I'm a layman.'

'Then let me clarify something for you. In layman's terms.' She assumed a businesslike tone he recognized from the boardroom. It was the sound of an implacable opponent preparing to deliver a death-blow. 'In the mid-eighteenth century a man named Edward Forsyth had a cheap printer's shop in a back street in a London slum. Forsyth printed a chapbook containing what he claimed were fragments from a book of prophecies by a medieval monk named Gervase. The book was called *A Viage to the Contree of the Cimmerians*. Stop me if I'm going too fast for you.'

The soul of graciousness, Edward nodded for her to continue.

'The fragments contained a sensational and occasionally salacious allegorical journey culminating in a mystical vision of the end of the world. Forsyth, an ex-convict and an employer of hacks, presented them as a prophecy of the apocalypse, accompanied by suitably sensational illustrations. The result was a nine-days wonder. The *Viage* was a bestseller, and Forsyth became a wealthy man.

'Since that time amateur bibliophiles and over-zealous graduate students have occasionally furthered their careers by speculating that there actually was such a mystical book, by the same title, and that the putative monk Gervase is identical with Gervase of Langford, a legitimate minor scholar of the early fourteenth century. Flights of fancy aside, however, serious academics agree that the *Viage to the Contree of the Cimmerians* is a fabrication.'

Now she did glance at her tiny silver watch.

'If you'll excuse me, my time here is very limited.'

She swept up the cards on the table, deftly restoring them to their original order, and began reinserting them into the catalog.

'Thanks for your help,' Edward said. *You incredible bitch.*

'Don't mention it.'

He bit his lip as she stood up and carried the heavy drawer back over to the catalog. He watched her heft it up into its proper place, and he saw how thin her arms and her shoulders were. The door to the Reading Room closed behind her, and Edward suddenly realized how cold he was. The distant, heatless sun of the skylights made him feel even colder. He went to retrieve his things.

He felt obscurely disappointed. There had been something tantalizing about this little project, this miniature quest. He hadn't expected it to go anywhere, really, but he didn't think it would turn to shit quite as fast as it had, either. The Reading Room was almost empty now, only Margaret Napier and the distinguished-looking white-haired man still remained, slowly paging through the same tattered old pulp magazine. Edward gathered up his papers and squared them off – not that there was anything useful on them, unless you counted his geometrical masterpieces. Margaret ignored him completely. He left and climbed the stairs up to the dark landing. When he pushed open the glass door to the street it seemed like he'd been underground for days. He was almost surprised to see that it was still only mid-afternoon.

CHAPTER 6

E dward woke up slowly on Tuesday morning. He was getting used to waking up late. He lay there on his back, slowly opening and closing his eyes, like a castaway who'd been washed up on a soft, gently sloping beach of white sand. He was awake, but he was dreaming, and every time he closed his eyes the dream would restart itself automatically, going back to the beginning and continuing on through the exact same course of events like a piece of looped film run and rerun over and over and over again.

In the dream he found himself on a fishing trawler, bobbing in a dark, choppy sea studded with whitecaps. His father was there, looking grizzled and irascible. He was dressed as a pirate in a cartoon, with a hat and a pegleg and a blue uniform – or was that the livery of the Wents' doorman? The clouds were low and dark, seeming to hover only yards above the wavetops. The light was failing.

They had a fish on the line, but it was so large and strong that it was dragging their boat through the water behind it. Sometimes they caught a glimpse of it when it came near the surface. It was enormous, ten or fifteen feet long, and slender and muscular like an eel.

After a while the fish got tired, and they managed to winch it up over the side. The ship's crew now included Zeph's wife, Caroline, as well as Edward's secretary Helen from work. The fish was olive green, with a beaked face like a turtle and bright yellow eyes. They laid it out on the deck, but even in the open air it refused to die. In fact, as they slowly made their way home through the mounting seas it gained strength, thrashing around and snapping at them and flaring its blood-red gills. No one knew what kind of fish it was. They weren't even sure it was edible. The waves were rising, and the ship was becoming dangerously overpopulated. 'Don't be such a child,' the Wents' housekeeper said, rolling her eyes in disgust. Edward could see the shore now, low green hills above the heaving whitecaps, but as it came closer he felt a sense of impending disaster. They would never reach the land. Somewhere in the distance a warning buoy was tolling and tolling . . .

The phone was ringing. He opened his eyes. The answering machine picked up.

'Howdy, playmate.' It was Zeph's voice. 'Re-telephone me, please, at your earliest convenience.'

Edward lay still for a while, staring blankly at the phone on his night table. The sheet was twisted up into a long rope that had gotten wound around his arms and legs somehow. With an effort he sat up far enough to see the clock radio next to his bed. It was almost one in the afternoon.

'Jesus,' he said, suddenly wide awake. 'Not again.'

He looked around at the furniture in his apartment, blinking. How could he have slept for thirteen hours straight? He went into the bathroom and splashed cold water on his face. Something must be going on deep in his subconscious, he thought, some kind of redecoration, refurbishment, reupholstering that required a lot of system downtime – some shadowy application running in the background, performing unknown operations, consuming huge chunks of psychic RAM.

The sheets had left a long crease in his skin, running from his crotch up to his collarbone, like the scar from some hideously invasive surgery. He came out into the kitchen dripping, rubbing his face with a towel, feeling the coolness on his face in the heat. He dropped the damp towel on the floor and plucked a pair of clean boxers from his dresser.

At any rate, he didn't feel sick. He should have been depressed after yesterday's disappointment, but instead he felt renewed, replenished, rejuvenated. The world looked crisp and washed, as if reality had been painstakingly restored and digitally remastered overnight for his viewing pleasure. He'd shaken off the feeling of defeat he had after yesterday's research. He was starting to enjoy his new double life – I-banker by day, book hunter by night – and he wasn't going to give it up that easily. He decided not to go to the Wents' apartment today. If he was going to tell the Wents that it was all over, that the book – whatever it was called – was lost forever, or never existed at all, he was going to do it with a full dossier on the subject in hand, complete with charts and tables and appendices and bound in leather' on triple-bond paper. And he knew exactly where to start.

He turned on his computer and Googled Margaret Napier. No luck in Manhattan, but Brooklyn had an M. Napier. It was a long shot – Brooklyn to Columbia was a long commute – but he wrote down the number anyway, pricking himself when the pen poked through the paper into his bare knee.

An answering machine picked up. She didn't give her name, but that low, affectless voice was unmistakable. He was about to leave a message when the voice cut off.

'Hello.'

There was a quick riff of feedback as the answering machine shut off.

'Hi. Margaret Napier, please.'

'Napier,' She corrected, pronouncing it to rhyme with *rapier*. 'This is she.'

'Margaret, this is Edward Wozny. We met yesterday at the Chenoweth library.' Silence. 'I asked you about Gervase of Langford.' He felt a twinge of embarrassment; after all, she'd never actually told him her name. 'There were a couple of things I wanted to follow up on with you, if you have a second.'

There was a long pause.

'I'm sorry, I'm not interested,' she said neutrally. 'Good-bye.'

'I'd like to discuss a job opportunity,' he extemporized hastily. There was another pause. A bass-heavy car stereo faded in and out under his window.

'I don't understand.'

'Let me explain,' he said. 'I'm under some time pressure from the Went Collection to resolve this issue of Gervase of Langford. I thought I might persuade you to act as a consultant on the project.' He wasn't exactly sure how the Went family would feel about this, but he forged ahead anyway. 'You have some reservations about the book's validity. I understand that. If anything, those reservations will make you that much more of an asset. We need somebody who can anticipate any possible barriers to authenticating the volume before they arise.'

Silence. His ear was getting slippery with sweat where he held the phone against it.

'Who are "we"?' she said.

'I'm sorry?'

'When you say "we,"' she repeated, 'to whom are you referring?'

'Myself, principally. And a woman named Laura Crowlyk who represents the Went family, the family that owns the collection.'

'How much can you pay me?'

He hadn't thought this far ahead, but the little he knew about graduate students suggested that this would be his chief source of leverage. He did some quick calculations.

109

'Let's say thirty dollars an hour.'

'And how much of my time would you require?'

'How much time can you give us?'

'Ten hours a week,' she said immediately.

'Ten hours. Fine.'

'All right.'

'All right.' Edward was a little taken aback. Things were progressing more rapidly than he expected. 'All right. When can you start?'

'Any time.'

'Today?' He might as well call her bluff.

'What time?'

'Four o'clock? Why don't you meet me at Café Lilas, on Eighty-second.'

'Fine.'

'Fine.'

Negotiations having been concluded ahead of schedule, there didn't seem to be anything more to say. He said good-bye and hung up.

She was already there when he arrived, sitting in one of the rear corners of the room, her long legs crossed underneath a tiny marble-topped table. Café Lilas was a long, bright, pleasant establishment fronted by tall picture windows divided into little squares. It was full of mismatched white wire tables and chairs jumbled together at odd angles in twos and threes. White ceiling fans spun slowly overhead in sync, creating an atmosphere reminiscent of an expatriate bar at a tropical hotel.

Margaret Napier was all business. She wasn't

interested in preliminaries, and that was fine with Edward. As they talked he realized he'd misjudged her. He'd mistaken her coldness and lack of affect for arrogance or just plain nerdiness, but he was wrong. It was more like a profound lack of interest. He had never met anyone so completely consumed by her work. She rarely made eye contact, and her voice always kept that low, almost mechanical tone he'd noticed when he first met her, as if she couldn't spare the extra energy to endow it with any real inflection. She spoke clearly, in long, elaborate sentences that she always took the trouble to complete, conscientiously redeeming any dangling clauses and firmly closing all parentheses, but it was all devoid of emotional investment. The effect was of somebody reluctantly reading a prepared statement off a teleprompter, a statement prepared by somebody against whom she had a bitter and longstanding grudge. He considered the possibility that she might be clinically depressed.

'Gervase Hinton, later Gervase of Langford,' she began, 'was born in London in the late 1330s. It was still the Middle Ages, but it was the Later Middle Ages. The Hundred Years War with France was just starting. Edward III had just become king of England by killing his mother's lover, Mortimer, who had become king by killing Edward III's father, Edward II, by sodomizing him with a red-hot poker.

'It's important to understand how different life was in the fourteenth century. London, the greatest city in England, had a population of about forty thousand, and those forty thousand had a hundred churches between them. The English thought of London as New Troy, a city founded by the descendants of Aeneas after the Trojan War. The average man was five foot three inches tall. People ate capons and suckling pigs at feasts and believed in goblins and fairies. The men wore stockings with different-colored legs. The population was made up of noblemen, knights, merchants, servants, and peasants, in that order. All of them lived in the Christian belief that the world was in a process of slow but steady decline, which would ultimately lead to the Day of Judgment and the end of time.'

'Right,' said Edward. 'King Arthur and all that.'

'No. King Arthur lived in the seventh century, if he existed at all. That was seven hundred years before Gervase of Langford was born. King Arthur was as far in the past from Gervase as Gervase is from us. In the fourteenth century King Arthur was already part of a legendary and sentimentalized version of English history. Think of *The Canterbury Tales*. Gervase was a close contemporary of Chaucer.'

A waiter brought them two glasses of white wine. Margaret sent hers back and asked for iced coffee.

'We don't know of anything unusual in Gervase's childhood. His family were dyers, and they seem to have made some money from it. His father and his uncle were prominent in the London dyers' guild. They owned property in the city and in Gloucester.

'When Gervase was around ten he witnessed the first outbreak of the plague that we call the Black Death, but which was then known simply as the Death. The plague killed somewhere between a third and a half of the population of Europe and created spectacles of unprecedented devastation. Whole villages were emptied. Ghost ships drifted on the open ocean, their crews dead. Cities were so depopulated that wolves came out of the forests and attacked the survivors. In Avignon the pope kept bonfires burning on either side of his throne to keep away evil vapors.

'Gervase was lucky. He survived the Death, and an uncle named Thomas survived as well, and when the plague receded in 1349 they inherited a fair amount of money and property from family members who died. Thomas became one of the more prominent merchants in London.

'Most of what we know about Gervase's life comes from official records and fragments of paper that have survived purely by chance. Family records were sometimes used as scrap paper to make book-bindings, and they can occasionally be recovered from inside old books. A psalter from Langford that was disbound for repairs gave us a receipt from the household of the Earl of Langford for pants and boots for a 'Gyrvas Hyntoun,' and from this we assume that Thomas Hinton sent the young Gervase north to serve as a page there. We can guess that Gervase probably took part in the siege of Paris in 1360, because the Earl of Langford and his retinue were there. We don't know anything more until 1362, when Gervase reappears as a law student at the Inns of Court in London.

'All this was perfectly ordinary for the ambitious son of a well-to-do merchant. But what followed was not. A young man in Gervase's position could have expected to become an esquire or a vallettus in the service of the king and eventually rise to a position of considerable consequence, as Chaucer did. But Chaucer was a go-getter, a company man, who knew how the game was played and played it well. Gervase was something else, something different. He gave up his position at court and went back north, back to the service of the Earl of Langford, where he became a kind of family associate and pet scholar. He helped manage the estate, he ran important errands for the earl, and in his spare time he wrote his books. Langford was not a prominent family, and Gervase was probably a painful disappointment to his uncle.'

Margaret stopped there. She seemed to lose her train of thought, staring vacantly out through the front window. A noisy crowd of college students was getting settled around a big table in the corner of the café. Edward waited for her to go on, but she didn't.

'Is that it?' Edward asked. 'But why did he go back to Langford, if he could have done better in London?'

'Nobody knows,' said Margaret. 'I think he left London under a cloud, some kind of political disgrace. No one knows exactly what. It must have been fairly severe to send him to the provinces – look at Chaucer, who was tried for rape and went on to become head of customs for all of London. Something different happened to Gervase, something worse, and it cast a shadow over his career from which he never recovered.

'Gervase accompanied one diplomatic mission, to Venice. I've even heard it suggested that he was involved in espionage, and that his undistinguished career was just a cover identity, but again, there's really no evidence to back it up. Maybe Gervase thought a less prominent position would give him more time to write, although from what I can tell the earl worked him like a dog. It's useless to speculate, there's no way we can know.'

Edward nodded. 'Poor bastard.'

He sipped his wine and studied Margaret's curiously pale oval face. The sun gleamed off her dark, straight hair. She met his eyes with her own unreadable stare.

'Well,' he said. 'So much for his life. What about his books?'

'By our standards, Gervase didn't write very much.' He sensed that Margaret was bored, but her speech remained as concise and composed as a prepared lecture. 'There are a dozen or so minor poems attributed to him, occasional verses which he may or may not actually have written. We know for certain that he wrote a book of animal fables, *Les Contes merveilleux,* which are witty in places but otherwise very conventional. His masterpiece, such as it is, is the *Chronicum Anglicanum*, an account of what was then England's recent history, the eleventh and twelfth centuries. He completed it in 1362. In those days Gervase was probably considered pretty unfashionable for his interest in the recent past – that kind of scholarship went out of style with the Venerable Bede.'

Edward had ordered a piece of dense flourless chocolate cake. He shaved off a thin slice with the edge of his fork.

'Have you read it?' he asked.

'Yes.'

'Is it as dull as it sounds?'

She didn't take the bait. 'It's an important document. It's a very scholarly piece of research in a period when serious scholarship was out of fashion. Is there something more specific I can tell you about it?'

'No. Sorry, go on. So he stayed at Langford for the rest of his life?'

She nodded.

'As usual, history only records the bad parts. He was robbed once, on the road from Langford to Hull. His losses were never recovered. He married a woman named Elizabeth who was very young even for that time. It seems to have been a marriage of convenience; she was a handmaiden to the countess. She died two years later, and there were no children. Gervase received the usual petty awards and annuities from his noble masters, but they were never sufficient to make him well-off. He engaged in the usual legal squabbles. Around 1370 he suffered some kind of serious injury on the castle grounds; possibly he fell from one of the walls. Some have called it a failed suicide. After that he kept to his bed.

'He died in 1374, in his mid-thirties. It's not unusual. People didn't live as long back then. It was a plague year, and that may be what finally killed him, but again, we don't know for sure. After all, he survived it the first time.'

So far, not a lot he could use. A waiter cleared away the dishes at the next table with a clatter. Margaret finally tasted her coffee.

'It seems like a shame,' he said.

'What does?'

'I don't know. That there wasn't more to his life.'

'Like what?'

'I don't know.' He frowned. 'Something more dramatic?'

Margaret shrugged unsympathetically. 'Most people had it worse than he did. A lot of them lived on leftover peas and radishes they picked up from between the ruts in some lord's field after the harvest. By any reasonable standard Gervase was extremely privileged.'

'I doubt that ever stopped anybody from being unhappy.'

She shrugged again, a tiny movement of one thin shoulder, obviously uninterested in this line of speculation.

The café was now bathed in yellow sunlight pouring in through the front windows, glinting off marble tabletops and discarded spoons. A large leafy tropical plant stood in one corner, half green, half dead.

'So Gervase wrote two books, and maybe a few poems,' Edward said, 'and he had a lousy job working for a minor nobleman. Why is he so important?'

Margaret arched her thin, dark eyebrows quizzically.

'What makes you think he's important?'

Edward hesitated, puzzled.

'I guess I just assumed – you're saying he's not important?'

Edward caught a faint flash of something in her eyes.

'He's a significant minor figure,' she said, calmly enough, and took another sip of coffee.

All right, he thought. *We'll come back to that.* He wanted another glass of wine, and he signaled the waiter and tapped his glass.

'And this other book, the one I'm looking for? Where does the *Viage* fit in?' He tried to imitate her pronunciation.

'The *Viage* is another matter entirely,' she said. 'If, for the sake of argument, we take seriously the possibility that it is genuine – and I suppose that doing so is one of the conditions of my employment – it would of course have real importance. There were only three really important writers in late medieval England: Chaucer, Langland, and the Pearl Poet. Together they essentially invented English literature. A fictional narrative of significant length from that period, written in English and not Latin or French, by a scholar of Gervase's general sophistication . . . its value would be inestimable. And of course,' she added pragmatically, 'the book itself could have some monetary value, as an artifact.'

'How much?'

'Hundreds of thousands. Maybe millions.'

'Wow.' Edward was grudgingly impressed.

'All right.' He could see her visibly remind herself that she was getting paid for this. 'The *Viage* purports to be the remains of a lost medieval narrative, a romance consisting of five fragments. It begins as a Grail legend. The quest for the Holy Grail involved many knights, hundreds, not just Lancelot and Galahad and the ones you've heard of, and they all had their own separate adventures along the way. Some successful, some less so. The *Viage* begins in the Grail genre, telling the story of a previously unknown knight, but it rapidly deviates into something else.

'The knight is a nobleman, never named, who leaves behind his wife and child in the dead of winter. After some preliminary wandering he stays for a while at the castle of a friendly lord who feasts him handsomely, with much boasting and swapping of stories in front of the roaring fire, while the ice-covered branches rattle outside. One night, from out of the darkness, a strange knight enters the hall. He has the body of an enormous muscular man, but his head is the head of a stag with a great branching rack of silver antlers. On the antlers is impaled the corpse of a footman who had been standing guard outside. His blood streams down over the strange knight's face.

'As you might imagine, everybody falls silent. The strange knight bows his horned head, dumping the footman's body unceremoniously onto the carpet, then straightens up and draws a long, slender sword. He speaks to them. He describes a strange chapel with stained glass walls, the place, he says, where St Maura Troyes wept her miraculous tears. He calls it the Rose Chapel. Between here and there are great perils, he says, but it is a holy place of great power. In short, he charges them to seek it out or forfeit their knightly honor. The stag knight speaks in a high, lisping voice, apparently one of the side effects of having the head of a deer.

'When he's finished the stag knight changes shape. Instead of a knight with the head of a stag, he becomes a stag with the head of a bearded man. He winks at the company, defecates on the lord's good red carpet, drags his hoof through it a few times, and bounds away into the winter night.

'No one sleeps in the castle that night. They forget all about the Grail and unanimously swear to take up the stag knight's challenge – in part for the sake of their honor, in part to avenge the footman, who turns out to have been somebody or other's nephew.

The servants are rousted out of bed and put to work packing food and strapping on armor and shoeing horses, and the knights put in some time praying for holy guidance. There's a lot of very technical discussion of the merits and demerits of various bits of armor and a fairly technical disquisition on hunting techniques – fewmets and prickers and things like that – but the gist is that they're all off and away into the forest the next morning, hounds baying, hoarfrost on steel, the bloody orb of the sun winking between the snowy trees, pennants of breath streaming from the horses' mouths. In a way, it's the high point of the story. It's certainly the happiest.

'They pick up the stag knight's scent quickly, but he turns out to be a past master at this game, and he leads them on an epic chase, in and out of streams and rivers, up and down mountains, doubling back on his tracks, laying false trails. Every time they think they have him he mysteriously vanishes, and every time they're about to give up hope he pops up again, posing cheekily on some distant promontory, and the chase is rejoined.

'At first everyone seems to be having a good time, singing round the campfire and handling little subquests on the side as they come up, slaying giants and righting local wrongs. But over time the knights start to feel run down. The chase has gone on for months now, and the strain is beginning to tell. It's worst at night. Asleep in their silken pavilions, the knights have troubled dreams. Glowing women drift out of the trees and tempt them to break their knightly vows. Grumpy hermits pop up wearing smelly hair shirts, demanding alms and posing thorny theological questions and telling them they're all going to hell. Then something truly terrible happens.'

'What?' Edward asked. He caught himself listening raptly, with his mouth open.

'One morning, early, the lord and his men pick up the stag knight's trail.' Margaret took another sip of coffee. 'It's fresh, and for once they actually seem to have a chance to catch it. They decide to herd it toward a blind canyon in the foothills of some mountains. They see the stag enter the canyon. The knights move in behind it to guard the entrance and settle in to wait. They sit there for several hours, till the sun is up and they're baking in their armor. The wind dies. Insects stop chirping. In spite of the bright sun the entrance to the canyon is dark and shadowy. In fact, it's black as midnight. For an instant the forest is still.

'Then the brush crackles, and the stag comes flying out of the dark canyon at enormous speed. Its eyes are rolling wildly in its human head. "Gyve over!" it shouts back over its shoulder. "Gyve over! For God's sake leave this place, if you value your lives!" There's something in the canyon that even the stag knight is terrified of. It runs straight at the crescent of armored knights, and the lord gives it a deep slash on the shoulder as it passes, but it breaks through and disappears back into the forest.

'This is the kind of situation knights live for. With typically short attention spans they forget all about the magic stag and the Rose Chapel and swear another mighty oath to brave the adventure of the blind canyon. They dismount and march shoulder-to-shoulder into the darkness.

'The next page of the book is entirely covered with black ink.'

CHAPTER 7

E dward blotted his forehead with his wrist. It was hot in the café, though Margaret didn't seem to feel it. She looked very cool and very still. She continued in her professional lecturing voice.

'No words, no pictures, just a solid page of blackness. It's an unusual device, very literary, even innovative – it's been written about quite often. Sterne probably borrowed the idea for the black pages in *Tristram Shandy*, though I don't think anybody's ever proved conclusively that he read the *Viage* himself. No one knows what it means, if it means anything, and there aren't many clues: That's where the first fragment ends.

'The second fragment is very short. It begins with the lord returning home. We don't know what happened to him on the black page, or what happened afterward, only that time has passed. His companions are now gone, presumed dead, and his quest for the Rose Chapel appears to have failed. As for the Holy Grail, he's forgotten all about it. He is a shell of his former self, a skeleton rattling around in his full-chested armor.

'What's more, his castle has been razed in his absence. When he left, one of his enemies apparently saw an opportunity and besieged it. It's nothing but a field of rubble, scorched earth and tumbled stones. His wife and child are dead. The invader was preparing to ravage the lord's wife when an angel appeared and slew her.'

'What?' Edward practically did a spit-take with his wine. 'Why?'

'To spare her from sin.'

He swallowed. 'That's insane. What about killing the invaders? That would have been a little more helpful.'

'The medieval God is mysterious.'

Edward snorted. 'That's one word for it. What happens next?'

'The lord gears up for an extravagant display of grieving, but we're spared the details, because the fragment ends there.

'Part three picks up on the theme of divine judgment. It's the most academic and theoretical of the five fragments, and it's also the longest, longer than the other four put together. It's similar in some ways to Dante's *Paradiso* – it's less a narrative than an attempt to sketch the outlines of the author's *Weltanschauung*. The fragment begins with the lord wandering the countryside, homeless and penitent. He believes himself cursed by God. He has been living outside, sleeping on pine needles and swimming in cold rivers. He is joined in his wanderings by the stag knight, of all people, who is still limping from the wound the lord gave him. This time the two get along like old friends. They're like two old soldiers who served with opposing armies in the same war. Now that the war's over, they're the only ones who really understand each other.

'They retire together to a hermit's hut on top of a mountain, where they keep the dialogue going in quasi-Socratic mode. There's a long excursus on the proper interpretation of dreams, largely quoted wholesale from Macrobius's *Commentary on the Dream of Scipio* – medieval writers didn't have any real scruples about plagiarism. As they talk the stag knight changes form at will, from stag knight to knight stag and back again as the mood strikes him. They cover a lot of ground: cosmology, theology, hermeneutics, and in particular eschatology, the theoretical discourse that deals with the end of the world. If the world were to end, how would we know it had ended? Is it possible that the world has already ended, and we are living in the after-math? Is this hell? Or worse, is this heaven? The stag knight is the authority here, being something of a mystical entity, but the lord gets in some good licks of his own. At one point he remarks – bitterly, but with a very eighteenth-century wink at the reader – that if he were a character in a romance he wouldn't care how his story ended, because no ending, not even the final reward of heaven, could recompense him for the loss of his wife and his child.'

Edward was starting to enjoy watching her talk. It was all so different from what he was used to: This was somebody who spent all her time just reading and thinking about what she read. In a way it seemed like a ridiculous waste of time; and in another way it seemed so much more urgently important than what he did all day. Or used to do.

'The fourth fragment is the most problematic, and the most written about, although I don't think the commentaries have done much to make it clearer. The tone is different from the rest of the *Viage*. It's more like a dream, or a hallucination, or one of Bosch's grotesques. It hardly seems to be by the same person – its repetitions and violence seem to reflect the mind of an infant, or a pathological grown-up. If an adult wrote this, he or she was very close to mental illness.

'The lord resumes his adventuring, though no longer with any quest at all in mind. He's just lost . . .' Margaret broke off, apparently at a loss as to how to continue coherently. She sighed and puffed aside her bangs, an uncharacteristically girlish gesture. 'The text becomes very repetitive, almost obsessively so: The lord slays one monster after another, giants, demons, dragons, on and on, over and over again. Sometimes he seems to kill the same monster twice or three times. Time circles around and doubles and triples back on itself. In places the verse degenerates into nothing more than a catalog of who or what the lord has fought or killed or saved, simple lists, stripped of any narrative or meaning.

'At one point we're told that the lord has re-married and rebuilt his castle, and he has raised a new son. He grows old and contented, and the narrative branches and follows the adventures of his son, who goes off on a quest of his own. But the son gradually grows up to become his father, who meets the stag knight and gives chase all over again, and soon the whole narrative has turned back on itself. Time swallows its own tail. Except that this time the lord succeeds in his quest – he completes the quest, finds the Rose Chapel and is accepted into heaven on the spot.

'But it doesn't last. The lord gets kicked out of heaven on some theological technicality that makes no sense, as far as I can tell. Back on earth he becomes a bitter man, and takes his revenge by hunting down the stag knight and killing him and eating his flesh.' Edward made a face. 'From this point on the text itself appears to go mad. People die and come back to life without rhyme or reason. The lord himself commits suicide, disemboweling himself with a misericord – a kind of slim dagger – only to be forcibly resurrected by a spiteful, sarcastic angel. The stag knight reappears, too, sounding a little petulant at having been killed off earlier, and he warns the lord that life is just a dream, that heaven is the only true reality, that he shouldn't take everything so seriously. Huge hosts assemble and do battle for no reason, described in minute detail.

The narrator is like a little boy with a chest full of army men, lining them up and knocking them down over and over again. We catch glimpses and echoes of a landscape devastated by war and plague.

'Finally the narrative loops back around once again, time curls in on itself, and we return to the fateful chase after the stag knight, exactly as before. In fact whole passages from the first fragment reappear verbatim, and the poem becomes a pastiche of itself. Just as before the stag knight is trapped in the blind canyon and rushes out in a state of panic. The lord appears to be aware that all this has already happened, but he is helpless, powerless to change its course. Just as before, the knights enter the canyon. But again, we never see what's inside, because that's where the fragment ends.'

'Curses,' said Edward. 'Foiled again.' He glanced at his watch. It was getting on toward six. It crossed his mind that if this went on much longer she could charge him for another hour. 'On to fragment five.'

Unflappable as ever, Margaret continued.

'It begins with the lord adrift on the open ocean in a boat. He has no oars, no sail, no rudder. He trusts in God to bring him safely to shore. Some time has passed. He's very far north, and there are icebergs all around him. Exotic Arctic whales breach and dive around him, belugas and bowheads and narwhals. Coleridge borrowed a few lines from this passage for 'The Rime of the Ancient Mariner.'

'And through the drifts the snowy clifts/Did send a dismal sheen:/Nor shapes of men nor beasts we ken—/The ice was all between.'

'Medieval authors often insert stories from classical works into their own, and here the narrator takes the opportunity to retell a couple of episodes from *The Odyssey*, the Sirens and the Lotus-Eaters. I can't really say why. He also retells the story of Paolo and Francesca, about a woman and her brother-in-law who become lovers while reading a book together. The woman's husband walks in and kills them both. It was a popular enough tale – Dante and Boccaccio both have their own versions of it – but Gervase's version is oddly bastardized: He gives it a happy ending, in which the literary lovers escape together and live happily ever after.

'The lord finally drifts onto the shore of a desolate country. All he can see from the beach is drift after drift of sand spotted with patches of snow. The sand is the color of iron, 'withouten toun, or hous, or tree/or bush, or grass, or eryd lond.' He walks inland for a while. Gervase takes a whole paragraph to describe the curious quality of the light – there's something about it that bothers him, it's pale and weak and a little unearthly. Eventually he comes to a place where people are living. They introduce themselves as the Cimmerians of the book's title.

'In Cimmeria, they tell him, it's twilight all the time – neither day nor night. It's a cold, hard, depopulated country. The lord wanders through the landscape, and we see it through his eyes. The inhabitants subsist on root crops and herds of shaggy sheep. The countryside is criss-crossed with icy streams, and he stumbles on the frozen corpse of a woman in a ditch. He walks through the ruins of a town, collapsed huts and stone walls that have been scattered and dispersed. He passes a field where the furrows are filled with snow, and he compares the alternation of black earth and white snow to lines of writing on a page.

'And that's where the last fragment ends. It's a very stark passage. Like the others, it's suffused with a sense of melancholy and longing, but with no obvious object. Parts of it are almost certainly allusions to Dante's *Inferno*. Which incidentally is another reason to think that it couldn't have been written by Gervase of Langford, because as far as I know the only man in England who had read Dante at that time was Chaucer.'

Margaret stared into her half-empty glass. Edward toyed with what was left of the cake. A heavy truck lumbered past outside, wheezing along the narrow street, its brakes snorting, temporarily blocking out the sun.

'What do you think it all means?' he said.

'What does it mean? I don't know. Read as the product of a medieval mind the *Viage* would probably be a religious allegory. The progress of the soul from sin toward grace. It might have had political overtones – usurpation, the plight of the agricultural laborer. And Gervase's psyche must have been profoundly affected by the spectacle of the

Death. He may have lived with unbearable guilt and shame at having survived when so many others died, as well as with fear that the plague would come back to claim him.'

'How about the Cimmerians? Who are they?'

'Nobody special. They have a basis in fact, if it matters: They were a nomadic tribe who invaded Asia Minor somewhere around 1200 B.C.'

'So they really existed?'

'Of course they did.' Margaret smiled thinly. 'The modern Crimea derives its name from Cimmeria. But the historical reality isn't nearly as interesting as the literary one. In the classical tradition the Cimmerians were thought to be a legendary tribe who lived in a land where it was always twilight.

'Ovid mentions them in the *Metamorphoses*, and Ulysses visits the land of the Cimmerians in the *Odyssey*. In the cosmology of classical myth the world was encircled by a river called Oceanus. The Cimmerians lived on the far side of Oceanus, and beyond Cimmeria there was only Hades. Pliny thought Cimmeria was in Italy, where there was supposedly an entrance to the underworld, but whoever wrote the *Viage* seems to be combining or conflating Cimmeria with Ultima Thule, the legendary northernmost land in the world.'

An argument broke out at the door between the maître d' and a man who wanted to bring his dog in. Margaret watched Edward steadily. He wondered if she were simply waiting for him to say she could go.

'So if I were looking for this book – just supposing for the sake of argument that it exists – what do you think it would look like?'

'Well, as far as the format goes,' she said, steepling her fingers, 'it would be a codex. It would probably be written on parchment, not paper. The covers would be wood covered with leather. It would be a manuscript – printing wasn't invented for another hundred years – and the writing would be Gothic bookhand. Very difficult to read for the nonexpert. Beyond that, it could look like almost anything. Making a book back then was like making a movie now: It took a lot of time and a lot of money and a lot of people with many different skills. You had to purchase the parchment and the pens and the ink. You had to have the text written out by a scribe, then it was illustrated by an illustrator, then bound by a binder, and so on.'

A waiter passed by and discreetly slipped the check onto the table between them.

'Could Gervase have done that? Could he have afforded it?'

She shrugged.

'It's possible. A young man from an upper middle-class family, serving a noble house. It's possible. But as for the text itself – I'm sorry, I don't know how I can convince you, and it's obvious you're not interested in being convinced, but it's simply not the product of a medieval mind.'

Edward pursed his lips and nodded. She believed what she was saying, and she was probably right.

133

She had no reason to mislead him; if anything, she had a financial interest in leading him on, in prolonging these sessions. He was disappointed. At some point, without fully realizing it or knowing why, he'd really started wanting the book to be real. He took out his wallet.

'So what do you think happened to those knights? I mean, at the end of the first part, in the blind canyon?'

'Much ink has been spilled over that black page, no pun intended.' Margaret swirled the dregs of her coffee. She didn't stop him from paying. 'There's at least one entire book about it, Capshaw's *Darkness Visible*. The Freudians think it's a womb, or an anus, or a grave, or all three. The Marxists talk about the rise of capitalism in England and the commodification of the novel. It's especially popular among the deconstructionists. I've seen it called a printer's error and a map of Africa and a protest against the Pragmatic Sanction of 1713.'

'What do you think it is?'

'I have no opinion.' All at once Margaret's flat affect returned. 'It's not my field.'

'All right. Okay.' The woman was starting to wear him out. He needed to go somewhere and think. Or better yet, go somewhere and not think. At the next table a young couple who looked like two lawyers were fighting in clipped whispers. 'Why don't we wrap this up for now? Are you headed back to Brooklyn?' She shook her head. 'Well, wherever you're going, take a taxi and keep the receipt.

Next time I'd like you to come look at the collection, assuming that the Wents are amenable. How would you feel about that?'

'Fine,' she said, exhibiting neither reluctance nor enthusiasm. She stood up, and he followed her to the door and out onto the sidewalk. It was almost six thirty, but it was a long summer afternoon, and it was still broad daylight outside.

'Can I—?' Should he? He gestured vaguely in the direction of the East Side while at the same time looking out for a cab.

'I'm going uptown,' she said. 'To Columbia.'

She turned away in the direction of the subway, her bag bouncing on her hip. Edward called after her.

'One more thing. You said before that the book would be a codex. What does that mean?'

'A codex—' She stopped and half turned. She seemed nonplussed at having to define so basic a concept. 'A codex is just – it's a codex. As opposed to a scroll, or a wax tablet, or a rock with words chiseled on it. A codex is a set of printed pages, folded and bound with a spine between two covers. It's what someone like you would call a book.'

CHAPTER 8

For their next appointment, two days later, Edward met Margaret on the sidewalk in front of the Wents' building. It was a warm day, overcast and muggy. Thunder hung in the air. The handle of an umbrella stuck up out of her leather bookbag, though it hadn't actually rained yet. Her hair was clipped back neatly in a tortoise-shell barrette. Pale and skinny as she was, he thought, she could have had a Goth thing going on without much trouble, but she didn't take the trouble. He ushered her inside past the doorman, who recognized him now and nodded them inside.

'Come and go!' he said, smiling under his bushy mustache.

Riding up in the elevator, Edward cleared his throat.

'I probably should have warned them you were coming today,' he said. 'But don't worry about it. Just be nice to Laura. You'll meet her – she's the Wents' Girl Friday.'

'Thanks,' Margaret said dryly. 'I wasn't worried.'

The doors opened onto a silent, empty apartment. They saw no one as they walked through the halls toward the spiral staircase that led upstairs. The light coming in through the windows was muted and gray, like moonlight.

He'd never really noticed the spiral staircase before, but it was a real wonder – maybe with Margaret here he was seeing it through her observant eyes. It was a genuine piece of old New York art nouveau glory, solid iron, cast all in one piece and dripping with serpentine Aubrey Beardsley ornaments. It must have weighed at least a ton. She followed him up it unquestioningly and waited in the dark while he unlocked the door and then fumbled around in the darkness for the one standing lamp.

It was oddly like bringing a girlfriend home to meet the parents – something he had done as rarely as possible when he was in college. Edward was relieved to see that he'd left the books in a reasonably orderly state. They filled the long wooden table in close rows of tall, neat, many-colored stacks, like a model city of miniature sky-scrapers. As he pried open the computer and started it up she went over to them and took the first book off the first stack on the nearest corner. It was a mossy green hardcover that looked fairly modern. She inspected it closed, all six surfaces, turning it over expertly in her pale, slender fingers, then she let the book fall gently open in her palm and studied a few of the pages. She bent her head and gave the central fold a delicate sniff with her long, elegant nose.

'It's been washed,' she said, making a face. 'Scrubbed with detergent. Disgusting French practice, ruins the paper. Should be illegal.'

She scanned the spines of each stack in order, carefully and without hurrying. She seemed to have forgotten he was even in the room. She stopped when she came to the wooden case that held the ancient book he'd unwrapped on his first day there. It was at the bottom of a tall stack of books, but before he could offer to help she picked them up and shifted them to the floor in one practiced motion. The books left a ladder of dusty smudges up the front of her dress, but she didn't seem to notice. She opened the case and looked inside.

'What do you know about this one?' she said, after a long pause.

'Nothing.' He cleared his throat. 'I can't figure out how to open it.'

'What does the catalog say?'

'There isn't one. I mean, I've been working on it, but I haven't done that one yet.'

She looked at him. It was very dark in the room: No light came in from the muffled windows, so there was only the lamp and the ghostly glow from the monitor.

'What do you mean? This book is undescribed?'

'So far as I know.'

'Are all these books—?' She looked around at the rest of the books on the table. 'They haven't been cataloged?'

'Nobody else knows about them, if that's what you mean.' Edward tapped nonchalantly at the computer keyboard, opening the file he'd made. 'I've been working on it. That's what I was hired to do here.'

'What cataloging standard are you using? AACR? ISBD?'

He shook his head. 'Beats the hell out of me.'

Margaret looked down at the book in the case and touched its cover with her hands. She sighed deeply.

'This is a very unusual situation,' she said finally.

'That's not all,' said Edward. 'Look over there.'

He gestured toward all the unopened crates at the other end of the room.

When she saw where he was pointing, she walked over and looked into the one opened crate, which was almost empty except for a few large, heavy packages at the bottom. A strange, slightly hysterical gasp escaped her, but she recovered her composure almost immediately and turned it into a cough.

She turned to face him.

'It's very unlikely that a collection this old and this large could have remained completely uncataloged,' she said evenly. 'There must be records of it somewhere.'

'You may be right. But then why would they have hired me?'

'I don't know. But there must be documents. A shipping manifest, sales receipts, insurance papers, tax returns. Objects like these don't just slide through history untouched, invisible, without a trace. They leave footprints behind them, tracks. How long have these books been here?'

'It all came over from England on a boat, right before World War II.'

He related what Laura Crowlyk had told him on his first day about the collection's history. As he talked she walked back over to the table and opened the drawers.

'What are you looking for?' said Edward.

'We should open up those other crates before we go any further.' She folded her arms. 'There may be documentation in one of them.'

'Okay.' Edward hadn't thought of that.

He retrieved the screwdriver from where he'd left it and handed it to her. The balance of power in the room had shifted, and not in his favor.

'Clean the dust off those bookshelves,' she said. 'We're going to need a lot of space.'

Edward came back upstairs carrying an aluminum bucket full of warm water, a squeeze bottle of Joy, two rolls of paper towels, and an unopened packet of fresh bright yellow-and-green sponges that the cleaning woman had given him when she found him rummaging around under a sink in a disused bathroom. Margaret already had the next crate open and was lifting out the books inside. He set down the bucket with a metallic clang, and she jumped.

They worked in silence in the hushed half light of the library. He overheard the creak of old screws leaving the soft wood and the dry rattle as she let them fall carelessly on the floor, and Margaret's breathing, deepened slightly by the physical effort. At first Edward tried to make conversation, but eventually he decided she might feel more comfortable if they didn't speak. He soaked a sponge in soapy water and slapped it down onto the first shelf. The coating of thick, oily dust came away all in one swipe. It was interesting, in a way. He spent all day every day in places that were cleaned by other people, people who emptied the trash and vacuumed the carpets and surreptitiously scrubbed the urinals while he was elsewhere, or while he averted his eyes and talked louder on the phone. He thought of the cleaning women who made the rounds of his office every night after work in the wee hours, chattering in Spanish and Portuguese and Ukrainian, pushing their gray plastic carts ahead of them. The only English words they seemed to know were 'excuse me' and 'sorry.' He wondered if they all had Ph.D.'s in microbiology in their home countries, and went home to write brilliant *romans fleuves* in their various native tongues.

When he'd finished one whole rack of shelves the water in the bucket was a solid gray. He dried them off with the paper towels. When he turned around Margaret was still working on the crates, deftly spinning the screwdriver with her slim, strong fingers.

'Find anything?' he said.

She shook her head without turning around.

'Who was Cruttenden?' she said.

'Who?'

'Cruttenden.' Despite the chill in the room she'd broken a sweat, and she paused to blot her forehead with her forearm. 'The name on the shipping label on all these boxes.'

'I have no idea. He or she or it was probably Crowlyk's predecessor. Probably several Crowlyks ago.'

'Crowlyk—?'

'Laura. The one who hired me, the secretary. I should probably tell you, the Wents don't seem to be around here much. They're kind of an absent presence. I gather they spend most of their time holed up in their estate in Bowmry. It's really Laura who runs the show.'

'In Bowmry?' She looked at him curiously.

'Bowmry. That's where they're from. The Wents are aristocrats or royalty or something. The Duke and Duchess of Bowmry.'

'Ah,' she said, as if he'd unwittingly given away a clue.

'What?'

'Gervase of Langford was in the service of the Duke of Bowmry.'

'I thought you said he worked for an earl.'

'Same person. Under the English system, one person can hold more than one peerage. Late in his career the Earl of Langford was created First Duke of Bowmry by Edward III. Edward was

142

crazy about dukedoms, probably because he invented them.'

'Oh. So does that mean the Wents might not be completely full of shit?'

'No. But it does give me a better idea of why they might think they have a Gervase.'

She went back to lifting books out of the crate in front of her and stacking them on the floor.

'Maybe you could move those books from the table onto the shelves you've cleaned.'

'Roger that.'

When Edward was done the books took up a full three and a half shelves on the wall, an uneven skyline of deep browns and greens and blues and umbers, chased here and there with traces of gold and silver like lighted windows. Margaret had stopped working on the crates and was unwrapping a package in the space he'd cleared on the table. The book was tiny, barely bigger than a pack of cards, with smooth, brown, cracked covers that looked like they'd been glazed and roasted in an oven. As Edward watched she gingerly laid it out on the tabletop like a wounded sparrow.

'There's a correct way to catalog a book,' she said. 'You might as well know it, if you're going to be doing it.' She took a notebook and a pencil out of her bag. 'A formal bibliographical description has four parts. Heading and title page; binding; collation and colophon; and the contents of the book. So beginning with the heading—'

As she spoke she printed fluently in her notebook,

and Edward watched over her shoulder. She had neat, pointy architect's handwriting:

Johnson, Samuel A Journey to the Western Islands of Scotland. 1775.

'Now the title page:'

[within double rules] A | JOURNEY | TO THE | WESTERN ISLANDS | OF | SCOTLAND. | [publisher's device] | LONDON: | Printed for W. STRAHAN and T. CADELL in the Strand. | MDCCLXXV.

'Now the binding.'

Sheep over marbled boards, warped, brown endpapers.

'This soft leather is sheepskin, very cheap stuff,' she added. 'See how it tends to crack at the joints?'

She went on exploring the book with her fingers, measuring it, noting the technical aspects of the formats and gatherings, the signings and the foliation and the pagination. She recorded them as she went in an arcane-looking formula consisting of capital letters, superscripts, and Greek characters:

$$\pi^2 \; \S^4 \; A^2 \; B-C^4\chi^2D-G^8 \; 2\chi^4H-M^8 \; 3\chi1$$

'A highly unusual collation,' she announced with satisfaction.

She worked with complete concentration and an almost mechanical intensity, all the time describing her actions aloud in the tones of a medical examiner performing an autopsy. Edward quickly lost track of what she was talking about, although he pretended to listen anyway. She was so absorbed in what she was doing she seemed to have forgotten that she was supposed to be explaining it to him, to have forgotten he was even there. When she concentrated her face was less severe – she became strangely calm, relaxed, almost happy.

When she was finished she tore the completed pages briskly out of her notebook and tucked them inside the little brown book. Then she set it aside and started unwrapping the next one. It had been shipped in a cardboard box stuffed to bursting with shredded old newspapers. When it emerged it was dark brown, almost black, and shaped like a cinder block, short and narrow but fully ten inches thick. The spine was worn down to just a few shreds and strips of leather stretched across the bunched, gathered pages.

Margaret treated it with a special delicacy. She carefully lifted up the front cover, supporting it with both hands. The printing inside looked different somehow, elegant and italicized, more like handwriting than printed letters.

'It's an incunable,' she said quietly, rapt.

'Edward, may I speak to you a moment?'

The moment froze and shattered. The voice came from behind them, and Edward turned around guiltily. Laura Crowlyk was observing them from the landing at the top of the stairs. Surprise entrances seemed to be one of her specialities.

'Laura!' Edward said brightly, to hide his annoyance. 'Laura, I'd like you to meet Margaret Napier. She's a medievalist from Columbia. She's helping me with the cataloging.'

Laura's eyes settled on Margaret. 'Hi.'

'Hello.'

Laura regarded Margaret frostily, sizing her up as a potential combatant. Margaret barely looked up from the book on the table. There was an uncomfortable pause.

'Join me in my office, please, Edward. In five minutes.'

She turned and descended the stairs without waiting for an answer. Her tinny footsteps faded away.

'Should I leave?' Margaret asked, when she was gone.

'No, stay here. Keep on doing – whatever it was you're doing. What did you say that book was?'

'An incunable,' she said, placing the stress on the second syllable. 'A book made in the first fifty years of printing. 1454 to 1501.'

'What book is it?'

'*Historia Florentina*. Poggio Bracciolini.'

'And who was Bracciolini?'

'Renaissance scholar. Worked on Quintilian.'

Her interest in keeping him updated was already flagging. He watched over her shoulder as she delicately separated the pages. She wore no perfume, but her hair had a not unpleasant smell, delicately sweet but with an edge of bitterness.

'I should go down,' he said. 'Back in a minute.'

As he climbed down the metal spiral, down into the relative brightness of the main apartment, Edward felt like a kid being summoned to the principal's office. He reminded himself that he was doing them a favor by being here in the first place. Laura's door was open, and she was sitting at her desk looking over a sheaf of papers with a pen in her hand, her brown hair gathered behind her head in a bunch. He had the impression she had deliberately posed herself for maximum severity. The blinds were lowered halfway against the gray day, and she'd turned on a desk lamp to give herself some light.

She waited a few seconds before she acknowledged his presence. She'd put on a pair of rimless glasses, but now she took them off again.

'I'll have to ask you to stop working up there,' she said.

Her voice was as dry as ever. Edward looked out the window at the brown roof of a building across the street. Disappointment stabbed him in the chest. He was surprised, but even more surprising was how much the news hurt. Something he'd been hoping for, without even really knowing it, had abruptly been ripped away from him.

'Laura, if this is about—'

'Of course you shouldn't have brought her here,' she said, tight-lipped, 'but no, that's not what this is about. I hope it won't be too inconvenient for you.'

'Not at all,' he said stiffly.

She looked down at her papers again. Edward couldn't think of anything to say, but he didn't want to leave it at that. It was up to him to take this news like a good sport, but somehow he'd forgotten how to do that. *This is a lucky break*, he told himself. *You're off the hook.*

'I'll write up a report,' he said finally. 'I mean, on my work up till now. Unless you'd rather—'

'That won't be necessary.' She gestured dismissively.

'Listen, I apologize about bringing Margaret here, but you have to understand, she's an invaluable asset to this project.' He placed his fingertips on the edge of her desk in what he hoped was a gently assertive gesture. 'I know I should have cleared it through you first, but I really think you should reconsider this.'

'It isn't that. I told you, that doesn't matter now. The fact is, I received a call from the Duke yesterday.'

'The Duke.'

'Yes. And he told me to stop work on the library immediately.'

'Oh,' said Edward, wrong-footed. 'Well, I guess that settles it then. But I don't understand, why stop now? I was just starting to make some real progress.'

'I don't know.' She began briskly transferring piles of papers from one wire tray to another. 'I just don't know.' He saw now that she really wasn't upset about Margaret. She was upset because Gervase could have been her ticket home, and he was slipping through her fingers. 'It's not my business to question the Duke's decisions. Perhaps he's bringing the books back to England ahead of schedule. Perhaps he's decided they're not worth the trouble after all. Who knows? Maybe he'll just sell the lot and have Sotheby's do the catalog for us.'

Edward nodded slowly.

'How's his health?' he asked, with miserable politeness. 'The Duke, I mean? You mentioned before that he'd been under the weather.'

She ignored the question.

'It's odd, isn't it?' she went on. 'He called last night – it must have been three in the morning at Weymarshe. He doesn't usually speak to me directly, you know. Technically I only work for the Duchess.'

'Is that where they live? In Weymarshe?'

She gave him a funny look.

'Most of the time. Weymarshe is the name of their estate in England.'

'Is it a castle?' Maybe answering questions about the Wents would make her feel better.

'You might call Weymarshe a castle.' She went back to her papers. 'It's been built over and added onto so many times, I don't know what you'd call it, really. It's a hodgepodge. Most of it was rebuilt in the late 1600s, after the revolution, but parts of it are very old – they say it was even built on some old earthwork fortifications. The academics are always wanting to dig it up, but the Wents won't let them.'

She looked up at Edward thoughtfully.

'You know, when you first came here I thought you might be after a career with the family. It's quite rewarding, you know. And of course I don't just mean financially.'

Edward blinked.

'You thought I was looking for a job with the Wents? A permanent position?'

He didn't know whether to be amused or insulted. Laura just shrugged.

'The Duchess has made arrangements like that before, with other young people. Particularly with young men.'

'What would that make me? A servant?'

'Well, call it what you like.' He considered, too late, the possibility that he might have just insulted her. 'If you played your cards right you might never really have to work again. The Wents like to keep interesting people around, to advise them if something comes up. It's not for everybody – I mean, it's not a regular career – but some people consider it very glamorous. Especially the Americans, I find.'

'I'm sure they do.'

Edward let it drop. There was no point in offending her while he was on his way out the door. He let his eyes stray to Laura's desk. On it was a picture of a woman in a plain black frame – drastically foreshortened, from his oblique angle, but undeniably the Duchess. He recognized her wavy dark hair, her wide, sensual mouth. In the photograph she was even wearing the same cream sun hat he'd seen her wearing before, when he'd met her on the street. There was something maternal about her, but also something undeniably sexy as well. She was like your best friend's mom, the one you fantasized about in junior high before you knew any better.

'But I suppose that's all off now,' Laura was saying. 'Look, I don't know what to tell you. The matter seemed so urgent when we made the initial arrangements, but now – well, everything's changed. I hope you aren't too disappointed?'

'No. No, of course not.' Edward's own voice sounded distant to him. He turned to go. 'You'll get in touch, if there's any change?'

She gave him a thin, sympathetic smile.

'Yes, of course.'

'I'll just get my stuff from upstairs.'

He slipped back up the spiral staircase to the library, where Margaret was still writing busily in her notebook. The incunable lay open in the pool of light from the one lamp, and as she leaned over it the light shone through the curtain of her dark hair.

He cleared his throat.

'We should go,' he said.

She finished the sentence she'd been writing, dotted the period, then looked up.

'Why?'

'Change of plan. We're off the case.'

'The case?'

'The library. They're terminating the project.' He couldn't quite keep the frustration out of his voice. 'I'm sorry, I had no idea this was going to happen. Word came down from the top, apparently. It's all extremely sudden. Even Laura seemed surprised.'

He felt embarrassed, but Margaret was outwardly unruffled. She simply nodded, closed the book, and dropped her notebook back into her bag. She stood up and straightened her skirt. Edward snapped off the lamp, and they made their way cautiously downstairs in the darkness. He looked around almost nostalgically. This was the last time he'd see the inside of the Wents' apartment. It was strange how attached he'd gotten to it.

'I just have to drop off the key,' he said, 'then we can go.'

'Wait.'

In the darkness of the hallway, Margaret put her hand on his arm. It was a strange gesture, awkward and sincere at the same time. He didn't think she'd ever actually physically touched him before. At first he thought she was trying to cheer him up.

'Don't give them the key,' she said. Margaret felt around in her bag and took out a large jingling key ring. She wrestled with it until she managed to pull off a gray metal tube key. It was indistinguishable from the Wents' key. 'Give her this instead.'

'What?' He dropped his voice to a hoarse whisper. 'What are you talking about?'

'I need to have access to this collection.'

'What? Why?'

'I need to be able to get back in here. To examine these books.'

He just stared at her. She seemed to have no idea that what she was saying made no sense.

'Margaret,' he began, in what he hoped was a patient and reasonable tone, 'these people are my clients. I narrowly escaped being in deep shit just for bringing you here. Whatever you have in mind – and I don't want to know what it is – if anybody found out about it—'

'They won't.'

She hadn't brushed away the dirt from the front of her dress, and there was a smudge of brick-red leather dust on her cheekbone like war paint.

'Margaret.'

'Look,' she explained, as if she were talking to a child. 'The keys look exactly the same. This one goes to a bicycle lock. This one is the Wents'. If they notice, just say it was a mistake. They got mixed up.'

He just looked at her dumbly, rubbing his jaw. Sensing her moment, she deftly plucked the real key out of his hand and dropped it into her bag. Then, taking his free hand between both of her own, she pressed the other key into his palm and closed his numb fingers over it.

'There.' She let go. 'All right?'

'This is insane.' He shook his head. It felt like it was full of buzzing bees swarming around in meaningless circles, lost and disoriented, queenless. 'What – so you're going to break into their apartment every time you feel like checking out a book?'

'If necessary. If we can't come to some other agreement.'

'What other agreement? What are you talking about? Jesus Christ, they're probably taking the books back to England anyway. That's why they're kicking us out.'

'Maybe they won't.'

'That's beside the point.' He looked nervously over her shoulder for signs of Laura. How long was this going to go on?

'Listen, we're not doing this,' he said in a furious whisper. 'It doesn't make any sense, and it's idiotic.'

'What are you going to do? Tell them that I have their key and I won't give it back?'

They stood and stared at each other.

'Edward,' she said earnestly. 'It's time you got a grip on what's really important here. These are people who inherited their money. This collection represents a tiny fraction of their total worth, and for all we know they're getting ready to liquidate it with little or no regard for its intellectual and cultural value. Do you know what happens to books like these once they're sold?' Her eyes burned. In the past thirty seconds they had acquired an incandescent intensity. 'They're disbound. Dealers dismantle them, cut them up and sell them off page by page because they're worth more money that way. Do you understand? They'll be gone forever. Dead. They'll never be reassembled.'

'I understand,' he hissed back, 'I also understand that my career cannot end over some stupid sitcom hijinks. And I don't mean to sound harsh, but I don't see what's up there that's so important that I should risk my whole future over it. And I don't understand why you're getting so excited about a bunch of—'

'It doesn't matter why!' she answered fiercely, her face flushing. If her eyes had burned before, now they were radioactive. She took a step forward toward the elevator. He moved to block her path and she grabbed his wrist, squeezing it as hard as she could – which wasn't very hard – and staring into his eyes.

'You don't understand anything,' she whispered, articulating crisply, spitting the consonants. 'You're an idiot and an ignorant greedhead! You don't care about books, you don't care about history, and you don't care about anything that's important. So if you're not going to help, then get out of my way.'

She flung his arm aside as an exclamation point. Taking a deep breath, she brushed back a strand of her hair out of her eyes.

'And I'm not getting excited.'

They glared at each other. It was a standoff.

155

Edward should have been angry, but instead he had to suppress a hysterical giggle. He didn't know whether to slap her or kiss her or burst out laughing. It was insane, but there was something a little magnificent about her and her speechifying and her academic zealotry. He knew it was wrong, he knew he should be taking things more seriously, but he also knew he was experiencing a moment of temptation, and to make matters worse it was the most diabolical temptation of all: the temptation to do nothing, to sit back and let things happen and get completely out of control. What would happen if he let her keep the key? Maybe the Wents weren't through with him yet after all. A giddy feeling came over him, like vertigo, as if he were an empty-headed animated character in a video game, and somebody somewhere else was playing him.

Somewhere down the hall a vacuum cleaner was turned on.

'What are you going to do about your bike?' he said.

'Excuse me?'

'Your bike. Without the key. How are you going to unlock your bike lock?'

'Oh.' She flushed. 'I have a spare key.'

'I have no knowledge of this. Do you understand?' Edward held up both hands, palms out. 'I don't know anything. If it comes down to it, you overpowered me with a Vulcan nerve pinch and took the key away by main force.'

She looked at him blankly. The sudden intensity was gone; she was just Margaret again.

'I know you think you're being clever,' he added. 'But you're not. This is very, very stupid.'

'All right,' she said flatly, in her old monotone. 'All right.' She patted him on the shoulder as she walked past him down the hall, as an afterthought. 'I'm sorry I said that. You're not an idiot.'

That, he thought, is where you're wrong.

CHAPTER 9

That night around midnight Edward found himself in a cab with Zeph heading uptown on Broadway.

'What beer did you bring?'

Edward lifted a sweating six-pack of Negra Modelo out of a brown paper bag on the floor. Zeph shrugged.

'It'll have to do.' He folded his massive forearms and looked out the window. 'These guys are real snobs about beer. They microbrew.'

'Where's this thing happening, anyway?' said Edward.

'Broadway and Fifty-first. Offices of Wade and Cullman, accountants-at-law, pillars of the financial community.'

Edward leaned back against the black upholstery and put his hands behind his head.

'What am I doing here?' he said, staring up at the cab's ripped fabric ceiling. 'I was going to start packing tonight. I have to be in London in a week. A week.'

'You haven't started?'

'I've been working at the Wents."'

'The Wents. That's a laugh. They're using you, man.' Zeph shook his fist in Edward's face. '*Why can't you see that?*'

Edward shrugged. 'I'm kind of getting into working there. Some of those old books are really beautiful.'

'I generally judge the worth of a book by how deeply the letters on the cover are embossed. Anyway, you need a vacation.'

Edward snorted.

'I need a vacation from my vacation. Jesus, do you realize it's been three days since I read the *Journal*?'

The thrill of his leap into the unknown, giving Margaret his key to the Wents' apartment, had already palled and congealed into a thin, greasy slick of dread and regret. The Wents had kicked him out, cut him off from the library, and instead of making a clean break, of salvaging at least his professionalism from the debacle, he'd left open the door for Margaret to fuck things up further. Letting her into the Wents' apartment was like giving an addict the keys to the pharmacy.

With the weight of that potential disaster hanging over him, he had allowed a few innocent pints with Zeph to turn into this decidedly dodgier and more compromising late-night excursion. The cab bogged down in traffic near Times Square. A brand-new skyscraper loomed over them, its lower third completely paneled with glowing video screens. The screens crawled, teemed, swarmed with restless multicolored information displayed in giant pixels, each one the size of a lightbulb. It was distracting, hypnotic, as if you could just fall into it.

'I should warn you about something,' Zeph said. 'You have to watch yourself around these guys. They've got a very strict social code, and they don't like outsiders. And you're an outsider. You think they're losers, but what you don't understand is, they think we're the losers. They tolerate me because I speak their language, and I understand math and computers – actually, they don't think I'm a loser. Just you. You – well, you've played a little MOMUS, and that's fine, but don't start acting all superior just because you were properly socialized and you went to the prom and you get laid once in a while.'

'But I don't get laid,' Edward said. 'I never get laid.'

'There could be chicks there, actually,' Zeph mused. 'Geek chicks can be *very* attractive. But forget about it, they'll loathe you even more than the guys do. They're like bees, man. They can smell your fear.'

'Uh-huh.'

'It took a lot of work to build multiplayer functionality into MOMUS. These are people who really understand how shit works.'

'Uh-huh.'

The cab lurched forward, then stopped short again.

'Maybe we should just walk,' Edward said.

'Suckers walk, man. Players ride.'

Five minutes later they got out at Fiftieth Street. The air was like warm bathwater. This close to Times Square the atmosphere was like a county fair, a constant, aimless celebration of nothing, with no object and no end. The sidewalks were packed with disoriented, jet-lagged tourists. Edward followed Zeph through the crowd toward the base of an enormous pink granite skyscraper. The actual entrance was quite small, a single unassuming glass door squeezed in between two stores selling off-brand gray-market electronics. Inside Zeph nodded at the young black man in livery who sat behind a marble desk in the foyer reading Cliff's Notes for *Wuthering Heights*. He showed the guard a card from his wallet, then signed his notebook, and they walked back to the elevator banks.

They waited. The buzz from the beer they drank earlier was starting to wear off.

'What did you call this thing again?' Edward asked.

'A LAN party.'

'A LAN . . . ?'

'L, A, N. Stands for Local Area Network.'

'Right.' Edward massaged his temples. 'Dude, I feel like you're leading me right into the heart of dorkness.'

They took the elevator up to thirty-seven and stepped off. Zeph held his ID up to a dark smudged spot on the wall, and it buzzed them through the glass doors to the office. The lights were off. The receptionist's desk was empty.

'This-all constitutes a misuse of company resources,' said Zeph in a half whisper as they walked down a silent corridor. 'Fortunately the IT guys are the only ones who keep track of said resources, so they can misuse them all they want. Ordinarily the sales staff would be here right now, grinding their souls away into magic gold dust, but fortunately they're all away at an offsite in New Jersey.'

They came out into a large bullpen filled with white cubicles. The overhead lights were off, but most of the cubicles were lit up from within by desk lamps. The room had no windows. The partitions were only shoulder height, and they could see the heads of people standing and conferring with each other over them.

As they walked past the first cubicle Edward felt something poke him in the chest. A tall, unsmiling man with long, wavy dark hair was holding a bright pink Nerf gun so that the tip of the Nerf projectile rested against the front of Edward's shirt. The man wore shorts and a sky blue Sea World T-shirt. He looked young, maybe twenty-five, but his hair already had streaks of gray in it.

'Give him the beer, dude,' Zeph said.

Edward handed over the brown paper bag. The man took it without lowering the Nerf gun and put it behind him. With his free hand he and Zeph exchanged an arcane secret handshake.

'Let's get you set up,' the man said, when they were done.

'I'm Edward.' Edward held out his hand, but the man just brushed past him.

'I know.'

They walked down the row of cubicles together. Somehow Zeph had disappeared; Edward glimpsed him walking into one of the offices with his big arms around two short fat guys with helmet haircuts who looked like twins. It was oppressively hot, and he was already sweating. A skinny kid who could have been in high school was walking backward along the wall, paying out wire between big stacks of speakers. Here and there stood racks of strobe lights, and a big black machine like a dehumidifier that Edward didn't recognize.

The wavy-haired man stopped at a cubicle. It had a chair and a desk with an ordinary workstation on it.

'This is yours,' he said. 'You may have to adjust the mouse sensitivity a little to get it to where you're comfortable. Whatever you do, don't quit out of the game. If it crashes, pick up the phone and dial 2-4444. Are you right-handed?'

Edward nodded.

'Know how to use one of these?' he asked, holding up a tangle of black wires. It was a telephone headset.

'Sure.'

'Okay then.'

Edward sat down and glumly started to untangle the headset. He didn't belong here. It wasn't Zeph's fault – Zeph hadn't exactly twisted his arm to come. In fact, Edward seemed to remember insisting in an inappropriately loud voice that Zeph bring him along. But now that he was here and sobering up it all felt like a mistake. He didn't belong here. These people didn't like him. He wished he were home in bed.

The chair had some kind of uncomfortable orthopedic pad strapped to it. The monitor showed a plain black screen with a menu of commands on it in a familiar white font. He looked around in-curiously at the clutter on the desk: pink phone slips, yellow stickies, a half-used packet of tissues, a squeezable blue rubber stress ball in the shape of a globe, a minitribe of Smurfs: Papa, Brainy, Smurfette. The red voice mail light on the phone was on. Tacked to the walls of the cubicle, which were made of fabric that would have been ugly as a carpet, let alone as a wall, was a series of gelatin-ous Polaroids showing a small black-and-white cat with staring red eyes.

'*Wozny!*'

He started. Zeph's shaggy head appeared over the cubicle wall. He was talking into a megaphone.

'I want that sales report and I want it now!'

'I don't think I get exactly how this works,' said Edward.

Zeph put down the megaphone. 'You'll be fine. Just remember: If you die, it's because you're weak and you deserve it. Come on, let's see about getting you a skin.'

Zeph's head disappeared. Edward got up and followed him, skirting the edge of the cubicles.

'So,' he said. 'Do you hang out with people like this a lot? Like, when I'm not around?'

Zeph wasn't listening to him. 'To think that these puny humans live like this, day in and day out. Poor beggars.'

He stopped and knocked on the door to an office.

'What's a skin?' said Edward.

'You know – skin. Skin flicks. Skin diving. Skin.'

There was no answer. Zeph pushed the door open.

It was a small square room with bare particle-board walls, containing a massive, squat work-station on it. To his surprise, Edward recognized the person who was hunched over in front of it: It was the gnome he'd seen at Zeph's apartment, the Artiste. It couldn't be anybody else; aside from his round face and thin black hair, he was so small his feet barely reached the floor. His childlike physique made it hard to guess his age, but Edward thought he might have been thirty or thirty-five. He barely glanced up when they came in.

There was a moment of silence. Even Zeph hesitated to disturb him. Then the little man looked up and calmly picked up something from beside the workstation. He held it up.

'So this is—,' Zeph started to say.

165

'Smile,' said the Artiste softly, and there was a blinding flash. It was a camera.

'Dammit.' Edward turned away, blinking green spots out of his eyes. 'Jesus. You could've warned me.'

But the Artiste had already turned back to his keyboard. He uploaded the picture of Edward onto the screen, then manipulated it with the mouse, tweaking it, sharpening it, pulling it like a piece of taffy, extrapolating it into three dimensions and spinning it deftly through all three axes.

'That's your skin,' said Zeph. 'That's what you're going to look like in the game.'

The game. Edward went closer, looking over the Artiste's shoulder.

'Can I change it?' he said. 'I mean, do I have to be wearing these clothes?'

'What would you rather be wearing?' the Artiste asked politely.

'I don't know.' The figure on the screen had on his clothes, khakis and a brown T-shirt from Barneys. 'I'm not exactly dressed to kill.'

The Artiste's tiny hands chattered on the keyboard, and the figure froze. Its clothes began flickering through a rapid succession of styles and colors.

'One moment please.'

Standing behind him, Edward could see the barest hint of a bald spot beginning at his crown. The Artiste tapped the back arrow a few times until the figure on the screen was wearing a black suit, a top hat, and a monocle. He was carrying a furled umbrella: the perfect English gentleman.

'Hey, wait a second,' said Edward. 'Why do I have to—?'

Zeph slapped him on the back, delighted. 'That's excellent! I love it! You look like Mr Peanut.'

With a little whine a Zip disk popped out of a slot on the side of the workstation. The Artiste whipped it out and handed it to Edward.

'We're done.'

He went back to typing. Edward and Zeph backed out of the office and closed the door.

'What's the deal with that guy?' Edward said as they walked back toward his cubicle. That first conversation they'd had at Zeph's had stayed with him, when the Artiste had mentioned looking through people's computers. The idea of this bizarre, autistic little elf as an omniscient being, gazing with X-ray eyes into the hard drive of his soul and spell-checking his most shameful secrets, was unnerving.

'He's always like that. Total genius. Makes me look like a fucking joker. You know what he does with his evenings? He moonlights running global climate simulations for the National Weather Service. Works on the serious supercomputers – the real Big Iron. For all practical purposes he's God.'

'But what was the deal with those clothes? Did you tell him about England?'

'Relax. You look good. You're doing the Bond thing.'

More people had arrived since they'd been in with the Artiste, and the cubicles were filling up. Devo's cover of the Rolling Stones' 'Satisfaction' stuttered from the big speakers in the corners. Zeph explained that the server could handle thirty-two people at once, and they'd probably have almost that many tonight.

'Jesus. You practically have your own subculture here.'

'You have no idea,' said Zeph. 'MOMUS is big. Nobody knows who started it, it just bubbled up from our collective unconscious via the Internet. Not even the Artiste knows about everything that's in it. It's bigger than books. That library you're messing around with? Obsolete information technology. We're witnessing the dawn of a whole new artistic medium, and we don't even appreciate it.'

Edward didn't answer. He thought about Margaret, and what she would think of him if she could see him now. In a way she kind of reminded him of the Artiste – she was as much a master of her own world, and as oblivious of everything else. As they walked past one of the cubicles, a skinny young man with a straggly red beard handed them each a bottle of beer, already opened, a can of Mountain Dew: Code Red, also open, and a bottle of water.

'These beverages will provide your body with all the caffeine, sugar, and alcohol it needs to stay healthy and alert,' he intoned.

Edward sat down at his desk again and braced

his feet on an orthopedic foot rest he found underneath it. His phone rang, and he let the voice mail pick up, but it rang again, and then again. He was thinking about taking it off the hook when he heard Zeph's voice from across the room:

'Fucking pick it up!'

Edward punched the speakerphone button.

'What?'

'Put on your headset.' This time Zeph's voice came from the phone. 'They're going to conference you in on the other line.'

'Look, how long is this going to take?'

'You have somewhere to be? Destiny is calling, you big pussy. Pick up the other line.'

Edward put on his headset and picked it up and immediately heard a babble of mostly male voices gossiping, boasting, talking trash, reciting Monty Python routines, and arguing over arcane network architecture issues.

'So,' he said. 'Any chicks on this thing?'

'*Hello, Cleveland!*' somebody yelled hoarsely. Edward could hear the voice echoed in real life from the cubicle next door.

'Are you there, Edward?' A calm, reassuring voice he didn't recognize cut through the chatter.

'Yes.'

'Click on the screen where it says "JOIN".'

He found the place and clicked. He felt a prickle of inexplicable nervousness in his palms.

'Yo, Geekstar Six! Let's do this!'

'We who are about to die salute you!' a bass voice intoned.

'Okay folks,' said the calm voice. 'Strap yourselves in. It's robot fighting time.'

The screen flickered black, and he heard his hard drive thrashing. A long, pregnant pause ensued during which somebody belched loudly. Then an error message popped up on his screen, and there was a collective groan.

'Goddamn motherfucking son of a goddamn mother-fucking bitch,' said the voice, calm as ever. 'Zeph, can you come here and see if these server settings are right?'

'I can access them remotely,' came the reply.

A hushed debate sprang up on the conference call.

'Someone should just rewrite the network protocols on this thing from the ground up,' said a woman's voice. 'There's no reason it should be this unstable.'

'I don't think it's a network issue, the bottleneck is in the protocols themselves. If they—'

'Protocols my rectum—'

'It doesn't have to be this slow, either,' said somebody else. 'Right now it's using cubic patches instead of bezier meshes—'

'All right, all right.' The voice was back. 'Everybody join again, please.'

The screen flicked to black again. In the blackness a hollow horizontal bar appeared, and the words LOADING MAP appeared above it. Edward

170

watched impatiently as it filled from left to right with an azure blue liquid. When the bar was completely blue it disappeared. There was a longer pause.

And then a scene appeared: a table set with many candles. Standing around the table in a circle, their pale faces illuminated by candlelight, were two dozen men and women dressed in a variety of outlandish costumes, like a coven of witches and warlocks. The walls were stone, with red and blue tapestries hanging over them. It looked like it might have been the banquet hall of a castle. Everything – the weave of the tapestries, the grain of the wooden table, the yellow candlelight that pulsed and glowed – had that same vivid, hyper-real quality he recognized from MOMUS. Edward understood from his point of view that he was supposed to be standing in the circle, too, and he saw that one of the men on the other side of the circle had Zeph's face. Zeph was dressed as a tall, fat monk, with a cowled robe and a rope tied around his waist.

Edward froze. For an instant no one else moved, then the circle broke and ran for the exits. He was left alone.

Edward blinked at the screen, then leaned forward over the keyboard. Using the mouse, he guided his virtual self out of the room by a long, straight corridor. All was quiet until he turned a corner and blundered in between two men. They were chopping at each other with long-handled axes. One wore an old-fashioned Apollo-style space suit complete with golden reflective faceplate. The other was Clint Eastwood in full ballroom drag. An explosion flashed near them, a bass beat sounded, and the force of it threw them apart in three directions. Something buzzed under him, and he nearly jumped out of his chair. What he had thought was an orthopedic cushion turned out to be an electric pad hooked up to his computer and synchronized with the sound effects.

'Watch it, hippie,' a voice crackled over the phone.

'You're entering a world of pain, my friend . . .'

Edward had gotten turned around. He couldn't find the men with the axes. He was in a stone corridor with arrow slits running all down one wall. A woman in low-cut Elizabethan garb ran toward him with a blue metal pistol in her hand, her décolletage bouncing wildly. A stream of metal nails issued from the pistol, and every time one hit him the bar at the bottom of the screen that measured his health got a little shorter.

He dodged past her and ran blindly until the nails were no longer hitting him in the back. He ended up on a high, thin walkway facing a burly man in a kilt and no shirt.

The big man stepped forward. So did Edward. He wasn't sure what to expect. When they were five feet apart the big man dropped to one knee with startling quickness and snatched Edward bodily over his head pro-wrestling style. The world blurred as it spun around him, and he saw that the walkway spanned a vast circular pit.

'*Luik!*' the man howled insanely in a Scottish brogue. '*I am yuir father!*'

He tossed Edward lightly over the edge. Bricks and masonry rushed past his face as he descended into the darkness, Alice's view falling down the rabbit hole, and then he was dead.

And then he was alive again. He woke up in a lavishly furnished bedroom, lying on his back in a four-poster bed. Beautiful yellow-tinted light poured in through translucent curtains. He pushed through them onto a stone balcony looking out over a perfectly manicured green courtyard. The sky was blue, and the grass was billiard-table green. Neat pathways picked out in white gravel radiated out from a central fountain. Sunlight flashed off the falling water. He was happy to have escaped from the fighting for the moment. He wasn't really in the mood anyway.

To Edward's surprise the Artiste was there in the garden. His skin wasn't surreal or exaggerated in any way: It looked exactly like him in real life. He was neither running nor shooting nor stabbing, just sitting perfectly still on a marble bench. He looked up at Edward, and their eyes met, but neither spoke. The sun was setting behind a distant line of puffy Claude Lorrain trees.

The screen darkened and faded to black. Time was up. The game was over. Statistics appeared on the monitor; next to Edward's name it said, in typical ungrammatical computerese: YOU DIED ONCE TIMES AND YOU KILLED ZERO ENEMIES.

He hardly had time to scan the list before the screen went dark again, and when it lit up he was back in the circle of players. This time they were deep underwater, suspended between the surface and the pale sandy floor of some great shallow ocean or lake. Across the circle from him, right next to Zeph – so close their shoulders were almost touching – floated a tall, broad figure dressed in armor. His face was hidden in the murk, but a towering rack of silver antlers sprouted from his head. Was it—? It looked exactly like he imagined the stag knight looked, that Margaret had told him about in the *Viage*.

Then the players vanished like a school of start-led fish, kicking and stroking away in all directions, leaving trails of silver bubbles that ascended slowly in their wakes. The antler-man was gone before Edward was even sure he'd been there.

He swam off on his own, through the murky light that seemed to emanate from all directions equally. The silence was broken only by the occasional dull *boom* and distant, burbling scream. It was almost restful. He swam upward, but no matter how persistently he tried he could never quite reach the shimmering, shifting surface above him, though he got close enough to see the pale underbellies of foaming whitecaps sweeping by above him. Sometimes a shaft of green sunlight would lance down from on high, through a break in the invisible clouds, and then disappear again. He spent long, tense minutes dodging through a network of luminescent caves, playing cat and mouse with a woman in a black wetsuit, until he was unexpectedly devoured by a giant green eel the size of a subway train. YOU DIED ONCE TIMES AND YOU KILLED ZERO ENEMIES.

They played again, and again, and again. In spite of himself he let the room, the cubicles, the headset, the Smurfs, everything fade away into the background. What was he, a moron? A violence junkie? The game, these little running pictures on a TV screen, took over his senses completely. Maybe Zeph was right, this was the real thing, the powerful mojo, a new medium for the new millennium. They fought on a featureless open plain, while schussing down an alpine slope, in the desert, in the jungle, with swords, with lasers, with no weapons at all, so that they had to punch and kick each other to death with their bare hands and feet. He died and was reincarnated instantly, like flipping a light switch off and on. He lived a hundred short, brutal lifetimes in one night. When a player died, the body lay where it fell for a few minutes before it disappeared, and once or twice Edward had the disconcerting experience of stumbling over his own nattily dressed corpse staring blankly up at him. For a while they all had white feathery wings, and they flew in silent circles around a meticulous re-creation of the floating cloud city from *Star Wars*. When the fighting got especially thick a thin white mist crept through the office: The geeks had set up a portable smoke machine.

Edward's thoughts drifted to buying into one of these computer games companies. Something this addictive must be disgustingly profitable. The initial hostility he'd sensed around him when he arrived had dissipated, and an ad hoc esprit de corps had settled over the room, embracing even him. It was no longer the geeks against the outsider. They were all in it together, a Local Area Network of brothers in arms, bound by the electric bond of virtual combat. Could a book do this?

It was five in the morning before it even occurred to Edward to check his watch. They'd been playing for four hours straight. He'd sweated through his shirt, and there were five beers and three empty Code Red cans on the floor around his chair. He didn't know how many times he'd gotten up to pee.

For the last game they played in the same castle where they'd started out. He woke up in a circular room in a high tower. He looked out the window at a sunless sky filled with swirling colors like the marbled endpaper of an old book. He was tired of fighting, and he wouldn't have minded just taking a virtual nap. He started down a long spiral staircase, but a nimble swordsman with a musketeer's mustache met him coming up and skewered him with a rapier.

Maybe it was the beer, or the lateness of the hour, but now Edward couldn't seem to go thirty seconds without getting himself killed. His luck had turned sour. Twice a sniper picked him off from above. Once he took a swim in the castle moat and a black current sucked him down and pinned him against an iron grate and drowned him. When he finally managed to arm himself with a decent weapon, a rocket launcher, he accidentally fired it point blank at a ballerina in a pink tutu and they both died in the blast.

He only saw Zeph once more, when they came face to face in the middle of a battle royal. They squared off.

'*I smell a wumpus!*' Zeph howled. '*Move or shoot?*'

'What the fuck are you talking about?' Edward muttered through clenched teeth.

They chopped at each other for a tense minute before someone waved a laser through the room at waist-level, cutting everybody in it in half.

'That was bullshit,' said Edward's headset.

'Nothing worse than a loser who won't admit it,' a high voice – the Artiste? – replied.

He was reborn in darkness, and for a long time he wandered alone in a low-ceilinged, heavy-timbered space that felt like an attic. Finally he reached a stone archway that looked like a way out. He peered inside, but there was nothing except pitch blackness. His headphones crackled.

'Stay away from that doorway,' the calm voice said in his ears. 'There's nothing there – the level's not finished. Could take down the whole network if you go through.'

Something about this reminded Edward of the black, blind canyon into which an entire company of bold knights had disappeared in the *Viage*. What happened to them in there? On a hunch he backed up and ran through the archway at full tilt.

It happened so fast that he never knew if he'd died and been reborn, or if he was magically transported to another part of the castle, but suddenly he was standing on a parapet on the very outermost wall of the keep. The dark, marbled sky was gone: This sky was clear and blue, and the sun was shining. The day was quiet. He'd left the fighting far behind.

Edward hadn't really noticed the landscape beyond the castle, but now it was all laid out in front of him panoramically. Peaceful wooded hills rolled away into the far distance, each one glowing a vivid emerald green. Some of them were farmland, divided up into squares like a green patchwork quilt, or like some fantastically complex mathematical function plotted in three dimensions, and others were dotted with tiny perfect trees, each one precisely the same as all the others. There was no fighting there, just endless electronic peace.

He wondered if this was what Weymarshe looked like. Could there really be somewhere this digitally perfect in real life? A rogue wave of childish, unironic longing suddenly welled up in him, rushing over him from he didn't know where and swamping him with melancholy before he was ready for it. God, what was wrong with him? All at once he was overcome by self-pity – he was embarrassed, but he couldn't stop it, he had to just let it happen. Empty tears washed down his cheeks. For the past four years it had seemed like time was standing still, but now it was rushing past him like a gale-force wind, like the wind from an atom bomb, tearing everything away and whirling it off to parts unknown, palm trees and roof tiles and fence posts, and suddenly he felt his whole future, his managership and his promotions and his year-end bonuses and his office parties, hanging like a lead weight around his neck, dragging him downward. He didn't want this. He only had one life, and he wanted it to be something else. Terror surged inside him, and in his panic he seized on something.

It was the Wents, they were his ticket out. He didn't know why, or how, or how he knew, he just knew that they were the key. He was going to find the book, the codex. He pressed the heels of his hands against his eyes, hard, until the colors came. The wave began to recede. He pulled a tissue from a packet belonging to the hapless cubicle-dweller whose desk he was sitting at.

After a long time he turned back to the landscape; for the first time all night he was conscious of looking at a screen. He turned away from the ramparts to face the interior of the castle and found himself gazing down into the same sunlit courtyard he'd seen hours earlier. Nothing had changed: There was the same stone fountain, the same grass, the same neat white gravel walkways. He wished he could find a flight of stairs down to it. He hadn't noticed before that there was a huge old tree, as big around as a tower and so massive that it actually formed a part of one of the castle walls. Its muscular roots had twined in between the stone blocks, both shifting them apart and locking them together in a crippling, crushing embrace. Its leaves were scattered on the grass beneath it.

The little figure of the Artiste was still sitting there on a marble bench, perfectly motionless, his hands in his lap, placidly watching the play of light on the water in the fountain. Edward cleared his throat.

'Hey!' he called out. 'How do I get down there?'

The Artiste looked up at him inscrutably and shook his head.

'You can't.'

CHAPTER 10

'And then, there he is, he-he-he-he comes out of Andy's house and he's wearing a Speedo!' Dan, Edward's boss, couldn't stop laughing. 'I'm not kidding! I mean, Andy does have a pool, but it's not like it was a pool *party*. Everybody else is standing around in their grays and their earth tones and their, and their, and their shoes that they spent ten hours picking out, because it's Andy, and everybody wants to impress him – myself included – and then he just walks right out onto the porch, and his-his-his-his package is, like, *straining* against the spandex, and he dives right into the pool. And everybody's just standing there stunned, just in awe of what an ass clown this guy is, staring at these bubbles coming up from the water where he dived in. And then – here-here-here-here's the best part – up comes the Speedo! It fell off! It's this bright red Speedo floating in the pool, and we're all staring at it like it, like it just fell out of the sky!'

Having gotten that off his chest, Dan sighed a long, satisfied sigh.

'I got Amanda to change his password to "speedo",' he added by way of an epilogue. 'So every time he logs onto the system in the morning he has to type "speedo" to get in.'

'Uh-huh.'

A lull in the conversation. Evidently Dan had been expecting a more appreciative audience for this gem, but Edward didn't feel up to it. Can you get a hangover from a computer game? He listened in contemplative silence, lying in bed and staring up at the blank white ceiling. It was noon.

'Anyway, Ed, reason why I called, I sent you an e-mail earlier but I didn't get a reply. So I thought I'd follow up by phone.'

'I'm sorry,' Edward lied. 'I had some problems with my ISP. I've been offline for a few days.' He hadn't been checking his e-mail. He imagined it piling up like a snowdrift, higher and higher and higher, in some virtual lockbox somewhere, but he felt no anxiety about it.

'Oh, yeah? My bad, I should have called before. Is everything okay?'

There was a pause. Edward covered the receiver and coughed. He felt like the voice on the other hand was reaching him from another era, over a wire strung across a void to his bedroom from an earlier period of his life, one that was inexpressibly distant and no longer really relevant to anything much that was going on here in his current dimension. He tried to picture Dan's face – broad, square, jowls just beginning to sag. In another ten years he'd look exactly like a bulldog.

'Did I wake you up?'

'No, no, not at all,' Edward said. He cleared his throat. 'Not at all. What's up?'

'Well, the folks from E & H in London have been trying to get in touch about the housing arrangements, and they haven't heard back from you. I guess it's what – less than a week now, before you start? They just want to know if you needed help getting set up.'

'Yes. I do. Tell them thanks, and I'll get in touch with them myself. Just give me their contact info, would you?'

Dan gave Edward a long transatlantic phone number. Edward pretended to write it down. He probably already had it somewhere. He lay back with his eyes closed as the conversation passed through its natural, inevitable stages: packing, then passports, then airfares, then airports, then customs, then finally, blissfully, closure. He hung up.

It was too hot to fall back asleep, so he just let himself drift, the bedclothes kicked down around his knees. One corner of the fitted sheet had sprung loose by his head. A breeze from the half-open window cooled the sweat on his forehead. An altercation was taking place on the sidewalk below his window, a man and a woman arguing about who knew what when, and when she knew it, and who told her about it, but it all seemed very, very far away. The voices floated up to him, light and shimmering, fading in and out of intelligibility.

He was going astray, he knew. The codex was

leading him astray. But a part of him had never felt more on track. To his surprise, his resolution of the night before had stayed with him. At the time it had felt like a moment of drunken wisdom, the kind that vanishes the following afternoon, but the sense of conviction was still with him. He had made his decision, and that was enough for now. He turned over on his side and went back to sleep.

At two Zeph and Caroline buzzed him from downstairs. While they were on the way up Edward hastily pulled on a pair of khaki shorts and a white T-shirt. He splashed water on his face and ran his hands through his hair.

Zeph lumbered through the door as soon as he opened it, breathing heavily, and pushed past him into the living room. His huge forehead was slick with sweat, and his purple and orange Hawaiian shirt was soaked through.

'Top o' the marnin' to ye,' he said in a bad Irish accent.

'We need water,' Caroline said hoarsely, heading for the kitchen. Her stripy tank top made her look rail-thin. She emerged carrying two tumblers full of musically clunking ice water, put one down on the coffee table and drained the other in one long gulp. Then she collapsed onto the brown velvet couch next to Zeph.

'Isn't it horrible?' she said. She indicated Zeph's shirt with one limp arm, then let it drop. 'We had a fight about it on the subway on the way over. God, it's murder outside.'

'I haven't been out.'

'I got it free,' said Zeph without moving. 'From a software company in Honolulu.'

He pointed to a spot on his stomach where the name of the company appeared in tiny letters twined in among the leaves.

'Hey, I lost track of you last night.'

'Oh. Yeah.' Edward remembered now. 'Sorry about that.' At the end of the night, after he'd seen the Artiste sitting there in the courtyard, he'd gotten up from his magic vibrating chair and stumbled like a zombie to the stale corporate bathroom. He'd looked into his own weepy red eyes in the mirror, and just like that the spell was broken. He slipped outside, flagged down a cab and made it home shortly before dawn.

'It was a pretty intense scene, even for that crowd.' Zeph pressed a water glass against his temple. 'We're doing it again next Friday. Some guys I know are renting a warehouse in Queens, they're gonna wire it up, hack the server code, try to get 128 players on the network at once.'

'Edward's going to be gone by then,' Caroline said. 'Aren't you?'

He did the math in his head.

'I guess I will,' he said.

Her gaze flicked around the room, floor to ceiling to bookshelves, suddenly suspicious.

'Have you started packing?'

'Not really.'

'You're being very relaxed about all this,' Zeph said. 'It's not like you.'

'Isn't it great?' Edward sensed that he was in imminent danger of a well-meaning intervention. 'I'm just going with the flow, grooving on a here-and-now vibe.'

Zeph and Caroline looked at each other.

'To tell you the truth,' Zeph rumbled, 'I don't know. We can't really tell.'

'I can't either. But it feels good.'

'Well, then,' Caroline said chirpily. 'It must be okay.'

Zeph toyed with two pads of stickies that were sitting on the coffee table, trying to mate them together into one seamless stack.

'Damn, it's hot,' he said. 'It's like that H. G. Wells novel, where the whole world is plunging into the heart of a giant flaming comet.'

'Comets are made of ice, love,' said Caroline. 'They aren't flaming.'

'Huh.' Zeph put the stickies down. 'Well, I guess it must have been some other novel.'

'Did you know,' she went on, 'that the tail of a comet is actually a stream of particles excited by radiation emitted by the sun? That means that when a comet is moving away from the sun, its tail actually precedes it along its trajectory, rather than streaming out behind.'

Edward and Zeph looked at her, then Zeph looked back at him.

'So Edward,' Zeph asked. 'Are you going to pack or what?'

'Yes, I'm going to pack.'

Edward lolled his head over the back of his chair. He knew they were being sensible. He'd had four straight years of sensible since college, he knew what sensible sounded like. A strand of cobweb dangled from a section of molding in his field of vision. He watched it waft in the nonexistent breeze.

'I'll do it over the weekend,' he said. 'Maybe I'll have somebody pack for me. You know you can pay people to come in and pack up your stuff for you? Anyway, I don't have all that much anyway.'

'One thing you can do,' said Zeph. 'Wrap up all your stuff in a red bandanna and then tie it on the end of a pole. I've seen that on TV tons of times.'

Caroline set her empty water glass aside on the floor.

'Actually, it's not really the practicalities of moving that we're so much concerned about,' she said. 'It's more the underlying ambivalence about this new phase of your life that your obvious reluctance to deal with those practicalities betokens.'

'Oh.'

'You could still back out if you wanted to. Just not go. Say you're allergic to warm beer. Say you're having a nervous breakdown. Are you, by the way? Having a nervous breakdown?'

'No,' Edward shook his head vigorously. There was no way to explain to them what he was planning, what he was thinking. Not yet. 'No,

187

that's not it at all. I want to go, I really do. I have to.'

He thought about Weymarshe. Overnight he'd built up a vivid picture of it in his mind, almost against his will, and based on no factual evidence whatsoever. The image was both strange and at the same time familiar, like a snapshot from a long-forgotten roll of film that he'd found at the back of some disused drawer years ago, and here it was, finally developed, as fresh and vivid as the day it was taken. The image was of a grand old English country house built out of gray fieldstone. Its roof was a mass of peaks and chimneys and dormers, and it was cooled by gentle mists and nestled in a labyrinth of light green lawns and dark green hedges that looked almost like the pattern on a printed circuit.

'Anyway, my sublettor's going to be here in another month, so I should probably be gone by then.'

'Probably,' Zeph rumbled. 'Well, at least you have boxes.' There was a waist-high stack of flattened cardboard boxes in the corner. 'Come on, let's get some of this stuff packed.'

'You guys don't have to do that,' said Edward. 'Really.'

'But we want to.' Caroline braced herself on Zeph's knee and pushed herself up.

'If you pay us,' said Zeph.

Caroline found some tape and scissors and started unfolding the boxes. Edward and Zeph took the books down off his shelves. Caroline put on a CD, and Edward set up fans by the windows. The room started to smell like dust and packing tape. A few times Zeph objected to something – a tie, a bowl, an alarm clock – and they stopped and argued over whether Edward should pack it, or leave it, or throw it away, or give it to Zeph.

'Are you taking that painting?' said Caroline. She looked critically at a huge print that Edward had had expensively framed.

It was a Northern Renaissance painting, Dutch or Belgian or Danish, one of those, he didn't know which. He had bought it online, an impulse click, and he was disconcerted at how big it was when it actually showed up, but since then he'd gotten attached to it. He didn't have much else in the way of decoration. The painting depicted a crowd of lumpy peasants at work in a wheat field. The wheat was a sunny golden yellow, and the artist, whose name Edward didn't even know how to pronounce, had obviously taken great pains to draw in every stalk individually with a superfine brush. Both the men and the women had hilarious bowl haircuts. Some of them were reaping the wheat with long scythes, others gathered it into sheaves, and others lugged the sheaves away, presumably back to some nearby village. The rest sat or lay around a giant gnarled tree in the foreground, in a quadrant of the field that had already been cleared, snoozing and talking and eating lumpy porridge out of wooden bowls.

Edward didn't think of himself as somebody who was particularly blessed with powers of aesthetic appreciation, but he was secretly proud of his painting. An air of contented resignation hung over the scene. Somehow, in the ongoing war to keep themselves alive and the world in some semblance of order, they'd managed to make a separate peace. These people were working, but they weren't miserable. They didn't hate themselves, and they didn't hate each other or the sheaves of wheat. They'd struck a balance. They could stand it. Every time he looked at it he saw new details – a bird or two flapping overhead, a tiny round moon hanging in a corner of the pale blue sky – as if the painting wasn't actually frozen in time but slowly evolving, imperceptibly, like glass flowing.

'It would be a pain in the ass to ship,' Edward said, 'but I hate to give it up.'

'I don't think I get it,' said Zeph.

'What's to get?' Edward shrugged. 'I just like watching those medieval suckers work.'

After a few hours they went across the street to a Japanese restaurant, where it was cool. It was late afternoon, and they were the only people there apart from some out-of-work hipsters and homesick Japanese tourists. Japanese covers of Western R&B hits played nonstop in the background. Edward and Zeph still felt a touch hungover, and they binged on salty miso soup, excruciatingly spicy kimchi, and steamed dumplings seared on

the bottoms and dipped in soy sauce and vinegar, washed down with rounds of bitter Japanese
beer.

When they were done Zeph sat back and yawned
in an exaggeratedly casual way.

'So I've been doing a little snooping on your
friends the Wents,' he said.

Edward poked at some waterlogged ginger with
his chopsticks.

'What about them? And how do you even know
about them?'

Zeph tapped the side of his nose with one thick
finger, meaningfully.

'Who are the Wents?' said Caroline.

'That's who Edward is working for,' said Zeph.
'The ones with the library. You know they're rich?'

'Of course they're rich,' Edward said.

'But do you know how rich?' For once Zeph sounded almost serious. 'The Wents are "rich" the way
Marvin Gaye was "attractive to women." Did you
know they're the third-largest private landowners
in England?'

'What?'

'You don't know the half of it. There's all kinds
of rumors about them online. Try searching the
royalty newsgroups sometime. You know they pay
Forbes to keep them off their annual list?'

Edward laughed.

'Zeph, that's ridiculous. Our firm handles a good
chunk of their portfolio. I'd know if they had that
kind of money. Anyway, that's just not how money

works. You can't hide that much of it. It finds ways to get itself noticed.'

'It's true! Edward, these people have one of the biggest private fortunes in Europe, and they're spending half of it trying to make sure nobody knows about the other half. And there was a scandal a few years ago – apparently they had a son who was kidnapped. The Duke wouldn't pay the ransom.'

'So what happened? Did they get him back?'

Zeph shook his head.

'He died. Apparently the kidnappers were hiding him in a meat locker and he froze to death. They kept it out of most of the papers.'

Edward glanced at Caroline. 'Zeph, you know most of that Internet stuff is bogus.'

'He's right,' Caroline said. 'Honey, remember the time you posted on that blog about how Bill Gates had been a child actor who played Batman's son on TV? You remember how many people believed that?'

'Batman didn't even have a son,' Edward said.

'But that was different! That was – look, I made that up! Jesus, I'm like the Cassandra of the Internet here. At least run their names through Lexis-Nexis sometime and see what comes back. They're worth *billions*.'

'Billions of dollars or billions of pounds?' Caroline asked.

'I don't know! Billions of euros, or sovereigns, or pieces of eight, or whatever they use for money over there! They have a huge private estate in Bowmry.

They're recluses – there's a famously huge hedge that runs all the way around their property. Their *hedge* is famous, for Christ's sake.'

'So where does all this alleged money come from?'

'That I don't know. Though *you* should be able to find out, Edward, if you tried,' Zeph said, still hurt. 'They keep it all over the place. A lot of it's pretty new – she comes from a big manufacturing family. He must have had some too, though – his family goes back forever. They probably cornered the market on blue face paint back in 1066.'

'Did I tell you they were thinking of offering me a job?' Edward said.

'A job? You mean on top of being chief scrivener, or whatever you are now?'

Edward nodded. Zeph and Caroline looked at each other.

'And you said no,' she prompted him carefully.

'Oh, of course!' Edward said, suddenly embarrassed. 'Anyway, they didn't exactly offer it to me. They were going to make some arrangement with the firm. I don't know what, exactly.'

'You know, some people say he's in a coma – the Duke, that is.' Zeph picked at a splinter on one of his chopsticks. 'That the family is covering it up for legal reasons. Some people say they have a child they keep locked up in an attic who's deranged. I read that there are whole families of servants who live on the estate grounds like serfs, and who haven't left it for generations. You know the kind of crap. The best one was a letter in the *Economist* that claimed they have their own currency on the estate – that it's a self-sufficient economy with its own money, so they pay no taxes to the crown.'

'Creepy,' said Caroline. 'How good is a duke, anyway? Is it higher than a count?'

Nobody knew. The conversation stalled. They all sipped their Japanese beer, and the waiter, a surly-looking teenager with a scraggly mustache, quietly slipped the check onto the table facedown and skulked away.

'Oh, Fabrikant wants to know why you didn't go to his party,' Zeph added.

'That guy,' Edward said. 'What does he want with me?'

'I don't know, exactly.' Zeph watched the people passing on the sidewalk. 'He's the one who told me who you were working for, though. I guess his company, InTech, does business with them. I think he's trying to get the Wents to buy into it. But that's strictly in confidence.'

Edward nodded.

'They do live in a castle. The Wents. I know that about them.'

'A castle?' For once Caroline sounded impressed.

'It even has a name. They call it' – he outlined a rectangular plaque with his thumbs and forefingers – 'Weymarshe.'

Caroline snorted.

'*Quel* anachronism.'

★   ★   ★

194

After they left Edward spent the rest of the day in his apartment watching TV in his boxers, lying on his couch and eating M&Ms out of a one-pound bag. It was a good couch. He'd ordered it from Pottery Barn in the hectic flush of his first bonus from Esslin & Hart, and it was still, four years later, the most expensive object he owned. It was gigantic, nine feet long and upholstered in brown velvet and, by any imaginable aesthetic standard, hideous, but there were times when he retreated to it for comfort. This was one of those times.

He was depressed. His job in London, the prize for which he'd worked so long and hard, was seeming more and more worthless every day, but at the same time his connection to the Wents and the codex was getting more and more tenuous. Except for Margaret. But now that she had the key to the Wents' apartment, it occurred to him, she had no particular use for him. So instead he watched old people playing golf. He watched shows about wildlife, about army ants building living bridges and giant squid lurking in the depths of the Marianas Trench and blue bower birds building their tufty earth-bound nests in Australian forests. Any time anything remotely financial came on he changed the channel, and he winced whenever he happened to land on CNNfn, with its slippery, poisonous blue serpent of fiscal data slithering across the bottom of the screen, rapaciously devouring its own tail.

Zeph called at around seven, but Edward didn't pick up. His answering machine was filled to capacity with messages from colleagues, invitations to the Hamptons from work-friends, desperate pleas for assistance from Andre, but he was way behind in returning them, so far behind he knew he'd never catch up. The more messages that backed up the harder it got to think about them, so they just sat there, a black hole of guilty, unfulfilled obligations on the wall that just got blacker and blacker and blacker.

For dinner he ate an entire jar of sweet Italian cocktail onions, evil-looking but infinitely savory little pearls packed in vinegar and still frosty cold from the fridge. At ten he filled a shot glass full of scotch and drank it. At eleven he got ready for bed.

Before he went to sleep Edward walked over to his desk and turned on his computer. He dumped his saved game onto the hard drive and opened up MOMUS. It seemed pointless now, not that it hadn't been before. He could hardly remember the last thing that happened. He'd gone looking for the library, and then it was gone, and then time started speeding up . . . ? Still, it was something to escape into. And he definitely felt like shooting something. He sat down at the keyboard.

He was still standing in front of the vacant lot where the library should have been, but instead of an empty field of rubble it was an explosion of greenery. Weeds and bushes and entire trees had sprung up from the ground where before there was nothing, as if he'd been standing there for years, rooted to the spot, while nature took its course around him.

The weeds were moving, rustling, visibly growing. In fact, something was badly wrong with time: It was racing forward at a ferocious rate. Earlier, back when he was on the bridge, he'd had the uncanny sense that time had lurched forward in his absence. This time he was watching it happen, and as it did so nature reclaimed the city in a monstrous orgy of fertility. Massive vines choked off the skyscrapers, wrapping around them in spirals, snaking in and out of broken windows. Trees erupted from manholes, rooted in the fertile mud of the sewers, waving their branches as they grew like movie zombies rising from the grave and stretching their stiff limbs. A green acorn the size of a Halloween pumpkin fell from somewhere above him and burst into a million woody fibers in the street.

As far as he could tell, he himself was not affected. The world was getting older around him, but he wasn't. He strolled back toward Rockefeller Center as the city literally went to seed around him. In the distance, somewhere uptown, an office tower sighed and quietly gave up the ghost, sinking gracefully in on itself in a cloud of dust. Whatever cosmic braking mechanism had existed to keep time running at a regular, reasonable pace had totally failed, and it was racing forward out of control.

Then as suddenly as it began, it stopped again. Time slowed down drastically until it was back to its usual crawl. Standing on the edge of Central

Park, which had become an impenetrable Sherwood Forest, Edward watched the rioting plants freeze in place and become still. Time was time again.

You know what? Edward thought. *This is lame. And it doesn't even make sense anymore.* He saved his game, shut down the computer, and went to bed.

The phone was ringing. It seemed like it had been ringing for hours, but it could only have been a few seconds, since the answering machine hadn't picked up yet. Edward opened his eyes and half sat up. The back of his head rested against the cool hardness of the wall. He cleared his throat loudly and lustily, then picked up the receiver and put it up to his ear. He closed his eyes again.

'Hello,' he said.

'Hello?'

The voice was grainy, staticky, like an old recording engraved on a wax cylinder. It spoke with an odd accent, somewhere between English and Scottish, that was both strange and familiar at the same time.

'Hello?' he said again.

'Hello? With whom am I speaking?'

'This is Edward. Who's this?'

'Edward? This is the Duchess.'

He opened his eyes. The apartment was dark and quiet, all its indistinct shapes and outlines re-assuringly present and accounted for. For a second he thought he'd been dreaming, but he was still holding the phone in his hand.

'Hello?'

'Hello?' She mimicked him girlishly. '"Your Grace" would be more proper if we were going by Debrett's, but I'm not going to stand on ceremony. Look – can you hear me? I can hardly hear you.'

He remembered the one time he'd seen her, out on the sidewalk, with her clingy cream dress and her heart-breaking smile. It already seemed like years ago. He could barely connect the person he was speaking to now with the one he had met then. The static was like a rushing wind, rising and falling, tides of white noise waxing and waning, swelling and receding. He closed his eyes again, and his thoughts formed themselves into a picture with the effortless draftsmanship of sleep. In his mind's eye he saw the woman in the cream sun hat talking to him through a snowstorm. She was all alone, lost in a blizzard of white noise that raged against a pitch-black sky. He wanted to help her.

'I don't have much time,' she said, 'so I'll make this quick. It was you I met the other day, wasn't it? Who found my earring?'

'I broke your earring.'

'Well, yes.' She laughed. 'I was going to let you off for that. Look, Edward, I need you to find the Gervase as quickly as you can. Can you do that?'

She spoke in the most ordinary, matter-of-fact tone imaginable, like a woman asking for a glass of water at a restaurant. He swallowed.

'But I thought—' He started over. 'I mean, sure,

yes. But what I was told was that you didn't want—'

'Look, forget whatever they told you,' she said impatiently. A voice of command. 'I'm telling you now. And Edward, the Duke can't know about this. All right? It has to be a secret. Between us.'

Something fell and clattered in the background, and she swore. There was a rustle as she bent to pick it up. Still half asleep, Edward nodded. A glowing green readout on his phone ticked off the seconds, seven of them, before he realized he had to say something out loud, too.

'All right,' he said. 'I mean, fine, sure. But—' He hesitated. What did he want to know? Was this real? Was he insane? Was she? It was all so very *dramatic*. It was as if the world had read his mind and granted him his most secret wish. He was afraid that if he said the wrong thing it would dissipate, that it would vanish and would never have been, leaving him clawing helplessly at wisps of smoke. This was his chance.

'But what?' she said, clipped. 'You want to know what you'll get paid, is that it?'

That wasn't it, not at all. But he didn't say so.

'You'll get paid what you earn,' she said, answering her own question. He could hear her smile, suddenly sweet. 'Don't try to contact me, I'll call you in a week.'

Then she was gone.

CHAPTER 11

It was late afternoon the next day when the phone rang again. Sitting at his desk, staring at the *Financial Times* web site without reading it, Edward let the answering machine get it.

'Edward, it's Margaret. Please pick up.'

She wasn't whispering, but there was a hushed urgency to her voice. Edward sat on the arm of the couch and picked up the phone.

'Margaret,' he said coolly. 'How are you?'

'I think I've found something,' she said.

'How exciting for you.'

'But I need your help.'

'You do.'

He stood up and walked over to the window. He still resented Margaret for blindsiding him so effectively over the Wents' key, even though a part of him was grateful for it. He decided to show his resentment by completely suppressing any of the excitement he felt at the sound of her voice. At the back of his mind, he also knew that every minute he stayed on the phone with her he was giving up a degree of plausible deniability that could be useful down the line, if their little ruse was ever discovered.

There had been a cloudburst, a momentary break in the heat wave, and the pavement outside was dark with wet gray stains like vast, unexplored continents.

'Where are you?' he asked.

'Where do you think I am? I'm in the Wents' apartment.' She managed to convey wintry contempt without changing her tone of voice in the slightest. 'Can you come here? I need some things.'

'I'm sorry, I don't think that's such a good idea right now.'

There was a long silence. He relished the inversion of their power dynamic, however temporary it might be. Edward watched an old woman wearing a yellow raincoat ride by on an old bicycle.

'Why can't you get them yourself?'

'Because I don't think I should leave the apartment right now,' she said. 'I had some trouble getting past the doorman this morning. I was forced to prevaricate.'

'What do you need?'

'Do you have a pen? I need a soft toothbrush, some wooden toothpicks, some mineral oil – Swan is the best – a can of compressed air if you can find one, a soft cloth, and a tack hammer. And a flashlight.'

'Is that all?'

'Yes.' If she was aware of his sarcasm, she didn't show it. 'You know what a tack hammer is?'

'I know what a tack hammer is.'

They were silent for a few more seconds. A dog barked in the street. The day hung in the balance, massive weights balanced on either side, like a tanker truck poised halfway off a cliff in a cartoon, waiting for a hummingbird to alight on the bumper. He sighed.

'I don't have a key,' he said. 'You'll have to meet me downstairs.'

'I'll be in the lobby in exactly one hour.'

She made him synchronize their watches.

This time when Edward passed the doorman he was positive he'd be stopped, but he just kept walking and tried to look self-assured and nothing happened. The man in the seedy livery never looked up from his Arabic newspaper, which he read with the aid of a magnifying glass. It was after six in the evening. Edward was carrying a bulky shopping bag.

A couple of table lamps were on in the lobby. He'd never seen it with the lights on, and it was surprisingly tawdry: a cracked marble endtable, an oriental carpet worn down to a grid of coarse burlap. A hint of stale cigar smoke hung in the air, left over from cigars that had been smoked in the 1950s. Margaret was standing by the elevators, looking very tall and thin. Her face was stony.

When she saw him she pressed the elevator button without a word. They waited in silence until it came.

'I wasn't sure you were coming,' she said gravely,

after the doors had closed. Then, with an obvious effort: 'Thank you.'

'I wish I hadn't.' Edward listened to the rumble of the machinery as they went up. 'You're sure this is safe?'

She nodded.

'There's no one here. The cleaning woman left at three.'

They stood shoulder to shoulder, staring straight ahead like two anonymous corporate drones on their way to the same meeting. They bumped shoulders getting out, and Edward stood aside and gestured for her to go first with exaggerated gallantry. She ignored him. The lights were off in the apartment.

He stepped gingerly onto the soft oriental carpet and then froze. Abruptly, and with no warning, he lost his nerve. He felt like a man whose foot was resting, gently but quite definitely, on an unexploded land mine. This was not a good place to be.

Margaret didn't look at him, just kept walking. He watched her back disappear down the hallway toward the stairs, her footsteps fading. All at once he found himself running after her pathetically, a puppy desperate not to be left behind.

'There's something I have to show you,' she said, when he caught up. 'Something I found when I started clearing out those crates.'

'How long have you been here?'

'Since this morning.'

'You've been here all *day*?'

'I came at six, before they were up.'

They stopped at the tiny door that led to the spiral staircase, and he followed her up the steps. She ran her hand familiarly along the railing, as if she'd already been up and down it a thousand times.

'They were here earlier,' she said. She gripped the doorknob, braced herself, and threw her weight backward. The heavy door jerked open with a crunching sound. 'In the apartment. Or somebody was. I heard people talking. There was a man speaking in an English accent. But nobody came up here.'

'Really? Did you overhear them planning a murder?'

Stepping through the doorway into the cool air of the library was like slipping into a pool of deliciously cold water. His sarcasm suddenly seemed overdone, and it vanished into the stillness. Margaret took off her shoes – sensible mary janes – and set them neatly aside. She wore dark stockings. He caught a glimpse of her pale heel where one of them was worn through.

'I don't want anybody to hear us walking around,' she explained.

She'd been working. The bookshelves were now full, and she'd laid down wrapping paper on the floor along the entire length of one wall. It was covered with stacks of books. All the wooden crates were now open, and the edges of the bookshelves were thickly furred with color-coded stickies. On the table were the laptop, Margaret's notebook, three cans of Diet Coke, and a crumpled-up, half-empty bag of fat free extra-dark pretzels, unsalted.

'Well,' said Edward. 'You've been busy. I hope you're not billing me for this.'

'I've gone through approximately two-thirds of the collection, and I've glanced at the rest of it. I've arranged them by period and country, then alphabetically. I keep my notes in longhand, but I put a basic catalog on the computer as well.'

Edward walked over to the table where the laptop was sitting. A window of the Wents' cataloging program was open. He ran a quick search for 'Gervase' in the database, but nothing came back. It wasn't going to be that easy.

'So,' he said curtly. 'What did you want to show me?'

'When I got here this morning I wanted to at least unwrap and open all the books and do a cursory inspection.'

'So you did.'

'Yes, I did. Look at this, it's particularly fine.' She picked up a small book bound in highly wrought leather. The cover was stamped with hundreds of tiny repeating swirls and squiggles and flourishes, arranged into squares and rectangles. 'Italo-Greek. After Constantinople fell in 1453 some Greek bookbinders set themselves up in Italy. They created their own highly distinctive decorative aesthetic. Look, the text is actually in English.'

She opened the book. The handwriting was

a cramped mix of pointy angles and looping flourishes. Edward couldn't read it.

'What is it?'

'It's a fishing handbook, fifteenth century. *The Treatyse of Fishing with an Angle.*'

'Is this what you wanted me to see?' Edward looked over at the door nervously.

'No,' she said, setting it aside. 'This is.'

She indicated a blank page torn out of her notebook lying flat on the tabletop. On the page was gathered a collection of tiny scraps of paper, four or five of them, hardly more than flakes. Some of them had fragments of writing on them, random shards of shattered black letters.

Edward squinted at them.

'What is this?'

'Paper,' she said, deadpan. 'I found these chips down at the bottom of one of the crates after I cleared the books out. If you hold some of them up to the light you can see fragments of a watermark.'

She paused, evidently expecting him to look for himself, but he didn't bother.

'And?'

'I recognized it. It's a known watermark, a boar's head and a flower. You can look it up in the *Dictionnaire historique des marques du papier* and find out when and where the paper was made. In this case the answer is Basel, around 1450. The texture is also distinctive – you can see here the laid lines' – she indicated one long fragment with her finger – 'and here the chain lines, wider apart.

Quite crude, in this case, not an aristocrat's paper, but I recognize the text from the fragments: It's Lydgate's *Life of Our Lady*, late fifteenth century. Terrible stuff, like medieval Jerry Falwell, but it would be a huge find. There are no complete copies in existence.'

'Huh,' he said, grudgingly impressed.

'But the book itself isn't here.'

Margaret turned to the thick old volume he'd looked at on his first day, the locked book that had its own case. She rested her pale hand on the rough, dark cover.

'This is the only book I haven't been able to examine. Based on the external evidence, it fits the text and the period, although the binding's a little fancy for Lydgate.'

Edward sat down on the edge of the table, which crackled loudly under his weight.

'Great. So here's Lydgate. Where's Gervase?'

She frowned a little and cocked her head, miming incomprehension.

'Gervase,' he repeated. 'You know, the *Viage* to the Whatever of the Whoever.'

'Edward,' Margaret said evenly. 'I'm not working for you anymore. That arrangement is over. So please listen to me: There is no *Viage*, and the sooner you accept that and stop looking for it the better.'

Their eyes met. He held her gaze long enough to hope that she thought what she was saying was sinking in.

'So what am I doing here?'

'You're here because Lydgate's *Life of Our Lady* is a rare book of immense value, and if this is it, I need your help to get it open. Did you bring the things I asked for?'

Edward picked up the shopping bag and set it on the table.

'I couldn't get a flashlight.' Actually, he had one in his apartment, but he'd left it at home it out of sheer mulishness. She sorted out the items and lined them up along the edge of the table like a surgeon preparing to operate.

'What were you shopping for at Henri Bendel?' she inquired conversationally. It was the name on the shopping bag. Edward was surprised – it was her first attempt at anything resembling small talk.

'Christmas presents. It was a long time ago.'

A vivid memory flared up of his first winter in New York: wandering up and down Fifth Avenue in mid-December, freezing rain, forcing his way through crowds of shoppers on the wet sidewalk, mob-strength crowds big enough and surly enough to have stormed a castle. He was looking for a Christmas present for his mother, and after three hours in one of the top three or four shopping neighborhoods in the world he still hadn't come up with anything that wasn't either too cheap or too expensive or too romantic to be appropriate. His feet were killing him, and his wool overcoat wasn't waterproof and smelled like a wet sheep, and he was painfully aware of not having a girlfriend to advise him about things like this. In a state of desperate exhaustion he wound up with a camel-colored cashmere cardigan from Henri Bendel, which he had brought home in this very same shopping bag. His mother adored it.

Edward had brought an old flannel shirt for Margaret to use as a soft cloth. She laid it out flat, its arms spread on either side, and set the old book on it like a baby ready to be diapered. At her request he dragged the floor lamp over closer to where she was working. She bent down and peered at the rusted, fused knot of metal that had been the lock.

'Why not just cut it open?' said Edward from a safe distance. 'I mean, saw through the wood?'

'Too invasive. Last resort.' She set to work picking at it with two toothpicks, one in each hand, pausing once in a while to blow out the accumulated rust flakes with the compressed air. 'It's already been damaged enough. Those scraps of paper are a bad sign as it is.'

'How long do you think it's been locked?'

She made a noncommittal noise.

'Under the right conditions rust like this can form relatively quickly. Do we know when the books were crated?'

'Not exactly,' said Edward. 'Or wait – yes, we do. Some of the books are packed in newspapers. Check the dates on the newspapers, and . . .' He tapped the side of his nose with his forefinger.

'Clever. Would you mind doing that, please?'

The newspapers were all from late 1938 and early 1939. Margaret dropped the toothpicks and began scrubbing the latch very gently with the toothbrush.

He watched her work for another minute – now she was wetting the toothbrush with mineral oil – then decided to take a stroll around the library. At the first footstep he realized he hadn't taken off his shoes the way she had, so he dropped to one knee and untied his black leather oxfords. He set them beside hers. The gesture felt incongruously intimate.

'I have this friend who's a paleoclimatologist,' he said at random, to nobody in particular. 'Studies the history of weather. He goes around looking for ancient samples of air so he can check the levels of oxygen and carbon dioxide in them.' He crossed his arms to feel warmer in the chilly air. 'He found some air from 300 B.C. once. It was trapped inside a hollow clay button.'

He felt conscious of being alone in a darkened room with Margaret, both of them in their socks, both of them implicated together in this furtive, clandestine activity. He was coming to appreciate her unconventional charms, in particular her out-landishly distinguished nose and the long, slender legs she was so careful not to flaunt, like a secret pair of wings that she had to keep concealed at all costs. As he walked around the room he picked up a book here and there from the tops of the tall, wobbly stacks along the wall. He glanced at the title pages before carefully replacing them. A thick science fiction novel in Cyrillic, printed on grim gray Soviet

211

paper. A volume of Ben Franklin's autobiography bound in red cloth ('I have ever had pleasure in obtaining any little anecdotes of my ancestors . . .'). When he reached the window he drew the curtain back with one finger and looked out at the dusky city with its lights just starting to come on, yellow and white and rose and the thousand different colors of thousands of different drawn curtains.

When he came back to the table Margaret had stopped working. She examined the rusted lock again from various angles, holding the tack hammer cocked back in her right hand. Then she tenderly folded one sleeve of the flannel shirt over the lock, steadied it with her free hand, and tapped it once, firmly. Edward couldn't see any change, but when she dropped the hammer and pulled back the sleeve, the catch opened easily.

They were both wrong: It wasn't Lydgate, and it wasn't Gervase. It wasn't a book at all. The cover swung open to reveal the corpse of a book, or the grave of one. It was hollow: The centers of the pages had been cut or carefully ripped out, leaving only an inch of blank margins on all sides and a void in the center. It had been disbound, and this was what was left, the hollow rind.

When Edward leaned over it he saw that the margins weren't totally blank. Traces of ink remained, motes and specks and single pixels of color: the black of text, but also rich Pompeian reds, fresh greens, deep welkin blues, and a very few precious flecks of gold.

CHAPTER 12

'There were originally twelve crates of books,' Margaret said, later that same night.

She was sitting on the wide windowsill of Laura Crowlyk's office with cardboard boxes of papers piled up on either side of her and on the floor around her stocking feet. Every few minutes she forgot where she was and leaned back against the venetian blinds, which made a horrible clashing noise, and snapped erect again. It was getting very late, after one in the morning. What had started as a casual and more or less constitutional plain-view search of Laura Crowlyk's office on their way to the elevators had turned into an exhausting, exhaustive, and deeply ill-advised itemization of every piece of paper it contained.

'Eleven. I counted.' After two hours of sitting cross-legged on the carpet, Edward's ass was on fire and his back felt like an S-curved length of red-hot cable.

'There were twelve, not eleven, according to this bill of lading. It's signed by Cruttenden.'

'You found the actual bill of lading?'

She continued to study the document in silence,

so he heaved himself up and went to stand next to her. The paper – which bore an elaborate baronial crest encrusted with hippogriffs – was headed THE MACMILLAN GRAND INTERNATIONAL TRANSLANTIC SHIPPING COMPANY and described twelve crates of similar sizes and weights, the contents of which were listed simply as dry goods. It was dated August 7, 1939. They were brought over on a ship called the *Muir*.

'I guess that's it,' he said, after a while. 'What kind of a word is "lading" anyway? Why not "loading"?'

'It's Middle English. An archaism.'

The room was lit only by Laura's desk lamp because Edward was worried that somebody would notice a light from outside. The air-conditioning was off, and the room was hot and muggy. Edward blotted his forehead with his arm. Margaret's hair was becoming unruly.

'All right then, so we're short one box,' he sighed, settling to the floor again. 'Any idea what happened to it?'

'No. Can you ask her?'

'Who?'

'Laura,' said Margaret. 'The woman whose office we are currently burglarizing.'

He shook his head. 'No. We can't let her know we're still interested in the collection. And certainly not that we've seen the actual bill of lading. Although—' He bit his lip – it was supposed to be a secret – then confessed. 'The Duchess called me last night. I wonder if she knows.'

'The Duchess of Bowmry called you?'

'Uh-huh.' He did his level best to imply that he conversed with Blanche, and possibly other members of the English peerage, on a regular basis.

'And?'

'And what?'

'Can she help us?'

'I don't know,' he said, blushing for no reason he could think of. 'It wasn't that kind of conversation. There's a lot I don't know about her yet.'

If Margaret felt any further curiosity about his conversation with the Duchess, she kept it to herself.

Laura Crowlyk's office had been disorderly before, but now it was a full-scale clerical catastrophe. Every available surface was covered with stacks of papers stuffed into every imaginable species of receptacle: manila folders, three-ring binders, cardboard pouches, weathered albums, shoe boxes, hatboxes, wooden trays, leather portfolios tied up with velvet ribbons. Most of the papers related to the apartment itself – taxes, insurance, estimates and bills for maintenance and repairs. Edward sifted through Laura's inbox. Its contents were utterly uninteresting: a lengthy CORRESPONDENCE with an airline over some lost green leather luggage.

The air was swirling with stirred-up dust, and Edward had to stop for a couple of minutes for a sneezing fit out in the hall. When he came back in he put the heels of his hands over his burning eyes and yawned.

'Which is better,' he said. 'A count or an earl?'

'What?'

'Counts or earls. Which is better?'

'Neither. An earl is what the English call a count, and a count is the Continental equivalent of an earl. The order of the English nobility is: baron, viscount, earl, marquess, duke, king.'

Edward stretched.

'I'm going. I have to sleep.'

'All right.' Margaret went back to her reading.

'Are you going to stay here?' he said.

'For a while.'

'All right.'

Edward lingered in the doorway. He could hardly keep his eyes open, but he felt guilty for leaving her there. He didn't completely trust her alone in the Wents' apartment, either.

'You've been here for eighteen hours straight. Don't you have classes to teach or something?'

'Not in the summer.' She sat up and stretched too, her narrow shoulder blades straining behind her through her sweater, and Edward involuntarily dropped his gaze to her slight bust. Oblivious, she kinked her long neck left, then right, popping it once on each side. 'And I have a fellowship this year to work on my dissertation. I won't be teaching this fall anyway.'

'How's that going?'

'My dissertation?'

She bent over her work again.

'That's not considered a polite question in academic circles.'

'Okay.' He leaned against the doorframe in what he hoped was a jaunty, insouciant pose and crossed his arms. 'How did you get here, anyway? I mean, what made you decide to become an academic?'

She sighed, but she didn't pause at all in the rhythm of her scanning and sorting. Apparently she was capable of maintaining the bare minimum of social niceties while the rest of her brain continued with the task at hand.

'I was home-schooled. My father worked in the Patent and Trademark Office. My mother spent most of her time on my education. They're very Christian, and I'm an only child, and I spent most of my time growing up reading. When I was fourteen my father died, and my mother became increasingly preoccupied with my . . . my moral development. I started taking classes at a local community college. It doesn't seem like much, but I suppose it was my way of rebelling. The curriculum was fairly rudimentary, and after a year an English professor there suggested I transfer to U. Penn. When I finished there I came to Columbia as a graduate student.'

Edward pictured Margaret's mother: an iron-haired, harsh-featured version of her daughter, her pale hand clutching a metal crucifix.

He had meant to leave, but instead Edward sat down again on the edge of the desk. He leafed half-heartedly through a thick, overstuffed manila folder labeled CORRESPONDENCE. Inside was a hodgepodge of miscellaneous letters, smudgy carbon copies of trivial business communications and thank-you notes. He stared at them irritably. Suddenly they seemed useless, primitive – crude ink scratchings on pressed wood pulp. What he wanted was a celestial keyboard, with which he could enter a query and search through the papers the way you could search a hard drive. Better yet, he thought, he should be able to go to the window, open the blinds, type 'FIND SECRET BOOK' and search the entire city. That's what he needed. Reality felt distinctly obsolete compared to the digital alternative.

Still, something about one of the letters nagged at him. He went back and reread it.

'Look at this,' he said.

'What.' She didn't look up from the document she was scanning.

'It's a letter from the Duke – the old Duke. It must be the father of the current one. It's to the Chenoweth.'

'Let me see it.'

He handed it to her, and they read it together.

Henry La Farge has informed me that facilities for the display of materials donated to the library in spring 1941 have not been constructed nor as I understand it have preparations for the construction of those facilities been undertaken. While I understand that an institution such as the Chenoweth has limited funds available to it you will understand if I express some concern over the lack of progress to date. Please respond

*at your earliest convenience with a full des-
cription of your preparations for the construction of those facilities and a preliminary
timetable for the construction of those facilities.*

It was dated 1953 and signed by the Duke of
Bowmry.

'He's no Gervase of Langford,' said Edward.

'He's not even a Lydgate.' Margaret set the letter
aside on the desk. 'All right. Let's suppose that's
it. Let's suppose the Wents sent that twelfth box
as a donation to the Chenoweth.'

'Let's suppose.' Edward went to an uncomfortable wooden chair in the corner of the room and
sat down. Then the implications of the letter
dawned on him, and he felt all the remaining energy
drain out of him. Stifling a yawn, he slumped down
so that the small of his back rested on the very
edge of the chair. 'All right. So the old Duke gave
the twelfth box to the Chenoweth.'

Margaret watched him.

'All right.'

'Well, that settles it, doesn't it? It's another red
herring.' He ran his hands through his short hair.
'If the codex were there, then they'd have it, and
it would be famous, and everybody would know
about it. Or you would, at least. And that would
be that. But you don't know about it, so it's not
there, end of story. Right?'

She didn't answer, just nodded thoughtfully.
Horns honked blocks away and far below them,

softened by distance so that they sounded almost musical. It was hot in the room, and Edward was hungry. He hadn't eaten since midday.

'It's possible,' said Margaret, looking thoughtful. 'But there's no Went room at the Chenoweth.'

'I'm sorry?'

'There's no Went room at the Chenoweth. The Duke's letter implies that when they made the donation, the Wents stipulated that some sort of special facilities would have to be built to house it. Unless I'm mistaken, that hasn't happened.'

'So – what?' said Edward irritably. 'What am I missing?'

Margaret shook her head.

'You don't understand how libraries work. People donate vast quantities of books and papers to the Chenoweth all the time, sometimes entire estates worth, most of which are either of questionable value or none at all.'

She stood up and began returning the office to a semblance of its former state.

'Evaluating and processing donations is extremely labor-intensive. If a book is obviously valuable and legally free and clear it might go directly onto the shelves, but more often it takes months or even years, and there's always a backlog. In a case like the Wents' donation, where the materials are encumbered with secondary financial conditions, it can take decades. In fact the Chenoweth has every incentive *not* to catalog them, so instead it buries them in a vault somewhere and hopes for some kind of change in the situation. A death, a new generation of heirs who might ameliorate the conditions of the bequest, or forget about them. Anything. Libraries live a long time, and time only makes books more valuable.'

'So you think the twelfth box could still be buried in the backlog? After fifty years?'

'The current administration probably doesn't even know it's there. In fact, it probably made a point of forgetting.'

Margaret was a wizard with paper. As she talked she squared off dusty stacks and realphabetized files and corralled stray sheets like a cardsharp shuffling and dealing.

'You have no idea what the Chenoweth vaults are like,' she said. 'Trunks and suitcases and bags and cardboard boxes stuffed with love letters and doodles and phone messages written on grocery bags, all of which may or may not be more or less tied up in pending legal disputes, none of which has ever been formally inventoried. And the books are the least of it. The walls are stacked to the rafters with paintings and beaver skins and old firearms and locks of hair that no one even knows how to properly care for. Once a colleague of mine found a beat-up old armchair in a corner of the vault and took it back to his apartment. It sat in the corner for six months before he noticed a tag on the back: It was Robert Louis Stevenson's writing chair. A couple of years ago somebody found Dante's ashes in a library in Florence.

They'd been sitting on an upper shelf in a back room for seventy years.'

'Fine.' Edward stood up. 'Great. So. What do we do? Can we get into the Chenoweth somehow and look for it?'

Margaret didn't answer. Until that moment Edward hadn't realized how tired she really was. Now she put both hands on the back of a chair and leaned on it. She closed her eyes, and her dark hair fell forward over her face.

'All right,' she said woodenly. 'If it's there, it's probably in the Annex facility, up in Old Forge. Overflow storage.' The chair creaked under her weight. 'I'll go there and find a way to get into the vault.'

'Good. How?'

'I don't know.'

'I can help you,' Edward said earnestly. He didn't want to make her do everything herself, and he needed to stay involved, to stay near her, to keep things under control, or at least within range of his general supervision, and he was afraid she would realize how little she needed him. 'I have the time. I know you have other work to do. Your dissertation, or whatever you—'

'Oh, who cares about my dissertation!' she snapped.

'Don't you?'

She didn't reply, just shrugged and stared at the shuttered window.

'What's it about, anyway?' he prompted.

'You wouldn't understand.'

'Try me.'

She sighed. He didn't really care what her dissertation was about, but she seemed angry about something, and he wanted to know what.

'All right. My dissertation' – she cleared her throat, a sarcastic schoolgirl delivering a book report – 'entitled *A Scholar and a Gentleman: Gervase of Langford and the Problematics of Secular Medieval History and Historiography*, explores the role that Gervase played in the revival of Scholasticism in late fourteenth-century England, a movement that helps mark the transition from the later Middle Ages to the early Renaissance. Gervase is in many ways an anomalous figure, a layman who pursued historical research at a time when—'

To Edward's relief, she broke off there.

'I know. It's boring.' To his surprise, Margaret actually looked chagrined, even embittered. 'Even my colleagues are bored by it, and believe me, their tolerance for soporific monographs is world class. Five hundred pages of solid scholarly competence.'

'You really wrote five hundred pages?' Edward was impressed. He'd never written anything longer than a twenty-page term paper.

She nodded and pushed her hair back behind her ears.

'That was eighteen months ago. I haven't written anything since. I'm blocked.' She brushed away a tear, angrily, as if a fly were buzzing in front of her face. 'I never thought I would be. I've never had trouble writing. Never.'

Edward felt an unexpected rush of sympathy for her.

'I'm sure you'll think of something.'

She shook her head impatiently.

'It's not me. It's him. It's Gervase. I've *never* had trouble writing,' she repeated. 'Something's not right. Something's missing. I stare at it, and it all makes sense, and it says nothing. There's something missing, something I'm missing about Gervase, I'm sure of it!' Unconsciously, her pale hands knotted into fists. 'And it's not my fault. There's something he won't tell me. No single thing that he says or does defies explanation, but it never entirely adds up, either. But what am I missing?' It was a rhetorical question; she was speaking to an unseen audience of her peers now, or possibly to Gervase himself. 'It's somewhere there, between the words, in the space between the letters. Why did he die so young? Why did he stay at Bowmry and never go to court? Why did he leave London in the first place? Why, if he did write it, is there so much pain and anger in the *Viage*?'

'Maybe he was just an ordinary person.' He knew he should be nice, he should comfort her, but for some reason, he didn't really know why, Edward goaded her instead, kicking her while she was down. He couldn't stop himself. 'Maybe he wasn't a genius. Most people aren't. He wasn't lucky. He wasn't important – you said it yourself. He wasn't even happy.'

She looked at him, and her eyes were un-attractively red around the edges, her downturned mouth solemn.

'I know what I said.'

CHAPTER 13

'Tell me something, Edward,' Joseph Fabrikant asked, leaning back in his chair. 'How much do you know about the Wents?'

The chairs at the Four Seasons were upholstered in fawn leather, and they were so extravagantly comfortable it was actually hard to sit upright in them.

'Not as much as I probably should.' Edward pressed his knuckles against his front teeth and stifled a yawn. It was eight thirty in the morning the next day, which was very early indeed on his new sleep schedule. He prodded his tomato and basil omelette with a fork and squinted at it blearily. Joseph Fabrikant, evidently tired of pursuing Edward through the intermediary of Zeph, had finally ambushed him by calling him at home and pressuring him into breakfast. Now he sat across the table from Edward, his highly symmetrical face half remembered from across woozy lecture halls, a snow-covered cross-campus walkway, a beery dorm-room party, leaving with the prettiest girl there. Fabrikant had been a natural

226

insider the same way Edward had never seemed to really be part of anything at all. The morning sunlight flooded through the high windows and fell on him at flattering angles, a tall, handsome, successful, affable blond demon.

'Why? How much do you know about the Wents?'

'As much as I've been able to find out,' said Fabrikant. 'Which is pretty damn little.'

The restaurant was half full, mostly with business-men and Upper East Side dowagers in pairs and threes, and the air was full of conversation and the clatter of heavy silverware muffled by expensive acoustical engineering. They'd already exhausted their store of college gossip. All that was left was business.

'Here's what I know,' said Edward. 'They're rich, they have a lot of old books, and they don't get out a whole lot.'

Fabrikant didn't laugh. His bushy yellow eye-brows lowered in concentration, and the muscles flexed in his square jaw. Edward wondered whether he had any sense of humor whatsoever.

Edward had ordered a mimosa with his omelette, aware that it was a wildly inappropriate drink for what was supposed to be a power breakfast. But he hadn't been feeling very empowered lately. It was clear why Fabrikant had asked him here: They were both junior members of New York's young financial all-star circuit, with a slight but definite personal connection between them. What would follow was a matter of ritual: a mutually beneficial exchange of mildly confidential information between respectful rivals, nothing too criminal, just part of business, one of the hallowed traditions of the fiscal fraternity. Information flowed like water these days, and sometimes even the best plumbers got their hands wet.

But information was something Edward was in short supply of these days, as regarded both the market – God help him if Fabrikant brought up the interest rates in London, he hadn't checked them in a week – and whatever nebulous sphere it was that the Duke and Duchess inhabited. And if what Zeph said was true, if Fabrikant really was trying to get the Duke to invest in his company, then Fabrikant was in play in both worlds. That only added another layer of complexity, and Edward was having trouble keeping them straight. He hadn't been tending his carefully nurtured sphere of influence lately anyway, and it was an effort to heave himself back into the world where Fabrikant lived, the world of work. It was a world, he vaguely remembered, that used to be his. The champagne flute containing his mimosa stood in a shaft of sunlight, and the bright yellow liquid glowed hypnotically.

'Just tell me what you know, and I'll tell you what I know,' Fabrikant said, as if he were talking to a child. 'How does that sound?'

'Look, you're going to get the short end of the stick here. I don't know anything you don't know.'

'Peter told me something about the work you've been doing for him. Tell me about that.'

'Peter? You mean the Duke of Bowmry?'

'Yes. Why, what do you call him?'

'I don't call him anything. I've never even met him.'

'You will.' Fabrikant set about methodically demolishing a towering edifice of French toast. 'Once he starts calling you, you can't get rid of him.'

'Does he call you in the middle of the night?'

'I don't think he ever sleeps. Wait till he starts instant messaging you.'

Edward cautiously sipped his mimosa.

'So what kind of business are you in with the Wents, exactly?' he asked, sidestepping. 'Aren't we competitors?'

'Not at all. InTech is very nichey. Strictly technology stuff. We baby-sit them on some of their high-tech holdings. A little biotech, a little Internet. Nothing you should worry about.'

'Okay.'

'As far as I can ascertain, we only deal with a tiny fraction of the Wents' overall portfolio. I don't think even your colleagues at E & H know about everything they have.'

Edward had forgotten how disarmingly handsome Fabrikant was. He looked heroic, almost knightly, with his symmetrical dimples and his deeply cleft chin. His suit was made out of a fine dark gray-green wool that seemed to soak up light from the rest of the room.

'So what's he like?' Edward said. 'The Duke, I mean?'

'The Duke? He's an asshole.' He chewed meditatively. 'Don't get me wrong, he's everything he should be – polite, generous, professional, whatever – but . . .' He groped for some word that was outside his executive vocabulary. 'He's a dick. You know what they say about him in London? That dogs are scared of him.'

'Huh.' Well, if there was fishing to be done, Edward wasn't above doing it. 'What about his family? Do they have kids?'

'Just the one son. You heard about that? Horrible.' Fabrikant shuddered and took another bite. 'I've never met the wife.'

They ate in silence for a minute. One of Edward's forks slipped off the table, and a waiter materialized to whisk it away almost before it hit the carpet.

'I was supposed to, once,' Fabrikant went on after a while. He regarded Edward with his freakishly pale blue eyes. 'Meet her, that is. He asked me out to his place in the country when we first started doing business. He flew me to London, but that's as far as I got. Something came up – I think he got sick again. The hotel had a videoconferencing room, one of those deals where you sit at one end of half a table, watching the other guy on a screen sitting at another half a table somewhere else. The Duke had one of these rigs set up at his house.'

'At Weymarshe?'

Fabrikant shrugged. 'They have a lot of houses.

It was weird. Here we are having dinner, and he has a Constable hanging behind him, and I have *Dogs Playing Cards*. He has hundred-dollar scotch, and I'm drinking the house red. He's eating off – anyway, you get the idea. Once I forgot and asked him to pass the salt.'

Fabrikant belched unselfconsciously.

'I hear he's not doing well,' Edward prompted. 'His health, I mean.'

Fabrikant nodded. 'He's in London now. Some Harley Street clinic, a new treatment.' Fabrikant's oddly guileless expression turned serious, like a worried child. 'Now tell me what's going on at that apartment.'

Edward caught himself before he could say 'What apartment?' Fabrikant was clearly several steps ahead of where he should by rights have been, and he wasn't going to let Edward leave the breakfast table without some kind of quid pro quo. Edward had no idea what he should or shouldn't tell him, or how close he was to the Duke, or whether or not that even mattered. He was picking up the rules as he went along. But he was clear on one thing: He was going to keep the Duchess out of it. Somewhere along the line he'd developed a fierce sense of loyalty where she was concerned. He grimaced. He was as bad as Laura Crowlyk.

As innocently as he could he explained to Fabrikant what Fabrikant probably already knew: what Laura had asked him to do, and that the Duke had then asked him to stop working on the project, and that he'd dropped the matter then and there. He left it at that. He said nothing about Margaret, or the phone call from the Duchess, or that he'd been back to the apartment since then.

Fabrikant studied him skeptically.

'So you're not still looking for – you know?'

'What?'

'That book?'

Edward shook his head slowly, seriously. Fabrikant stared at him, trying to hold his gaze. Edward kept his face blank. The moment passed. Fabrikant nodded, looking thoughtful but not convinced.

'That's probably for the best,' he said slowly.

And there it was, Edward thought. Fabrikant wasn't here on his own behalf. He was here for the Duke. Edward was being reconnoitered, and not particularly subtly, to make sure the Duke's prohibition was being respected.

'He talks about it sometimes, you know,' Fabrikant said.

'Who, the Duke?'

'He was here a few weeks ago. Came by the office, met the staff, treated everybody to dinner at Lespinasse and a lorry-load of British charm. All those "don't you know's and "my dear boy's that he can't seem to get through a sentence without. You know how he is.' He did a bad imitation of the Duke's upper-crust accent. 'Or I guess you don't. Anyway, we all ate it up. Afterwards I went up to his apartment with him alone and we sipped brandy out of giant snifters and smoked cigars and he ordered the servants around. I was humoring him. We're trying to put a deal together. He talked a lot about his ancestors – he's crazy about that genealogy stuff.

'Anyway, he mentioned you. I don't know how you came up. It seemed to make sense at the time. He told me that hiring you was all his wife's idea, that you're one of her pet projects.'

Edward froze. He looked up from his breakfast. 'I don't follow you.'

'Told me you were her latest hobby. One of her "phases". He said that if you ever found that book, he'd rip it up, right in front of her.'

A terrible, icy fear crystallized in Edward's brain, of what he didn't know. He chuckled as casually as he could, but it came out a little hysterically.

'That's ridiculous. I've never even met the Duchess either, just her assistant. Crowlyk.'

It wasn't completely true, but it might as well have been. It was at least plausible. Fabrikant nodded sympathetically.

'I was embarrassed for him, to tell you the truth. Most of the time the Duke's a classic gamesman. One of the best close-to-the-vest players I've ever seen. You could learn a lot from him actually,' he added guilelessly. Edward winced inwardly. 'I don't know what he was really getting at, but whatever he was after, the delivery wasn't up to his usual standards. Makes me think there's something else going on here. Something besides money.'

'Besides money? Like what?'

Fabrikant shrugged.

'I didn't ask. Maybe he was drunk, or whacked out on medication or something. Anyway, it wasn't one of those conversations you want to prolong unnecessarily, if you know what I mean.'

Fabrikant was doing a lot of talking – much more than he really had to. Why? Clearly, his primary allegiance was to the Duke. He had his company to look out for. But something else was going on here as well – Fabrikant seemed genuinely confused about what the Duke was really up to, and genuinely concerned about what Edward's role in it might be. The Duke was his client, but Fabrikant could still think for himself. Maybe he and Edward could help each other out without compromising their respective loyalties too egregiously. Fabrikant obviously knew more about what Edward had been doing than he was letting on, and less about what the Duke was doing than he was comfortable with. Could there be something else on offer here – a tentative, unspoken truce? An alliance between pawns?

'At the time I had only the vaguest memory of who you were, but somehow the Duke figured out that we went to college together, and he had the idea we were best buddies. Anyway, he told me Blanche had hired you to find this book, and that I was supposed to invite you to this party I was having. To make sure you were there – he was pretty emphatic on that point. Somebody

234

was going to meet you there. But you didn't show.'

'Yeah. Sorry. Short notice.'

Fabrikant pushed his plate away and leaned forward confidentially.

'He's a very strange guy, Edward. I'd drop him as a client if I could, but he's too rich, and we need the money.' A cloud of worry crossed his fresh, unlined face. 'I'm trying to get InTech off the ground. There's no VC anywhere. I'm two months away from missing payroll here. But you – I don't get it. What's the point? You don't need him. You're set. You're golden. And you're getting caught up in something that could fuck up your career in a very serious way. It just doesn't make sense.'

Edward hedged.

'What's the big deal?' He tried a chuckle. 'It's just a bunch of books, right?'

'Exactly my point,' Fabrikant said. 'Think about it. How much is one book worth to you? Why not get out now?'

'I *am* out. What more does he want from me?' A note of huffiness crept into Edward's voice. 'How much further out can I get?'

'Further. A lot further. Look, just think about it. That's all I'm asking.'

Edward was silent for a minute, rubbing his chin, defiantly not thinking about it. The whole subject was uncannily resistant to serious, sober, analytical thought of any kind. Edward had the impression that Fabrikant wasn't so much concerned about him anyway. It was more that the very idea of somebody not acting in their own professional self-interest was offensive to his sensibilities, a blasphemy against his personal creed of greed.

Gauging his moment perfectly, a passing waiter paused long enough to whisk both their plates away. When the check arrived, shockingly large, they argued over who would pay, and to his surprise Edward won. He kept the receipt, told himself he'd find some way to expense it later. They walked out together.

The power breakfast crowd was just beginning to thin out. Nine-to-fivers and shoppers charged past them, heads lowered, already laden with brief-cases and bags from Barneys and Bloomingdale's and Crate & Barrel. The ordinary commerce of ordinary people. Edward considered the distinct possibility that he might go back to bed when he got home. He and Fabrikant squinted at each other appraisingly in the bright sunlight that sparkled off the polished door handles of parked cars and the stainless steel implements on display in the windows of Restoration Hardware and Williams-Sonoma.

'So you really don't know what this is all about?' Fabrikant said. 'Why he's so worked up about that book, or whatever it is?'

Edward shrugged.

'It's probably worth a lot of money.'

'Is it?'

'Isn't it?'

'It'd have to be worth a hell of a lot,' said Fabrikant, 'for them to care this much.'

'Six figures. Maybe more.'

Fabrikant snorted derisively.

'I'm surprised at you,' he said. His concerned look came back, and this time Edward wondered if Fabrikant might actually pity him. 'This really is all you know, isn't it? I thought you were a pro at this stuff, but you're just an amateur. You're worse than I am.'

He shook his head sadly. It wasn't meant as an insult, and Edward found that he didn't particularly resent it.

'Look, just try to watch out for yourself,' Fabrikant said. 'And whatever you do, stay away from the Duchess.'

'I thought you said you never met her.'

'I haven't. And I never, ever want to. You know she has a reputation?'

'What kind of reputation?' Edward asked numbly, feeling more and more like he was out of the loop, that he'd missed the meeting, was flying blind.

'She eats guys like us alive.' Fabrikant winked broadly. 'For breakfast.'

He turned away, squaring his broad shoulders and thrusting his hands into his pockets, which made him look even more dashing than ever, if possible.

CHAPTER 14

The next day Edward and Margaret left the city.

They took the West Side Highway uptown until it became Route 9A, which runs north out of Manhattan along the Hudson River. The further north they drove the faster the traffic moved and the thinner it got, and soon they were racing at highway speeds past the monumental facades of Riverside Drive apartment buildings, then past Grant's Tomb, with cloverleaf exits peeling off east into Harlem and north into the Bronx. A perfect little red tugboat bobbed around in the water under the George Washington bridge, looking exactly like a bath toy.

The car was a rental car – a cheap, snazzy, green Ford Contour, not much more than a stereo on wheels – but Edward loved to drive, and he didn't get to do it very often. He rolled down the window, weaving and fighting for position with the other drivers, and thought about nothing at all. It was a relief to get out of the city. Breakfast with Fabrikant had been an awkward reminder of all the responsibilities he was neglecting, not to mention a warning of future difficulties to come, but now he almost managed to forget about them again, or at least to section them off in a carefully quarantined area of his brain where his thoughts never went without strict supervision.

It was a perfect, golden summer day. The air was hot and dry, and the road swooped breathlessly up and down the steep side of the Hudson Valley. He drove it like a race course, but Margaret didn't seem to mind. They took a lumpy old macadam highway through Van Cortlandt Park, a three-laner worn slick and shiny with age. The morning sun shone down through the pollen-dusted air, through the leaves of giant prehistoric trees that leaned out from the hillside over the road, flourishing on the carbon dioxide released by the millions of breathing humans nearby.

Margaret looked blankly out the window, not talking, lost in her own thoughts. There was less hostility between them now after the day spent in the Wents' apartment. There was a bond of amiable resignation – nothing shared, nothing exchanged, but a tacit, temporary acceptance of their odd-couple partnership. She wore a blue and green plaid skirt and blue stockings. She couldn't seem to fit her long legs comfortably under the dashboard.

'Who would name a town Fresh Kills?' said Edward for no reason as they passed a road sign.

' "Fresh creeks". "Kill" means "creek" in Dutch.'

'Why'd they put this place all the way upstate in Old Forge anyway? The Annex, I mean.'

'I don't know.'

'Do you go up there a lot?'

She shook her head.

'The Annex doesn't have much that interests me. No significant medieval holdings. It's mostly just a repository for the Hazlitt papers, of which there are several hundred feet, and for overflow storage. I went up once or twice back when I worked at the main library, on business.'

She looked out the window again. Edward expected her to fall silent, but she didn't.

'I wanted to tell you something,' she said. 'I've been doing some work on the pressmarks in the Duke's library.'

'Pressmarks?'

'Call numbers. Most private libraries don't use a standard classification like the Dewey decimal, they have their own unique filing systems, made up by the owner more or less arbitrarily. Librarians call them pressmarks. Each bookpress – bookcase – has a name or a number assigned to it, or a letter, or a Roman emperor, or a part of the body, or what have you. They can be quite idiosyncratic. Did you read *The Name of the Rose*?'

'Saw the movie. Sean Connery. Christian Slater.'

Margaret refrained from comment.

'In the Wents' system each bookpress is named after an Arthurian knight: Lancelot, Galahad, Gawain, Bors, and so on. I've been able to figure out where just about everything used to be, originally. But there are some interesting gaps.'

240

She passed him a piece of paper. He glanced down at it, caught a glimpse of a fearsomely complicated diagram in colored pencils, and handed it back.

'I'll take your word for it.'

'It's a rough map of the library's original layout. Missing books are marked in red. Most of a whole bookcase is gone, here, and a few scattered volumes here and here. If it comes to that, we can learn more about these two by looking at the books on either side of them – they probably left traces of their covers behind. I've also been rereading the text of the *Viage*. The eighteenth-century fragments.'

Edward kept his eyes on the road.

'All right.'

'There's something—' She hesitated. A moment of fierce internal struggle ensued, which she quietly but decisively lost. 'There's a certain amount of evidence, both linguistic and historical evidence, that might suggest – if one were to interpret it that way – the possible existence of an older precursor text to Forsyth's version of the *Viage*.'

After that short speech she straightened up primly in her seat, like a nun who had been forced to refer, however euphemistically, to something obscene. She fixed her eyes on a point directly in front of her. Edward recognized this as a sign that she was getting ready to lecture, and it was.

'From a linguistic point of view, the text looks like a fake. Why? Because it's not written in the Middle English of Chaucer or of the Pearl Poet.

English varied a lot from place to place in the fourteenth century, but the *Viage* doesn't sound like any kind of medieval English I've ever come across. It sounds more like a half-educated eighteenth-century hack doing his best impression of what he thinks fourteenth-century English should sound like.

'But that doesn't necessarily mean that the publisher, Forsyth, wasn't working from a genuine fourteenth-century source text. Even if he did have one, he wouldn't have followed it very closely. More likely he would have translated it into modern English, badly, and then added whatever archaic touches he thought were necessary to make it sound "authentically" medieval – more authentic, for his purposes, than the real Middle English text. Like a novelization of a movie based on a novel.'

'So you're saying there's no way to tell.'

'I'm not saying that at all.'

She reached into the back seat, rummaged in her leather bag, and took out a thick volume with a plain library binding: pine green with a white call number stamped on the spine. Its edges were frilled with yellow stickies.

'Listen.' She opened the book and ruthlessly cracked the spine. 'Although the Middle English of the *Viage* is bad, it's not quite as bad as it should be. There are echoes of something authentic in the meter. In Middle English you generally pronounce silent *e*'s, and a lot of the lines here scan better with the silent *e*'s pronounced. It could be just a nice archaic touch – except that in 1718, when the *Viage* was published, no one knew how to pronounce Middle English correctly. They just thought Chaucer wrote unmetrical poetry and couldn't spell very well.'

'Good. I like it. I'm sold.'

'There's more.' She brushed back a strand of hair and kept flipping through the book.

'Take this phrase: "the kyng Priamus sone of Troye." What the narrator means is, "King Priam of Troy's son," or "the son of King Priam of Troy," but he doesn't say that, he has "King Priam's son of Troy." You see the difference? The grammar is pure Middle English: The object of the possessive comes before the genitive modifier. Only a scholar would have known that, and Forsyth, whatever else he may have been, was no scholar. He couldn't possibly have gotten it right. He couldn't possibly.'

Edward smiled.

'You're arguing my side now.'

'I know.' She crossed her arms exasperatedly and slouched down in the seat, putting one knee up against the glove compartment and staring at it.

'So what if we're right? Why don't you write something about it? An article or something? Isn't that what you people do?'

She laughed at this, exactly once: 'Ha. I'd be laughed out of the profession.'

'Well, we'll clear everything up tonight, if it's there.'

She nodded.

'If it's there.'

They were on a narrow two-lane highway now, loosely following the Hudson River north into Washington Irving country – pine-infested towns with names like Tarrytown and Sleepy Hollow perched on the steep sides of the Hudson Valley. Neighborhoods of rich old colonial homes alternated with tiny pre-fabricated houses in bad pastel colors, with gazing balls in the garden and Camaros on the lawn wrapped in blue tarps.

Edward cleared his throat.

'You said one of the bookshelves was missing,' he prompted. 'In the library.'

Margaret didn't answer immediately. After her brief spell of talkativeness she'd lapsed back into her usual melancholy affect. She toyed unconsciously with a strand of seed pearls around her neck, the only jewelry she wore.

'Sir Urre,' she said, after a while. 'That's what the shelf was labeled. The missing one.'

'Urre? What kind of name is that?'

'Hungarian. He was a very minor knight. He didn't even make the Round Table until late in the game, which makes his inclusion in the cataloging scheme a little strange.'

'I didn't even know Hungarians could be knights,' said Edward. 'If he wasn't a knight of the Round Table, who was he? Some kind of freelancer? A minor leaguer?'

'Malory wrote about him. Sir Thomas Malory was a very strange man, a knight who wrote mostly

244

from prison, where he landed for looting and raping and pillaging, but he was also one of the greatest natural prose stylists who ever lived. It was Malory who stitched together the various French Grail legends into a single English masterpiece, the *Morte D'Arthur.*

'As a knight, Sir Urre only had one moment of glory, and even that wasn't very glorious. He was cursed – he'd received some wounds in a duel, seven of them, and the curse (as administered by his opponent's mother) stated that the wounds wouldn't heal until they'd been touched by the best knight in the world.'

'And that was—?'

'Well, that's the question, isn't it? Sir Urre came to visit Arthur's court. There was a contest to see who could heal him. It was all for Sir Urre's benefit, in theory, but of course the knights just saw it as a convenient way of figuring out who the best knight in the world was. Anyway, he was carried out on a kind of portable pavilion with bees on the curtains – that was his coat of arms, a golden bee – so that all the different knights could take their shot at healing him. Everybody expected Sir Lancelot to win, because he was the local hero, but only Lancelot knew that he couldn't win, because he was a sinner – he'd slept with a woman named Elaine, and he was sleeping with Arthur's wife, Guinevere, and he was probably prideful on top of that.

'So all the knights lined up to try, and they all

failed, and finally it was Lancelot's turn. Lancelot knew he would fail, too, and his sinfulness would be revealed, but he had no choice. He had to try anyway.'

It was getting hot inside the car, and Edward rolled up the windows and groped around on the dashboard for the AC. Margaret reached over and punched it for him.

'Now here's the twist,' she said. 'When Sir Lancelot laid hands on Sir Urre, the wounds did heal. God had forgiven Lancelot and allowed him to perform his miracle. Nobody else was surprised, but of course Lancelot knew what had happened, he knew that God had spared him when He could have humiliated him. He could never be the best knight in the world, but God had allowed him to pretend, just for a minute, that he was. It was too much for him, and he started to cry. 'And ever Sir Lancelot wept,' says Malory, "as he had been a child that had been beaten."'

Edward swerved the Contour around a dead branch lying in the road.

'It worked out pretty well for Sir Urre, anyway,' he said. 'What do you think it means that they named the bookshelf after him?'

'Who knows?' Margaret smiled a tight, private little smile. 'It makes a good story. Not everything means something, you know.'

With that she closed her eyes, squared her slender shoulders, and promptly and efficiently fell asleep.

It had been a long time since Edward ventured out of the city – weeks, months, he couldn't even remember the last time – and the green fermented smell of grass and fields and hay and sap was like a warm bath. His eyes watered, and he enjoyed a satisfying sneeze. Everything looked more vivid in the natural sunlight, unobstructed by skyscrapers and power lines: finer, clearer, with exciting textures and superior cinematography. In the distance the rock cliffs on the far side of the Hudson were a rich, old, wrinkled red. The sky was cloudless except for one decorative feathered wisp. They whipped past corn shacks, rural churches, general stores, a dilapidated warehouse with a sandy front lot half full of rusting old plow blades, abandoned by their snowplows.

Edward looked over at Margaret. Her pale, sleeping profile was perfectly silhouetted against the green blur of the landscape: her long, swooping nose, her downturned mouth, her elegant neck, pale with one tiny brown mole. She was wearing her customary T-shirt-and-cardigan uniform, even in the summer heat. A tender, protective feeling came over him. He would watch over her while she slept.

Eventually he turned off Route 87 onto 116, crossing the river on a high iron bridge that arched up over the blue water. He pulled up at a red light, and Margaret sensed they'd stopped and opened her eyes. She pushed her glasses up onto her forehead and covered her face with her hands.

'I'm sorry,' she said through her fingers. 'I must have fallen asleep.'

'That's good,' said Edward. 'You'll need it for tonight.'

'Yes.'

When they were moving again Margaret rummaged in her bag and took out another book. She began turning pages at an impossibly rapid rate.

'So you really think it could be there?' Edward said, playing the kid brother who wouldn't shut up. 'What would you say the odds are?'

'Who knows?' She flipped another page irritably. 'We'll find out soon enough.'

'Well, right. But—'

'You really want to know? No, I don't think it's there. And I'll tell you why.' She snapped the book shut on her finger. She seemed to need to get something off her chest. 'Because it's just too modern. People in the Middle Ages didn't use books for the same things we do. We read books for fun, to escape from the world around us, but back then books were serious business. In Gervase's time literature was for worship and instruction, for moral improvement. Books were vessels of the Truth. A book like the *Viage*, a fictional narrative written to be read alone in your room, for pure enjoyment, would have been considered immoral and unhealthy, if not positively satanic.

'Off in France they were busy formulating a sinister invention called the romance. Pure escapism: knights in armor, quests, adventures, all of it.

That kind of thing was fine for the French, but it hadn't caught on in England yet. For the English the idea of fiction, of using a book to escape into another world, was new. It was wild, illicit, even narcotic. You can see it in Chaucer. There's a scene from *The Book of the Duchess* where the narrator is reading in bed, reading a story about a queen whose husband dies. He gets so caught up in it that he confuses what's real and what's on the page:

> *That trewly I, that made this book,*
> *Had such pittee and such rowthe*
> *To rede hir sorwe that, by my trowthe,*
> *I ferde the worse al the morwe*
> *Aftir to thenken on hir sorwe.*

'Fiction was hot stuff, wild and new and dangerous, and the lines between what was made up and what was real were all tangled up. Edward III had a real Round Table in his castle, to be like King Arthur. Mortimer, Edward III's stepfather, told people that he was *descended* from King Arthur. And God knows, if there was ever a time to escape from reality, the fourteenth century in England was it. War, bubonic plague, anthrax, famine, relentless rain, civil unrest – it was probably the worst time and the worst place to be alive in the last two thousand years. A little escapism would have been perfectly understandable.

'But I know Gervase. He wasn't the type to get mixed up with a book like this.'

It was almost three o'clock, and by now Edward had turned off the highway onto a back road lined with pine trees on both sides, and occasionally a gas station or a farm stand offering unshucked summer corn in cardboard boxes. With Margaret giving directions they wound their way toward the center of Old Forge. It turned out to be a double row of antique shops and restaurants, some quaint and some just tawdry, with a single traffic light at the halfway point and a movie theater showing the big blockbuster from two months ago, slightly misspelled on the marquee.

Eventually a motel appeared up ahead on the right, a neat one-story building with a row of shrubs along the front growing in a moat of wood chips. It was called the White Pine Inn. Edward hauled the wheel over and pulled into a fresh black asphalt parking lot. Theirs was the only car in it. When he shut off the engine it was strangely silent. They took their bags inside and checked in.

Back outside in the parking lot, it was three in the afternoon, and the sun was still high in the sky. It was weird to see Margaret standing there on the hot asphalt dusted with green pine needles, drenched in sunlight, holding her bookbag. She looked a long way from her native element, hushed stacks and chilled air. The air was rich with biological stuff, pollen and insects and fluffy motes, and Margaret sneezed quaintly. She squinted pallidly in the pale light like a little girl just waking up from a nap.

'What now?' Edward said.

She looked him up and down critically.

'Don't you have anything to carry? A bag, or a notebook?'

'No. Why would I?'

'It would add some verisimilitude. You're supposed to be a visiting scholar.'

She gave him a pencil and a spiral notebook from her bag, then led him down the motel driveway and out onto the sandy shoulder. They picked their way along it. Fragments of glass glittered in the gravel, and a massive tractor-trailer hauling logs almost killed them as it roared past. It honked deafeningly and threw billows of fine road dust in their faces. A sheet-metal guard rail ran along the other side of the road, and the sun flashed blindingly off the unpainted steel. Margaret took mincing steps in her good leather shoes. Edward was about to ask her if she was sure she really knew where they were going when they pushed past a colossal tuft of ragweed and he saw for himself.

He hadn't realized how close they were to the Hudson River. It was the first thing he saw, a broad flat expanse like a lake sparkling far below them down in the valley. They were standing at the foot of a long, curving gravel driveway that ran between two parallel rows of trees. Beyond them he could see spacious grounds, manicured lawns dotted with modern sculptures in iron girders and polished marble that looked like giant alien punctuation marks. In the middle distance stood a pink granite building, a two-story modernist oblong with large tinted windows. He could have mistaken it for a software company or a high-priced rehab clinic.

'This is it,' Margaret said.

She set off up the driveway, her feet making soft crunching noises in the quiet.

'Damn,' said Edward under his breath. He hurried to catch up with her. 'There's a lot of money in this place.'

She nodded. 'Yes, the Chenoweth is very wealthy.'

'Wealthy enough to build an extra room for the Went collection?'

'Wealthy enough. Too stingy.'

They walked side by side. The landscaper had left several natural-looking stands of pine and birch trees in place. A bird sang three sweet solo notes, then repeated them.

'You're sure this is going to work?' Edward asked.

'Of course. Security here is virtually nonexistent.'

'But you're sure—'

'They know me. They'll let me into the vault, no questions asked. There's a side door. Meet me there twenty minutes before closing and I'll let you in. If they ask you what you're looking for, tell them you're interested in Longfellow. They'll show you some letters. Have you read "The Song of Hiawatha"?'

'No.'

'*Grapes of Wrath?*'

'In high school.'

'Well, say Steinbeck then. The curators will love you. They have his journals here. They were very expensive, and no one ever asks for them.'

There was a sweeping view of the river valley below them. Edward turned to look downstream, where a bridge supported by two stone towers crossed between the two steep banks, silhouetted against the bright silvery water. Tiny cars zipped across it at irregular intervals. An icy shock of recognition ran through him. All of a sudden he knew where he was, but it was somewhere he couldn't be, because it was somewhere that wasn't real. He stood stock-still.

'My God,' he said, half to himself. 'My God. This is part of the game.'

Margaret looked at him suspiciously over her shoulder.

'Just keep walking.'

CHAPTER 15

E dward sat on a hard plastic chair at a computer terminal. His eyes refused to focus on the monitor in front of him. He couldn't type, for the simple reason that he was so nervous that he couldn't feel his hands. This was all happening much too fast. He pressed the keyboard with all ten of his frozen carrot fingers – fjj;dk safskl – and hit return. THAT COMMAND WAS NOT RECOGNIZED.

Margaret was up at the front desk talking to the staff. He watched her slim, straight form from where he sat. Despite himself, he was impressed: She handled herself like a pro. She was holding up better than he was. There had been a minor stir when she came in, when the staff recognized her and gathered together on the other side of the counter to say hello, but she looked perfectly composed. She even seemed to be smiling, something he hadn't known her to do in civilian life. Where in that cloistered academic soul of hers had she found such heroic reserves of sangfroid? Maybe she didn't have enough of a soul to be terrified, he thought meanly. He noticed the way the curved

254

wings of her shoulder blades showed through her thin cardigan.

The library turned out to have been built right into the side of the river valley, making it bigger on the inside than he expected. The far side of the building, the side facing the river, was one single sheet of smoked glass three stories high that looked out on the water. As it descended through the trees the sun shone weakly through the gray-brown translucence, creating dramatic circular lens-flare effects.

After a few minutes Margaret came back and sat down at the terminal next to him. She pretended not to see him.

'You see the circulation desk?' she said quietly, looking only at the screen in front of her. 'Follow it with your eyes. Look where it would meet the far wall if it continued on. There's a door there – you can't see it from here because it's paneled wood like the wall, and there's no handle on this side, but it's there. That's the door you'll go through.'

'Okay.'

'I prepared a map for you. I'm going to leave it under the keyboard of this terminal—'

'Oh for fuck's sake,' he snapped. 'Just give it to me.'

Margaret hesitated, then slid it to him sideways along the tabletop. It was drawn on the back of a yellow index card.

'There's the desk,' she said. 'There's the door.' She could have been a knowledgeable former employee initiating a neophyte researcher in the mysteries of Boolean operators. 'If you keep going along that wall there's a room where people hang their coats. If something goes wrong you can pretend you were just heading back there.'

'I didn't bring a coat. It's summer.'

'Well, think of something else.'

'An umbrella?' Edward had never seen a day that looked less like rain in his life.

'If you like. Check your watch. Mine says' – she looked down – '3:47 exactly. The library closes at 5:30. At 5:00, I want you to go up to the front desk and sign us both out at the registry. Then, at 5:05 exactly, I will open the door. You will step through. I will close it after you. If you're late, I won't wait.'

'What if somebody sees me go in?'

'They'll probably assume you belong here. Just look like you know what you're doing.'

As she talked Edward felt like he should at least pretend to use the computer he was sitting at. His fingers automatically typed the word 'blimp,' and the search returned a list of memorabilia from famous dirigibles: the *Dixmude*, the *Shenandoah*, the *Hindenburg*. That last seemed like an omen of disaster. We're stealing a book from a library, he thought. A very valuable book. I could lose my job over this.

'Once you're through the door what you do next is very important, because there are cameras in the stacks. Turn left immediately, walk as far as the corner, and wait for me there.'

'Okay.'

A tall man wearing a maroon fez sat down at a terminal opposite from Margaret's, his long, Levantine face ravaged with deep acne scars.

'What should I do till then?' said Edward.

'Try not to be noticed. Consult the reference books. There's usually an exhibit on the second floor, go look at that. If you get in trouble, remember Steinbeck. I have to go now, they're waiting for me in the vault.'

'Fine. Go.'

She hit a key. A dot matrix printer on a nearby table chattered insanely and spewed out paper. She stood up, tore off the printout, and took it up to the circulation desk where she was swiftly ushered back through a swinging gate and then through a doorway into the stacks.

This is unwise, Edward thought lucidly. *Nothing I could gain by finding the codex could possibly be worth the chance I'm taking now.* He mentally rephrased and amplified and expanded on this thought in a variety of ways, and in every form it took it seemed equally true, if not truer with every passing second.

What was he going to do for the next hour and thirteen minutes? He looked around furtively at the lobby of the Chenoweth Annex, feeling lost and abandoned. It was almost empty, and the air had the sterile chill he recognized from his visit to the main branch back in the city. The walls were all paneled in pale blond wood. The ceilings were high and lit with lots of teeny-tiny track lights. There was a row of low, comfortable-looking couches along the glass wall facing the river.

The exhibit upstairs turned out to be closed for a private function, so he stood up and went over to a bookcase along one wall. The books were all books about books – bibliographies of obscure literary figures, catalogs of long-dispersed scriptoria, histories of printing and publishing and bindings and typefaces. Taking one down at random, *Twelve Centuries of European Bookbindings 400–1600*, he walked over to one of the couches. He still had the notebook Margaret gave him, and partly to be convincing and partly to relieve the tension he scribbled down some notes on its contents: *The Book of the Dead, Le livre de Lancelot du Lac*, Richard de Bury's *Philobiblon*, Hugh of Saint-Victor's *Didascalicon*, the Samaritan Pentateuch, the Lindisfarne Gospels . . .

A massive double-decker Rothko hung on the wall to his left, balanced by a brown, two-lobed *mappamundo* on his right. In spite of himself Edward started to relax. There were a few terrifying moments when members of the library staff seemed to be about to say something to him, but none of them ever actually did. He wondered what it would be like to belong here the way Margaret did. Settling back into the overstuffed leather, with the notebook in his lap, he imagined another life for himself as one of these silent scholars, buried in his research like a guinea pig in its wood shavings, nibbling away steadily after some arcane piece of knowledge in the hope of making an addition, however imperceptible, to the collective pile. It wouldn't have been so bad. A summer breeze silently ruffled the coarse green grass that clung to the steep slope of the valley. After a while he stopped even pretending to read. Down below, the river glittered in the late-afternoon sun; it was only the smoked glass of the window that allowed him to look directly at it. A white power-boat was forcing its way vigorously upstream, bouncing across the water, swell by swell, surging against the current, the sun flashing rhythmically off its wet hull.

He looked at his watch again. It was almost five. All the panic that had drained away gradually in the past hour came back in one freezing splash. He shot up out of the couch and looked around. He was the only patron left: The room was empty except for staff. An olive-complected young woman walked by pushing a wooden cart with squeaky wheels. She offered to reshelve the book he'd been reading. He let her take it from his numbed fingers.

Edward sat down again at one of the computer terminals and waited, checking his watch every few seconds. His investor's mind was intimately familiar with the calculus of risk, and it was urgently flagging this expedition as a very bad one. This wasn't making poker bets with somebody else's pin money. This was real life. Sweat prickled on the palms of his hands. The letters on the dusty monitor screen burned a lurid, hallucinatory green. He had to go to the bathroom.

At 5:03 he stood up and walked to the far end of the room. This was it. The time was now. A random phrase from a poem he'd read in college came back to him involuntarily, like acid reflux: *It was no dream. I lay broad waking.* He was suddenly preternaturally aware of his peripheral vision – the walls, the furniture, the faces, everything seemed to be jumping wildly in the corners of his eyes.

He walked parallel to the circulation desk, trying to keep his eyes fixed straight ahead of him. He couldn't have felt more conspicuous if he were walking a tightrope or doing a series of flying *jetés* across the room, though in reality he could barely manage even basic bipedal locomotion, because his arms and legs were suddenly stiff and wooden like a toy soldier's.

A crack opened in the wall in front of him. Inside was nothing but intense blackness. It reminded him of something.

The air was cold. It was pitch dark, and there was an intense smell of damp leather. He could literally see nothing – it was like swimming in a deep sea of oil. He was on the other side. Edward reached out into the darkness and his knuckles clanged painfully against something metal. He turned left, robotically, and started walking, the way Margaret had told him to.

White light flashed behind his eyes, and he reeled backward. He had smacked face-first into a

concrete wall. He sat down backward onto somebody's feet.

'Ow!' he whispered hoarsely.

'Ow!' hissed Margaret.

He struggled to get up, and the top of his head
caught her hard under the chin. He heard her
teeth click together.

'I'm sorry!' he whispered. He put out his hand
to reassure her and encountered her breast. He
snatched it back.

A door opened on the other side of what was
suddenly a large room. Bright light spilled towards
them between rows of tall metal bookcases. Then
it closed, and he was blind again.

'What's going on?' he said.

'They changed it,' she whispered angrily. She
rubbed her chin. 'I think they changed the layout.
Put up new partitions.'

Edward stood up, more carefully this time. That
hadn't felt like a partition. He rubbed his forehead and leaned against what felt like the end of
a bookcase.

'Are you sure you remembered right?'

She didn't answer.

'Who was that who opened the door?'

'I don't know.'

Edward's knuckles and forehead throbbed
warmly in the chilly air.

'It's cold in here.'

'"A sunny pleasure-dome, with caves of ice,"'
she said oddly, but her voice was reassuringly calm

261

and even again in the darkness. He reached out his hand and this time found her elbow. He held on to it. Together they listened to muffled conversation from the public area, on the other side of the door, suddenly a world away.

'Did you sign us out?' she said suddenly.

'Shit.' Edward made a face that she couldn't see. 'No. I forgot.'

'Do it now.'

'I can't go back out there!'

'If we're not signed out there's no point in going through with this. They'll be looking all over for me. For both of us.'

'I think there are still people out there.'

Nevertheless, he felt along the wall with his fingertips until he found a crack, then down the crack until he found the doorknob. As he eased it open a line of light appeared. He pressed his cheek against the rough cinder-block wall and peered out. Miraculously, the coast was now clear.

'All right,' he said. He felt for her warm hand, found three of her fingers and squeezed them. 'Promise you'll wait for me.'

'Go.' She pushed him.

Unbelievably, he slipped back out from the safety of the darkness into the light. The late-afternoon sun flooding in through the picture windows was painfully bright now, and he half ran to the circulation desk, stooped over like a doughboy dashing along a trench under enfilading fire. The heavy leather registry book was gone. Fearless now, he went around behind the desk and rummaged through the forbidden boxes of call slips and metal stamps and yellow pencils until he found it. Sitting down cross-legged on the thick carpet, he found their names, signed them out, and tucked the book back where it had been.

He stood up. He felt foolish: The library was empty. There was no one here. He inhaled and let it out in short, open-mouthed breaths: *ha ha ha.* The air-conditioning was so severe he almost expected to see his breath in the air. Somehow the absence of other people made him feel the presence of the books all around him more keenly. He imagined he could hear the rustle of each volume furiously poring over itself, muttering monomaniacally as it reviewed its own contents for all eternity.

Up to this moment, he realized, he hadn't done anything wrong. He was still legally free and clear. There was a line to be crossed, beyond which he would be irrevocably and incontrovertibly entangled, but he hadn't quite crossed it yet. He strolled out from behind the desk, swinging his arms vigorously forward and backward like a swimmer loosening up for the fifty-meter butterfly. That line was very, very near – he could sense it, smell it buzzing dangerously like a downed power line, yards away in space and minutes away in time.

He found himself climbing the shallow flight of steps in the direction of the exit. The sun was starting to set behind the red cliffs on the far side of the Hudson, and beams of light streamed sideways through the room, making Giacometti shadows spring from his feet and from those of two librarians he passed on their way in, a man and a woman, chatting about nothing, a party for the library's donors upstairs, perfectly unsuspecting. Nothing was keeping him here, he thought. He could still walk out if he wanted to. The freedom of it was tempting. Maybe this whole thing was all part of somebody else's story – Margaret's, the Duchess's, somebody's, not his. He could leave now, get on a bus, be back in Manhattan by night-fall. He felt bad about Margaret, but she still had the car, and she'd be better off without him, they both knew it. He pushed open the double doors at the end of the hall and stepped out onto the gravel path.

A small army of black and midnight blue limousines with smoked windows was parked all along the driveway and on the lawn. Men and women in fancy dress were standing and talking and walking along the gravel paths holding champagne flutes. Waiters wove between them with trays of hors d'oeuvres. Leaning against one of the limousines, gazing pensively down at the cigarette tucked between his knuckles, was a man with an unusually weak chin. Edward recognized him instantly. He'd seen him outside the Wents' apartment the first day he went there. It was the Duke's driver.

Edward froze. What was he doing here? If the driver was here, was the Duke here too? Why wasn't he in London? Was he healthy again? Was he following the same trail of clues they were, looking for the codex? Everything that had seemed clear and fixed and right to him a moment ago reversed itself in a dreamlike rush, like an hourglass being inverted. He backed inside, back over the threshold, and the doors boomed closed behind him like a pair of curtains closing on the final act of a play. He was wrong, his place was here. His leather shoes slipped wildly on the carpet as he ran. The hidden door to the stacks was still ajar, and he clawed it open, ducked inside, and carefully closed it behind him. He waited a few minutes, breathing hard. Then he called Margaret's name as loudly as he dared.

There was no answer. He felt his way further into the safety of the room, using the bookshelves as a guide. In the absolute blackness everything – the floor, his feet, the cold metal shelves – felt over-sized, enormous, half real, as if he were an intruder in a giant's house, like Jack from 'Jack and the Beanstalk,' wandering around among titanic chairs and tables. Where was she? His mind, which had locked up when he saw the Duke's driver, began racing again, trying to catch up. He kicked over a plastic footstool, and it clattered away into the darkness. He let his fingers trail along the shelves on either side, his fingers brushing nameless volumes, hanks of dust piling up under his fingertips.

In another minute he reached the far wall and started along it, patting his way past more shelves, a filing cabinet, mop and broom handles, and then a door. Voices were audible behind it.

'Well, I'm sorry, but you should have planned better. Next time leave yourself more time to work.' He recognized the peevish voice of one of the librarians he'd passed earlier. He had a French – Belgian? – accent.

'But there's far more material here than I could possibly have anticipated.' Margaret sounded as even-keeled as ever. 'The catalog is very misleading. I've drafted a replacement entry that's much more comprehensive, but—'

'The alarms come on at six thirty. I am sorry, but there is no time for this now.'

'Ellen told me she reset them for eight in case the donors want to see the vault.'

She said something else that Edward didn't catch.

'All right,' the librarian said. He sighed heavily. 'All right. But do not reshelve anything. You understand? Just leave it all on the cart when you are finished.'

'I understand.'

'All right. Come and join us at the party afterwards,' he added grudgingly, 'if you have the time.'

Edward waited for the librarian's footsteps to recede, then gingerly opened the door a crack. He was now in the library's inner offices. Margaret was alone. She didn't even seem surprised to see him.

'Come on,' she said.

'What happened?' Edward said angrily, trailing after her toward the back of the office. 'Why didn't you wait for me?'

'I watched you out in the lobby. I thought you left.'

Edward blushed. She'd seen him almost abandon her.

'Well, I didn't,' he said defensively. 'Listen, there's something I have to tell you. I think the Duke of Bowmry may be here.'

She stopped.

'I thought you said he was in London.'

'I know it doesn't make any sense, but I saw somebody who works for him. I think he saw me, too.'

'He saw you.'

He glanced nervously behind him at the door to the lobby. Her sangfroid was starting to irritate him.

'Look, let's just forget about this for now and get out of here. We'll come back some other time.'

'Edward. We're in a library.' She waved her hand at the room around them. 'It's just books. The worst thing that happens here is a strongly worded overdue notice.'

She kept walking.

'Margaret.' Edward didn't move. 'I'm serious—'

'No, *I'm* serious,' Margaret said coldly, without looking back. 'You're the one who's losing his nerve.'

She led him through a large, unkempt work space crammed with computer terminals and bulky microfilm and microfiche readers. They wove between desks piled high with teetering towers of books, each volume stuffed full of stickies and manila cards and white Xerox paper. On the walls hung bulletin boards shingled with *New Yorker* cartoons as thick as old-growth moss. Edward stopped to examine one. Young man in rowboat passes mermaid on rock. Mermaid is talking on a cell phone. Young man says—

'Edward.' Margaret called his name. She was struggling with the top drawer of an unassuming gray metal filing cabinet.

'Turn it over,' she said.

'What?'

'Turn the whole filing cabinet upside down.'

Edward hesitated, then bent down on one knee and wrestled the filing cabinet over onto its side. It was extremely heavy, and its contents rattled around ominously inside it.

'I place entirely too much faith in you,' he said.

When it was completely upside down, Margaret squatted down and tried the top drawer again. It opened easily, and a jumble of office supplies poured out onto the floor. So did a key chain with a well-worn Pikachu fob on it. Margaret plucked it out of the mess.

Edward watched her, grudgingly impressed.

'How did you know that would work?'

'I read a lot.'

Somewhere down at the other end of the long office a door opened, accompanied by the sound of many voices.

'That's the tour,' said Margaret, checking her watch. 'It's starting.'

'The tour?'

'The tour for the donors.'

'Do you think the Duke is with them?'

'I really have no idea.'

Keys in hand, they jogged down a hall that ended in a pair of dingy steel elevator doors. Edward ran ahead of her and punched the elevator button.

'They'll be coming this way,' she said calmly. 'It's the main entrance to the stacks.'

The doors seemed to open in slow motion. Margaret pressed the button for the sub-basement while Edward frantically mashed the CLOSE DOOR button. Somebody called for them to wait. The doors shut.

When they opened again it was on a long, low-ceilinged room lit by fluorescent lights and full of endless ranks of metal bookshelves painted battle-ship gray. Edward propped the elevator doors open with an office chair. They munched on it noisily in the silence like a monstrous baby gumming a chew toy.

Margaret chose an aisle and they set off down it at a fast stiff-legged walk. The first thing Edward noticed was that there were no books on the book-shelves. Instead they were filled with an eclectic, dreamlike collection of objects: a stuffed owl, a narwhal horn, Victorian pocket watches, hairy South Seas fetishes. One long shelf was occupied by an ancient blunderbuss with a flared muzzle like a trombone. A stupendous matched pair of smoky brown globes stood in a corner, one terrestrial and one celestial, each one five feet in diameter. Soon the voices of the tour echoed behind them – they must have taken the stairs – but they faded again as Edward and Margaret pressed on deeper into the stacks. The shelves whizzed by on either side of him with exaggerated speed. They were through the looking glass.

The first room opened onto a second crammed with thousands of identical boxes stacked up in perfect rows. Each one had a tiny typewritten label on it held in place by a neat metal clip. Out of curiosity, Edward opened one. It contained nothing but a manila folder, inside of which was a single thin envelope, pressed flat like a dried leaf, brown with age and stamped all over with multicolored postmarks.

'Letters department,' said Margaret. 'Come on.'

She took them down an echoing concrete stairway, deeper into the earth, and through a heavy metal door like an airlock into a massive subterranean warehouse. It was like descending into the depths of the ocean in a bathysphere: Everything became quieter, darker, more pressurized, stranger. Racks of bright, buzzing lights lit the space from thirty-foot ceilings. It was more like a bomb shelter than a library. The bookshelves were solid steel and bolted to the floor. They ran the full height of the room, like the pillars of a cathedral, with rolling ladders to reach the upper stories.

Margaret took his arm collegially, like Hansel and Gretel in the dark forest, and led him through a section filled with oversized books: bound volumes of illustrated newspapers, census records with brown and black leather spines stamped in flaking gold, giant atlases of vanished countries. Some were collapsing under their own weight; most were too tall to stand upright and had to be stored on their sides. The cold air was heavy with the rich, dank smell of slowly decomposing leather.

Margaret glanced up at call numbers as they walked.

'What are you looking for?' he asked.

'Uncataloged Materials. It's somewhere near here—'

She checked her printout.

'I've pulled books from down here before, but I can't quite remember—'

Her voice trailed off.

'Is it on this floor?'

'I said, I can't remember,' she snapped. 'When I remember, then I will know, and I will tell you.'

It was more like visiting a morgue than a library. The shelf next to Edward held a long black box like a musical instrument case with the word TENNYSONIANA written on it in black magic marker. Next to it was a cardboard carton with one corner crushed. A masking-tape label read AUDEN, W.H. AND SEALED UNTIL. 1/1/2050.

'All right.' Margaret stopped. 'We're on the wrong floor. Come on.'

The long, straight lines of the metal bookshelves flickered past on either side, exaggeratedly perspectival. The industrial lights buzzed in the stillness. Margaret hit a switch when they reached the wall, plunging the room into darkness. Down two more flights to the very bottom of the concrete stairwell, then into another ware-house. The fluorescent lights flickered on, seemingly in random order. In one corner was a cubical shed made out of what looked like aluminum siding.

'That's a blast freezer,' Margaret explained, following his gaze. 'Every book that enters the library has to be frozen first to kill any parasites.'

'Bookworms?'

He was being facetious, but she nodded.

'There are a number of maggots that feed on paper or library paste. "Bookworms" is the generic term for them. If that doesn't work, they put the books in a partial vacuum until the insects suffocate.'

The stillness was even deeper here, further underground. He looked at his watch: It was past seven.

'What about those alarms?' he said. 'Should we be worried?'

'Nothing we can do about them now. We'll be here until seven in the morning.'

'Jesus! I thought you said security around here was a joke.'

Margaret shrugged. She let go of his hand and looked up at the numbers on the nearest bookcase.

'All right,' she said. 'We're here. Most uncataloged materials are stored in the quadrant defined by this row and this aisle, as far as that wall.' She pointed.

'What now?'

'Now we start looking for what we came for.'

'Will I know it when I see it?'

'This isn't buried treasure,' said Margaret. 'It's not hidden, it's just lost. Look at the call numbers, look for something obvious, like "Uncat Went." If it's here, we'll find it.'

She set off down one aisle and came back dragging a tall aluminum stepladder on wheels. Edward took the next aisle over, where there was another ladder. He climbed up to the top step, where he could look out over the very tops of all the shelves in the room, rank after dim rank, receding into the distance a few feet below the ceiling. Each one was covered in its own drift of silent dust. They looked as if they'd lain untouched for decades, like a silent, sleeping, snowbound city, Pompeii buried under the ashes.

Most of the boxes were clearly labeled and easy enough to eliminate. Every couple of minutes he had to climb down and move the ladder, and the little shopping-cart wheels it ran on shrieked horribly in the silence. He could hear Margaret working directly opposite him, on the other side of the bookcase, just inches away. He caught glimpses of her through the gaps between the books and boxes: the hem of her skirt, a pearly button from her blouse.

'It's like the end of *Raiders of the Lost Ark* in here,' he said after a while.

'With all these boxes,' he added lamely.

His voice rattled dryly and faded away. He didn't really expect her to answer, but after a while she did.

'Did you notice those red metal canisters along the walls?' she said. 'They're in case of a fire. If the smoke detectors go off, the doors will seal themselves automatically. All the air in this room will be replaced with an inert gas. We have thirty seconds to get to an exit before it happens.'

The cold was starting to chill him through his clothes, and he sneezed.

'Gesundheit,' said Margaret, with a very correct German accent.

They worked quickly, making their way down each shelf to the wall, then moving on to the next one. Margaret worked faster than he did, and soon she was two shelves ahead of him.

'Edward?' she asked suddenly. 'You once asked me how I became an academic. How did you become a private banker?'

Her voice was farther away now, he could no longer tell exactly where. It echoed in the forest of steel shelves like a will-o'-the-wisp. He had almost forgotten she was still there.

'How does anybody get to be a private banker?'

'I don't know. How does one?'

He stopped working. His forehead itched, and he rubbed it with the back of his hand, the only clean spot left.

'You don't have to tell me if you don't want to.'

'There isn't much to tell,' he said. 'I grew up in Maine. My father was an engineer, my mother was a graphic designer. Still is. She did a collection of aprons and potholders that sold well. She has a special way of drawing vegetables, peppers and onions. You've probably seen them.

'My father took over the manufacturing and marketing. They probably shouldn't have gone into business together. They sent me to boarding school for high school, then they split up – some dispute about patents and copyrights, look and feel. She was getting ready to sue him when he died suddenly. Diving accident.'

'I'm sorry.'

'They called it a freak accident.' Edward cleared his throat. Reciting it out loud, his own past seemed strange to him. 'But there isn't really anything freakish about dying when you're spearfishing in a lava tube at a hundred meters, is there?' He paused, surprised at how bitter he sounded. 'I guess I'm still angry about how careless he was. Anyway, she moved to California, I went to Yale. I haven't seen her for years. When I graduated I guess I was just looking for stability. A sure bet. I-banking seemed like as sure a bet as they come. Most of my friends were doing it, or something like it.'

'There's no such thing as a sure bet,' Margaret said.

'Everything's a sure bet if you're the bookie.'

It was a glib response. Silence resumed, somehow deeper than it was before.

'Margaret,' Edward said, 'do you still think the codex could be a fake?'

Margaret cleared her throat.

'It would hardly be the first of its kind,' she began. 'History is full examples of pseudepigrapha.'

'Pseud—?'

'Fakes. Hoaxes. Literary forgeries. The *Culex*, which claimed to be Virgil's juvenilia. "The Letter of Aristeas," which was a false account of the composition of the Old Testament. *The Travels of Sir John Mandeville*. Annius of Viterbo, who pretended to be a Babylonian priest. Jacob Ilive's *Book of Jasher*. The so-called Jacopo of Ancona's *City of Light*.

'In the 1700s people were crazy about the poetry of a third-century Scottish bard named Ossian. They called him the Celtic Homer, and he was a major influence on the Romantics. After he died it turned out he never existed. The man who claimed to be Ossian's translator – a well-known academic named James MacPherson – made it all up.

'Around the same time an impoverished teenager from Bristol was producing some very accomplished poems that he claimed were the work of a fifteenth-century monk named Thomas Rowley. He said he found them in an old chest. The boy's name was Thomas Chatterton. Of course, the poems were fakes. Chatterton thought he was a failure, and he poisoned himself when he was seventeen. Keats wrote *Endymion* about him.

'Books don't have to be real to be true. Gervase

would have understood that. Was Rowley's work real? It was real poetry.'

He heard the screech of her stepladder as she dragged it along the floor like a large, recalcitrant pet.

'I suspect the *Viage* will end up as what bibliographers call a ghost,' she said, her voice becoming more and more distant. 'A book that has been documented, and attested to in the literature, but that never actually existed.'

They worked silently in parallel for another hour. At first Edward was curious about each of the boxes he was checking, snooping around in the contents when they looked interesting, but he got over that in a hurry. Now he just wanted to eliminate them as fast as possible and move on.

Margaret was waiting for him at the end of the next row with her arms folded.

'That's it,' she said.

'What?' He tried not to show his disappointment. 'You mean that's all?'

'For this section.'

He absentmindedly wiped his hands on his pants before he realized they were covered with black dust.

'Okay. What's left?'

By way of answering she indicated a dark corner of the warehouse that Edward had previously ignored. A large square of floor was partitioned off from the rest of the space by a chain-link cage that ran halfway up to the ceiling. It had evidently been used as a kind of in-house junkyard, a place to put things that were broken but not broken enough to throw away, or too big to haul up to the surface: discarded shelving units, dented filing cabinets, extended runs of obscure and damaged journals. A massive, medieval-looking steel press squatted amid the detritus.

Edward walked over to the chain-link fence and put his fingers through it.

'You think it's in there?' he said. He had a sinking feeling.

'I don't think it's out here.'

'Can we even get in?'

There was a door in the fence held closed by a large steel padlock. After a few tries Margaret found the right key on the Pikachu key ring, and the lock popped open with a well-oiled *snap*. The door moaned dismally as it swung open.

Inside the jumbled heap sloped upward toward the corner. It was worse than he'd thought: There were brooms and mops and old cleaning supplies and just plain trash inside – broken chairs and busted-in globes and gutted, discarded bindings, all covered with a thick layer of greasy dust. There was actual dirt here. Edward picked his way gingerly through the edges of the pile.

'This is hopeless,' he said. He glanced at Margaret, half hoping that she would agree and admit defeat, but she started clearing it away with surprising vigor.

'Let's work our way to the back,' she said. 'Where the big stuff is.'

They stacked the junk against the walls of the cage as best they could, working together to lift the heavy furniture, old chairs and tables. Margaret broke a nail on an old two-by-four and stopped to smooth it down, swearing under her breath. Soon they could make out a row of trunks and crates along the two rear walls. When he got close enough, Edward opened the top drawer of a battered filing cabinet with a horrific screech. It was full of old call slips and yellowing interlibrary loan records from the 1950s, all blank, never used.

He had a terrible premonition that they were wasting their time.

'Margaret—'

Margaret ripped open a rotten cardboard box that belched out a cloud of dust like a puffball spewing spores. She extricated a stack of red leather-bound books from its interior, glanced at their spines, then dumped them to one side. The more exhausted he got the stronger she seemed to become. She pushed the hair out of her eyes with her forearms.

'Nothing yet!' she said gamely, breathing hard.

Edward felt like they had slipped into a parallel dimension where time was elastic. It seemed like they'd been down in the vault for days, and the cold and the silence and the darkness and the tension were getting to him. Any trace of the fear and excitement he'd felt at the outset was gone. He worked in a dreamlike state. He had no idea what time it was. He guessed two in the morning, then checked his watch: It was only ten thirty.

He spent five minutes with a steel bookend trying to lever open an antique wooden box that looked vaguely Chinese. It turned out to be packed with brittle, translucent glass negatives individually wrapped in tissue paper. He slipped one out and held it up to the light. The ghostly image of a busty blond with a twenties hairstyle materialized, winking back at him. She was perched on a rock, squinting at the seaside sun with one pale, wobbly breast exposed.

Edward frowned. He glanced over at Margaret. She had stopped working.

She was standing in front of a big black suitcase half as tall as she was, studying the bundle of tags that was hanging from the handle. The suitcase was stamped with faded luggage stickers from old transatlantic lines. In the cold, dusty basement of the library it gave off an impossibly remote air, of sunbathing and canvas deck chairs and shipboard romance.

'What is it?'

'"Cruttenden",' she said. 'It says "Cruttenden".'

Edward dropped the negative. It shattered on the cement floor.

'Thank God,' he said, with more emotion than he meant to. 'We're saved.'

They worked together to clear a space for the suitcase, then carefully rocked it out away from the wall and laid it down on the floor on its back.

It was a formidable object, bound in heavy brass, and it weighed a ton. Edward tried the latch, but it was locked.

'I don't suppose you have the key—?'

Margaret picked up an empty fire extinguisher. He snatched his hands away just in time as she gave the lock a solid two-handed blow with its butt-end. Something metal sprang off it and tinkled away musically into the darkness. She put the fire extinguisher down.

'Try it now,' she said, breathing heavily. The lid yawned open on two cleverly constructed hinged arms. He saw why it weighed so much: Inside it was full of books, a solid mass packed tightly together like a Chinese puzzle, each one carefully wrapped in its own fine paper nest.

This was it. He wanted to prolong the moment of the unveiling, but Margaret apparently didn't share his delicate feelings. She chose a book at random, tore the wrapping off, and squinted at the spine: It had a series of numbers and letters, some of them Greek, printed on it in gold.

Margaret grimaced.

'These press marks are wrong. They're not even close to what they should be.'

'You mean this isn't—?'

He didn't dare to finish the sentence.

'No,' she said, still shaking her head. 'I mean yes, this is the missing box. It has to be.' She looked up at him helplessly. 'What else could it be?'

Edward had no answer for her.

They worked together to unpack the books, starting at opposite ends. Kneeling next to the suitcase, Margaret ripped the wrapping paper off each book with both hands and threw it behind her. Edward was seeing a new side of her: She had scented blood, and something serious and primal was coming to the fore, an angry shark spiraling up out of the blue depths. Edward stayed out of her way as she worked. She'd been looking for this longer than he had, he thought. It was her victory more than it was his.

He used his sleeve to clear the dust off a table where he could stack the books as she unwrapped them. She went through the volumes in the suitcase with the ruthless efficiency of a child looting the broken carcass of a piñata. Some of the books, the ones that were obviously modern, she tossed aside without even opening. She spent longer on the older volumes, then threw them behind her, too.

And then it was empty. The blank bottom of the suitcase gaped at them in the dimness. They both felt around in the shadows inside it, patting the sides, looking for a book they'd missed, or maybe – could it be? – a secret compartment? But there was nothing to find. The codex wasn't there.

Edward was almost too stunned to be disappointed. He'd been so sure, he hadn't even stopped to consider what would happen if they were wrong. Margaret obviously hadn't either. She pawed through the huge pile of wrapping paper she'd thrown aside, like a cat in a pile of leaves, but there was nothing solid.

'It's not here,' she said in a small, odd voice.

'I guess not.'

Edward tried to sound casual. He got to his feet, dusting off his hands, okay, no big deal.

She stood up with a dazed expression on her face, looking around at the jumble of trash and discarded objects.

'I don't think it's here,' she repeated, as if she hadn't heard him the first time. She looked like a shell shock victim stumbling out of a bomb crater.

'Margaret, it's obviously not here,' he said. 'There's still a few more filing cabinets. We could—'

She took a running step and kicked the empty suitcase. Dust flew up out of it, and it boomed hollowly in the silence. Then she kicked it again, and a third time, with increasing force. Edward watched, fascinated, as she slammed the suitcase closed. He'd never seen anybody so angry. With more strength than he would have thought possible in her slender arms she picked it up and threw it bodily against a row of filing cabinets. A huge crash echoed through the vault, like the collapse of a colossal machine.

'This is bullshit!' she screeched. 'Bullshit!'

She kicked the suitcase again and again where it lay on the floor until Edward finally snapped out of it and grabbed her around the waist. She struggled, trying to pry his arms away, but she was too light, and he was too strong. For a second her cheek pressed against his. It was wet with warm tears that turned cold in the chilly air.

'*Shhh*,' he said. '*Shh*. It's all right.'

'No, it's not! It's not all right!'

She finally pulled away from him and sat down on an old desk chair. Sobbing, she put her head in her hands. They were both covered with black dust and dirt. She sniffed and wiped her nose on her sleeve. Her hands were trembling.

'I'm sorry,' she said. She sobbed once, convulsively. 'I'm sorry. God damn it.'

Edward stood the suitcase up on its side and sat down on it. He shouldn't be here, he thought wearily, watching her. He was tired and cold and unhappy, but even so, he didn't deserve to be here. She wanted the codex more than he could have guessed, more than he'd ever wanted anything in his life. She was right: She was the serious one, he was just along for the ride. He felt like an acquaintance at a funeral who realizes for the first time that he'd never really known the deceased, that he'd been invited along merely out of politeness.

He wanted to comfort her. The distance he so often felt between himself and other people was reasserting itself, and he didn't want to let it. He went over to where she was sitting and put his hands on her shoulders, then around her waist. The position was awkward, but he couldn't let go of her. How old was she? From what she'd told him she couldn't be more than nineteen or twenty.

He wanted to protect her from the hurtful, disappointing world around them. He stayed like that for what seemed like a long time. She didn't move. After a while his neck got tired, and he rested his head on top of hers. From time to time she sniffed wetly, but she didn't try to pull away.

Finally she turned around. He shifted his weight to an old crate next to her, and they kissed. It was a soft, tender kiss. A good kiss. After a few minutes she moved his hand up her slender ribcage and placed it over her small, soft breast.

Another long time later they broke apart. Margaret's eyes were closed. She seemed to be half sleeping, half dreaming. They didn't speak, and the silence was deep around them. They were like two slaves buried alive together for all eternity in the tomb of some cruel Asiatic king. She leaned her head against his chest, and he put his arms around her shoulders. He was grateful for the warmth.

He looked up at the shadowy ceiling far above their heads, then carefully, so as not to disturb her, he glanced down at his watch. It was one in the morning.

At 6:58 a.m., two dirty, shivering refugees stood at an out-of-the-way fire exit in an obscure corner of the basement of the Chenoweth Rare Book and Manuscript Repository Annex. Margaret stood slightly apart from Edward. He carried the heavy suitcase containing the Wents' books, looking like a bedraggled immigrant with chalk marks on his coat waiting to be processed at Ellis Island. She carried a rare copy of De Quincey's *Confessions of an English Opium Eater* in her folded arms; she'd picked it up at some point the night before and refused to part with it. They watched and waited. At exactly 7:00 a tinny electronic tone chimed, and a tiny red light over the door winked out.

The door opened onto a thick evergreen hedge covered with dew. They pushed their way out through it and across a moat of brown wood chips. It was daylight, but no one saw them, or if they did they didn't raise the alarm. The air was as warm and humid as a rainforest after the dry chill of the library, and they shivered uncontrollably as they warmed up. Margaret's face was streaky and red where her tears had dried. A bird called sweetly from further down the riverbank, nearer the water, where a mist was burning off in the morning sun. The grass was drenched with moisture that soaked into their socks. Edward would happily have murdered for a sip of scotch.

Margaret walked ahead of him through the carefully manicured grounds, whether out of embarrassment or eagerness to get out of there, he couldn't tell. She limped slightly; she must have hurt her foot when she kicked the suitcase. Edward hadn't slept much, and he hadn't eaten since yesterday afternoon. Now the hunger and fatigue caught up with him, and he felt faint. His mouth flooded with saliva. She waited impassively, sphinxlike, while he puked into a rhododendron.

A half-dozen cars were lined up in the motel parking lot like suckling pigs. All the windows were dark, the curtains drawn. Edward had the key. There were twin beds in their room, covered with synthetic floral bedspreads, fresh and unslept-in. Two water glasses stood on the dresser, still wrapped in hygienic tissue paper.

Edward sat down on the nearer bed.

'Just give me a minute,' he mumbled. He'd get up in a second. 'I just need to close my eyes for one minute.'

The mattress was hard, and the bed was made so tightly it was an effort to pull back the covers. Finally he just lay down on top of them, still wearing his shoes, and put his hands under the flat, flaccid pillow and closed his eyes. A warm, glowing, pulsing pattern appeared behind his eyelids. He heard the shower come on.

After a while he felt hands untying his shoes, urging him under the covers, tucking him in, and then Margaret lay down next to him, warm and pink and clean, and they fell asleep together in the bright white sunlight streaming in through the windows.

CHAPTER 16

The day after they got back Edward came down with a summer cold.

It might have been the chilly air in the library, or the dust or the stress or the lack of sleep, or all of them combined, but when he woke up the next morning everything around him felt different. He knew that his apartment was full of sunlight and heat, but he couldn't feel it. Time was slower. Gravity was weaker. His head felt like it was full of some thick, heavy, viscous liquid.

For two days Edward lay on his couch with his head on the cushions and his legs hooked over one of the arms, his blue office shirt unbuttoned and his hair unwashed. He wore plaid flannel pajama bottoms and drank cartons of orange juice in little sips because he couldn't breathe through his nose. He ate once a day. He left the TV on all the time, watching shows he'd never seen before, or even suspected existed. One show was devoted exclusively to horrific sporting accidents captured on videotape. Every episode followed the same formula: a festive occasion, bright sunlight, crowded bleachers, 'loving' family members present. Often the fateful incident took place in the background while the amateur cameraman, oblivious for the first few seconds, focused on the loved ones chattering away blissfully in the foreground, while behind them a funny car un-expectedly spewed burning fluid all over itself, or a double-hulled speedboat took graceful flight and floated toward a beach packed with sunbathers, or a privately owned Cessna lumbered into the air, overloaded with happy hunters bound for a carefree weekend upstate that they would never, ever enjoy.

After two or three days of this he lost all remaining sense of connection with his old working life. He should have been in a panic. It was almost time for him to go to England; a glance at his offer letter, disinterred from his briefcase, confirmed that he was due there tomorrow. With a casual mendacity that was totally uncharacteristic of him, he called Esslin & Hart in London and gave them an exaggerated account of his illness. Afterward he couldn't remember exactly what he said, but they agreed that he sounded terrible and that he could postpone his arrival for another two weeks, to the beginning of September.

One strange thing: He called Margaret and left messages, but she never picked up and never called him back. He didn't understand. It hurt that she was ignoring him – or at least, it would have hurt if he'd really been able to feel much of anything, but not much got through the soft, warm blanket of illness that was wrapped around his brain. He felt physically unable to think about the codex, either. He forgot about the past and the future; only the miserable, meaningless present existed. And when even that was too much, he played MOMUS.

Time was in free-fall in the game. The sun raced by overhead, faster and faster, until it blurred into a single glowing band, a burning streak across the sky. Day and night, clouds and sky, sun and moon blended together into an even gray-blue luminescence.

Talk about wasting time. He had climbed up to the roof of a skyscraper, and from there he watched as centuries passed like minutes. Entire ages arose and subsided, millennia came and went, civilizations waxed and waned. The city became a jungle crowded with towering ginkgo trees between which sailed enormous birds of paradise trailing long feathered plumes. Then the trees withered and fell away, and New York became an oasis in a vast desert. Scalloped dunes of yellow sand hundreds of feet high drifted by like great waves, one after the other, mountains of dust marching inland over the horizon, driven by the wind. Finally, when it seemed like the desert age would never end, the sea rose and covered everything, until he could have leaned down from his rooftop perch and dabbled his fingers in the salt water.

Edward was joined by a strange man – his presence was never satisfactorily explained by the narrative – who moved the story forward in genteel, surprisingly cultured tones.

'It's actually pretty simple,' the man said. 'Aliens are planning to invade Earth, but first they need to make it habitable. They come from a cold planet, and Earth is heated by the hot molten lava at its core. When that core cools and hardens, millions of years from now, Earth will be cold enough for them to colonize. So the aliens are accelerating the passage of time until Earth has cooled down enough to be comfortable. If they're lucky, humanity will have died out by then, too.'

'Right, okay,' Edward typed. 'So how do we stop them?' He wasn't interested in the details. He was tired of being a passive observer. He was spoiling for a fight. But the man – whether out of stoicism or because of some gap in his programming – didn't answer him.

Tens of thousands of years slid by. With oceans covering the land masses, mankind evolved a society that lived entirely aloft in massive dirigibles made from whale skins sewn together and inflated with hot air. Edward left his high tower and joined a band of aerial buccaneers, and together they cruised the jetstream, miles above the glittering seas, preying on smaller craft. For food they dragged the oceans with massive nets and snared seabirds from the endless flocks that darkened the skies. They flew jury-rigged gliders made of bamboo harvested from the peaks of the Himalayas, the only mountains that still poked their tips up above the water.

After a while he forgot all about the alien invasion. After all, he reasoned, from his point of view, within the accelerated time-stream, he had millions of years to go before they would even begin to be a threat. He could go on like this practically forever – bronzed by the sun, knife clenched between his teeth, living by his wits, caring for nothing.

Then one morning Edward woke up feeling better. His sinuses were clear. His head had returned to its normal size. The dull yellow scrim of fever had lifted.

In fact, he felt fabulous, if a little light-headed. His momentum was back, and with interest. My God, he'd wasted so much time! It had rained torrentially the night before, and the sky was still overcast. The air smelled moist, and the day had a freshly washed look to it, as if it had been vigorously scrubbed with a steel brush. Edward showered, dressed, and did ten push-ups.

He picked up the phone and dialed Margaret's number. No answer, as usual. No problem. A quick search online yielded her address in Brooklyn.

Bounding out the door, he felt – for no particular reason, and despite quite a few reasons to the contrary – relaxed and happy and refreshed. Purged. It was the first time he'd left his apartment in a week, and he was exploding with energy. Armed with a bundle of newsprint – the *New York Times*, the *Journal*, the *Financial Times* – to bring him up to speed on the world at large, he jogged down the steps to the 6 train. An hour later he re-emerged, blinking, in Brooklyn.

Zeph was exaggerating when he said Edward had never been to Brooklyn, but not by much. Apart from a night or two of artsy slumming in Williamsburg, and one accidental detour the wrong way down the Brooklyn-Queens Expressway, he'd almost never crossed the East River. He looked around at a sinister cityscape of brownstones and row houses receding away from him in all directions at strange off-angles, and he wished he'd thought to bring a map. Clearly he was in foreign territory, *terra incognita*, way outside the easy Cartesian grid of Manhattan. The streets were leafier, with a ginkgo or some other hardy urban flora planted every twenty yards, and dirtier.

When he finally found Margaret's building, he had another problem: She wasn't in it. He rang her bell for a good five minutes with no answer. It was mid-afternoon. The strolling mommies and elderly stoop-sitters scrutinized him, then looked away when he looked back. Staring up at what he assumed to be her window, Edward felt anger infecting his sunny post-recovery mood. How dare she disappear on him now! Was she just going to cut him off like this? Was she even in town? Had she lost interest in the codex? Or had she left him behind to go off on her own, pursuing some more promising lead?

In the end he wedged a note under her door and got back on the train. Somewhere around Soho he

293

realized he was ravenous – he hadn't had a real meal in days – so he got out and ate a huge late-afternoon lunch sitting at the counter in a cheap Japanese diner in Chinatown. He watched as a short, wide man with a shaved head and strangler's arms cooked dumplings in a frying pan the size of a manhole cover. He thought about Zeph and Caroline – he'd been ignoring their calls the way Margaret was ignoring his. He called Margaret on his cell phone, but she didn't answer. The hell with her, he thought. He was having a fine old time without her. He called Zeph and Caroline, but they didn't answer, and that was fine, too. He didn't feel like talking. Talking would just lead to explanations, and discussions, and sober evaluations, and stock-taking, and other things he wasn't in the mood for.

By that time it was getting dark, so he took the subway up to Union Square and saw a pointless action movie about CIA assassins. Then he stayed for another one about good-looking teenage surfers, and by the time he got out it was almost midnight. On his way back to the subway he stopped at a bar that was barely wider than its front door, with a cheap-looking papier-mâché dragon hanging from the ceiling, and ordered vodka gimlets – the favored drink of the CIA assassin from movie number one – until he was drunk. Then it was late and somehow he'd teleported onto the subway platform. A team of men and women in fluorescent vests hosed down the platform, and the air smelled comfortably of warm, soapy water. A blind Chinese woman picked out 'The Girl from Ipanema' on a hammered dulcimer. A gray pigeon floated by weaving hopelessly between the pillars, a lost soul trapped in the underworld.

Tomorrow Margaret will call, Edward thought. Tomorrow I'll get back on track. Staring dreamily at the lights that glittered far down in the subway tunnel, he felt like he was gazing into the secret, jeweled interior of the earth.

But Margaret didn't call, and Edward didn't get back on track. Instead he spent five thousand dollars on an expensive laptop, a tiny technological masterpiece: black, wicked-looking, nearly weightless, and so thin it seemed almost occult – it felt like it was constructed out of the chitin of some monstrous black tropical beetle. He bought a high-tech laptop case for it, too, made of black synthetic gel-filled fabric, and he started carrying it around with him. Its function, as he saw it, was to maximize the efficient use of his increasingly abundant free time. Whenever he had the urge – in a café, on the subway, sitting on a park bench – he would crack it open, boot it up, and play MOMUS.

After a certain point, though, he got stuck. Times had changed since his days as a high-flying buccaneer of the jetstream. The cooling of the earth continued, and with it yet another age had arrived, an ice age. A secondary phenomenon was accelerating the process, too. In the sky, next to the sun,

hung a ghostly circle. It was almost transparent –
it was visible only along its round edge, which was
defined by a slight but definite distortion in the
air. As Edward watched, the disk's edge touched
the edge of the sun and began to pass over it. The
disk was slowly eclipsing it, sliding into place on
top of it like a contact lens over an eye. The portion
of the sun that it covered was whiter, paler, colder,
less painful to look at.

The genteel man reappeared.

'It's the aliens,' he explained matter-of-factly.
'They're covering the sun with a special lens. To
accelerate the cooling,' he added helpfully.

From then on the sunlight changed, became
colder and grayer. Clouds rushed in, low and white,
and the temperature dropped. Light, powdery
snow began sifting down from the sky. The humans
now eked out an existence among the cold ruins
of New York, which had survived improbably intact
during the millennia the city spent under sand and
water. Civilization had fallen good and hard, and
it wasn't getting up.

Edward's role in the game had become less that
of a military leader and more that of a mayor, or
a tribal chieftain. The humans who inhabited the
New York of the future weren't concerned with
resisting an alien invasion. They were concerned
with staying alive on a day-to-day basis. They lived
underground in the subway stations, where it
was warmer and they were safer from predators.
His job was resource management: finding food,

collecting firewood, building tools, salvaging supplies from office buildings. He micromanaged, breaking out the spreadsheets and the actuarial tables. It was almost like his old job. As he played he manically hummed the theme from an old animated Christmas special:

> *Friends call me Snowmeiser*
> *Whatever I touch*
> *Turns to snow in my clutch—*
> *I'm too much!*

Edward would stay up all night playing MOMUS and finally force himself to quit at eight in the morning, in broad daylight, with morning rush hour in full swing under his window. If he could have billed the hours he spent playing MOMUS, he thought, he'd be a millionaire ten times over. When he finally closed his eyes he saw the game on the insides of his eyelids, and when he finally fell asleep he dreamed about it.

Life in the game mimicked the bleakness of his real life. Wolves had returned from wherever they'd been living during happier times, and now they prowled the streets in search of the old and feeble, pink tongues dangling from gray muzzles. Icebergs as tall as skyscrapers crowded into New York Harbor. In Central Park the ground was hard as iron and streaked with light, powdery snow. The only color was the trace of blue that showed through where the snow had formed low drifts, which the wind blew into the shape of breaking waves. Edward knew where he was now, knew it with a bizarre, delusional certainty. He was in Cimmeria.

CHAPTER 17

Edward's phone rang, and messages were left, but never by Margaret. He'd called her often enough now that it was pointless to call her again, but he couldn't think of anything else to do. Her phone numbers (he'd managed to pry an office number for her out of a stuttering secretary at Columbia) felt like his sole connection to anything that mattered. He was feeling the pull of the codex again, more than ever, and he needed her to find it, and he missed her, too. Was she embarrassed by what happened at the library? Angry? Ashamed? At this point he didn't care, he just wanted an answer.

He was sitting on his couch noodling aimlessly on a guitar he'd never learned to play when the phone rang again. His answering machine picked up.

It wasn't Margaret. The voice was clear, sensuously sweet, and oddly ageless, neither young nor old. He snapped awake, and every nerve in his body fired at once. It belonged, unmistakably, to the Duchess of Bowmry. It seemed like the first real sound he'd heard in weeks.

The Duchess seemed nonplussed – she didn't

seem to really understand that the answering machine wasn't a human being. He picked up.

'Edward,' she said, flustered. 'You're there.'

'Yes.' He was wearing only his boxers, and he looked around for some pants to put on. It seemed wrong to address her while looking down at his pale, bristly legs. 'Uh, Your Grace,' he added.

'You don't have to call me that, you know. Peter insists on it, but I never got used to it. Growing up I was just a baroness.'

He sat back down, still in his underwear.

'So – Baroness Blanche?'

'I was called Lady Blanche.'

He waited for some clue as to what she wanted, but nothing came.

'So are you a baroness of . . . somewhere in particular?' he hazarded. 'Or just a baroness? I mean, not that you could ever be *just* a baroness—?'

'Of Feldingswether,' she said. 'It's a horrible little place. I never visit. They make tennis rackets there, the whole town smells like varnish.'

'So how did that work when you got married? I mean, if you don't mind my asking. Did you have to give up being Baroness of—?'

'Of Feldingswether? Not at all.' She laughed. 'One person can hold more than one title, thank God, so I'm Baroness of Feldingswether in my own right and Duchess of Bowmry by courtesy.'

'And so is your husband the Baron of Feldingswether by courtesy?' Edward asked, mani-

300

cally following the logic to its bitter end. He didn't seem to be able to shut up.

'Certainly not!' she said triumphantly. 'Men don't automatically assume their wives' titles the way women do. That's why if you marry a king you're a queen, but the husband of the queen of England gets fobbed off with some silly little title like "prince consort". Anyway, it's all very complicated.'

'So what should I call you?'

'Call me Blanche,' she said. 'It's what my friends call me.'

Edward did. To his surprise he and the Duchess had a long, meandering, fairly pleasant, and utterly ordinary conversation. He could hardly believe it was happening. She could have been a friendly aunt – affable, voluble, slightly flirtatious, a world-class conversationalist, obviously the product of centuries of breeding and decades of training. True, there was a slightly manic quality to her speech, but at least it had the advantage of making up for any awkwardness on his part. She had obviously set out to charm him, and even if the gesture felt a little forced, he wasn't in any position to put up a fight. Before he knew it he was explaining about his job, about his vacation, about his plans for the future, such as they were, and she had the gift of making it all seem improbably fascinating. It was a relief to talk to somebody who – unlike, say, Margaret – knew how to make him feel paid attention to for a change. And so what if she was an enigmatic foreign plutocrat?

She steered the talk around to Edward's upcoming move to London, to the vagaries of air travel, the various neighborhoods he might consider living in, the relative advantages and disadvantages of country life over life in the city, and so on and so forth. She told a long and actually fairly humorous story about renovating an ancient garderobe at Weymarshe. In the background Edward heard the *yip yip* of a tiny dog jumping up and down for attention.

Inevitably they came around to the subject of the codex. He told her the story of his and Margaret's trip to the Chenoweth Annex, and their disappointment there – leaving out the part about his close encounter with the Duke's driver. She sighed.

'I sometimes wonder if it's real.' The Duchess sounded tired. 'The *Viage*, that is. It was once, I feel sure, but do you think the poor thing has really survived all this time? Books can die so many ways, they're like people that way. Though they remind me of mollusks, too – hard on the outside, but with those delicate articulated innards . . .'

She sighed again.

'This is going very badly, Edward. We're running out of time.'

'I don't know what to tell you.' Edward could hear the concern in her voice, and he imagined her pale brow furrowing. 'We've pretty much exhausted all our leads.'

'What about Margaret? She sounds very clever.'

'She is. But she . . . I don't know where she is. I haven't heard from her in days.'

'What's she like?' A hint of something – could it possibly be jealousy? – crept into her voice. 'Can we trust her? I just love the *idea* of her – she sounds like a cross between Stephen Hawking and Nancy Drew.'

'She's a hard person to read.' Edward felt guilty talking about Margaret behind her back, but really, why not? What did he owe Margaret, anyway? 'She's very serious. Very earnest. A little strange. But she's read practically everything anybody's ever written about anything.'

'She sounds intimidating.'

'She is. She makes me feel like a complete idiot, to tell you the truth. But it's not her fault. She can't help it if I'm ignorant.'

'Don't be silly. You're not ignorant at all.'

'Well,' he finished up haplessly, 'maybe you'll meet her someday.'

'Well, I hope I will,' the Duchess said graciously. 'Is she coming with you when you come to England?'

'I don't know. At least, I don't think so.' The idea had never even occurred to him. 'She has her own work to do here. I could never drag her away from that.'

'But you would if you could, wouldn't you?'

'You mean, bring her with me?' He balked. 'I don't think so. I mean, I wouldn't want to assume—'

He broke off, flustered. The Duchess laughed.

'I'm teasing you, Edward!' she said. 'You're much too serious! You do know that about yourself, don't you? You're much, much too serious.'

'If you say so,' he said, chagrined. He felt like he needed to turn the conversation around, regain the initiative. 'Blanche, why doesn't your husband want me to look for the codex?'

There was a long pause.

'He said that?' She sounded distracted – maybe it was the little dog's turn to bask in her attention. He sensed that he'd broken an unspoken rule, that their temporary rapport was fragile and could disappear in an instant. 'Well, I'm sure he didn't mean anything by it. So you talked to him, did you?'

'No, of course not! It came through Laura. But why don't you want him to know I'm looking for it?'

'Look, I appreciate your concern, Edmund—'

'Edward. Good, because—'

'And if at any point you feel that you'd rather not be involved with this project, you're free to go, as long as you agree to keep the substance of our dealings confidential.' She spoke in a warm, full, obtrusively generous tone, a warning tone, and he could tell her impersonal manner was meant to wound him. The friendly aunt was suddenly far away. 'But as long as you're working for me, you'll do so on my terms. I have a lot of other irons in the fire right now, Edward. I have resources beyond anything you know about. You're not the only one looking for the codex, you know. You're a very small part of this.'

Edward hesitated. He wondered if it was true, that she had other people like him working for her. He strongly suspected that it wasn't, that the Duchess was bluffing him, but that was almost beside the point. She was testing him, ascertaining to a precise tolerance how much of her bullshit he was willing to put up with, and how little information he could get by on before he balked. And he realized to his dismay that he hadn't reached his limit.

Once he apologized the Duchess reverted to her cheery, unaffected manner, and he sensed her starting to steer the conversation toward a graceful ending. They talked for five or ten minutes more. She showed him her flirtatious side again. He must call her when he came to London. They must meet. It would be wonderful. She had a few thoughts about where to look for the codex – she would send him a letter. He was almost embarrassed by how easily he succumbed to her wiles, giving himself up to the blissful illusion that they could trust one another. He found himself admitting that he was already supposed to be in London, that in fact his job was already supposed to have started, and she laughed as if that was the most hilarious thing she'd ever heard.

'I was wrong about you,' she said, when she recovered her composure. 'Maybe you aren't too serious after all.'

'Maybe I'm not serious enough,' Edward countered.

'Well, I don't know,' said the Duchess. 'But it can't be both. I should think it would be either one or the other, as a matter of logical principle.'

He sensed that she was getting ready to hang up, but he couldn't let her go, not yet. Not before she gave him something more.

'Blanche,' he said gravely. 'I need to know something. Why did you ask me to help you find the codex? Why me and not somebody else?'

He expected her to snap at him again, but she just smiled instead – he could hear it in her voice – and suddenly he suspected that he was treading dangerously close to something he didn't want to know.

'Because I know I can trust you, Edward,' she said, her voice low and thrilling over the phone line.

'But why? Because of that deal I did for you, at Esslin & Hart? The one with the silver futures? And the insurance company?' He was grasping at straws now.

'No, Edward. It was—' She hesitated. 'Well, that was the reason at first. Peter wanted you. But when I saw you that day, I knew you could help me. I could see it in your face. I just knew I could trust you.'

Edward was silent. That's it? he thought. Was she making fun of him? Was she trying to seduce him? Was she insane? What kind of a fool did she take him for? It had been a serious question, and he dearly wished she had a better answer for him. Her answer made him want to hang up the phone, badly.

Was she really so alone, so helpless, that she had nobody else to turn to but him? A twentysomething banker she hardly knew? She must be completely cut off from the world outside Weymarshe, he thought. She put a brave face on it, but she must be utterly isolated. There was nobody else to help her.

Sitting on his couch, staring up at the ceiling in his apartment, Edward felt a pang of real fear.

Whatever spell he'd been under, the sound of the Duchess's voice had broken it, and time began ticking forward again. Suddenly the game was back on. Seconds after they hung up, before Edward even had a chance to put the phone down, it rang in his hand. It was Fabrikant: He wanted to meet again, another breakfast at the Four Seasons. Edward temporized – they could at least make it a beer after work, for God's sake, something at a reasonable hour – but Fabrikant pleaded a tight schedule, and Edward gave in. After all, their last meeting had been informative. Maybe Fabrikant had a few more scraps he wanted to throw Edward's way. They agreed to meet tomorrow morning, a Thursday. Edward hung up and took a deep breath. He eyed the phone warily, but it didn't ring again.

The next day he woke up early. It took him longer than expected to deal with the wispy beard that had somehow sprung up in the mirror, and even longer to tear himself away from an early-morning MOMUS session – hey, his tribe needed him, he had mouths to feed. He got to the Four Seasons ten minutes late. The host eyed him frostily, as if he could see right through him, sense that he didn't really belong there anymore. Instead of showing him to a table he led Edward to a padded leather door at the back of the dining room and through it into a private room.

Fabrikant was waiting there, but he wasn't alone. Sitting on either side of him were a woman in a gray Armani suit, dark-haired and frowning, and a man about Edward's age in a rumpled tweed sport jacket, with long, floppy blond bangs that fell over his forehead. All three looked up when he came in, and Edward had the distinct impression that an awkward silence had been in progress before he opened the door. A pitcher of pulpy orange juice and a plate of pastries stood on the ivory tablecloth, untouched. Fabrikant nodded at him. To Edward's surprise, he looked uncomfortable. He didn't think anything was capable of penetrating Fabrikant's sunny sense of personal perfection, but apparently something had.

'Edward,' said the man with the tweed jacket, smiling warmly and sliding a business card across the table. He had a plummy, well-educated English accent – he was almost a parody of the well-put-together Oxbridge graduate. 'Nick Harris. I'm here to represent the interests of the Duke of Bowmry.'

Edward sat down at the table, leaving the business card where it was. So the Duke was intervening directly now. Well, it was about time; it was almost surprising that he hadn't done it already. Edward looked over at Fabrikant, but Fabrikant just stared back blankly. No help there.

Edward cleared his throat.

'So,' he said. 'You work for the Duke.'

'We've worked together in the past. He asked me to meet with you on his behalf.'

Nick reached into a pocket on his vest, took out a round golden pocket watch on a fob, consulted it, and put it back. The gesture was so ridiculously affected that Edward thought it might be a joke, but nobody laughed. A waiter came in and silently laid place settings for the extra guests.

'Are you in his New York office?'

'In a manner of speaking.' Nick smiled at him, friendly but sober, a concerned parent. 'Edward, I don't want to mince words. We have reason to believe that you're in contact with the Duke's wife.' He held up a hand as if to cut him off, even though Edward wasn't trying to say anything. 'Please don't confirm or deny this. That would only complicate matters for you from a legal standpoint—'

'Of course I'm in contact with the Duke's wife,' Edward said. 'She called me just yesterday. How could that could possibly be a legal matter?'

'Oh, believe me, it isn't. For the moment. Although you should know that if such contact continues, we are prepared to seek a restraining order, in both countries.'

'This isn't to frighten you, Edward,' the woman added gently, speaking for the first time. She was an American. 'But it is meant to show you how serious the Duke is about preserving his wife's safety.'

Edward sighed. So they were going to patronize him. He'd forgotten how much he hated businesspeople. His corporate infighting reflexes, which had lain dormant for the past three weeks, began to reawaken themselves.

'All right. You're suggesting that I pose some kind of a threat to the Duchess. Let's talk about that.'

'Not a threat in the sense that you mean,' Nick said, unfazed. 'But you are a threat, though you may not know it.'

'Look, I'm running a little late,' Edward said, the soul of fake politeness, 'and Joseph and I have a lot to talk about. Why don't you tell me what you need from me and we can all get out of here.'

Nick and the woman exchanged glances. They were both such obvious lightweights, so obviously ill-equipped for rough-and-tumble negotiating, that Edward didn't feel especially nervous. This could even be fun. He rolled his eyes conspiratorially at Fabrikant, who glanced at Nick and shook his head nervously. Meanwhile Nick frowned and steepled his fingers on the white tablecloth, like a news anchor preparing to introduce a touching human interest story.

'I think we're all aware of the supposed existence of a book supposedly written by one Gervase of Langford. None of us knows its exact location, or whether or not it actually does exist. Always assuming, that is, that you don't.' He glanced pointedly at Edward.

'Right. Sure.' Despite himself Edward admired the perfect way Nick's blond hair fell over his forehead.

'The Duke has asked you to stop searching for it. We don't think you have. And why should you? Maybe you feel a sense of allegiance to the Duchess. You're on her side, and you want to carry out her wishes. Maybe you sympathize with her for personal reasons. Certainly you have no reason, no particular reason, to feel any loyalty toward the Duke. All this is perfectly understandable. But I think if I tell you a little more about what's been going on at Weymarshe you might feel differently.'

'I'm all ears,' Edward said pleasantly. He sat back and folded his arms. He couldn't deny that Nick had piqued his curiosity a little, and he wanted to keep him talking. Fabrikant silently crumbled a danish onto his plate.

'Has the Duchess told you why she's looking for the *Viage*? No? The Duchess is looking for the *Viage* because she believes it is a steganogram.' Nick pronounced the unfamiliar word crisply. 'I don't expect you to know what that means, so I'll explain it. "Steganogram" is a technical term from the field of cryptanalysis. It refers to a message that has been encoded in such a way as to conceal or camouflage the presence of the encoded message itself. In other words, not only can you not read the message that a steganogram contains, you cannot tell that the message is there at all. It's woven into the very fabric of the medium onto which it is inscribed in such a way as to be indistinguishable from that medium itself.'

'Like that cartoonist,' Edward volunteered. 'The one who put "NINA" in all his pictures.'

'Just so. In the case of the codex, the coded message might be incorporated into the text of the book, or into the illustrations, or the watermarks, or the binding, or the choice of materials, or the recipe of ingredients used to make the ink in which it was written. We have no way of knowing. Only a person who knew exactly where and how the message was encrypted would be able to find it, and even then they might not be able to decipher its contents.'

'So what does this message say?' Edward asked.

'There is no message,' Nick said, suddenly stern. 'There is no message, and there is, in all likelihood, no codex. Gervase of Langford, servant to an unfashionable fourteenth-century country squire, did not compose a fantastical work of literature containing an encrypted message which has since then been lost to history. The Duchess has concocted a fantasy, a fantasy based on very little evidence and some very strong emotions, and in which, I am sorry to say, she has involved you. I must tell you, Edward – and this is in confidence – that the Duchess is not entirely sane. I say this with all due compassion, but she is unstable, and she has become emotionally attached to the idea of the codex in a way that is very unhealthy. And although you may be acting with the very best of intentions, you're not doing her any favors by encouraging her.'

Edward kept his face as blank as possible. He wondered if he should just get up and walk out, but something stopped him. It couldn't possibly be true – it was too bizarre, too convoluted, like something out of a spy thriller. Occam's razor just wouldn't allow it. Granted, there was something a little odd about the Duchess – the manic edge in her speech, the way her moods changed a little too rapidly from moment to moment – but he couldn't believe she was really insane. The codex was real. He could almost feel it, like a compass sensing magnetic north from half a world away. It was out there. He had to talk to Margaret. Margaret would know what to believe.

The real question was, why was this ridiculous fop sitting across from him at the Four Seasons chattering away about steganograms? He was trying to discredit the Duchess in his eyes, but why? The whole situation was spinning out of control, getting too complicated to analyze on the fly. He needed time to think. He pulled himself together with an effort.

'Back up,' he said. 'Why does the Duchess want

the codex? What does she think is in this secret message?'

'The specifics there don't matter,' said the woman. 'Let's just say it's something that would be very, very hurtful to the Duke.'

'Like what?'

They looked at each other again.

'It's not the kind of thing one discusses in polite company.'

'Oh, for Christ's sake,' Fabrikant said disgustedly, breaking his silence. 'Spit it out.'

'You'll remember I asked you not to contribute to this meeting,' Nick said.

'I don't work for you,' Fabrikant replied calmly.

'Let's just say that it's something that would be very embarrassing to all concerned,' the woman continued. 'Something that could be very damaging to the fortunes of a great man, a man who deserves better. And to the reputation of a prominent English peerage.'

'I don't get it,' said Edward. 'If it's so terrible, why would she want to find it?'

'Because she hates him!' said Fabrikant. He chuckled hollowly, and Nick glared at him. 'Don't you get it? He's an asshole, and she can't stand him!'

He stood up abruptly.

'I apologize for this, Edward, I really do. I was blindsided – the Duke's participation in my company gives them leverage over me. They told me to set it up, and I did, but I'm not—'

'That's enough,' said Nick.

314

'She's going to ruin him, Edward. If she finds the codex. He'll lose everything he has—'

'That's enough!' Nick's peaches-and-cream complexion flushed red. 'You're through, Fabrikant. Done. Got it? We're out. No more.'

Fabrikant looked at both of them, nodding lightly, his chin hardly dipping. Slowly, with incongruous delicacy, he refolded his white napkin on the tablecloth. Edward thought he looked a little pale, and he moved with the precarious dignity of a man in a Western who'd been shot in the gut but refused to give his enemies the satisfaction of seeing him fall down. Edward watched him go helplessly. As he left the room he tried to slam the door behind him, but the leather-paneled door had been carefully engineered to make no noise whatsoever when it closed.

Nick rebuttoned his blazer and sat down. The woman acted as if nothing had happened, and Edward did likewise. With Fabrikant gone the whole scene suddenly seemed much less funny. He wanted to get it over with.

'So the codex is – what? Some kind of tabloid bombshell, waiting to go off?'

'The codex is an absurd fantasy,' Nick said patiently, as if he were speaking to a child. 'A fantasy conceived by a very fine woman who is very sadly no longer herself. How can I make that any clearer to you? Believe me, the Duke has nothing but the Duchess's best interests at heart. All we ask is that you stop communicating with her immediately. Do you see, now, how important that is?'

Edward hesitated. Should he just play along?

'Don't you see what this is doing to her?' Nick's partner said contemptuously. Her elegant eyebrows made an angry, accusing V. 'Everything you say feeds into her delusions. You're just making it worse.'

Edward nodded vaguely, but he was hardly listening anymore. His mind was elsewhere. What were they going to do, tap his phone? Why wouldn't they just leave him alone? The truth was, he was having trouble connecting to any of this – the whole scene seemed so staged, it was getting more and more like a cheap paperback mystery novel every minute. Well, if he was the gumshoe, it was going to take more than Sir Goldilocks here to shake him off the case.

'All right,' he said finally. He sighed. 'Whatever. I promise I won't contact her.'

He could say that – after all, he'd never actually called the Duchess. She'd only ever called him. He wouldn't have known how to reach her anyway.

'All right then,' said Nick. The woman stood up. 'All right.'

She held out her hand in an awkward, conciliatory gesture. Edward shook it. Order was restored. Against all odds, the meeting finally seemed to be over.

'So where does the Duke keep his offices in the city?' he asked Nick collegially.

'I wouldn't know,' said Nick. The woman – he'd never gotten her name – took care of the check. 'I've never been there. I'm sort of a consultant for him. It's a flexible arrangement. I spent most of my time over at E & H.'

'At—' He must have heard wrong. 'You mean at Esslin & Hart.'

'That's right,' said Nick, his accent sounding just like a foreign correspondent for the BBC, reporting live from Ouagadougou. 'What, didn't they tell you?' He grinned. 'I used to be in the London office. I'm the fellow they sent here to take your place.'

That evening, back in his apartment, Edward was staring at his computer screen as usual. But this time Zeph stared at it with him. Zeph sat in Edward's office chair, and Edward watched over his shoulder.

'Dude,' Zeph said. 'This is unbelievable.'

'I know.'

'No, I mean it's really fucking incredible.' His face was a mask of shock and outrage. 'Really! I mean I literally cannot believe it!'

'I don't know how to explain it.'

'Neither do I!'

Zeph prodded halfheartedly at the controls, rotating the point of view back and forth. Even Edward, who was looking for something to distract him from the storm of complications that had descended on him that afternoon, was sick of looking at it. He had decisions to make, hard ones, and soon, but instead he stared at the monitor. What he saw, when he could bring himself to look, was the same thing he'd been staring at futilely for the past week: the broken-down encampment of the tribe he was supposed to be leading. Snow filtered down from street level through sidewalk grates and melted on the cement platform where his fellow humans sat disconsolately awaiting his orders. A smoky fire built with wooden subway ties burned sullenly down on the tracks. It was a flat little world in a box, a pitiful, pixilated simulacrum of three dimensions.

'How could you have let this happen?' Zeph said reproachfully. He was growing a beard, sparse and curly, which made him look even more ogreish than usual. 'This is the most pathetic spectacle of incompetence I have ever witnessed in the context of a computer game. And believe me I've seen a few. You should be ashamed of yourself.'

'I am ashamed of myself.'

'You shouldn't even be here!' Zeph went on. He smacked his enormous thighs with both hands. 'Since I gave you this copy I've won MOMUS three times – once on each difficulty level! Let me explain something to you: You should have bases on the moon by now. You should be mining the comets and having sex with alien babes.' He was so upset he was spluttering. 'You should have a satellite-based planetary defense system! You should be on the offensive! Instead it's like *Clan of the Cave Bear* in here.' He shook his head sadly. 'This is over. It's just fucking over.'

'Good. I want it to be over.'

Zeph was right. He hadn't been paying attention. He'd made mistakes, he'd missed his cues, and now it was too late to fix them. He never paid close enough attention when it mattered. What clues was he missing right now?

'It's been like this from the beginning,' Edward knew he sounded petulant, but he didn't care anymore. 'I didn't have any weapons, or I didn't have the right ones, or I didn't know where they were, or who to use them on, and when I finally got there it was too late, everybody was gone, and the aliens were off blowing up something else, or messing up time, or God knows what! Now even the other humans are beating on me.' He ran his hands through his hair. 'Plus there's this whole thing with the sun.'

Zeph's eyes went wide with horror.

'You let them fuck with the *sun*?'

'Look for yourself.'

Edward reached past him to the keyboard and guided his character up the stairs and outside. He pointed his gaze upward: The weakened sun, behind the alien lens, was streaming down its empty, heatless rays. While they watched it a band of feral humans from another tribe came by and killed him. He fell down backward onto the snow, bleeding but still looking up at the sky.

'For fuck's sake,' said Zeph. 'I've never seen that before.'

'Why else do you think it's so cold?'

Zeph pushed himself back, stood up, and strolled over to the windows with an expression of enormous gravity on his face, his hands clasped behind his back like an emergency room doctor facing the greatest diagnostic challenge of his career. It was late in the evening, and the apartment was dark.

'How did you get here?' he said after a while. 'Tell me from the beginning.'

Edward described the opening scenes of the game. Zeph listened carefully, then held up a hand to stop him.

'So you didn't get the letter that was in the mailbox? You didn't save the bridge?'

'No, I didn't save the goddamned bridge. How could I have saved the bridge?'

'You were supposed to be under the bridge. Killing the goddamned munitions expert.'

'What munitions expert? What are you talking about? How could I have killed a munitions expert?'

'With the pistol,' said Zeph. He shook his head. 'It was all supposed to fit together, like clockwork. But forget it. Forget it, I can't even explain it. You fucked it up from the beginning. You never had a chance.'

They were both silent for a while. Edward had a couple of strategically placed fans going, but even at night it was still oppressively hot. The summer air smelled damp and heavy, as if it had already been breathed by eight million other Manhattanites in turn. He went to the kitchen and came back with a bottle of scotch and two tumblers with ice in them.

Zeph accepted a glass.

'Don't feel too bad,' he said, jingling his ice philosophically. He sank into an armchair. 'It's like this one time, when I was right on the verge of conquering medieval Japan. But this one *daimyo*, he built a land bridge across – actually, it's easier if I draw it for you—'

'Zeph.' Edward kept his voice steady with an effort. 'Try to focus. I don't care about medieval Japan. Just tell me how to win MOMUS.'

'I don't know if you can. In fact, offhand I'd say you were totally and permanently fucked, except for one thing: The game should have ended already. A long time ago. By rights it should have just stopped.'

Zeph rubbed his large, woolly chin thoughtfully.

'Okay,' Edward said sulkily. 'So what?'

'Don't you see? Somebody bothered to code this whole elaborate scenario you're playing through. Why? Usually by now, when it's this hopeless, you'd have gotten to the point where your character flops down dead and a voice intones, "Mortal, you have failed!" or something to that effect. Instead somebody deliberately created all this stuff you're seeing – all these elaborate maps and textures and backgrounds and sound effects. They scripted it all out in advance. Why, when it's all so useless?'

'I don't know. Unless there actually still is a way to win from here.'

'Exactly.' Zeph finished his scotch, stood up, and clapped Edward on the shoulder. 'Exactly. It's not over, my friend. Not by a long chalk, as your English associates would say. There's a story here, a plot that's been laid out, which means there must be some way to finish it. But you need help, help that I can't give you. There's somebody you have to go see.'

'Who?'

'You can't call him. He doesn't have a phone. His apartment only has data lines.'

'I'll e-mail him.'

'He won't accept it. Your crypto isn't good enough. You'll have to go see him in person.'

'I don't know, you're not making him sound like that sociable of a guy.'

Zeph shrugged.

'It's your choice. But he's your only chance. He knows as much about MOMUS as anybody I can think of. He's part of the online collective that manages its code base. He moderates the MOMUS newsgroup. As far as I can tell he even wrote most of the graphics engine himself. You have a pen?'

Edward gave him a pen. Zeph looked around for a piece of paper, then took a cheap science fiction paperback out of his back pocket and ripped out one of the endpapers. He wrote out an address on the Lower East Side in block capital letters, along with a name: ALBERTO HIDALGO.

Then he paused, pen poised fatefully over the page, as if he were contemplating an additional last-minute revision.

'I think you've met him, actually.'

CHAPTER 18

That night Edward received a letter from the Duchess.

He found it when he went to walk Zeph to the subway, a cardboard FedEx envelope strapped to his mailbox with thick red rubber bands. Well, she had said she was going to write him, but he hadn't actually been expecting anything. He didn't open it right away, instead he saved it until he was sitting up in bed with the envelope in his lap, balanced on his knees. Inside were several pieces of stiff, expensive white paper, foolscap, covered with writing in dark blue fountain-pen ink. The handwriting was large and feminine, written rapidly, with many extravagant swoops and loops and a few blots, but still quite legible.

The paper was letterhead from Weymarshe. At the top was a shield with a single thick-trunked tree letterpressed on it in black ink, no motto. Their coat of arms? he thought, Or their seal, or whatever it's called? Somehow it looked familiar. He must have seen it before, months ago, when he'd worked on their account for Esslin & Hart. Underneath it were the words WEYMARSHE CASTLE in a clean, classic sans serif font. He reflected that as time went by the Duchess seemed to be receding away from him instead of getting closer. First he'd met her in person, then he'd heard her voice on the phone, and now she'd dwindled away into handwritten words on the page.

There was no salutation at the beginning of the letter, or even a date. The writing just started at the top of the page.

Edward was coming home from a long day of work.

He frowned. That wasn't quite what he'd expected. He bowed open the envelope to see if there was another page in there that he'd missed, but it was empty. He sorted through the pages, to see if he'd somehow gotten them out of order. But no – in fact they were numbered, and this was page one.

He read on.

Edward worked for a large financial firm in Manhattan, in New York City, in the state of New York, in the United States of America. He was tall and handsome and his hair was dark. It was almost ten o'clock in the evening, and he was very tired. He strolled along the sidewalk by Central Park gazing up at the sky.

He was feeling sorry for himself. He was very

successful, and at the early age of twenty-five he was well on his way to acquiring a sizable personal fortune, but he had to work very very hard to do it, and after a long day of listening to difficult clients and studying patterns in the market and that sort of thing he sometimes found himself wondering whether or not it was really all worthwhile.

It was summertime, and moderately warm out, but there was something strange about the weather. A warm wind was blowing, and there was a kind of indescribable sort of electrical feeling in the air. A storm was coming on.

Edward felt something strike him lightly between the shoulder blades. He turned around to see what it was. It was a sheet of paper blown along by the wind.

A beautiful dark-haired woman was running toward him along the street. She was no longer in her first youth, perhaps older than him by more than a few years, but she was still possessed of a mature and really rather bewitching loveliness. She wasn't really running, more taking little girlish steps as rapidly as she could, which was all she could manage in her long skirt. She carried a leather portfolio, and it had somehow come open, and the wind had taken the papers that were inside and scattered them all up and down the street. Now she was trying to gather them up again, with the assistance of a small man in dark livery who followed along after her.

'Help!' she cried. 'Please, my papers!'

Edward joined in the chase, and the three of them dashed about madly after the flying sheets, which filled the warm summer air like autumn leaves. The street was empty, and Edward darted out into the middle of it, nimbly snatching the pages out of the air and tucking them under his arm. His tiredness vanished. The exercise felt good. It was a relief to run around and stretch his long legs after a day spent with them tucked under a cramped little desk.

After a few minutes they had caught all the pages. Panting, Edward brought his bundle back to the beautiful woman like a faithful hound delivering a fallen duck.

'Thanks ever so much!' she said. She was breathing hard too. 'I don't know what I would have done without you!'

'It was nothing.'

'Now please,' she said, putting her hand on his arm, 'let me ask you one more favor. Take me back to my hotel.'

Edward hesitated.

'All right,' he stammered. 'I mean, if—'

'Please!' She gripped his arm with her tiny hand. It was cold, and surprisingly strong. 'I am not well! I really am not myself tonight!'

He looked into her eyes. They did seem unusually bright, and her face, though lovely, was worryingly pale against her dark hair.

Edward got up and tossed the rest of the pages onto the comforter. What the hell was this? What the hell kind of game was she playing? He went into the kitchen to get himself a glass of water. He'd had another glass of scotch after Zeph left, probably a mistake, and now he could feel a headache coming on. He drank a tumbler of luke-warm tap water, then another. Then back to bed with just one more scotch.

She wasn't making it easy on him, he thought. Was she crazy? Was it a prank? Some kind of elaborate joke? If so, he didn't get it. Could it really be from the Duchess? The Duke's people had tried to make him doubt her sanity; this could be more of the same, a forgery planted in his mailbox. But somehow he doubted it. It had a genuine feel to it.

But what did it mean? Was it supposed to be some kind of fantasy? And if so, was it supposed to be his, or hers? Was it a novel-in-progress? Some kind of coded message, designed to foil an eaves-dropping reader? He tried to remember what Nick had said about steganograms. If there was a hidden meaning here, he couldn't see it. Maybe she really wasn't all there.

Or did it make a deeper kind of sense? Maybe he just wasn't looking hard enough. Something about the letter chilled him, even through the summer heat.

The small man in livery took away the port-folio, now stuffed full of papers, and returned a minute later driving a limousine. He opened the door for the woman, and Edward followed her into the dark interior of the car. It was silent there, and it smelled of sweet tobacco and leather. The summer night outside was murky behind the smoked glass. The limousine slid smoothly and silently through the city, like a gondola along a Venetian canal, a dark, sheltered canal deep in the heart of San Marco. They were there together.

'What's your name?' Edward inquired politely.

'Blanche. What's yours?'

'I'm Edward. Edward Wintergreen.'

She said nothing more, just gripped his hand tightly, trembling a little in the darkness.

The driver took them swooping down through the park to the Plaza. He held the door open for them, and the mysterious Blanche led Edward out onto the carpeted sidewalk and into the foyer. He saw that she was very slender and dressed in the most glamorous and stylish clothes. She leaned on him as if it were all she could do to support herself, but at the same time she somehow hurried him along through the lobby with irresistible speed, with dark purpose, past the reception desk and the hotel bar with tinkly piano music in the background and down a plush red corridor like a throat. It was all a dream, the most wonderful, delightful, impossible dream. They entered an ornate cage elevator and the door crashed to behind them.

Instantly Blanche pressed herself against him. Her body was soft and warm and ripe, and he hungered for it. He put his arm around her, still awkwardly holding his briefcase with the other hand. His thigh slipped between her legs, and they kissed. It was heavenly.

Then the doors opened again, and she broke away and led him out into the hall.

'Now,' she called over her shoulder. 'You must come to my room and help me sort these papers. They are all out of order!'

'Out of order?' Edward said stupidly. His face was flushed. What could she possibly mean?

'Please!' she said. 'I must get them properly sorted!'

'But why?'

At the end of the hall she opened a door upholstered in red leather and went inside. He followed her.

Inside, the ceilings were twenty feet high, and the walls were hung with rich medieval tapestries. On one Edward could make out the woven shape of a riderless horse frozen in the agonies of battle, all rolling eyes and flared nostrils and bared white teeth. A vast, dark oriental rug spilled across the stone floor, woven with patterns that repeated themselves again and again, tinier and tinier, until they vanished altogether.

Moonlight and starlight flooded in together through high windows. The first drops of rain from the storm were just beginning to spatter against them. Now at last they were alone.

Blanche turned to Edward and took his head between both of her hands, standing on tiptoe to reach him.

'Now listen to me, Edward. The real world isn't nice like this. It's chaos, it's all out of order, just like my pages were. The whole world has been disbound, Edward, its pages scattered to the wind. It's your job to put them back in their proper order.'

She put her arms around his neck and whispered, her lips brushing against his ear:

'Now make love to me!'

CHAPTER 19

The next day Edward took a cab down to the Lower East Side. It let him off on the empty corner of Fifth Street and Avenue C, and he stood there for a minute looking through his pockets for the address Zeph gave him, which he had managed to misplace during the ride over. It was a Friday, mid-afternoon, and the sunlight was hard and white and bright, but the steel shutter was already down in front of the bodega on the corner. An amputated refrigerator door stood propped up against a parking meter. Rancid rainwater was pooled in the butter compartment.

Edward finally found the address wadded up in his back pocket. The paper it was written on was a cheap, pulpy off-white, already starting to go yellow with age. On the back was a sentence printed in bold type, all caps:

TO SAVE THE EARTH, FIRST HE MUST SAVE
ITS FIFTEEN DUPLICATES!!!

A van from a bakery rattled by, and the large technicolor painted loaf on the side reminded him wistfully of the bread the peasants were eating in his wheat field painting. A gust of wind blew up and pushed the dust around in the street. It was warm out, but there was the faintest hint of a chill in the air, so faint that it almost wasn't there at all. It reminded him that summer was almost over: Tomorrow was the first day of September. Time was passing.

The building was tall and thin and made of brown brick, a turn-of-the-century tenement that leaned visibly out over the street. Alberto Hidalgo's name appeared next to the topmost doorbell. All the other slots were blank. Edward rang the doorbell and waited.

Standing on the corner, surrounded by shattered crack vials and fluttering Slim Jim wrappers and multicolored dog shit, Edward heard the inaudible but unmistakable sound of his life hitting bottom. What was he doing here? Everything about the whole situation was wrong. Was it worth the effort to come all this way downtown, all the way to the edge of the known universe, just to get help with a computer game? No, it was not. But what else did he have to do? Margaret wasn't speaking to him. The Duchess was a question mark. The codex was more lost now than it had been before they'd exhausted their only lead in Old Forge. He was cut off from everything that mattered. It was time to go to England. He'd even taken the drastic step of booking himself a flight in a few days, but he knew he couldn't get on the plane. Not yet, not without the codex. Maybe if he ran as far as he could in the opposite direction he'd run into the codex coming the other way. And why did he know that name, Alberto Hidalgo? He leaned on the buzzer, half hoping that nobody would answer.

After a minute or two Edward noticed a small video camera staring down at him through a grimy pane of glass set in the door. He waved at it, and the lock buzzed.

He pushed his way inside. The staircase was narrow and steep. The ceiling was covered with old sheets of tin stamped with a repeating floral pattern and painted pale green. It was dark and silent as he walked up, his shoes rasping dryly on the worn marble steps. Now that he was inside he saw that the security system had a home-brewed look to it, as if it had been put together from parts ordered out of different catalogs. A pair of wires ran out of the camera, a power cord and an Ethernet cable stapled together into the angle between wall and ceiling, and he followed them up the stairs. They ran all the way up to the sixth and final landing.

One of the doors on the landing stood slightly ajar.

'Come in,' said a high, androgynous voice.

He did. The apartment was cool and dim, with a dropped ceiling. The walls were white. Light filtered in through windows almost completely blocked by tall, unsteady stacks of paperback books that let in only occasional chinks of white light.

The floor was covered with cheap shag carpet, pale blue and brand new-looking, littered with crumpled pieces of paper, ballpoint pens, brightly colored hardware catalogs, CD-ROMs, the colorful internal organs of several computers, and many, many empty orange bags of Jax. Alberto Hidalgo had tacked power strips along the walls, just above the floor, so there was an electrical outlet every few feet. Every single one of them was in use. Alberto himself sat at a long white IKEA desk with half a dozen monitors of various shapes and sizes lined up along it. Edward recognized him immediately.

'I know you,' Edward said.

'I know you, too,' the Artiste replied calmly.

It was the tiny man from Zeph's apartment and the LAN party. He was dressed as neatly as the room was messy, in a gray suit and a neatly knotted pink tie, like a kid dressed up for a bar mitzvah, except that his feet were bare. He was so small that they barely touched the floor.

Edward stood in the doorway, less sure than ever that he wanted to go ahead with this.

'Zeph told me you were coming,' the Artiste said. 'Please sit down.'

Edward picked his way over to a broken-down velvet couch against the opposite wall, feeling like a first-time visitor to a psychiatrist's office.

'Do you have your saved game with you?'

Edward nodded. He took a disc out of his shirt pocket and handed it to him. The Artiste slipped it into a massive, squat PC that sat under his desk giving off an audible hum.

'That's quite a machine you have there,' Edward said.

'It's a KryoTech,' the Artiste replied. He seemed perfectly at ease. 'They're faster than most off-the-shelf systems. It's built around a refrigeration unit that cools the microprocessor to around forty degrees below zero. Reduces the resistance in the silicon. At that temperature even a standard chip can be reliably overclocked to speeds much higher than factory spec. You don't see a lot of KryoTechs, though – they make a lot of noise, and they use a lot of power. They also weigh a ton. And they're expensive.'

The disk drive whirred as it read Edward's disc.

'Now,' he said. 'Let's see where you are.'

His hands hesitated for a moment, poised over the keyboard.

The Artiste typed faster than anybody Edward had ever seen. The individual clickings and clackings of the keys merged together into a single high whine. The massive monitor screen had ten or fifteen windows open on it and after a few seconds Edward's game appeared in one of them, shrunk down to the size of a postage stamp. The Artiste grabbed a corner of the window with his mouse and dragged it open until it covered most of the screen. He studied it critically.

'Uh-huh,' he said, with precisely the manner of

a radiologist examining an X-ray of a crushed spleen. 'Uh-huh. Uh-huh.'

He spun the point of view around 360 degrees. 'Huh.'

'What?'

'Well,' he said. 'This is certainly a fucked up situation you've gotten yourself into.'

A tiny, lopsided smile appeared on his face, then disappeared, then reappeared again – a secret joke. The Artiste suppressed a giggle. Edward got up and walked over to stand behind him. On the screen, large wet snowflakes sifted down out of the blank gray sky.

'What,' Edward said.

'I'm sorry.' The Artiste cleared his throat. 'Do you know what's going on here? You're trapped in an Easter Egg.'

Edward shook his head. He just wanted to get this over with.

'An Easter Egg. I don't know what that is.'

The Artiste leaned back and clasped his hands behind his head.

'An Easter Egg is something that a programmer will sometimes insert into a program he or she is writing. Did you ever have an Atari 2600 when you were younger?'

Edward blinked.

'I don't remember. But you're not the first person who's asked me that question.'

'If you had, you would have played a video game called *Adventure*.'

'Okay.' Whatever.

'The object of *Adventure* was to find the Holy Grail.' The Artiste pushed himself back from his desk, so that his chair rolled a few feet across the carpet. 'However, on your way to get the Holy Grail, you would pass a couple of mysterious walls with no doors. To get through them you had to find the black key, enter the black castle, and kill the red dragon with the sword. Then you went and fetched the purple bridge, brought it into the black castle, into the darkened labyrinth, and used it to enter a wall. Embedded inside the wall was an invisible magic dot.'

Edward sat down on the couch. He wasn't paying the Artiste for his time, so he might as well let him talk.

'When you brought both the invisible dot and the Holy Grail into a room at the same time, the mysterious walls would disappear, and you could enter a secret room. Inside the secret room was the name of the person who wrote *Adventure*, spelled out in multicolored flashing letters.'

'That must have been kind of a letdown, after all that work,' Edward said, just to prove he was still paying attention. Three weeks ago, he reflected, he would have found the idea of somebody seriously lecturing him about a video game completely implausible.

'It was somewhat anticlimactic,' the Artiste agreed. 'But the point is, that room was an example of what programmers call an Easter Egg: a secret signature, a hidden message within the larger whole, there to be read by those who knew where to look. Most programs have them – but you have to know where to look.'

'Kind of like a steganogram,' said Edward.

'In some respects, yes,' said the Artiste. If he was surprised that Edward knew what a steganogram was, he didn't show it. 'Now you have found an Easter Egg in MOMUS. The entire virtual environment you're exploring – the cold, the starvation, the wolves – is like that hidden room in *Adventure*: something secret that most people who play MOMUS never see.'

'But I don't see how I could have discovered anything secret,' Edward said patiently. 'I didn't do anything special. I barely did anything at all.'

'I can only surmise that you must have stumbled into it by accident. But to me the real question is, why would somebody go through the trouble of building an Easter Egg of such size and complexity in the first place?'

The Artiste paused and coughed once discreetly into his fist. He got up and went into the apartment's small kitchen, where he removed a disposable paper cup from a sealed plastic package and filled it with tap water. The kitchen faucet was fitted with a large and expensive-looking water filter. Edward hadn't noticed before that he wore an artsy-craftsy embroidered-leather carpal tunnel brace on his right wrist.

'Was it for his or her own private amusement?'

Somewhere beneath his blank exterior the Artiste was obviously enjoying playing the shrewd Sherlock Holmes to Edward's witless Watson. 'Perhaps. But would such private amusement really be worth all the work necessary to create such a detailed virtual environment?' The Artiste's diction had an overly rhetorical, almost scripted quality, as if he'd learned to talk from listening to TV news anchormen. 'Might there have been another motive? Is there a message here, and if so, how can we read it? And how can we get you out of the Easter Egg, so you can go on and finish the game?'

'Right,' Edward said. 'All good questions.'

He waited, but the Artiste didn't respond immediately. His train of thought had evidently veered off into its own private tunnel. He sat glassy-eyed in his desk chair, occasionally taking quick, rabbit-like sips from his paper cup. Edward noticed that one of the windows on his desktop was a Web page with plane reservations to London. Another one showed a grainy real-time view from the security camera in the foyer. It added to the Artiste's weirdly omniscient quality.

'This is a nice building,' Edward prompted.

'Thank you,' the Artiste replied absently. 'I own it. I was employee number seven at Yahoo!'

He put down the cup and gazed up at the image on the monitor, tapping fitfully at one of his keyboards.

'Well,' he said, 'you can still win. If you want to. Slow down the flow of time again. Defeat the aliens.'

Edward sat up, surprised.

'I can?'

'Quite easily. Look, I'll show you.'

One hand began to play over the keyboard while he kept the other on the mouse. It was a fancy wireless model, streamlined and studded with silvery buttons. On top of the monitor rested a pink piece of tissue paper, an invoice, with a tree at the top.

Something clicked in Edward's mind.

'Holy shit,' he said. 'You're Alberto Hidalgo.'

'Yes. I don't understand why Zeph uses my name when I prefer to be called "the Artiste." It may reflect his sense of humor.'

'But you're the Alberto who used to work for a family called the Wents.'

There was no discernible pause in the rhythm of the Artiste's keystrokes, and he kept his eyes unwaveringly on the screen. Things were connecting in Edward's mind, almost against his will, things that had no business connecting with each other.

'Yes. How did you know?'

'I work for them now.'

'Oh.'

Edward watched the Artiste carefully.

'They contracted with me to design some custom software for them,' the Artiste volunteered. 'A database for a library catalog. I fulfilled my contract to their satisfaction.'

'I know. I'm using it now. They hired me to catalog their library.'

341

'I see.' The Artiste adjusted a dial on the monitor with exaggerated care. 'I hope you're finding my software to be adequate for your purposes.'

'It's fine.' Edward's heart beat deafeningly; he felt like it must be visible through his shirt. The Artiste swung his short legs rapidly as he worked.

'Let me ask you something,' Edward said, trying to keep his voice casual. 'Did the Wents ever talk to you about an old codex they were looking for?'

'Codecs,' said the Artiste. 'Plural of codec, an abbreviation for "compression/decompression," which refers to an algorithmic process for reducing file size by eliminating redundancies . . .'

'That's not what I meant. I meant a codex, singular. A codex with an *x*. As in a book.'

'I know what you meant,' the Artiste said quietly.

Edward sensed that suddenly, unbelievably, hidden in this shabby Lower East Side apartment with its eccentric technophile shut-in, he had found something. He didn't know what it was, except that it was fragile, and that he would have to play things perfectly or lose it forever. The hair was standing up on his forearms – he felt like a man on the verge of being struck by lightning, invisible thunderbolts gathering in the air over his head and massing in the ground beneath his feet.

'But you worked with their library.'

'Yes.'

'With Laura Crowlyk.'

'That's right.'

'And the Duchess.'

'And the Duchess,' the Artiste agreed. He whacked an arcane key combination using both hands. He'd somehow increased the clock speed in the game so that events inside its tiny world unfolded at a frantically accelerated pace. The tiny figures leaped around spastically like jitterbugging dancers in an old newsreel.

'So – did you get to know her at all?' Edward asked, circling his prey.

'A little. Not much. They say I don't work well with other people.'

The Artiste stopped typing, and the screen was still again. The disk drive whined and grated as it wrote to the disc, then spat it out.

He took it and turned to Edward.

'You should be all set. I've put you in the head-quarters of the human resistance movement,' he explained, rapid-fire, 'and I've activated the emergency generators, so you should be able to get the subways running. Visit Bulgari on Fifth Avenue and take the diamonds that are in the safe. The combination is in the clerk's pocket, though you may have to kill him to get it. Don't worry, he's a collaborator. Once you have the diamonds, take the subway to the airport. Use the diamonds to pay a flight crew to repair a plane and fly it to Cape Canaveral in Florida. From there you can ride the space shuttle into orbit. It should be self-explanatory after that.'

The Artiste held out the disc. Edward eyed it warily without taking it. He sensed that the Artiste wanted him to leave. The audience was over.

'That's it?'

'What more were you expecting?' the Artiste asked reasonably.

'Well, but you still haven't answered those questions. Like where does all this stuff come from? And who put it there? And why?'

For an instant the Artiste registered something like impatience.

'Why does it matter? I told you how to get out of it.' The Artiste gazed at the screen, his face pale in the monitor's light. 'Though I don't know why you would want to. The snow. The empty streets. The silence. It's beautiful in its own way, don't you think?' For a moment he looked like a beneficent princeling showing off the view from the window of his mansion. 'You can see the stars from the middle of Times Square. I doubt anybody has done that in 150 years.'

'I guess.'

'Why let yourself be trapped by conventional notions of "victory" and "defeat"? Would you really win by repelling the aliens and saving the world? Why not just let it go? Let the humans die out. Give the wolves a shot at running things for a change. And the narwhals – the narwhals are coming south with the cold. Did you see them? You know they're one of the only whales that lack a dorsal fin? Along with beluga? They would have been here soon. They like the cold vestibulary currents.'

Edward looked at the monitor screen. He saw,

to his surprise, that something about the 'head-quarters' the Artiste mentioned looked familiar. The distinctive molding, the high ceilings, the leather chairs – it looked like the Wents' apartment. In fact, that's exactly what it was: a virtual replica of the Wents' apartment.

'You made this,' he said.

He was starting to get it now. The similarities, the echoes, the connections between the game and his life and the codex. The ruins where the Chenoweth library should have been. The landscape outside the Annex building in Old Forge. The man with the antlers he'd seen at the LAN party. Something, a shape, was emerging out of the darkness. He shook his head, torn between anger and exasperation and sheer admiration.

'It was you – you made this whole thing. You made it, you put it in the game, and I got trapped in it. My God. You complete fucking bastard.'

The Artiste watched him impassively, but he was blinking a little too frequently.

'Why?' Edward wanted to shake him. 'Do have any idea how much time I wasted on this thing?'

'Nobody was holding a gun to your head.'

That was true. 'But why? Why even bother? What's wrong with you?'

'I had my reasons.'

'Yes? Such as?'

Instead of answering the Artiste stood up and walked over to a window, where he pretended to study the spines of the paperback books stacked up there. Edward noted with surprise that they all, without exception, had the pink and blue spines and swirly gold lettering of mass-market romance novels.

'Because I wanted to,' said the Artiste, with an air of childish sincerity. 'I thought one day maybe I would show it to her. She might like it. There were things I always wanted to tell her. But after a while she stopped coming to the office, and I didn't see her anymore. I never knew why she didn't come. And anyway I thought better of it.'

'You made this for Blanche.'

Edward's anger was starting to fade. It was too pathetic, too funny. He tried to imagine the Artiste demonstrating his computer game for the Duchess.

'You said you wanted to tell her things. Like what?'

'Like where the codex is.'

Time, which had been rushing ahead uncontrollably for the past minute, froze abruptly in place. Its engine seized and melted. Edward's mind felt very clear. He held consciously still, afraid he would startle the Artiste like a rare bird, scare him out of saying what he was about to say next. On the wall opposite the Artiste's desk hung a vast whiteboard covered with illegible scribbles and diagrams and flow charts and symbols written in red, green, and blue marker. A humidifier stood in one corner, noiselessly breathing out puffs of white mist, one after the other, miniature clouds that dissolved into the air in slow motion.

'It didn't take me that long to find it,' the Artiste went on. 'I'm very good at puzzles. This wasn't even an especially hard one.'

Edward could barely speak.

'It wasn't?' he croaked.

'No. Not really.' The Artiste sounded neither proud nor boastful, just honest.

'So you – you have it?' Edward said.

'I said I found it. I didn't say I have it.'

'Where is it?'

'You don't know?'

'Jesus Christ.' Edward clutched his head frantically. He was going insane. He didn't know whether to strangle the Artiste or beg him for mercy. 'Just tell me where it is!'

The little man smiled sadly and shook his head. 'I've already said too much.'

'You haven't said anything!'

'I wish I hadn't.'

Abruptly the Artiste sat down on the carpet, which was the pale blue of a lightly chlorinated swimming pool, and leaned back against the bare white wall. The strength seemed to leave his tiny body. He looked like a magically animated doll whose enchantment was fading, Pinocchio in reverse.

'The Duchess hired me to work on their computers, but Laura told me all about the codex. Or enough, anyway, and I guessed the rest. I've been everywhere you've been. I shouldn't have done it. At first I thought I'd be doing the Duchess a favor – she likes having young men do her favors. You found that out. I thought I'd be her hero, but I was wrong. I realized that just in time. It was almost too late. Maybe it was too late.' He sighed, and Edward was surprised to hear a trace of unsteadiness, a telltale shudder in his voice. The Artiste was trying not to cry. 'It took me so long to make it. I used climate patterns from the Ice Age as a model. The Wisconsin Era.'

He sniffed.

'Incidentally,' he said, 'I think you're the only one who ever found it. You have to be very, very bad at MOMUS to find my Easter Egg.'

'Thanks a lot.'

The Artiste began to describe the lengths he'd gone to accurately model the effects of the alien sun filter on the earth's biosphere. It made sense – Edward remembered what Zeph had said about the Artiste's day job, something to do with the National Weather Service – but he was only half listening. Something else was nagging at him, and he leaned down to look at the Artiste's monitor again. The re-creation of the Wents' apartment was amazingly detailed. Tapping at the keyboard, he guided himself down the corridor, opened the half-sized door, climbed the spiral staircase – which took some tricky mousework – and up into the Wents' library. It was there, just like in real life, but empty, stripped: no crates, no table, no lamp, no curtains. Just bare floor, walls, ceiling, windows, though all meticulously drawn. The only furniture was the bookshelves, which were themselves vacant. A virtual bee buzzed and beat itself impotently against the virtual window. Why a bee?

'But I don't understand,' he interrupted. 'Why didn't you tell the Duchess you found it?'

'I'm sorry, Edward.' The Artiste shook his round little head. 'I can't tell you that either.'

It was pointless, like arguing with a recalcitrant voice mail system. But something was assembling itself in his mind, something that had been broken into separate pieces and scattered was being gathered up and made whole again. Isn't that what the Artiste said about e-mail, the first time they met? Scattered bits of information, gathered up and re-knit into a message to be read. Chaos becomes order. Or what the Duchess said in that ridiculous letter – it was like a book being disbound, the pages scattered, and then reclaimed again and made whole. He thought of Margaret again, and the story she told him about Sir Urre. Didn't he have a bee on his coat of arms—?

Edward picked up the disc with his saved game on it and turned to the Artiste, who was suddenly standing between him and the door. Now he was ready to go, and it was the Artiste who wanted to keep him there, like a host who had suddenly remembered his manners and was making up for lost time.

'Do you know why this game is called MOMUS?' he asked, his voice calm and soft again, the way it was when Edward first walked in. They were standing face-to-face. There was no way the Artiste could physically stop him; Edward had at least a foot on him, probably more. 'There's a place you can get to where you see the word "MOMUS" written on a wall as graffiti. No one knows who put it there, or why. But do you know who Momus was? He was a Greek god, though of a generation older than Zeus and his children. His mother was Nyx, which means Night, and his father was Erebus. Erebus was the personification of the darkness of Hades.

'Momus was the only one of the Greek gods who dared to criticize the created universe. He even suggested a few improvements. He thought that bulls should have horns on their shoulders instead of on their heads, so they could see what they were attacking better. He told Aphrodite, the goddess of beauty, that her sandals squeaked. He said that humans should have been made with doors in their chests, so you could open them and see what they were really feeling.

'Eventually the other gods got tired of listening to Momus complain, and they got together and threw him out of Olympus. I don't know what happened to him after that, but I think there's a lesson there somewhere, Edward. Maybe it's that the world is an imperfect place, but if you spend all your time looking for something better you'll only end up somewhere even worse.

'I'm sorry about the codex, Edward. I really can't tell you where it is. I've told you too much already.'

'But why not?' Edward asked, not wanting to give away more than he had to. In his mind he was already out the door. He knew where the codex was.

'Because I know you'll tell the Duchess.' The Artiste's smooth, childlike face turned grave, and his voice was urgent. 'I can't let you do that. Your replacement Nicholas is right, though for all the wrong reasons. The Duchess is far better off without the codex. If she found it, she would try to use it against the Duke, and the Duke wouldn't stand for that. Anything she could do to him is nothing compared to what he would do to her. He could hurt her, Edward.'

'That's ridiculous,' Edward said shortly, feeling like the world's sole surviving voice of reason. He had to get out of here before his head exploded. He took the disc and tucked it into his shirt pocket. He was barely listening now. 'It doesn't make any sense. What could he possibly do? The Duke is an invalid. He's sick. And anyway he's at some clinic in London. She's at Weymarshe. He can't do anything to her while she's there.'

He turned and walked purposefully toward the door, toward the Artiste, picking his way through the junk scattered on the carpet.

'Thanks for all the help,' Edward said, not wanting to seem ungracious. He squeezed awkwardly past him. 'With the game.'

'You're wrong,' said the Artiste. He stepped aside reluctantly. 'Wake up, Edward. Working for the

Wents taught me something. I've been through all this before you. I found the book, and I let it go, and so should you. Forget about the Duchess. This isn't a game, Edward, this is real life. Go back to work.'

Edward didn't look back. He didn't need a lecture on real life from somebody who looked like a hobbit. He jogged down the first flight of stairs, then gave up and bombed down the rest, picking up speed, taking them three at a time, skidding wide on the turns, grabbing the banister to stay on his feet. The Artiste followed him out onto the landing, shouting down the stairwell after him.

'I loved her too, Edward!' he called down. The Artiste's voice boomed and echoed off the marble steps. 'Work is God's curse on us! Remember that, Edward! Don't ever try to escape it!'

Then Edward was outside on the sidewalk, running.

CHAPTER 20

In the cab on the way over Edward left yet another quixotic message on Margaret's answering machine, trying to infuse it with a sense of the urgency of the situation. He hadn't been to the Wents' building for two weeks, and there was a new doorman out front, though he wore what looked like the same shabby suit that the old one had. Edward wondered what had happened to him. The new doorman was a stocky man, with the bland pink face and thinning white hair of an accountant, and unlike his predecessor he spoke excellent English when he stopped Edward on the way in. To Edward's surprise his name was still on the Wents' list. Even more surprisingly, he saw Margaret's name on it, too. The Duchess must have managed to have her added.

He blundered into the darkened lobby, and there she was. It was as if the sight of her name on the doorman's battered clipboard had summoned her into being. She was waiting for him in the lobby, sitting in a cracked brown leather chair, cool and unruffled as a stone nymph. She stood up when she saw him, her large leather bag slung over her hip. He half expected her to still show signs of the disaster at the Chenoweth – dark circles under her eyes from sleepless nights, unwashed hair, a shadow of her former self – but she looked exactly the same as when he'd first met her: demurely, almost frumpily dressed in a skirt and cardigan, with her dark hair chopped off severely at chin-level. She had the same resigned, indifferent expression on her pale oval face, the same perfectly straight-backed posture.

He wrapped her in a bear hug which she neither invited nor avoided, pinning her arms against her sides. He clung to her, his eyes shut tight against the tears that unexpectedly prickled in them. He said nothing, just held her, not caring whether the emotion was in any way requited. His faith in something, he didn't know what, had been on the verge of crumbling, and her unexpected presence had instantly restored it intact as if it had never flagged. He felt like he'd been wandering in a mist without her, without any expectation of being rescued, and she had appeared out of the fog to lead him back to safety.

'I missed you,' he said finally, into her hair. He released her. 'I missed you. Where have you been?'

'I was away.' She dropped her eyes. 'I'm sorry. I didn't want to see you.'

'I thought you'd abandoned me.'

He'd forgotten how pretty she could look, with her long, serious face, her extravagant swoop of a nose. How could he ever not have seen that?

They walked over to the elevators and rode up together. The *ping* of the passing floors was deafening in the silence. Inside, the apartment was deserted, and they made no real attempt to conceal their presence. It was clear that the Wents were already gone. They must be selling up, he thought. The big oriental rug in the front room had been rolled up and stood in a corner; a slight bend in the middle made it bow politely to them as they passed it. A fine haze of plaster dust hung in the late-afternoon light that filtered in through the windows, left over from the commotion of the movers. They passed Laura Crowlyk's office on the way to the staircase. It was bare except for a couple of bright yellow plastic moving crates with descriptions of their contents scribbled on the side in black Magic Marker. A sense of imminent and drastic change permeated the air.

'I hope they didn't take the books,' Edward said. The absence of rugs or curtains had subtly changed the acoustics, making it sound like he was addressing an empty concert hall.

But the books were still there. When Edward hauled open the heavy metal door at the top of the spiral staircase, the library was waiting for them, apparently undisturbed since the last time they were there. Heavy curtains still muffled the tall windows.

'Have you been back here?' he asked. 'Since we got back from the Annex, I mean?' Despite his best efforts he felt himself blushing in the darkness. He groped around for the standing lamp, his arms held out in front of him like a sleepwalker.

'Once,' Margaret said. She indicated the old suitcase that had contained the books they'd liberated from the Chenoweth. It was empty; she'd already reshelved them.

'Do you realize how many times I called you?' Suddenly all the anger he'd been nursing came rushing back. He glared at her. 'Why didn't you answer me?'

She shook her head.

'I'm sorry, Edward, I just – I'm sorry. I thought it was over. I thought the codex was gone, and I just – I wanted to move on. I wanted to forget about it.'

She pursed her lips.

'I went home for a while.'

'Well.' He wasn't going to say he forgave her. But. 'I'm glad you're back now.'

An hour ago Edward had been burning to tell her everything he'd just learned, but now that she was actually here he felt tongue-tied. In the end it was Margaret who spoke first.

'I've been reading Richard de Bury,' she said quietly. 'You've probably never heard of him. He was Bishop of Durham in the fourteenth century and an advisor to Edward III. He was also the first great English book collector. He was ruthless about it, he'd ruin a noble family just for its library, and after he died he left behind several lists of books that he had intended to acquire. One of them sounds like it might have been our codex. *A Viage to a Fer Lond*, one volume, no author, from the library at Bowmry. But his papers don't say whether or not he ever managed to get it.

'There's also something in the papers of a John Leland, keeper of the king's library under Henry VIII. He was charged with creating a register of England's historical artifacts, books included, but he went mad before he could complete it. His papers are in—'

'Margaret. Wait.' He put a hand on her arm to slow her down. 'There's something very important I have to tell you.'

He took a deep breath and forged ahead. He started by telling her about his breakfast with Fabrikant. He found himself picking and choosing the truth carefully, not wanting to tell her more than she needed to know. He explained the Duchess's theory about the steganogram, as the Duke's representative had described it, but he skated around the question of what it might mean, or why the Duchess wanted it.

When he finished Margaret was looking up at the ceiling, her lips moving silently.

'A steganogram,' she said to herself softly. 'A steganogram. What a ridiculous idea.' She was thinking out loud. 'Trithemius's *Steganographia* was later than Gervase, much later. Though Bacon's *Nullity of Magic* was a hundred years earlier – Roger Bacon, not Francis. And the coded section of Chaucer's *Equatorie of the Planetis* would have been a close contemporary. If it was really Chaucer who wrote it.'

She sat down at the worktable.

'To tell you the truth, I don't think it's absolutely impossible,' she said finally, shaking her head. 'Technically speaking. But it is very, very unlikely. No, it's preposterous. It's outrageous! And what does it say? And why does the Duchess want it? And why did they tell us to stop looking for it?'

Edward sighed. 'I don't know.'

'What do you think she would do with it? If it were real?'

'I don't know,' Edward said again, with a guilty pang. He was a bad liar, but she didn't even seem that curious. Margaret looked down at the little silver watch on her wrist, toying with it.

'Well, it doesn't matter, does it?' she said bitterly. She sat down on the creaky old office chair and crossed her legs. 'We're still no closer than we were.'

'But we are.' He paused for a second, selling the line. 'Margaret, I think I know where the codex is.'

She flinched, physically, as if he'd just thrown a drink in her face.

'You found it? Where is it?' She gripped the seat of the chair, leaning forward.

'Not me,' he said, talking quickly. 'Somebody else found it, or he says he did. Somebody who didn't want it. He didn't tell me where it was, but he did give me a clue. If I'm right, it's in this room.'

She looked around nervously as if the book

might be lurking in a dark corner, ready to jump out at her.

'All right,' she said, settling herself with an effort. 'Tell me your theory.'

Edward was enjoying his big moment. He paced, his footsteps echoing in the large, empty space.

'You once told me that some of what we know about Gervase comes from documents that were re-used in the bindings of other books. Books that were disbound to recover the original papers.'

'Yes,' she said slowly, 'that is true. Although such cases are relatively rare.'

'Well, what if the same thing happened to the codex? What if somebody used it to make the binding of another book?'

'Why would anyone want to do that?' Margaret looked scornful, a professional scolding the bumblings of an amateur. 'The procedure you're talking about was for waste paper. The codex would have been written on parchment. There's a big difference. Parchment is essentially very fine leather – it was expensive, and it has very different physical properties from—'

'But listen.' Edward cut her off. 'Just listen. What if they did it as a way of hiding the codex?'

She took an instant to process this notion.

'Well,' she said more slowly, 'it would entail some damage to the original pages. The paste causes discoloration, in addition to any holes that would have had to be cut. And why would anybody bother?'

'Forget about that for a second. Let's just assume that they did.'

Margaret stood up, with her characteristic unlimbering motion, so that she could pace as well.

'There's far too much parchment in a book to be concealed even in a very thick binding. You could fit eight or ten leaves at the most.'

'Right. I thought of that. So you break up the codex, split the pages up and scatter them, disperse them throughout a whole series of volumes.'

'Okay.' She stopped and folded her long, slender arms. 'All right. Suppose such a procedure has been carried out on the codex. Now we're looking for any number of books instead of just one. We're worse off than when we started.'

'Exactly.' Edward walked over to the old suitcase. 'Margaret. What if you were right all along. What if the codex was in the twelfth box after all?'

He let his voice trail off; the thought finished itself. He could see his words starting to sink in. Margaret walked over to one of the bookshelves and put her small, pale hand up to touch the row of worn, motley spines, softly, as if she were caressing the weathered scales of a sleeping dragon. She bent to look more closely at their yellowing gray labels. A pink stickie stuck to the shelf gave up the ghost and fluttered gracefully to the floor. She ignored it.

'Damn it,' she said, but softly, without heat. 'Those call numbers. I knew they were strange. I knew it.' She studied them in the dim light. 'It's so obvious,' she whispered. 'They put the codex into the books in the twelfth box and gave the twelfth box to the Chenoweth, knowing it would get lost. These numbers and letters aren't call numbers, they stand for signatures. And these words must be catchwords!' She looked up at Edward. 'If it's really in here, these are the collations, right on the spine. These aren't call numbers, they're the instructions for reassembling the codex.'

Their eyes met, and Edward felt goosebumps rising on his arms. He'd thought he was right, but now the thought was becoming reality, and suddenly there was a third and slightly supernatural presence in the room with them: The codex was here, the ghost of a book, disemboweled and dispersed but waiting to be brought back to life. Bracing herself, Margaret pulled out a massive tome from the Urre shelf – an odd volume left over from the diaspora of some forgotten encyclopedia – and carried it over to the work table. She laid it flat with a resounding *whoomp*.

'All right,' she said. She opened it and began studying the inside cover. She ran her fingers along the edges, feeling their texture and thickness. 'These boards are pasteboard, not wood. If they're here the pages of the codex are part of the cover, under the leather.'

She took a steel penknife out of her bag and with a single confident gesture made a long, straight slit along the hinge of the inside endpaper. She put down the knife and worked her fingertips inside. Holding the rest of the book down by leaning on it with her forearm, she roughly jerked the slit open with her other hand. Fine dry dust flew out.

She held the wound up to the lamp and peered inside. A long moment passed, then she looked up at Edward.

'We're going to need some cash,' she said.

It took both of them working for half an hour to get all the books down to the sidewalk and into a taxi. In the end they had to rummage through the Wents' apartment for old shopping bags to hide them in. Evidently the process of removing the Wents' possessions had been going on for some time, because the doorman saw nothing suspicious in what they were doing. He even called them a cab.

Margaret wouldn't risk putting the books in the trunk, at the mercy of rattling tire irons and oozing motor oil, so they had to stack them up in the back seat and then wedge themselves in afterward. The soft springs of the old upholstery twanged and sagged under their weight. Margaret was squeezed up against one door in the back, and Edward had to sit in the front seat next to the driver, crushed under a stack of books that reached up to the ripped vinyl roof.

They took Third Avenue downtown to where it turned into Bowery, then Canal Street across to the Manhattan bridge. Every tiny bump in the roadway transmitted itself with the precision of a seismometer up through the car's clapped-out, overloaded suspension and directly into Edward's ass, but he didn't care. For weeks the codex had been an abstract thing, mystical and vaporous; now he closed his eyes and felt the solid, reassuring weight of the books in his lap and pictured their taxi soaring across the bridge in a long, dramatic helicopter shot, the viewpoint pulling up and away, the end of the movie, cue the theme song, roll credits. *This is it*, he thought. *It's finally over.* Weymarshe was just around the corner. On cue the cabby started singing along loudly and unselfconsciously with the radio in a Near Eastern accent: Wings' 'Another Day' segueing seamlessly into 'Band on the Run' and then Thomas Dolby's 'She Blinded Me With Science,' doing the keyboard part for good measure. As they crossed the bridge the metal mesh embedded in the asphalt whined musically under their tires.

All of downtown Brooklyn seemed to be under construction. Traffic inched along through a tortuous morass of jersey barriers and gravel pits and sawhorses with orange lights on them blinking at each other out of sync. Traffic stopped dead for five solid minutes while Edward, paralyzed under the weight of the books, was forced to stare out the window at a restaurant called 'For Goodness Steak!' It was dark by the time the taxi pulled up in front of Margaret's building, on a narrow street of identical brownstones. She unloaded the back seat while he paid off the driver, and together they ferried the books upstairs, walking quickly, legs bent, steadying the teetering stacks under their chins.

He'd seen her building once from the outside, but he'd never seen the interior, and he had lazily imagined it as a kind of scholarly bolthole, a one-room cloister paneled in dark wood, with a reading table upholstered in green baize. Instead she led him up three flights of stairs – two folded-up strollers haunted the gloomy stairwell like a mated pair of giant spiders – and into a dark, undecorated, and disorderly studio on the fourth floor of what must have once been a comfortable bourgeois residence before it was carved up into separate rentable apartments. The walls were white and the ceilings were low. Everything was slightly undersized: The fridge was half as big as a regular one, and the futon-bed wasn't much bigger than a child's cot. Makeshift bookshelves, unstable edifices of pine planks and cinder blocks, reached up to the ceiling.

The only full-sized piece of furniture in the apartment was a colossal wooden desk pushed up against the front windows. It must have weighed half a ton; it looked like it came from the office of the president of a midwestern bank. Margaret swept the papers off it onto the bed and started rummaging through a closet for supplies, which she rapidly assembled in a neat line along the desktop: rolls of white tape, big shiny metal alligator clips, soft paintbrushes, knitting needles, a jar of paste, assorted spatulas, scraps of exotic-looking paper, sheets of stiff clear plastic, and a small, thin black case that opened to reveal a shiny surgical scalpel snug in a velvet nest.

Edward was ready to begin the unveiling, or excavation, or reassembly, whatever the appropriate term was for the project they were about to commence, but Margaret sent him out to the nearest bodega for Diet Coke and Q-tips. He went without protest, but as he wandered the dirty, urine-smelling aisles, full of off-brand paper towels and expired cookies and bins of nameless Caribbean roots, he wondered if he should try to contact the Duchess and tell her what was going on. On his way back he stopped at a payphone and tried the number of the Wents' apartment. Nobody answered – which made sense, since he'd just been there and it was empty. Feeling stupid, he left a terse message for Laura to call his cell phone and hung up.

When he got back Margaret was bent over the first of the books, a handsome edition of Tennyson's *Idylls of the King* with illustrations by Gustave Doré, which lay like a surgical patient in a pool of light from a halogen lamp. She showed it no mercy. With a few economical strokes she sliced the spine and the covers free of the block of pages inside.

'I'm violating the first law of preservation,' she said in a low voice.

'Which is?'

'Never perform any operation on a book that you cannot reverse.'

She carefully set the stack of freed pages to one side and concentrated on the covers.

'I'll never tell,' Edward said.

He stowed the Diet Coke away in her miniature fridge. The only other contents were a box of baking soda and a Tupperware container of what looked like cottage cheese. When he was done he sat gingerly on the bed, which was neatly made and covered in a lumpy, well-worn quilt, possibly handmade.

'At some point in the Middle Ages people decided it was too expensive to keep making book covers out of wood,' Margaret said, 'so they started using paste-board instead, which is glued-together sheets of paper covered with leather. They were also switching from parchment to paper for the pages – paper doesn't warp the way parchment does, so they didn't need those heavy wooden covers anymore to keep the pages flat.'

She sliced the front and back covers away and set aside the now disembodied spine, first making a note of what was written on it. Edward winced, but Margaret had the scholar's callousness for the physical well-being of books – she'd seen so much bibliocide that nothing shocked her.

'It's astonishing, when you think about it,' she went on. 'They couldn't have cared less what paper they used. They weren't interested in preserving history. They just cut up whatever books nobody was reading at the time. Sometimes they used works of literature that were hundreds of years old, books that we would have kept under glass in a museum even then, let alone now. They were so *strange*.'

She frowned and shook her head, as if she took the perplexing behavior of earlier eras personally.

'We forget that not every age was as obsessed with who owns what as ours is. In Gervase's time an author was concerned only with the truth: He was its steward, its temporary curator, not its owner. They had no conception of plagiarism. If one man copied something somebody else wrote, it wasn't a crime, it was a service to mankind. And he regarded his own writings the same way.'

While he was out Margaret had prepared a batch of clear solvents in a stainless steel mixing bowl. Working quickly and carefully, she used a sponge to brush the clear liquid around the edges of the pasteboard covers – now just two empty blank panels – then applied a thick layer of mushy white paste over it, which she let sit for a minute. When the pasteboard was good and saturated she scraped off the paste and set about separating the edges of the endpaper from the pasteboard with the narrow edge of a kitchen spatula. She went around all four sides, then she lifted the endpaper away and hurriedly blotted the damp parts with the paper scraps.

When she took away the blotting paper, Edward and Margaret were looking at the first page of the codex.

He'd been searching for it for so long that he'd stopped thinking of the codex as an actual physical thing, something that could be seen and

touched and handled and read. When he thought
of it at all he'd imagined the codex as something
out of a Scooby Doo cartoon, a mystical volume
floating unsupported in midair, illuminated from
within by a ghostly green glow, serenaded by celestial choirs, its pages turning themselves as if by an
unseen hand. But there it was: It lay in front of
him on Margaret's desk, as limp and bedraggled
and apologetic as a newborn baby.

He hadn't expected it to be so beautiful.

The page itself wasn't especially large, not much
bigger than the standard 8½" by 11" of a sheet of
white Xerox paper, but it was infinitely more
fragrant: A sweet, damp, musty odor billowed up
when Margaret uncovered it. She had warned him
that it might be damaged, and it was, a half-inch-
wide strip running along three of its edges was
stained a deep, burnt brown, but the rest of the
page was a smooth, mottled cream color. The
Tennyson had been a big book, so whoever had
hidden the page there hadn't had to fold it to fit
it in. The page bore two dense columns of handwritten text, perfectly centered both vertically and
laterally and neatly squared off as if they'd been
justified in a word processor. They were surrounded
by wide, spacious margins and written in ink that
might once have been black but which had faded
to a rich mahogany. Scattered at random across the
page, a letter here and a sigil there was picked out
in deep red or smooth, metallic gold.

The writing was a dense script that looked like

nothing so much as a tangled hedge of thorny black branches, or the wrought-iron curls of a fire escape. It was almost completely illegible; only when he stared at a single word did one or two of the pointy squiggles slowly resolve themselves into recognizable letters. What did it mean? He stared at the text, and it shimmered on the very edge of making sense, promising everything but divulging nothing, the symbol of a symbol. It was like the chess problems that he'd solved so ridiculously easily when he was seven, and which he now stared at in the newspaper with impotent incomprehension. For some reason he wanted to know what it said so badly his eyes burned, but the codex resisted him – it was like the frost of meaning, pure significance, condensed and collected and frozen on paper into this black tracery, the darkness of it so bright it was blinding.

Halfway down the left-hand column, the scribe had turned a big *Y* into a miniature tableau: A miserable hunchbacked peasant was lugging a dry tree branch over his shoulder through a snowy landscape. He was bent double under his burden, as if the weight of what it meant was too sorrowful to bear.

'It looks very genuine,' Margaret said clinically.

Edward snapped back to reality. He wondered how long he'd been standing there gazing at it. She handled the page casually, but he thought he could see her fingers trembling.

'Exceptionally fine vellum,' she added. 'We'd need a microscope to know for sure, but it looks like unborn calfskin.'

'Unborn—?'

'Vellum made from the skin of a fetal cow. It was highly prized.'

Working carefully, soaking and blotting, teasing and tugging, she loosened and removed a second page from the same binding, and then a third. If she felt any of the electric anticipation Edward did, her methodical, unhurried pace betrayed none of it. By nine o'clock Margaret had finished with the Tennyson: It had disgorged six sheets of parchment in all, withered and stained but intact. They lay drying on paper towels laid out on her bed. In one or two places the ink had eaten all the way through the page – iron-gall ink could be highly corrosive when imperfectly mixed, Margaret explained. As she spread them out Edward saw that the pages were actually double-sized sheets, each one folded in half and covered with writing on both sides, making a total of four pages in all, with holes running up the middle where they had once been sewn into the binding.

Four cans of Diet Coke lay scattered around her chair. There was nothing else to sit on in the apartment, and the futon was taken, so Edward sat on the cracked linoleum kitchen floor with his back against the humming fridge and his feet braced against the opposite wall, watching her. Unable either to leave or to help in any way, he hovered uselessly.

Margaret's apartment provided few distractions. The one good-sized window over the bed looked out on the rear end of a diner, where Mexican kitchen hands emptied tubs of dishwater and listened to mariachi music. Margaret's shoulders and arms worked as she sliced and tore and blotted the old pages. Her hair was pulled back into a stubby ponytail held together by a pink rubber band, from which a few floating strays had escaped.

'I'm going to go get us some dinner,' he said, after a while.

'There's a Chinese place around the corner on Vanderbilt. Wah Garden.'

Edward heaved himself up.

'What do you want?'

'Number 19, chicken with garlic sauce. And steamed dumplings. And maybe you could pick up some more Diet Coke.'

At midnight Edward realized he'd fallen asleep sitting up with his head canted backward and his mouth wide open. The Chinese food was gone, the empty white cardboard containers lined up neatly on the counter in the kitchen area. A tall glass full of something cloudy and vaguely lime-colored stood on Margaret's desk.

Margaret worked with precisely the same level of energy and concentration as when she'd started six hours earlier. The stack of intact books on her left was shorter now, and the pile of gutted, dismantled books to her right was taller. He watched her work, oblivious to him, and wondered how many nights she'd ground away like this, one after the other, until nothing was left but the dawn, with nobody there to watch over her the way he was watching over her now. She was driven forward by sheer will, impelled by some inner engine the workings of which he could only guess at. It occurred to him that for Margaret, this – this sustained, obsessive, masochistic act of labor – was what passed for happiness. He was looking for a way to escape from work, but work was all Margaret had. He wondered if it was all she wanted.

He stood up, put his hands on his hips, and arched his stiff back.

'You're awake,' Margaret said, without looking up.

'I didn't even know I was asleep,' he said stupidly. He cleared his throat. 'What are you drinking?'

'It's a Tom Collins. Without the vodka. I just like the mix,' she added, sounding a little embarrassed.

He used her bathroom – one of Margaret's long dark hairs was pasted to the wall of the molded-plastic shower stall – and cleared away the remains of dinner, then went over to the bed to examine the pages.

'Well,' he said, feeling giddy, 'here it is.'

There were twenty or thirty of them now, in various states of preservation and deterioration. Some, like the first one he'd seen, were almost pristine; others had been folded two or even three times to fit inside smaller books and had suffered the effects of moisture and acidity, so that they ranged in color from a too-new-looking cream to a deep burnt brown. A few were so riddled with dark, blooming mold stains that they looked like maps of the surface of the moon.

The best parts – the only parts that meant anything to Edward – were the illuminations: an *H* transformed into a stony castle, or an *F* into a squat, sturdy tree. The animals seemed to have more personality than the people: eager whippet-like dogs; amiable sheep; serious, pious-looking horses. On one page a sinuously smiling vermilion salamander lurked along the bottom edge of the text. The pigments were so fresh and vivid they looked wet; in places the colors were laid on so thickly that the page under them was stiff and warped.

Eventually Margaret took pity on him and stood up to look at the pages, too.

'There's something strange about these images,' she said. 'But I can't quite put my finger on what it is. From the penwork it looks like the scribe and the illuminator were the same person, which is unusual but hardly unheard-of. The quality is high. See that bright blue sky? The color comes from crushed lapis lazuli, imported from Afghanistan. That pigment was as expensive as gold.'

'Can you read the writing?'

'Of course.'

He sat down gingerly on the edge of the bed.

'What does it say?' he said nervously. 'I mean, is it the same text as the *Viage*?'

'I think so. Parts of it are the same, at least. I've barely had time to glance at it.'

'What do you mean, parts?'

She frowned. The corners of her downturned mouth dipped lower.

'It's too soon to say tonight.' She waved her hand, which was still holding the steel scalpel. 'I've been reading bits and pieces as I go. There are things here I don't recognize – things that aren't in the modern text. In this version there's a lot more about the lord's child who was killed off while he was away chasing the stag knight. It goes on for pages about what a mighty hero he would have been. Sentimental stuff.

'And here – this passage.' She pointed to one of the pages. 'The lord meets a woman on his travels who gives him a seed. He thinks the woman is a holy virgin, but when he plants the seed a giant tree springs up, with demons living in its branches.'

'But what about that secret message? The steganogram, or whatever it is?'

She shook her head.

'I wouldn't even know where to begin looking for it, Edward. Even if it is real. If it's here it could be anywhere – hidden in a drawing, or written in invisible ink, or stippled in tiny pinpricks, or in any number of medieval alphabetical codes. Each word could stand for a letter, or each letter could stand for a word, the number of letters in each word could in turn stand for a letter. Authors of medieval codes were very resourceful. And Gervase spent time in Venice. The Venetians were the master cryptographers of the medieval world.'

Edward bent over the page with the *F* on it and studied it closely. At the most he could spell out a word or two at a time: *. . . anone . . . gardeyne . . . sprange oute . . .*

Margaret saw him squinting at it.

'It's beautiful, isn't it? That script was never intended for laymen. It was designed to be written as quickly as possible and to take up as little space as possible, to save time and paper. Some words are abbreviated, others are fused together – the technique is called *littera textura*, "woven words." It's lovely, but it takes a lot of practice before you can decipher it. And look here.'

Margaret picked up one page, supporting it carefully on her flat palms like a priestess making an offering. She held it up to her desk lamp so the light glowed through it, showing the texture of the parchment.

'Look closely,' she said. 'This is something I didn't expect. I can't read it yet, not without an ultraviolet light.'

Edward looked. Behind the dark letters and running perpendicular to them, vertically down the page, were faint brown stripes, so light that they almost faded into the paler brown of the parchment around them. When Edward looked closer he saw that the stripes were made of letters, bands of ghostly writing floating behind Gervase's crisp black script.

'Curiouser and curiouser,' Margaret said dryly. 'This paper has been re-used. There was something else written here, an earlier text that was scraped away to make room for the *Viage*. Our codex is a palimpsest.'

Despite his best efforts, Edward's pitch of excitement gradually gave way to exhaustion, and he faded as the night wore on. While Margaret pushed on in an orgy of work, he slumped further and further down the wall. He closed his eyes; his shoes came off; somehow he found himself on the bed, curled up to keep clear of the precious pages, his arm flung over his eyes to keep out the light. The mariachi music had finally reached a climax and ceased for the night. He stared up at Margaret's ugly styrofoam dropped ceiling. He'd never felt so tired. The pillow he rested his head on smelled marvelously like Margaret's hair. He closed his eyes, and he felt the room revolving slowly around him as if he were drunk.

He imagined the pages of the codex floating all around him, like limp brown leaves on the glassy surface of a pond in which he lay face up in a dead man's float, or a backyard swimming pool that was going to seed in those first early weeks of September. Those were punishing weeks in the Maine of his childhood, when the weather reminded you that summer was a temporary anomaly, not to be gotten used to, and that Bangor, while it appeared to be superficially civilized, shared its chilly latitude with such northern fastnesses as Ottawa and Halifax. Later he would have vague, stillborn memories of Margaret not reading but talking to him – lecturing him? pleading with him? – shaking her head in disapproval, or disbelief, or disappointment. But he could never remember what she was talking about, or even whether it was real or just a dream.

He woke up to find her clearing away the rest of the pages from around him on the bed and stacking them on her desk. He crawled under the covers without opening his eyes, like a baby. After a while he heard the light click off and felt her climb into bed next to him.

In the darkness, in her narrow twin bed, it was like Margaret was a different woman: warm, soft, nuzzling, both comforting and needing comfort, nothing like the dour, difficult day-Margaret he was used to. Her long legs were bare and stubbly. She turned over on her side, away from him, and he rolled up against her and snuffed the warm nape of her neck. She was still wearing panties and a T-shirt, but the bareness of her legs made her feel naked. Her cold bare feet mingled with his warm socks. Then she turned over to face him.

She kissed him, and he felt again, as he had that night at the Chenoweth, the urgent need inside her, just underneath her placid surface. She bit his shoulder, scratched at him fiercely like an angry little girl. He helped her slip her T-shirt up over her head, and the world shrank to the tiny tropical island of bed that sheltered them and bore them up in the middle of a dark, rocking sea.

Margaret was shaking him. He looked at the clock radio. It was four in the morning.

'Jesus,' he said. He rolled over and put a pillow over his head. 'Don't you ever sleep?'

'Edward,' she said. There was an unfamiliar, urgent note in her voice. 'Edward, you have to wake up. I need you to look at something.'

Edward opened his eyes. He was warm and tired and comfortable, but the novelty of Margaret asking for his advice did have some appeal to it. He sat up. The glare from her desk lamp was painful. In the half light he thought she looked frightened.

Margaret had a magnifying glass in one hand – it reminded him of when the Duchess compared her to Nancy Drew – and a stack of pages from the codex stood on her desk. She'd changed into a plain gray sweatshirt of no particular affiliation and put on a pair of uncharacteristically hip rectangular glasses he'd never seen before. She must wear contacts during the day, he thought. She smelled delightfully like minty toothpaste.

'Edward,' she said melodramatically, looking him in the eye. 'I found it.'

'What did you find.'

'I found it. I found the steganogram, the hidden message. The Duchess was right: It's real.'

Edward's stomach tightened. The final glaze of sleep vanished.

'What? What are you talking about?' he said. 'It can't be real.'

'I know it can't. But it is.'

He stared at her, wanting to share her enthusiasm, but instead he felt only cold. He realized he hadn't really wanted the message to be real. His victory was already complete. They had the codex. He didn't want all the rest of it: the secret message, the intrigue, the alarums and excursions and revelations. They could only lead to more problems.

'What does it say?'

'Wait. I'd rather show you.'

She took the first page from the stack of pages on her desk. Edward went over and stood behind her, letting his hands rest on her shoulders.

'You remember,' she said, 'something was bothering me about these historiated initials – the large illuminated letters.' Her voice gradually found its way back to her calm, lecturing tone. 'If you look at them, you'll see that there's nothing very unusual about their placement, or their execution. This *O*, for example, which forms a frame around a mother and child.'

'Okay.'

'It's not the picture that doesn't make sense, it's the context. The subject of a historiated initial usually follows from that of the text around it, but here I can't see any connection at all. The passage doesn't have anything to do with a mother and child, it's about the hero crossing the ocean in a boat.'

'Right. Okay, well, maybe it's a metaphorical

connection,' he said glibly. 'Ocean as mother, something like that.' He shaded his eyes as they got used to the light.

She frowned.

'I don't think so. It would be anachronistic to—'

'Fine, fine! Hurry up, you're making me nervous. Just tell me what it means.'

'It means nothing in itself. But I checked the other illuminations, and the same thing is true of them. None of them has any real relationship with the text around it.

'After I stared at them for a while, I decided to make a list of all the letters that the scribe had chosen to illustrate. I was thinking of the *Hypnerotomachia Poliphili,* in which the author spelled out a love letter using the first letters of each chapter. He was a monk, and no one noticed until after he was dead. But that's not what happened here. The codex has thirty-four historiated initials, but they don't spell anything at all. Look, I wrote them out in order.'

Margaret showed him a page from her notebook with the letters copied out in order:

W M H G E G O M E O A Y N O D S L O D E D E
C F R H R M E A V N I O

'I kept turning them over and over in my head, playing with them, trying different combinations. I don't know why. It took me a long time, but eventually I came up with this.'

She turned a few more pages, all of them densely covered with letters and scribbles and erasures. At the bottom of the last page, underlined twice, was this sentence:

GOD SAVE MYN OWNE GOODE CHILDE FROM HARME

Edward looked at the page, then at her, then back at the page again. He relaxed. His chest filled with a warm puddle of relief.

'Margaret,' he said gently. 'You don't understand, this could just be by chance. You could make any number of words by rearranging those letters. It's like a Rorschach blot – it doesn't prove anything. And even if it did, what would it prove?'

'I thought of that,' she said. 'But there's something else, something I need to show you. I tried to think of a way to test the theory, so I went back to the illustrations. I reordered the pages of the codex so that the illuminated letters spelled out the words I came up with. I want you to look at what I found.'

She stood up and indicated that Edward should sit down in her place. He did so, reluctantly, and she put a stack of pages in front of him; given their condition, it was more of a heap. He began to read through them in order, ignoring everything except the illuminated letters.

His resistance crumbled. He saw what she saw, and what she saw was real. Arranged in their new order the pictures formed a coherent, recognizable narrative – a story. The first illustration was of a young man with short wavy hair and a fringe of reddish beard, standing by himself inside the arc of a giant red G. He had the simple cartoon eyes that faces in medieval paintings have, plain but expressive – he looked a little apprehensive, as if he had a fair idea of what was in store for him and he wasn't all that happy about it. He was dressed humbly, and he held a quill pen in one hand and a small knife in the other. On a table beside him lay an open book. Its pages were blank.

'G for "Gervase",' whispered Margaret.

He shushed her.

'I get it.'

The second letter – an O – introduced a noble couple. They were posed like figures in a cameo, the woman pretty and slender, with a becomingly weak chin, the man very erect, with dark ringletty hair and a long, sharp nose. He wore a navy blue doublet and a weird floppy hat. He regarded Edward from the page with dignity.

Over the next few pages the same three characters recurred again and again, alone and in groups, posed in a variety of settings. Sometimes there was a miniature castle behind them, waist-high like a doghouse and hopelessly nonperspectival; once the nobleman was alone, hunting, surrounded by a circle of whippet dogs. The young man joined the couple, apparently in the capacity of a high-ranking servant. He was shown laboring at clerical tasks, treating with merchants and counting stacks of coins. Sometimes he wrote with his pen in the book, and sometimes the noblewoman read from the book. The whole effect was like seeing a montage of still frames from a movie. Time passed. The sun rose and set. Seasons changed. After a while the husband with the ringlets appeared less and less often.

Edward knew what he was looking at. It was an Easter Egg, just like the Artiste's, but hidden inside the codex for him to find. It reminded him of something the Duchess had written in that bizarre letter – hadn't she said something about getting her pages properly sorted, getting them back in order? How much had she known? At least, he thought, this proves she wasn't crazy. Halfway through the story there were two especially lavish and realistic paintings set inside the twin *Os* in the word GOODE. In the first the young servant and the pretty, weak-chinned noblewoman were posed alone together. Her hand rested protectively on his chest. In the second she was nursing a child, her hand supporting a neat hemispherical tit like a Madonna's. As if the point needed any further clarification, the child had wavy red hair.

Edward paged through the rest of the codex quickly. The remaining pages recapitulated a similar sequence of images, but in reverse order: The young man was seen less and less often, and when he appeared he was alone, writing. The film was running itself backward. The Duchess was pictured more often with her husband, or reading by herself. The penultimate image showed the noble couple together, with the growing child between them. The very last initial, a lavish golden *E*, showed the young man alone again, quill in hand. His eyes were the same as before: hooded, unhappy, penetrating. The sky behind him had darkened to an inky blue-black, swarming with bright white stars. The book open on the table next to him was now full of writing.

Edward looked at the last picture for a long minute. The blank eyes of Gervase of Langford looked back at him, and their gazes met across the centuries. Edward folded his arms and stared back at the page. *So?* he thought. *What do you expect me to do about it?*

Or maybe Gervase wasn't asking him for something, maybe he was trying to tell him something. Maybe he was trying to warn him. Despite the lateness of the hour, Edward made an effort to concentrate. After all, this was the great secret that they'd rescued from within so many other nested secrets within secrets – from a game within a game, then a book within a book, then another book hidden inside that one. Gervase had tried to escape out of his own world with the Duchess, and in the end he'd finally done just that. And look what it had gotten him. The eyes just looked blank now, but there was darkness there, black misery, Edward recognized it – misery was still misery, and six hundred years of history hadn't done anything to improve it. The more he stared the more the blackness in Gervase's eyes frightened him, like the darkness of that blind canyon in the *Viage* that the knights had plunged into, never to return. Pain was there, Edward thought. And death. He shifted uncomfortably on Margaret's hard chair. Gervase knew about escape, he knew about trying to live out a fantasy life, and all he'd gotten for it were loss and hurt and an early grave. He'd wandered off the straight path, and he'd fallen on the sharp hungry rocks that waited below. There was danger there for him too, for Edward, and it was close, very close . . .

Edward closed his burning eyes and shook his head. Snap out of it, he thought. No point in making connections where there weren't any. As Margaret would say, not everything means something. He pushed the pages away from him.

Margaret lay on her side on the bed, her eyes closed. He thought she'd fallen asleep, but somehow she sensed he was done and raised her head.

'Did you see it?' she asked.

'I saw it.'

'But did you *see*?' She sat up all the way. 'Do you see what this means? My God. Gervase of Langford fathered the Duchess of Bowmry's child and left it to be raised as the Duke's. He must have been in love with her after all.'

'I saw.'

'But it's so perfect. It makes so much *sense!*' Her

385

hands were pale fists on her bare knees, and her eyes burned with scholarly zeal. 'There's so much longing in the *Viage*, such a sense of loss! Why? Because it was written by a man who'd lost his child and his lover, but who still had them in front of his eyes every day, and could never touch them! His life was an emotional wasteland. That's where Cimmeria came from. Maybe this was for his son – Gervase must have thought he might find it one day.'

'Right.' Edward rubbed his sandy eyes. He checked the windows, but it was still dark out. It felt like a week had passed in the last twelve hours.

'This could be it – don't you get it? The missing piece of the puzzle! No wonder his reputation was ruined in London, it must have been all over the city. My God, this changes everything. Instead of writing pious little fables, or press releases in verse for his patrons, or love poetry, he was writing this – this glorious, godless, escapist romance about knights and monsters. No wonder he was passed over! Gervase was the first educated man in England to discover reading for pleasure. The Duchess must have known, too.' He could see the gears of her mind gripping and turning, picking up speed, gathering mental torque. 'Maybe that's how he won her – like Paolo and Francesca, remember? The couple who were seduced by a book?'

'That's a big leap to make from a bunch of cartoons, don't you think?' Edward said. He should have been elated, but instead his mind was muzzy and irritable. He found himself perversely wanting to deflate her, to poke holes in her theory.

'Maybe.' Margaret flopped down on the bed and stared up at the blank white ceiling. 'It's right, though, I know it is. It's too perfect. What do you think the Duchess will do with it?'

'I don't know,' he lied. 'I'm not sure.'

Of course he knew what she would do with it. It would become a weapon, or a hostage, in her little internecine war with the Duke. If the Duchess had borne Gervase's child, then the Duke's precious lineage was compromised, tainted by bastardy and infidelity, and she had the means to prove it. God knows when or if Margaret would ever get her chance at the codex. Edward sat at her desk and rested his chin on his folded hands. He had decisions to make, but he lacked the will to make them. He gazed dumbly at the ancient leaves. He could sense her rewriting her dissertation in her head. She probably wanted him to leave so she could get to work right then and there.

'It's an amazing discovery,' he said, playing along. 'If it's true. It'll absolutely make you famous.'

She nodded, but he could tell she wasn't listening. Outside in the night a distant siren wailed. Somebody or something knocked the lid off a trash can and sent it rolling noisily for an improbable length of time, on and on, until it finally came to rest with a grand tympanic crash. It was after five now, and the sun would be up soon. A crushing wave of fatigue rose up and broke over him, obliterating all further thought. He stood up, switched off the light, and collapsed back into bed.

Margaret lay facing away from him. Her ponytail poked him gently in the face, and he tenderly disentangled the pink rubber band that held it together and launched it away into the darkness with his thumb and forefinger.

'You can't stay here,' she whispered after a while.

'Why not?'

He kept on stroking her hair.

'I have people coming tomorrow morning.'

'What kind of people?'

'Just people. Visitors.'

She wriggled a little under the covers, getting more comfortable.

'That's okay,' said Edward. 'People like me. I'm a people person.'

There was a long pause. He was almost asleep.

'Just a couple of hours,' he whispered. 'Then I'll go. I promise I'll go.'

She didn't answer, but he heard her setting the alarm clock she kept by her bed.

CHAPTER 21

'Edward, what's happening?'

Edward didn't even sit up in bed. He just turned over on his back and put the phone in the general vicinity of his ear and left it at that. He was back in his own apartment: Margaret had kicked him out at dawn, as promised, and after searching for a cab for what felt like hours up and down shuttered, deserted, trash-strewn stretches of Flatbush Avenue he'd finally given up and taken the subway home. He'd been asleep for half an hour, a delicious, cloud-strewn, rainbow-tinted half-hour of unconsciousness, when the phone rang.

'Edward?' the Duchess repeated, less patiently. 'Are you there?'

'I'm here.'

'You sound strange. Is something wrong?'

Edward thought about that for a while, weighing both sides of the question equally and taking into account the full scope and complexity of the circumstances before he answered.

'I'm fine,' he said.

'You left a message on the machine.' She was in

her imperious mode, her voice hard and urgent, brushed steel. 'What's happening? Do you have another lead?'

He was still at the disadvantage of an asleep person talking to an awake person, but he cleared his throat.

'Blanche, I have it,' he managed. 'We have the codex. We found it last night.'

'Oh, thank God!' she whispered.

The Duchess disappeared, and there was the clunk of the phone hitting something hard. In the background he heard a big, theatrical sigh of relief, then a hysterical laugh which sounded scarily close to a sob. Edward sat up in bed. He thought he could hear her breathing heavily. It took another half minute for the Duchess to pick up the phone again.

'Thank God, I thought we'd never find it!' she said cheerily, as if nothing had happened, as if he'd just told her that he'd found his lost contact lens. 'Not that I was much help, was I? Where are you?'

'I'm in my apartment.' He lay back down. 'You called me here.'

'You're right. My God, I'm losing my grip. Is your girlfriend there?'

'Is who here?'

'"Is who here?"' She mimicked him and laughed again, not quite as pleasantly. 'I meant Margaret. Is she there with you?'

'She's not—' He sighed. Never mind, whatever. 'No. I'm here alone.'

'What are you going to do now?'

'I don't know.' It came out sounding more plaintive than he meant it to, but it was true. So much had happened yesterday that he hadn't even thought it through yet. 'You tell me. Should I come to England?'

After what sounded like a moment of mental calculation, she replied:

'Yes. Why not.'

'But isn't that what you wanted?'

He was guessing now, taking stabs in the dark.

'Of course it is,' she said soothingly. 'How soon can you come?'

'I already have a flight booked, in a couple of days – E & H is flying me over. Hang on a second and I'll get the flight times.'

'A couple of days? I need it sooner than that.'

'Well, I suppose I could try to find an earlier flight.'

'Never mind,' she said brusquely, 'I'll take care of it.'

The playful, girlish tone was gone again, replaced by a firm, wintry tone of command, the voice of someone accustomed to using money to compress time and distance to her own specifications. He could imagine her ordering around legions of maids with that voice.

'Stay where you are until you hear from me, and don't talk to anyone. How does that sound? Can you manage that?'

She hung up without waiting for an answer.

'Roger,' he said into the dead telephone. He turned off the ringer and fell back asleep.

Somebody was pounding on the door of his apartment.

'All right, *all right!*' he yelled without opening his eyes. He lay there for another few seconds, angrily savoring the last moments of sleep, then levered himself upright.

Edward walked to the bathroom, splashed water on his face, and wrapped himself in a fluffy white bathrobe. His eyes felt like they were full of dried rubber cement. Five messages on the answering machine. For a few seconds he didn't even remember what had happened the night before, then it all came rushing back to him. There was no time to think about it. He peered through the peephole.

The person at the door was Laura Crowlyk. Her long, freckled face was wide awake and flushed with excitement. He opened the door.

'Edward!' she cried. She reached up to put both her hands on his shoulders and kissed him long and resoundingly on the mouth. 'You found it!'

Flustered, he took a step backward, and she bustled past him into his apartment.

'The Duchess called me.' She stopped and hugged him again, as if they were having a long-awaited reunion. 'I knew you were the one!' she said into his terry-cloth shoulder. 'I always knew it was you.'

'You did?'

'I can only stay a minute.' She pushed him away. 'We have a great deal to do.'

Laura was utterly transformed, her haughtiness gone and replaced by manic good humor. Her serious features weren't suited to such an extreme state of glee. She plunked her buff-leather Coach bag down on his kitchen table.

'I'm going to get dressed,' Edward said.

He gathered up some clean clothes and retreated backward into the bathroom, holding them protectively in front of him in a defensive posture. When he came out, wearing a T-shirt and jeans and feeling marginally more human, she'd put the coffee on. He leaned against the counter, feeling dizzy from lack of sleep.

'So what can I do for you?'

She took a cream-colored envelope out of her bag and handed it to him.

'Plane ticket,' she said.

He opened the envelope. It was to London, one-way, business class. This must be what the Duchess meant when she said she'd take care of it.

'Jesus. This flight leaves in five hours.'

'It was the first one we could get you on.'

'Look, you don't have to do this,' Edward explained patiently. 'The firm is already paying my moving expenses to London. I have a flight leaving on Tuesday.'

'It can't wait till Tuesday,' she said primly. 'It can't wait another minute. Everything is starting now, Edward. If you can't go, we'll send someone else.'

'No, I'll go,' Edward said, stung.

'Good. A limo will pick you up here at noon to take you to the airport. We'll have a car waiting at Heathrow.'

She handed him a second envelope, this one considerably thicker.

'A thousand dollars and a thousand pounds,' she explained. 'For any expenses.'

Edward didn't open it. He didn't have to. He wasn't an idiot: He knew it would all be there. He glanced down at the two envelopes, the money in one hand, the ticket in the other, then up at Laura's flushed, expectant face. A rarefied, intoxicating gas was filling his lungs and carbonating his bloodstream: happiness. It was finally happening. He was passing through the doorway, crossing over into her world, the world of the Duchess. He squared off the envelopes with a businesslike crispness and set them aside before he could do anything stupid, like hold them up to the light or sniff them for their new-money smell.

He sat down at the kitchen table, gripping the most familiar object within reach – his coffee-hot souvenir Enron mug – with both hands as if it were the only solid fulcrum in an otherwise swiftly tilting universe. The last twenty-four hours had been so rushed and dreamlike that they hadn't really sunk in, like a barrage of unread e-mail, but now they were hitting him all at once. The money was nothing, of course. Grossly more than the circumstances called for but infinitely less than a snipped fingernail to the Wents. It was what it stood for, the ease with which it was dispensed, evoking by synecdoche the unimaginable sums that stood behind it. He thought back to the first and only time he'd actually seen the Duchess in the flesh. The dark locks beneath the brim of her sun hat, her pale upturned face, that wide, heart-breaking mouth. She was waiting for him. Not just waiting, she was impatient.

He stared down at his coffee, feeling his pulse start to race. Things were moving too quickly, blurring at the edges, getting away from him. He knew he had to take a giant step backward and get some perspective on the situation. He needed to go in with a plan. He would meet with the Duchess at Weymarshe, formally. He would present her with the codex – or should he leave it in London in a safe-deposit box, show up empty-handed? Which was the stronger position? They'd have to discuss terms, remuneration, a place for him in her organization. He'd need to see some paperwork. He would want to talk to a lawyer.

And then, if all went well, back to London to resign his position at E & H. And then – what? He grimaced. There were too many variables here and too few constants. He was out of his depth. Nick was right: The Duchess hadn't made any promises, or none she couldn't break. *Your instincts are better than this,* he told himself. He'd gone through a lot of trouble and expense to acquire first-class instincts, weapons-grade instincts, and they were telling him to cut his losses here and now. Even Margaret knew better: Never do anything that you can't reverse.

And yet. Something was still pulling him forward, something he couldn't name or describe, a motivation from way out in deep space, way beyond the familiar constellation of desires – hunger, lust, greed, ambition. It was telling him to throw his career away, and he was doing it. He was going through with it. He would never, ever forgive himself if he turned back now. He pictured himself in a bedroom at Weymarshe, sipping coffee by himself in the early morning, in the silence of the deep countryside. Cool stone floors. A large white bed like a white marble tomb, rich linens tastefully disarrayed, white light flooding in through tall windows, green allées receding into the undulating distance.

There would be problems, he knew that. He wasn't delusional. But they'd be new problems, better problems than he had now. He rubbed his chin. He needed to shave. And his stuff – he'd never finished packing. Edward looked around at his chaotic apartment with dismay. There were half-filled boxes everywhere, stacks of books and CDs spilling onto the floor. A crippled coffee table stood with two legs on and two legs off, where he and Zeph had abandoned it.

'I'll never be ready by noon,' he said.

'Not to worry!' said Laura, trilling like Mary Poppins. She covered his hand with hers. 'We'll send your things on after you. Or you can stay at the castle, why not? You have a passport?'

Edward nodded dumbly. He felt the apparatus of the Duchess's money swooping down, safely enfolding him in its protective wings. He'd spent his whole career playing with obscene amounts of wealth, counting it, manipulating it, pouring it from account to account, then parking it neatly like a valet and surrendering it to its rightful owner. This must be how it felt from the inside.

'Well, then,' she said. 'I think you're all set.'

She stood up to go. Edward stood up with her, taking a deep breath. He felt drunk.

'Ms Crowlyk—'

'For God's sake, call me Laura.' She beamed at him fiercely as she shouldered her bag. 'You're a part of the family now.'

'Laura,' he said, as seriously as he could with his head swimming, 'what exactly is going to happen now? Once the Duchess has the codex? I mean, what's she going to do with it?'

She paused, looking at him appraisingly.

'I don't think that's really any of your business,' she said carefully. 'Or mine, for that matter. We've done our jobs. We've done what we had to do. Now the Duchess will do what she has to do.'

'But why? What's going to happen to the Duke?'

'Only what he's got coming to him. Only what he deserves. He'd do as much to her if he could, and worse.'

'So – it's all okay?' he said helplessly.

'Of course it is!' She touched his arm, and her face took on an air of maternal concern. 'Of course it is! As long as you have the codex. You do have it, don't you?'

Edward nodded weakly, his mind racing again.

He went to let her out, but at the threshold she stopped and turned to face him. For a moment she seemed much older, almost haggard. The points of her collarbone showed above the neckline of her dress, and the skin above it bore a flushed red patch the shape of Australia. She took a step toward him, her eyes glowing with mysterious expectation, and for a second Edward thought she was going to kiss him again.

'Can I see it?' she asked.

Edward blinked. 'See what?'

'The codex, foolish boy. Can I see it?'

'It's not here.'

'It's not?' A flicker of doubt crossed her gleeful eyes. 'Well, where is it?'

'Margaret has it. It's at her apartment.'

'Margaret—?'

'Margaret Napier. The woman from Columbia.'

Her head reared back. She looked like she wanted to spit in his face.

'You complete bloody fucking bloody idiot. When can you get it back?'

'Whenever I need it,' said Edward.

'Well.' Laura's face was contorted, almost frightening. She was literally shaking with disgust. 'Go on and go get it!'

She tried to slam the door on her way out, but Edward caught it before it could close.

'Laura,' he said, 'it's just over the bridge in Brooklyn. It's fine. We still have plenty of time.'

She pursed her lips and said nothing, then she opened her leather bag and rummaged around in it furiously for a few seconds. Edward waited. What the hell was she looking for? A gun? A compact? A glove, with which to slap him across the face? She came up with a small square packet wrapped in pink tissue paper.

'There,' she said icily. 'The Duchess asked me to give you that.'

He unfolded it standing in the doorway. Inside was a single earring in the shape of a tiny, exquisite silver hourglass. He turned it over in his hands, tenderly, then he looked up again just as Laura slammed the door in his face.

Edward took a long, lukewarm shower. His whole body felt dull and achy after his mostly sleepless night. Edward's building was equipped with immensely powerful pre-war plumbing, and his shower was capable of dispensing torrents of warm water at crushingly high pressure for indefinite periods of time. He let it sluice down over his face, smooth as glass, flattening his hair, spilling down his cheeks, gently closing his eyelids. He felt like one of those intrepid explorers who, bayed by cannibalistic pygmies, discovers a secret hideaway in the pocket of space behind a waterfall.

He blinked. He'd drifted off on his feet. It was time to get moving again. He only had five hours to catch his plane, less than that now. He shut off the water, dried himself hurriedly, and got dressed. Before he left he sent an e-mail to Zeph and Caroline letting them know what was going on.

It was after ten when he stepped out onto the side-walk, his head still spinning. It was a Saturday morning, and the street was empty. A broad fat leaf, still green, came flipping down out of the clear blue sky and flopped gracelessly onto the pavement. He felt like he was walking on the moon.

A large, shiny black sedan was parked by the curb. As he passed it one of the rear doors opened.

'Wait,' said a voice. 'Edward.'

Edward turned around to find the tall, lanky form of Nick Harris jogging to catch up with him. He wore a rumpled gray suit that looked like he'd slept in it, and not especially well. His hair was longer than Edward remembered it. In his dark glasses he looked like a blond vampire.

But he was smiling. Edward just smiled back at him. At this point he was past surprise. He just accepted the fact that the world had resorted to simply flinging people at him at random.

'What?' he said.

'Need to talk to you.'

Edward didn't want to stop, and Nick was unwilling to let him go, so they walked along the sidewalk together in step. Nick had a small black

400

cell phone in his hand. He said something into it and tucked it away in his jacket.

'Were you waiting for me?'

'Yes. Do you have the book?'

'You actually staked out my apartment?'

Nick took off his glasses. His eyes were blood-shot from lack of sleep.

'Yes. Parking's a nightmare around here, have you noticed?'

'I don't have a car.'

'Have you got the book?'

'So now you're saying it does exist?'

There was an uncomfortable pause. The morning sunlight was painfully strong, and Edward shaded his eyes with his free hand. He wondered if he was actually as good at this as he thought he was.

'This isn't a game to us, Edward.'

'Not when you're losing, anyway. But to answer your question, no, I don't have the codex.'

Edward couldn't help noticing that the big black sedan was now pacing them down the block.

'But you know where it is,' Nick said. 'You can get it.'

'I might be able to.'

'Well, we have to get rid of it. Burn it, if we can.'

'It won't burn.'

Nick blinked at him. He pushed back his floppy bangs.

'What do you mean?'

'The codex is written on parchment, not paper.

It's not flammable. Listen, I'm in kind of a hurry—'

The cell phone reappeared in Nick's hand.

'I have His Grace on the line,' he said. 'He has a straight cash offer for you. I think you'll find it surprisingly generous. We want to settle this in a friendly way.'

He scratched the back of his head unselfconsciously. Edward had last seen Nick only a few days ago, but those days had apparently been difficult ones. He hadn't shaved, and his famous pocket watch was nowhere in sight. Edward didn't feel especially sorry for him. He sighed and closed his eyes. All he wanted was to bring this scene to a timely close – it had really ceased to be at all interesting in any way. Why were they still after him? He'd found the codex. It was real. Whatever was inside it, whatever Margaret had brought to light with her secret decoder ring, it was his. He groped for words. *How can I put this? Game over. I win.*

'Give it to me. Give me the phone.'

Edward stopped walking and held out his hand. Nick gave him the cell phone. Edward hung it up, snapped it shut, and handed it back.

'I'm sorry,' he said. He spread out his arms. 'We have nothing to talk about.'

Nick didn't seem surprised. He watched Edward with the hardened cheeriness of somebody who was accustomed to rejection. Now he was scratching his shoulder.

'I think we do. Have you ever wondered how you got that cushy job in London, Edward? The Duke arranged it for you. He could rearrange it just as easily.'

'I don't believe you,' Edward said, smiling sunnily.

He didn't. It had to be a bluff. He was reasonably positive it was, anyway. Not that he was overly attached to his job at the moment, but he was still proud of having won it in the first place, and he was damned if he was going to give that up. Either way, he had no time to get his balance back, because while Nick was delivering this carefully calibrated bombshell Edward heard the little flurry of sounds associated with the halting of an automobile – the ratchet of the emergency brake, the car door opening, the keys-still-in-lock chime – and out of the sedan climbed a short Turkish-looking man with a mustache: the Wents' ex-doorman.

In retrospect the scratching had probably been a prearranged signal. The doorman joined Nick on the sidewalk, threading his way jauntily between two parked cars.

'We need your help on this one, Ed,' Nick said with the avuncular manner of a soccer coach. 'You could save yourself some real trouble.'

Edward waited, but neither one of them said anything more. Looking from one to the other, Edward was visited by the creeping suspicion, almost unbelievable on the face of it, that he was being physically menaced.

'Where were you headed?' Nick went on casually. 'Why don't we give you a ride? We can talk in the car.'

It was much, much too early in the morning for this, but Edward sized up his options, trying to get himself into the spirit of things. What the hell, neither of them was as tall as he was, and the Turkish doorman looked like his best scrapping days were behind him. He could probably just shove his way out of it. But Nicholas was toned and pink, and as Edward watched he set himself in a sparring stance, suggestive of some kind of old-fashioned English martial arts training. Edward was exhausted, and he hadn't been in a fight since grade school.

He backed up a step. Nick and the doorman spread out on either side of him to cut off his escape routes. His mind wandered back to his days as a swashbuckling air pirate in MOMUS. What would his virtual alter ego do here? He was sick of running away.

Then the two men weren't looking at him anymore. Their gaze had shifted to something over Edward's shoulder.

'*Top o' the marnin' to ye, lads!*' boomed a vibrant bass voice in an atrocious attempt at an Irish accent. The voice stopped, then tried again, sounding exactly as bad as the first time. 'Wait. I'll get it. *Top o' the* – wait. *Top o' the marnin' to ye!*'

Edward risked a quick look behind him.

As enormous as he was, it had never occurred to Edward that Zeph's appearance could be in any way threatening. Now he was forcefully reminded of the effect Zeph's considerable bulk had on strangers. Granted, Zeph was wearing Teva sandals and a black T-shirt with the words GENERIC HUMANOID CARBON UNIT on it in yellow block letters, slanted perspectively to look like the prologue to *Star Wars*. Nevertheless, he was six and a half feet tall and well north of three hundred pounds, and he was sporting an extremely scary-looking beard. From where Edward stood he actually appeared to be partially blocking out the morning sun.

Edward turned back to face his adversaries. The standoff was over. He cleared his throat.

'I never liked you,' he said to the Wents' doorman, 'and I don't think much of your boss either. So why don't you and James Blond here get back in your carriage and go back to the Duke of Earl and you can all have tea and crumpets together?'

It was all he could think of on the spur of the moment.

At this hour on a weekend the drive to Brooklyn didn't take long, even stopping to drop Zeph off at his apartment downtown, and in half an hour he was standing on the crazed, cracked cement sidewalk in front of Margaret's building. A ginger cat twitched its long white whiskers at him from its perch behind a window box. Next to the column of doorbells he found the name 'Napier' written on a paper slip in her neat, pointy handwriting. A raindrop had fallen on it and then dried, blotting the black ink into a delicate blue watercolor bloom.

Edward pressed the button. From the depths of the house came the distant echo of an answering ring.

A silent interval followed. Shock and fatigue were making his mind wander, and for a long, terrifying flash he thought she might be gone, that she might have just taken the codex and left town – where would she go? back to her mother? – but an instant later Margaret appeared. Evidently the buzzer wasn't working, because she came down to let him in herself. Her face was puffy from sleep, and her slender body was hidden under a baggy T-shirt and gray sweatpants. She didn't seem particularly surprised to see him. He followed her upstairs.

Her apartment, so disorderly the night before, was clean and neat now. The Chinese food was cleared away; the dishes were stacked in the drainer; her clothes were out of sight. The remains of the gutted books were arranged in two neat piles on the floor, one of leather covers and spines, one of discarded pages. Only the bed was rumpled.

'Sorry I woke you up,' Edward said.

She waved aside his apology.

'Did you sleep enough?'

'Enough,' she said. 'There's a lot to do.'

'What about your friends?'

'They didn't come. I told them not to.'

She didn't offer any other explanation. Her voice

was husky, and she ran herself a glass of water at the kitchen sink. The water pipes clanked loudly.

'There's something I have to talk to you about,' he said. 'I need to take the codex.'

Her expression didn't change. He went on.

'About an hour ago Laura Crowlyk woke me up. The Duchess's assistant. She came to my apartment and handed me a plane ticket to London and told me to bring the codex with me. I'm supposed to give it to the Duchess.'

Margaret nodded. Her face showed no expression, no reaction, not even blankness.

'When is your flight?'

'This afternoon. Margaret, the codex isn't ours, even though we found it. The Wents still own it.'

'I know that,' she snapped, but halfheartedly.

She turned to the desk where she'd been working. There was a package on it, wrapped in a canvas tote bag from Target, and Margaret unwrapped it. It was the case he'd found on his very first day in the Wents' library. It was made of fine-grained wood, plain but finished and polished to a buttery yellow glow in the Saturday morning light, with delicate metal hinges on one side and a single cleverly wrought catch on the other.

'I brought it with us yesterday when we took the rest of the books,' she said quietly. 'When we were leaving the Wents' apartment. The case is modern, of course, but it's quite nice all the same, and that binding is almost certainly original. It fits perfectly.

Goatskin, I think, over oak boards. So it wasn't Lydgate after all.'

She opened the box to reveal the covers of the hollow book, nestling in the velvet interior.

'I should have guessed the first time. This was the codex all along. Minus its contents, of course. But I suppose it's really the binding that makes a codex a codex, technically speaking.'

Edward nodded and touched the dark, gnarled leather surface of the cover, with its dense ornaments and indecipherable icons and images, worn smooth with age and handling. He'd been so fascinated by them the first time he'd seen them in the Wents' library. Now he wanted to ask Margaret what they were, who made them and how, and what they meant, but it was already much too late for that. He was out of time.

He flipped the case closed again and latched it. Her eyes followed his hands, as if she were hoping for a last look or a last-minute reprieve. He felt worse than he expected. He took a deep breath.

'I can't thank you enough for everything,' he said, the words sounding all wrong even as he said them. 'You know the Duchess will pay you for all the work you've done. Just send them an invoice – take whatever we agreed on and multiply it by ten. She won't mind now. Chances are she won't even notice. And God knows you've earned it.'

They were standing face-to-face, Margaret cupping the tumbler of water with both hands, her dark hair flat and unwashed but still lovely. There was so much more that he wasn't telling her, and so much more after that he wanted to tell her and didn't know how.

'What do you think she'll do with it?' she asked.

'I don't know. Probably have it assessed. Maybe arrange to donate it to a museum. Maybe she'll keep it for her personal collection. I really don't know.'

With each fluent lie he told, Edward felt like he was losing her, like his words were rolling time backwards, erasing everything they'd been through together and leaving them strangers again, the way they had been that first day in the library. But he couldn't tell her the truth. It was the Duchess's secret to tell, not his, and Margaret was better off not knowing it anyway.

'I don't want money, Edward.' She couldn't meet his eyes. He wondered if she'd prepared this speech. 'I just want to spend time with it. I know it wasn't my discovery' – she cut him off – 'no, it was you who found it in the end. I know that. But I can read the codex, Edward. I can speak for it. I can speak for him, for Gervase. No one else could do that as well as I could.'

'I know, Margaret. Believe me, I'll do everything I can for you.'

'Then take me with you.'

Even as his heart was breaking, a stream of words was coming out of his mouth that he felt no identification with or control over whatsoever. 'Consultancy,' 'core competencies,' 'client

409

relationship,' 'maintain ownership of the process.' It was like a robot talking. He, or it, talked faster and faster, trying to stay ahead of his own feelings of shame and doubt, which loomed over him like a breaking wave curling above a surfer.

'Listen,' he said, desperately trying to bring the horrible speech to a close, 'I think I'm staying at Weymarshe. I'll call you when I get there, we can figure out the terms. All right?'

She gave him a small, forced smile.

'We'll talk about it when you get there,' she said.

'I'll call you. However you want to do it.'

Edward slipped the case back into the canvas tote bag and hoisted it jauntily onto his shoulder. It was almost time to go.

'Did you have time to read any more of the book?'

'Some.' She nodded, seeming as relieved as he was to talk about something other than their future. 'Some of the pages need restoration work before they'll be fully legible.'

'Did you figure out how it ends?' he asked. 'We last left our hero in the middle of a frozen wasteland, right? Something like that? Don't keep me in suspense.' Everything he said and thought made him cringe.

She pursed her lips.

'It's interesting. I've been teasing out some of the earlier underlying texts, before this one. The palimpsest. It looks like Gervase toyed with a few different endings. In one of them the protagonist goes native and marries a Cimmerian woman. In

410

one he becomes very holy and converts them all to Christianity. In one it turns out – I think – that Cimmeria was really England all along, only it was so devastated by plague and winter as to be unrecognizable.'

'Very *Planet of the Apes*.'

'Isn't it? But Gervase scrapped all those versions. In the final draft, the hero wakes up one morning and realizes it's Easter Sunday. It's been a long time since he's been to Mass, and he needs to go to confession. He doesn't know if the Cimmerians are Christians, but he asks, and they agree to lead him to a church.

'They take him to a miraculous chapel, telling him that to pray there is his only chance for a safe return home. The chapel is mysteriously constructed entirely out of stained glass, without a single stone. I don't know if you've ever been to Paris, but I imagine it looks something like the Sainte-Chapelle. The windows depict stories out of classical myth: Orpheus and Eurydice, Pygmalion, the fall of Troy, and so on. In a way the whole structure is like a codex. Gervase points out the resemblance: "Hyt was as a very boke hytself, a volume boonde wyth walles, with leeves of glas."

'It is, he realizes, the Rose Chapel. It's the mystical church that the stag knight described at the very beginning of the story, that was the object of his quest all along. He's finally found it, long after he stopped looking for it. The quest is finally over.

'It's hot inside, which makes a certain kind of

literal sense – I imagine a glass building like that would function something like a greenhouse. The lord feels warm and safe for the first time in months. He prays, and as he prays he lets go of the things he had been looking for. All at once he no longer misses his wife, or his home in England. He no longer cares about anything on earth. He lets go of everything that had ever been important to him. Maybe it's a spiritual epiphany, a shedding of all his earthly, material bonds, or maybe he's just exhausted. In a mixture of faith and disillusionment, ecstasy and disappointment, he takes off his armor, curls up, and falls asleep in front of the altar. As he sleeps, his soul leaves his body and is accepted into heaven.'

Edward shifted from foot to foot. There was something satisfying about the ending, but also something sad about it.

'So that's it? He never gets to go home?'

She shook her head slowly. 'He doesn't get to go home.'

He felt like he should have something intelligent to say about it, but he was drawing a blank.

'What do you think it means?'

Margaret shrugged.

'I know what my colleagues will think,' she said guardedly. 'On a dialectical level the Rose Chapel is the inverse of the black page in the second fragment: light where the black page is dark, sheltering where the blind canyon is destroying, legible where the blackness is unreadable . . .'

412

'Okay, okay. I get it. But what do you think?'

She turned away to her desk and discreetly swept some book dust off it into the palm of her hand.

'It's strange. It feels almost more existential than Christian. I don't know. I like it.'

'Well,' he said uncomfortably, 'but don't you think he should have gotten to go home? In the end?'

She rounded on him without warning.

'Is that what you think? You think he should get to go home?' She threw the fistful of dust at him. He flinched. 'Look around you! Is that what the world is like? Everybody gets what they want, everything works out fine, everybody gets to go home. Is that what you think?'

'Well, no,' Edward said, brushing himself off, hurt and baffled. 'I mean, I don't know—'

'You don't know? Well, you'll find out!' she retorted bitterly. 'Or why don't you ask the Duchess? Maybe she can tell you.'

Her anger came almost as a relief. He wanted her to be angry. He was angry at himself.

'All right,' he said. 'All right. I'm sorry, Margaret. I have no choice about this. You know that. I'll do everything I can for you.'

She nodded. She dusted off her hands over the trash.

'I know,' she said. 'I know that.'

A stillness fell over the room. The constant background wash of street noise, always audible in Margaret's apartment, mysteriously ceased for a second, leaving them alone in a conspicuous silence. He shifted the bag on his shoulder.

'I should go,' he said. 'My flight is in a couple of hours.'

'All right.'

'We'll talk soon. I'll call you when I get there.'

'All right.'

She took a graceless half step forward and kissed him with unexpected tenderness. He held her for a moment, then turned and unlatched the door. There was nothing else to say. Anyway, she knew it wasn't his fault. There was no real reason for him to feel guilty.

CHAPTER 22

Two hours later Edward was sitting in a Chili's on the concourse at J.F.K. wearing his most expensive suit – a black four-button Hugo Boss – and his best black leather shoes, with an impeccable pink silk tie rolled up in his pocket. He had two bags with him: his laptop case, into which he'd also managed to stuff his toothbrush and an extra change of socks and underwear, and the tote bag with the codex in it. He stowed them safely under the table, clamped between his knees, and ordered a huge frosted mug of pale Mexican beer with a chunk of lime floating in it. He felt like he should have something quintessentially American before he left.

He glanced surreptitiously at his reflection in a mirrored beer ad. The pain of leaving Margaret behind was still with him, but it was starting to pale next to the thrill of what was happening next. It was all coming together. Now that he was actually on his way the whole past month seemed like one long, dreamlike ordeal that was finally ending, and thank God. Even the past four years that he'd spent working at Esslin & Hart seemed unreal, like a jail sentence he served for a crime he never even committed. Forget about it. That time was gone. He was facing forward, ready to start over. God, he was so tired. He felt like an astronaut waiting on the gantry, his rocket sweating liquid nitrogen on the launch pad, waiting to boost him up and out and into the next world.

A voice called his flight over the PA. A flight attendant was waiting for Edward beyond the security checkpoint, and she accompanied Edward personally to his seat, squiring him past the long line of passengers who shuffled obediently down the telescoping corridor to the airplane. Nice touch. Once he was on board Edward didn't want to stow the codex in an overhead compartment – in an ideal world, he thought, he would have had it handcuffed to his wrist, secret agent style – but he was determined to keep his laptop with him, so he reluctantly consigned the case with the codex in it to the luggage rack. A nozzle over his head blasted him with dry, frozen air. The seat next to him was empty, presumably having been bought up by the Duchess for his traveling comfort. He thought about trying to call Esslin & Hart on his cell phone to tell them he was en route, but at that same moment the announcement came to turn off all electronic devices, and he put it away. The day had gone dark, and a couple of raindrops left fine stitches of water down the thick plastic window. Through it he watched the runway crew driving around in their weirdly shaped baggage-handling vehicles, like alien golf carts.

When they finally took off the acceleration pressed him gently back into his seat. His long night was finally catching up with him, and he closed his eyes. They seemed to be rising up, up, up into nothingness, and he felt as if at any moment he might just vanish, just blissfully cease to be, draw the curtains, bring up the houselights. The story was over, and it wasn't perfect, but well, things were never perfect, were they, except maybe in books. By the time they were above the clouds he was asleep.

He woke up again in the middle of the in-flight movie. He watched it lazily, not even bothering to put on the free headset. It was a big-budget martial arts movie, easy enough to follow even minus the dialogue. The young hero was being trained by an ancient fighting master who set him a series of torturous exercises. He played the flute while balancing on the point of a sword. He shattered a giant ruby by smashing it with his forehead in slow motion. He kicked tropical fruits off the heads of the masters' servants without ruffling their bowl haircuts.

The time came for the disciple to compete in a big tournament. Not only did he fail miserably, he was publicly humiliated by the star pupil of the ancient fighting master's archrival, a shadowy figure possessed of sinister mustachios. The old master shook his head sadly. All that time and training – wasted. But just when all hope seemed to be lost, when the master's pretty daughter was struggling to hold back tears, the disciple re-appeared. The purpose of his training had become clear to him. His dormant abilities manifested themselves. He re-entered the ring. Victory in the big tournament. Defeat of the archrival's student. Joy with the pretty daughter. Knowing smile of the master. The movie ended.

It was dark inside the plane. The window shades were drawn – glowing red with the high-altitude sunset behind them – and all the reading lights were off except for one single one, far up toward the front of the plane. The dry, sterile air was cold, and each passenger snuggled up underneath his or her individual gray fleece blanket. On the monitors the arc of their trajectory was approaching the Arctic Circle, and the sound of the engines had become a dull, soporific, reassuringly steady roar. The stewardesses clustered together silently at the ends of the aisles, slipping off their shoes to massage their shapely, aching feet through their stockings.

But Edward wasn't sleepy – he could already feel his circadian rhythms drifting out of whack – and he fished out his laptop from under the seat in front of him and booted it up. He slipped in the disc that he'd remembered, with the addict's presence of mind, to bring with him in his lapel pocket. The cool gray light from the liquid crystal screen flooded over him in the darkness like a bath of milk. MOMUS was waiting for him, as it always was, just where the Artiste had left it. Now that he had the means and the know-how and the free time to finish it off, he might as well do it.

To his surprise, Edward found that he remembered everything the Artiste had told him about how to win the game with absolute clarity: how to reactivate the subway, where to find the diamonds, how to get to the airport, how to fly to Florida, how to take a rocket into orbit. He still had four hours left till London, and now that he was free of the Artiste's Easter Egg it was all ridiculously easy. He felt like a tremendous weight had been lifted off his shoulders. He won every fight, found every clue, dodged every trap without even half trying.

Before he knew it he was up in outer space. The swirly blue-green marble of earth rolled beneath his feet. Missiles flew, lasers flashed. He had mustered a crack army of warriors and engineers, and now he bent them to his will: Using a superpowerful magnetic field they lassoed a passing asteroid – it was conveniently rich in ferrous metals – hauled it out of its trajectory and sent it hurtling into the center of the orbiting lens that the aliens had used to deprive the earth of sunlight. It was like the rose window of a cathedral shattering: A lattice of fine cracks spread out from the center – a jewel with a blinding bright flaw, or a great eye bloodshot with capillaries of molten gold – then it broke apart, letting through the pure intolerable burning brilliance of the sun.

419

Satisfaction. It was over. The earth was frozen and dead, but at least the aliens were gone, and soon the sun would be back. Life would re-emerge. He guessed. Anyway, he'd done his part, he'd won the game. He yawned and stretched.

Except that the game wasn't over. It was still going on. Edward frowned. Logically – at least according to Zeph's logic – there must still be something left to take care of. But what?

He studied the situation. It was nighttime, the night before the first new dawn of the old, un-filtered sun. Edward watched his little figure struggle along on the screen, tireless as ever, crunching robotically through the light, powdery snow that covered the ground. He guided it up the frozen river that led north out of the city, walking for miles along the ice, leaving a dotted line of miniature footprints behind him.

It took a long time, and he lost track of the minutes and hours in the monotony of the moonlit landscape, drift after drift, like waves or sand dunes, interrupted only by the occasional stand of ever-greens or a collapsed farmhouse half covered by a blanket of snow like a restless sleeper. And maybe time was the problem. He'd destroyed the giant floating lens and routed the invading aliens, but the aliens had speeded up time, too, and he hadn't fixed that, had he? For that matter, even if he did manage to stop time, hadn't the damage already been done? He tried to think like a science fiction geek for a minute. The earth was cold and dead.

Nothing was going to change that. Maybe it was too late after all. A creeping fear stole through him. Had he won the game, or had he lost it?

He rounded the last bend in the river valley. He was almost there. The ruins of the old bridge were long gone, but he recognized the shape of the bluff: This was where the game had started. The summit was still covered with grass that had somehow survived the cold – coarse, green, thick-bladed tufts, hoary with frost. It really was like Cimmeria. He wondered if the Artiste had stuck in a model of the Rose Chapel somewhere for him to find. Edward watched as a flat pink sunrise tinted the frozen field a delicate rose-gray. As he walked through it the frost crystals began to melt into dewdrops. When he stooped down to examine one, he saw in each gleaming droplet – and he'd long since stopped wondering how this degree of detail could even be possible – the reflection of the entire world around it, and in every other droplet appeared the reflection of that reflection, and on and on into infinity.

The old mailbox was still there, still empty. The thin birches and aspens he'd walked through at the very beginning of the game were bent almost double with the weight of ice and snow, so that they formed an arched colonnade roofed over with heavy drooping branches. Beside them was a great old tree, now overthrown and on its side, lying next to the pit its hideous roots dug as the weight of the trunk ripped them out of the earth. Edward settled deeper into the comforting embrace of his business class seat and closed his eyes.

But still the game went on. He ducked and dipped his way deeper into the grove, spilling branchloads of snow on himself. Isn't this where he came in? he thought. Maybe he could get out the same way. He'd messed up this world, now he'd just quietly slip out the back exit and try again in a new one. Better luck next time. But no, it was just trees and more trees. He put his hands on his hips and gazed up at the blank gray dome of the sky. Well, it was a puzzle, but you know what? He was tired of solving other people's problems, jumping through their hoops, prying into their secrets. He was tired of his own secrets, too. He took a deep breath: good, dry, crisp cold air.

Dawn came on, and snow began to fall. It fell and fell, light dry flakes, not the big mushy stuff that never sticks, that melts into slush before it has a chance to mount up into the big, solid drifts you really need. This was the good stuff, and it showed no sign of stopping. He leaned on the familiar white porch railing, brushing off the skim of snow that had already collected there, and looked out over the frozen river. It was all so pleasantly familiar, and why not? This was where he grew up. Apparently time had raced so far forward that it had looped back on itself, because here he was back in Maine again, and his father was alive, and his parents were still together. *Maybe I won the game after all*, he reflected, his dream-self formulating hazy dream-thoughts, *and this is my reward.*

He needed only one more thing before he was completely happy, and it was on its way. He watched the snow fall and listened to the special hush it brought with it. It was almost a sure thing now. There was no possible way there could be school tomorrow.

A bell rang. Edward opened his eyes. The FASTEN SEATBELTS sign was on. The plane was beginning its descent into Heathrow.

Something wonderful was happening inside him. He took a deep breath to try to calm himself down, but he couldn't stop grinning. He couldn't help it. He couldn't remember the last time he genuinely couldn't wait for something to happen. He wished he could stop time, prolong this gentle, stomach-lifting descent forever, the better to savor the anticipation. He stood up and hefted the bag with the codex in it down from the luggage rack and held it in his lap, feeling its reassuring solidity. The plane banked over the London suburbs. His window flooded full of sleeping gray roofs and scurrying white headlights.

Five minutes later they were on the ground. The plane taxied to the gate, and a line of disembarking passengers formed. Edward shouldered his bags and joined them. It was a relief just to stand up. His knees ached deliciously. By New York time it was only nine in the evening, but it was two in the morning in London. Outside in the waiting area everything looked subtly different and European. The payphones were red and white, and there were complicated, high-tech cigarette machines all along the walls. The snack bar had a fully alcoholic wet bar behind it. Beards were plentiful, and everybody seemed to have a cell phone and sunglasses.

Edward was in no hurry. He stood by the gate and waited while the crowd streamed out of the plane around him. Like all airports, Heathrow was rich in arrows and signs, branching trails, forking paths, into which his anonymous fellow travelers busily sorted themselves. They passed him by as if he were just one of them, just part of the crowd, instead of somebody with a critical and highly secret mission to carry out. He was ready to join the general flood, to allow himself to be swept along and sorted, but he paused for just a minute. He was in no hurry. He could afford to take his time. He watched silent news on a TV suspended from the ceiling. Across the room a figure in the exiting crowd caught his eye.

A tall, willowy young woman was struggling determinedly across the floor of the waiting area with a heavy bag. Her nose was long and interestingly curved, and her straight dark brown hair swung at chin-length as she walked. She had no particular expression on her face, but the naturally downturned corners of her mouth gave her a melancholy look.

He watched her cross the carpet to where a man

was waiting for her at the far end of the gate area. Edward had seen him before. He was tall and handsome, an older man with a stiff brush of white hair. He was very thin, almost haggard, as if he'd recently recovered from a serious illness, but his posture was ramrod-straight. When Margaret reached him he took her bag and hefted it easily up onto his shoulder with a single muscular gesture. His pink cheeks glowed with rude health. A silvery bell rang, and a rapid-fire voice spoke dispassionately over the loudspeaker. After a cursory exchange Margaret and the Duke of Bowmry left the gate together through the exit marked CUSTOMS.

Edward watched them go from where he stood. It was strange, but he couldn't move. It was as if a colorless, tasteless toxin had entered his body, the silent sting of an invisible jellyfish, and left him completely paralyzed. He stood where he was, observing them from a distance. He couldn't take it in yet. It was just colors and shapes, which his mind couldn't translate into anything that made sense.

Then they were gone, headed toward customs, and his paralysis vanished, replaced by fear, fear of what he knew was already happening, had already happened. Only then did his body jump into action. As he walked a part of his brain kept up a neutral commentary on what was going on. He wanted his brain to grapple with this new mystery, to wrestle it into the shape of something bearable, but it refused to leave its corner, was in fact desperately trying to climb out of the ring. Everything around him was very clear and sharp, like a mosaic of broken glass. There was no time. He should really say something. He needed inspiration, a tactical masterstroke that would reverse the situation – not just reverse it but make it so it never happened, explain it and neutralize it and make everything all right again in one fell swoop. She must have thought I was getting a later flight, he thought. She wouldn't have wanted me to see this. He felt like a camera with its shutter stuck open – he couldn't shut it off, couldn't turn away, couldn't stop taking it all in.

For a long moment he thought he'd lost them in the crowd, but then they reappeared in the line at Passport Control. He tried to catch Margaret's eye, but the angle was bad, and she was wearing sunglasses, which he'd never seen her do before. They looked terrible on her – they made her look blind more than anything else. She said something to the Duke, and he searched his pockets solicitously and handed her a fresh handkerchief. Edward could hardly look at her – her outline shimmered, she was an incandescent sunspot of pain. She didn't understand. He needed to warn her.

'Margaret,' he said. Then he shouted, 'Margaret!'

Ten thousand people turned around to stare at him. Margaret glanced in his direction and looked away hurriedly. A uniformed agent approached the Duke, they spoke, and he and Margaret stepped out of the line. They disappeared through a separate doorway, bypassing the crowd completely. He watched them go, one hand raised like a man frozen in the act of hailing a cab. There was a sudden commotion at one of the customs windows as a child – no, an unusually small man – tried to force his way through the line and was vigorously restrained by two uniformed customs officials who had no trouble overpowering him. They escorted him away.

Suddenly Edward's bags felt very heavy. He found a bench and sat down. Some urgent action was still required, some input on his part; an inner alarm was ringing more and more insistently with every passing second, but he didn't know what to do or how to shut it off. It seemed incredible to him that time was still rolling forward at all, that this new development hadn't brought it to a shuddering halt, with a grinding noise and a smell of burning insulation. His brain mechanically catalogued meaningless details in the comfortingly dull airport corridor: ads for Lucky Strikes and Campari, patterns of speckles in the linoleum floor. His nose itched. Outside on the runway, workmen were doing something to an exposed truck engine under the glare of a spotlight. He stared at it till it hurt, deliberately making afterimages on his retina. They looked like balls of blue fire.

A meaningless echoing racket in the background gradually resolved itself into the sound of a man's voice speaking over the PA system. He forced himself to understand it.

It was calling his name.

Astoundingly, despite everything, the crude mechanisms of real life were still functioning at maximum efficiency, turning and slicing, shunting and processing. A series of painted arrows, courteous officials, and gratifyingly rapid lines whirled him through customs and out into the receiving area. A chauffeur with the usual crudely lettered sign was there to meet him at the baggage claim. It was his old friend the driver with the weak chin, wearing a stylish leather jacket over a ludicrously inappropriate cable-knit turtleneck sweater. Another man, a debonair footman who looked uncannily like Clark Gable, took his bags. They didn't speak to him, or to each other for that matter, just led him down to an underground garage full of heady gasoline fumes. A midnight-blue limousine waited there, a feline Daimler-Benz crouching on gleaming spokework paws. He was ushered decorously into the back seat, while they sat together in the front. The car started with a genteel cough.

They drove him round the city, through darkened suburbs with half-familiar names – Windsor, Watford, Hemel Hempstead, Luton – into the countryside north of London. Edward felt like he'd been sitting down for days, and his ass was starting to hurt. He did his best to keep his mind studiously blank. At that moment there were no possible

428

avenues of thought he was even remotely interested in exploring. He wondered what lie the Duke had told Margaret about what he'd do with the codex, how he wanted to preserve it, would let her write about it, would treat it as the national treasure it was. How could she be so brilliant and so naïve at the same time? The Duke would shred it as soon as he could, of course, just as he told Fabrikant he would.

They drove for hours. The stars were startlingly bright this far from the city, but he didn't bother to admire them. He didn't get out when they stopped for a cigarette or for gas, or petrol, or whatever it was. He didn't register the heavenly smell of leather and sweet tobacco in the back seat of the car. Instead he just stared straight ahead at the seat back in front of him, or closed his eyes and tried to doze. In his now-rumpled black suit and his good white shirt, half untucked and open at the collar, he looked like a disheveled guest on his way home from a long and utterly disastrous party.

In spite of his best efforts, Edward's thoughts wandered ahead to his imminent arrival at Weymarshe, and the inevitable practical difficulties. Would she even let him in without the book? He tried to picture it. The Duchess would look up from where she sat curled on a Sun King sofa with a blank, annoyed expression on her face as the butler announced his name. How dare he show his face at Weymarshe now? Or maybe it wouldn't be so bad, he thought, as the Daimler-Benz whisked him ever closer. He was on the losing team, but so was the Duchess. They were in it together. She still had her money, and that counted for something, right? And she was in nominal possession of Weymarshe, while the Duke was still in London. It was a setback, but not a disaster, not a deal breaker. It was time for the Duchess to retrench, rally her forces, reconsider her options, and he could help with that. She needed a sympathetic ear and a fresh set of eyes, now more than ever. He forced himself to take a deep breath, and some of the tightness in his chest eased up. Maybe it would all be all right after all.

He played the scene of his arrival again in his mind, but this time she answered the door herself (the servants having already gone to bed) in an evening gown, with cocktails in both hands, the light glowing through them from behind. The codex had only been a passing fancy, she confessed, just an aristocratic whim, that's all, nothing more. She was horrified at his distress. Think nothing of it. She would dismiss it with her musical laugh, with a playful kiss on the cheek. Never speak of it again. Drink up. Cheers.

An ambulance howled past going the other way with its dismal, dopplered, off-key European siren. It made him uncomfortable. Suddenly it felt like the car was crawling along, like they were moving backward or driving on an endless treadmill, past a revolving set of cardboard hills and plywood houses and the same hedges over and over again.

After an eternity the car finally slowed down, then drew up at a gate. White gravel popped and crackled under the tires. It was the moment before dawn, the moon had set and the sky was glowing blue. A spasm of doubt and self-preservation gripped him. What was he getting himself into? He couldn't face her yet. It was too soon, he wasn't ready. Before they could go through the gate Edward grabbed the door handle, jerked open the car door, and jumped out.

It took him a couple of stutter-steps to find his feet. The air outside was unexpectedly cold and brisk, and the shock revived him a little. It was the first fresh air he'd breathed since he got on the plane in New York twelve hours ago, and just inhaling it made him feel calmer. The gleaming car immediately scraped to a stop beside him.

Edward straightened up and looked around almost calmly, getting his bearings. A high, dense hedge surrounded the property, looking like it could have turned back a German tank, with the top of a crumbling brick crenellation visible just above it. What was he doing? Should he call for help? Just walk away? A whispered conference was taking place in the front seat of the Daimler-Benz. The chauffeur rolled down his window halfway.

'Shall I wait, sir?' he inquired politely.

The other man – Clark Gable – got out on the passenger's side, his jacket still unfairly neat and crisp after the long drive. He looked at Edward across the car's smooth, glossy roof with an expression of mild concern.

'Shall we run you 'round to the front of the house, sir?' he asked. 'It's a fair ways. Take you half an hour at least on foot.'

Edward took another look around. The man had a point. The nearest house had to be ten miles back. Well, he was going to have to see this through sooner or later. *What's the worst that could happen? Don't answer that.* He climbed back into the car and closed the door.

The footman wasn't exaggerating: It took them at least half an hour to reach the house by car, let alone on foot, even though the chauffeur attacked the winding, intermittently paved road like it was the Autobahn. It was almost five in the morning, and sunrise was bearing down on them fast, and here and there along the way he could already distinguish artfully decayed tableaux through the twilight: a struggling orchard, a field full of neat hayrolls, an Edward Gorey garden full of amorphous, poorly tended topiary. Edward sat up straight now, shoulders squared. The last thing he wanted was to be caught gaping at the scenery. Whatever happened, he was going to salvage as much of his dignity out of this as he could.

At one point the car screeched to a halt so abruptly that Edward almost banged his forehead against the seat in front of him. A stag was standing foursquare in the middle of the road, as if it had been waiting for them. The car's high beams bounced off its proud, furry white chest. The deer was huge, and Edward found it strangely unnerving – it must have wandered out of the Wents' famous deer park, he supposed, but it could have stepped directly out of the pages of the *Viage*. The driver honked at it vainly, but the animal took its time getting out of their way, not at all intimidated by its mechanical adversary. It cocked its head away, as if it were receiving inaudible transmissions on its dark, spreading antlers, then turned back to stare at them. Its eyes seemed to seek out Edward alone with a message of lordly contempt.

Then they were moving again, and the road divided and became a wide, circular, white gravel driveway, embraced by a pair of open colonnades on either side. In the center of the circle stood a modest fountain, travertine nymphs and satyrs enacting some unreadable mythological allegory, with a tall, obtrusively masculine water god presiding sternly over the proceedings. At the head of it all stood the house itself. This time Edward waited for the car to stop for well and good before he got out. He let the footman open the door for him.

After all that, he thought, Weymarshe was nothing like his dog-eared mental snapshot of it. He was a little disappointed: It was a looming gray juggernaut of a house, more massive than grand, all bulk and no poise. He had a blurred impression of many columns, many windows, urns, ornaments – the house had acquired a neoclassical facade at some point in its history – and a wide, shallow stone staircase below a large pair of double doors. It looked more like a university library than a mansion. Edward had half expected it to jibe with something in MOMUS, but no, he realized, the Artiste had never gotten this far. He'd never seen Weymarshe firsthand. Edward was in new territory.

A door opened. He thought she would come out through the big central doors – that's how he would have staged it – but instead the Duchess emerged through a smaller one to the side; he supposed there must be some architectural term for it. She must have waited up for him, or gotten up early. She looked magnificent silhouetted against the warm light from inside the house. He'd imagined her in evening wear, something royal and sweeping, but instead she wore a decidedly practical outfit: a long dark skirt, gloves, and a light overcoat against the chill. Her earrings were sensible studs.

In fact, he thought, she was dressed to travel.

'Edward.' She stopped and smiled a silly, chilly little smile, with the corners of her mouth only. 'Well, well. You're the last person I expected to see here.'

He thought she was joking, but after a beat he saw that she was just telling the truth. She really was surprised to see him. He mounted the steps toward her. She was smaller than he remembered, her shoulders narrower, though the extra step she stood on made up for it. She was older, too, he thought ungallantly, then added quickly: but no less beautiful.

'Didn't Laura tell you?' he began. 'She gave me the ticket you sent. My flight got in a few hours ago. We drove straight here.'

'Oh, Laura!' She waved her hand dismissively, effectively canceling the idea of Laura from the universe. 'I heard what happened at the airport. I didn't think you'd really come after that fiasco. I mean, really. Poor strategy, poor tactics.' She shook her head sadly. 'Poor taste!'

The Duchess took a step forward but stumbled over the first step and put a gloved hand against his shirt front for balance. He smelled her breath, and he realized in a cold flash that she was truly and profoundly drunk.

'Well,' he said, with forced breeziness, 'now that I'm here, maybe you could show me around.'

He offered her his arm. The cold air was trying to steal his voice. He couldn't catch his breath.

'I don't think we'll have time for that. Dennis?' Apparently she meant the chinless driver, because he turned around. 'Is everything ready?'

'Ready Freddy,' came the jaunty reply. 'Your Grace.'

Belatedly the Duchess took his arm, but her attention was clearly elsewhere. She looked past him to where the footmen were now fussing over her multifarious green leather luggage, which stood in heaps along the top step in the luminous pre-dawn light.

A bird cheeped. Weymarshe was built on a slight natural rise, affording Edward a sweeping view of the grounds, and they looked out at them together, standing side by side for all the world like the lord and lady of the manor. The sky was now a lush, luminous blue, the bluest blue he had ever seen, and the lawn and the driveway and the marble fountain seemed to be washed in pure indigo ink.

'The truth is, Edward, I was just on my way out,' she said. 'I'll have to leave you all *on your lonesome,* as you charming Americans say.'

For that one phrase, 'on your lonesome,' she hazarded a Texan accent.

'Where are you going?'

'I'm going away, Edward.' The Duchess cut her eyes toward the waiting chauffeurs. 'Far away. Truth to tell, it's high time I took a vacation. God, I need some time away from here.'

She looked around at Weymarshe, her lip practically curling with disgust.

'You're really going?' Edward said. He tried to force her to meet his eyes. 'But what about the codex? What are we going to do about the Duke?'

The blow arrived out of nowhere. It was a serious slap, not just for show, a quick hard right with some shoulder in it, and it left his ear ringing.

'How could you come here? How?' Her face was suddenly close to his, and her breath was thick with gin and expensive cigarette smoke and contempt. 'He'll kill me, do you know that? And Laura, too. If he can catch us. You've ruined us both!'

She drew herself up, her nostrils white and flaring. She was shaking, but her voice was steady as ever.

'It's over. Don't you see that? I suppose it's not the American style, but where I'm from we know how to make a decent exit. Nothing worse than a loser who won't admit it.'

And as suddenly as it came the storm was past. She was herself again. Mercurial as ever, the Duchess quirked her eyebrows at him.

'What is it?' she asked. 'You want to come along, is that it?'

Edward shook his head.

'I think I've had enough time off for now.'

She leaned toward him, evidently meaning to give him a kiss on the cheek, but he stopped her with a firm, assertive forearm. There would be none of that. He was a slow learner by any standards, but if he'd learned nothing else from all this, he'd learned that much.

'It's just as well,' the Duchess said, straightening up. 'Where we're going I don't suppose they'd let you in anyway.'

She turned away abruptly and tripped – almost literally – the rest of the way down the steps to the waiting limousine. The chinless chauffeur opened the door for her. She paused on the threshold and – did he imagine it? – rested her hand for a moment on the chauffeur's ill-shaven cheek before she half stepped, half fell into the darkness inside, and it swallowed her up.

Edward watched the car go. He jogged a few steps to one side so he could see past the fountain in the middle of the driveway, following the ruby tail-lights as they receded along the road down which he had just come, two pale ruts with a crest of green between them, exquisitely groomed and straight as a ruler. He put his hand in his jacket pocket and fingered his good silk tie. Now he wished he'd remembered to put it on before he saw her, but it was too late. The Duchess was running away, he thought, and he wondered if she would ever be able to stop running now. He doubted it, but the truth was, he would probably never know. The endgame of this match would be played without him.

He sat down on the cold stone steps. He still had the bag with the case for the codex in it, and he set it on his knees. Was it really empty? Tiny brave crickets chirped deafeningly in the grass. Had Margaret found that copy of Lydgate she was looking for after all? Maybe that would be his consolation prize. He flipped the latch and was faced once again with the gnarled black cover.

The hollow inside wasn't empty. It was full of paper, but it wasn't the codex, or Lydgate, or any book at all. It was full of bills, a hundred dollars each, in stacks of – he thumbed one and took a well-educated guess – a hundred each, fifty stacks in all. Five hundred thousand dollars, give or take a few hundred either way. It must have been Margaret's price. Well, she always had been a good negotiator, and knowing her it was the full amount. She'd said it wasn't about the money, and he supposed she must have been telling the truth. He thought about making some kind of grand gesture with it – tearing it up, maybe, or scattering the bills across the lawn like leaves, or burning them on the steps of Weymarshe – but instead he tucked them safely back in the box and put it away. Edward felt a newly pragmatic mood coming over him.

He looked up at the tops of the trees and the sky arching up over him. He felt like he was waking up from a dream. The air smelled like autumn, and the sky was now a rosy-gray color like the inside of a seashell. He hugged his arms across his chest. It was cold, but it would get warmer as the sun rose. He would have to start carrying a flask of scotch with him for occasions like this, Edward decided. To his surprise he felt almost pleasantly numb inside. He looked over his shoulder: Behind him invisible hands had closed the door through which the Duchess had come, and the stone facade of Weymarshe was as lightless and dead as an Easter Island head. The blankness of Edward's mind was like the blankness of the endpapers at the end of a long, long book. He wondered idly if anything interesting would ever happen to him again.

There were still a few stars visible, and he could sense the cold winter constellations lying in wait below the horizon, just out of sight, ready to rise.

It was funny to think that they were still expecting him at the office tomorrow morning, he thought. Early, before the markets opened. He pulled the lapels of his jacket tighter around him, but the chilly fall air cut right through the thin fabric. It was even funnier to think that he would probably be there.